P9-DNV-885

Every Past Thing

Pamela Thompson

Unbridled Books

Every Past Thing

This is a work of fiction. Names, characters, places and incidents either are the product of the author's imagination or are used fictitiously, and any resemblance to actual persons, living or dead, business establishments, events, or locales is entirely coincidental.

The painting on the cover of this edition is "Mourning Picture" (1890) by Edwin Romanzo Elmer, reproduced by permission of Smith College Museum of Art, Northampton, Massachusetts.

Unbridled Books
Denver, Colorado

Library of Congress Cataloging-in-Publication Data

Thompson, Pamela
Every past thing / Pamela Thompson.
p. cm.
ISBN 978-1-932961-39-3
1. Wives–Fiction. 2. New York (N.Y.)–History–1898-1951–Fiction.
3. Middle age–Fiction. 4. Domestic fiction. I. Title.
PS3620.H685E94 2007
813'.6–dc22

2007019499

1 3 5 7 9 10 8 6 4 2

Book design by SH • CV

First Printing

for Mark

Why should we grope about the dry bones of the past, or put the living generation into masquerade out of its faded wardrobe? The sun shines to-day also.

—RALPH WALDO EMERSON, "NATURE"

With the ones we love, we know from the start the Story's end. Death will come to one of us, and we Three will be Two, and the Two finally One. The sun will set and rise again and after our sleep (if there be sleep) we will stir only to find that heartache knows no rest: Still it sears straight through and burns hottest along the edges of our shoulder blades. How fragile we are, there. The wings we once had have been broken, and the sky is far beyond us.

We will not see that place again.

I would not have seen that sunrise if I hadn't been watching over her. It wasn't meant for anyone human to see—its brilliance, the orange Fire of it, was not of this world. Or if it was, if it was only our own sun rising in the sky, then Life was so terrible, so Wide, so Beyond us that death itself seemed very small. More human. For how, lit by such fire, nestled in such power, could such small beings hope to survive? How long could we expect Life to stay in the delicate and precise arrangements that are our bodies?

Every rise and every fall of her chest I watched. I unfolded and refolded a damp cloth to press to her brow. And I watched her skin for Signs.

What Economy created her—only two shades, cream and brown: her skin utterly pale, with no bloom or agitation or bite; her brown eyes the same golden brown as their lashes, the same as her two brows kicking up as if to touch in the center, the same as the soft long hairs loosed from her braids and sticking to my cloth. I leaned down next to her, my head to her breast, as if she were the mother and I the child. I couldn't let her see the worry that ran shock-through me. Was there some curing touch—? She needed more air. I unbuttoned the tiny mother-of-pearl buttons down the center of her chest, fumbling, my fingers all clumsy. Why had I attached nubs the size of milk teeth, and worked button-holes smaller even than her fingertips? Why such fuss?

When I put my ear to her heart, it was rubbing. Not beating. As if something were squeezing and muffling that muscle whose effort pushes Life through our limbs. When I heard that strange sound (which was the absence of rhythm), I knew what the Doctor would not say. That this sickness would not ease. That her words and bloom would not return. That the rubbing too would stop.

Do not think I guessed this day would come. She had been such a healthy child! Last I knew, it was Summer and she and Maud were skipping along the road to Goodnow stream, big girls, bold, with thick braids and loud voices and enormous appetites. Or she was rolling down the hill with her father, the two of them cock-a-doodling like roosters. Their voices came to me through the kitchen window.

But that morning, in the presence of the terrible orange light, no voices came. All sounds below muffled. Imagined—at most. Yet they had been, once, all of my existence.

I understood then how small my own part in this Life.

After she died, the sky was gray and cold. I noticed this only later, in the afternoon, among people. Edwin, the Doctor, Samuel, and his Maud with her giant lily. And then I wondered, Was that Fire her leaving? Or had the Fear inside me dreamed such a Sun? I left the parlor and went outside and stared up at the sky. The empty gray expanse that Fire's diffusion. How was I to believe a winter sky so dull contained all that light?

I knew then something about people and their quiet. How little we know of anyone. Each of us with our skin covering and fixing us in place, and our eyes, carrying us by. Our small lives and—such brilliant light.

"Come, Mary," Samuel said, wrapping a dark shawl about my shoulders. "You'll catch a chill. Come inside." I let him lead me there, tho' I did not see why.

THE GREEN BOOK OF MARY JANE ELMER
Effie Lillian Elmer, dearest.
29 June 1880–3 January 1890

New York City

November 1899

Monday

Alice waits by the parlor windows with the heavy velvet curtains nearly closed, so she can see but not be seen. Three times she has leapt to her feet, certain she heard the carriage—Samuel had sent his own to fetch them. Three times certain and three confounded, so now the waiting has become a trial and a degradation. It demands of her a patience that makes her neck itch. Though nothing actually disturbs her neck: not hair escaping from the careful pile atop her head, not her dress, which plunges low in front and back, symmetrical but for the body's asymmetry, and all silk: Why not, luck provided?

It was luck, she grants, luck and not anything else that brought her to these comfortable surroundings, husband upstairs and dinner waiting in the kitchen and orange silk wrapped snug about her and then flowing to the floor. With every reason not to itch, she itches. (Though vanity prevents the indulgence of scratching. Her chest must not be scrawled over with pink gashes.)

How can she be expected to make a good impression on his family, she wants to ask Samuel. Dinner cold an hour ago. But he does not leave his study.

She must not succumb to scratching. Or to pacing. She sits down on the sofa and opens her book. She will not look out the window anymore, nor stand in the foyer. She will slow her breathing; she will not be bothered by the lateness of famous Edwin Romanzo Elmer the painter, nor Mary, his worshipped wife. It was in poor taste, she must screw up her courage to tell Samuel, to speak of a woman as though she were a saint. Her child dead not her choice. Her name, either. Mary, mother of God. The chestnut purée will be wasted on them. She should have settled on a plain consommé and been done with it. Strangers they are to her, after all: Samuel's brother and his wife, who did not even come to their wedding.

She is reading the *Lives of the Painters* in preparation for meeting Edwin. Distemper not madness but a paint mixed of egg or the milky juice of fig tree twigs. Michelangelo recommended that wives be "ten years younger, healthy, of a good family" (surely twenty years younger—as she to Samuel—that much better). In every life, Alice notes, these artists were failures first, and refused the paths laid out for them: Neither scholars nor wool merchants would they become. Perhaps then Samuel's hopes for Edwin were not misplaced, because Edwin *has* proved to have a genius for worldly failure.

It was all very well for Giotto, who could sketch his sheep with a stone, as they flocked about him, grazing. "That's it! That's all Edwin needs," Samuel had said, when she read aloud Giotto's unlikely story, how the great painter Cimabue had happened upon the boy shepherd drawing on a rock on a hill in Vespignano. "To be seen. We'll bring him down from the hills. We'll find him a master." She would see. They would all see, how astonishing it was that years after their boyhood home had burned to the ground, Edwin could render it precisely from memory.

Very well. She has no comment on talent, or boyhood. But she does know that the portrait of Samuel that hangs in their hallway has something about it not at all a likeness. It's not a portrait of the Samuel Elmer she knows.

When Alice pushes aside the curtains again (though she had promised herself she would read until a knock came), a woman and a man standing on the bottom step so surprise her that for a moment it seems impossible that they should be real. Impossible that they are they and she is she. Impossible that they should matter to her at all, this small woman and this dark-haired man with the top hat just slightly out of fashion. (Too tall, she judges.) Impossible that they plan to approach her door. Yet they look up in her direction, as if their steps toward her had already been approved by a divine order, to which everyone save she is privy. All the people who are not Alice Elmer, and see as she does not. If she were consulted, she does not remember.

All because she had once taken off a stranger's hat. Alice stops to think of that moment, as someone else might drink for courage—to think that she was a woman of such audacity (and beauty—but could she help that?) that once she had walked up to a man she desired and removed his hat; to think that this very man, father of a grown daughter, had married her soon after! From this distillation of the past, Alice draws fortitude. Filling in the substance of Samuel's frame, the intensity of his brown eyes—how exceptional had been their meeting! How quickly they had fallen in together!—she strengthens herself.

And looks again at the man and woman on the bottom step. The woman's back to her. She's tiny, clad in a dark wrap. A pinch to her shoulder blades, as if they were folded wings, delicate, poised for flight. Fragile, Alice decides. This is what Samuel dared not say. So this is Mary, on Alice's step, a sister now. Because of a hat. Because Alice had lifted Samuel Elmer's top hat from his head, and brushed back the hair that fell across his forehead before the thought came to either of them what it meant, for a man to be so touched by a woman he did not know. The familiarity of it—smoothing his hair! Because of that, Alice peers through the opening in her curtains at this woman and this man. They are not coming up, Alice realizes with quick relief. They must have taken down the wrong number. They must be someone else's guests.

When the small woman reaches to touch the end of the man's thick dark mustache—not at all streaked with white like Samuel's, does he color it?—the gesture takes Alice by surprise. Though nothing is more ordinary than a wife touching a husband, she supposes. The woman's hands small and purposeful. She must offer to take Mary's gloves—if she be Mary—and look to see if Edwin's mustache has streaked them black. She supposes his color could be natural: He is a year younger than Samuel. And softer, she thinks. Slighter. Vague where Samuel is definition and substance. How much she prefers the brother who is hers! And how much she prefers the brother who is not hers to his wife. Her tininess makes Alice feel too large. And the fragility of her bones, clumsy. She, Alice, is not fine enough, not acute enough. Well!—she cannot help if she prefers not to sigh or grieve or think about life as it might have been. She grants Mary virtue—she cannot say that applying oneself to libraries and political committees and Lord knows what else is not virtuous. But she, Alice, is the one Samuel has chosen. She had taken his hat, and he had taken her.

Samuel always spoke of Mary softly, as if to raise his voice to its usual daylight volume would chase away the few words that came: "Light and quick. And—"

"And?"

"And then—then Effie died. Just nine years old. Their only. After that—"

When Alice saw that Samuel was somewhere else, making she knew not what of the border between wainscoting and the papered walls above, she frowned, impatient with his silence (though if she had seen her reflection, she would have softened the furrows between her brows and parted her lips slightly, to suggest the ease with which words might pass, to indicate her willingness to hear all he might say).

"What happened to Edwin then?"

Samuel squinted at her, as if he did not understand whom she meant.

"Edwin. Your brother."

"Oh, well. Edwin." Samuel rolled his eyes and moved as if to stand, then reached toward her instead, dragging his thumb across her lip. Though perhaps he had not meant to dismiss Edwin in favor of making love to Alice, the possibility pleased her: that he might, with her, forget all that came before.

"Some things cannot be told," he said after.

Alice tightened the quilts over them, as though the past were a wind.

"Shall we?" asks Edwin, as he and Mary pause before mounting the steps to Samuel's house.

"Here we are," she says, as if that alone were assent. "Central Park West."

Samuel is at his best with women, Mary thinks, as she watches him across the room with Alice, his head inclined, all slowness and attention. How wrong she and Edwin had been not to have encouraged him to remarry sooner. He should not have been alone all those years after Alma died. Alone as far as people knew (Mary inserts a space for his life across the road, behind the closed doors of the Whiting house, and in the New Haven boardinghouse, and goodness knows what other places he traveled). Alone, after Alma's parents had called the day a day, and Maud was tucked into bed, and Nellie had finished in the kitchen and gone home. Samuel stayed awake, next to the light that glowed in the big front window, reading with his chair pushed back and his feet up on the table. Other nights, he sat at the table leaning over his account books. And in the summer, when she took the dishtowel out to hang it over the porch rail and stood very still, she could hear the creak of his rocking chair out on the porch, and through the lilac bush she could make out Samuel's silhouette, as though the creaking illumined the chair and its inhabitant.

How clever Edwin had been to build the house where a lilac bush already stood: an atheist's prayer, she thought; his salute to nature's pace. She looked for Samuel through its branches. If she could hear him and see him, she realized late one summer, he must know that she was there, too. Hello Samuel, said the scrape of her kitchen door, where it scratched gray arcs into the floorboards. Mary, she understood the creak of his reply. Hello, dear Mary.

Sometimes she wondered what it was that had kept them both from crossing the road late at night. Neither of them ever lacked things to say. Perhaps for him it was no comfort to hear the noises of his brother's house. At least not the same sweetness it was for her to know he was there. When he left for good and took Maud with him, she decided that he must not have known of her presence, must never have thought of the nighttime noises as a kind of conversation between them, because otherwise he would not have kept the lamp lit all those nights later on—he could not have meant for her to see him with Nellie like that.

With a woman, he is in his element. She and Edwin should not have been surprised or hurt when he announced that he was moving away. Alma still walked at night there. Edwin said as much. Mary, too, had started out the door and stood, looking across the road and down the hill, realizing she'd come out to tell Alma something. Then she would have to recite the facts: Alma with her cloud of black hair will not walk down these steps again, nor open the door to the porch, nor yell *Cocorico,* the French rooster's dinner call. She will not answer any call; she will not sneak in the back door and sit at the kitchen table until someone finds her. Still, when she heard Samuel's chair creaking late at night, it seemed to Mary as if Alma's chair moved beside it.

Who inhabited that darkness? In the night, even after Samuel had finally moved away, she liked to stand on the porch listening. Sometimes Nellie left late after tending to Ma Whiting. The world was not small, then.

When we think of someone, Mary wonders, don't they know, wherever they are, whatever far realm is theirs? Aren't the ones we love with us always—Jimmy Roberts, she blushes to think, and looks at Edwin. He brushes something from his boot. She turns away before he catches her eye, and looks back at Samuel. Did he think of Nellie? Of her baby? Instead of Gracie, it is Effie whom Mary sees: a small girl with long brown curls leaning over the basket to admire the sleeping baby. You fit in there once, Mary must have told her. For an instant, Mary sees Effie, looking up from the basket in inquiry, turning from Gracie to her. And then she is gone. Mary cannot imagine her anymore. Only her brown eyes (always they were darkness, even the night she was born, when Mary looked into them and saw the question, *Why did you bring me here?*)

Though Mary's faith goes so far as to say, *The dead are always with us,* she is puzzled by her belief. They come down the same staircases and speak in the same mortal voices. But out of time. And if out of time—where? Effie by now or by yesterday grown and aged and born again. The plump sturdiness of a girl about to become woman, unbounded.

Mary watches Alice laugh and Samuel touch her bottom lip—she sees that Alice cannot keep her eyes from him and Samuel's own crinkle with delight—and she feels old, older than she should be, old enough to be his mother and Edwin's both. Well: Hadn't she known them both always? At least since the War's end.

Alice watches Samuel as he shifts and stretches his arms back behind his head: He looks happy, she supposes, and yet is not content herself with that description. Something is different about him tonight. A flavor she's not tasted—something foreign to their lives together. At least Maud is not here to see. Impossible, that would be. Alice could not have stood all of the Elmer family together at once—Samuel's daughter, brother, sister-in-law, all talking about a life she would never know, no matter how long she and Samuel live together. Certainly they would have taken pity on her and narrated the necessary scenes. But without Maud to shift the balance irrevocably toward the past—Why not call it that? It was over and done, wouldn't they see?—they had slipped into the comfortable conventions of civility reserved for dining couples of little intimacy but circumstantial favor: The husband had grown up with Samuel; the wife had been sent an introduction by neighbors. This, Alice could well manage.

"Excuse me."

Samuel's words startle Alice, though she had been waiting for him to speak. But she had thought that he would say something to *her*. Not this half-swallowed apology directed toward—whom? She had thought he would signal her—fold up his napkin and drop it on his plate, touch her sleeve—before embarking on the evening's summation, before suggesting easily, but without commitment, future plans. They might take a ride in the park together. He would see about introducing Edwin to Sinclair, who wished to add to his fine collection of paintings.

"Not at all," Mary answers, withdrawing her feet from under the table and shifting her chair back.

His feet touched Mary's, Alice thinks. Bony Mary. See that she doesn't break.

"I'll make some room over here—" Samuel hauls his feet out from under the cloth and starts to put them right up on the table with the china plates. "Oh-oh," he laughs, pulling them back just before his heels make a smear of the potatoes. He makes a show of how civilized a clown he is. A thoroughly citified man joking about the country boy he still is at heart.

Mary waves a hand, dismissing Samuel.

Like a mother, thinks Alice. Like a mother clucking disapprovingly over the antics of her beloved son, all the while aglow with the very fact of his existence, that central amazement that cannot be diminished, no matter how bad his behavior.

"Samuel, stop." Alice slaps his thigh. "Now—" She hesitates before suggesting that the men retire to Samuel's study, and in her hesitation, Samuel goes over to the sideboard, takes a bottle from ice, and pulls the cork. She claps her hands together in pleasure.

Slipping the stems of the champagne flutes between the fingers of one hand, he shows off: how beautiful and large his hands, that he can hold the glasses so, barely clinking. The glasses are made insubstantial in his hand, the spokes of a wheel or the rays of the sun, she knows not which. She watches and thinks, Here is happiness, as he pours from high above each glass a precise cascade of the cold wine.

She sees Edwin and Mary exchange a look: This is what they do; very well, this once.

Yes, Alice silently adds. Let them see us as we are.

When Samuel finishes pouring, he sits back comfortably.

He should say something now. He should welcome her to the family, Mary and Edwin to the city. But Samuel acts as though nothing deserves comment, not the fact of their first dinner all together, not having poured champagne—this just another moment in the series of moments that make a dinner or a lifetime. They look into their glasses and concentrate on sipping the champagne, embarrassed for him, Alice thinks, embarrassed that he has not seen the requirements of the moment he himself created. No one asked him to do it!

He sits back in his chair, as comfortable as if he'd been born to it.

"Ah, Mary. How I will enjoy watching this city of ours come out refracted through your great"—he reaches out with his hand, as if it is from the air that he must pluck the proper words—"scattering intelligence."

Edwin feels everything in him pitch forward. Leave it to Samuel. Leave it to Samuel to deliver the moment for which they had all been waiting, without even knowing it (thus his success in business). He says something unexpected. All evening, all four of them, too timid to move beyond the most circumscribed of territories, as if each had been told the other three were invalids and so dutifully followed doctor's instructions not to startle the patients. They must be protected from chills, from sudden movements, from shocks. Which of them hadn't known the parameters of each answer before the question asked? And so arranged a look of interest that was not itself interest but falsely elaborated patience. How can he hope to produce paintings of any worth in these circumstances. "Your trip was good, I trust?" "You are settling in on 23rd Street?" Leave it to Samuel to blow that all up. Goading Mary.

Damn him, Edwin thinks. His provocation is deliberate. In one sentence—harmless enough; he can already hear Samuel's "What on earth did I say?"—he will upset both Alice and Mary. Though innocence is always his stance, his acumen, his successes, belie it. "Great" will bother Alice, who will not bear to have Samuel's attention turn to another woman, and Mary, too, who will assume that Samuel is mocking her. "Scattering"—Edwin shuts his eyes against the commentary that will produce. Likely for their entire stay in New York.

Everything in him tenses as he looks from Samuel to Mary. He had known when Samuel sat back in his chair. He knows that posture. The way Samuel settles into his own frame. Impervious to the world. A powerful will in him. And in Edwin, a parallel stiffening that is not power but a kind of primitive terror. As if Samuel could make his heart stop, could bring life as he tries to live it lurching to a halt. He tries to unspool the last minutes, to Samuel's first settling into his great wing chair, to the lift of his brow. Brother provocateur. He tries to loosen Samuel's hold on them all. What Samuel said was not so terrible, surely. In fact, wasn't it kind for him to have called Mary's intelligence great. *Great.*

So this is what Samuel makes of this buttoned-up woman, the neck of her crisp shirtwaist holding her head aloft. These women with their books and degrees and sensible clothes. Alice hadn't thought of intelligence as any explanation for Mary's quiet. She didn't think she had gone to college. But Alice has become accustomed to the generous strokes with which Samuel paints the magnificence of others (qualities invisible to her, and others, too, she suspects): the banker with his passion for botany, that boring gentleman who did not get up from the armchair for the whole of the Stanfords' party ("But how splendidly happy he keeps his wife"). Samuel had only to come up to her, nod in the direction of the woman wearing the dull red dress, and whisper, "Poet," to entirely transform the woman sheathed in that unfortunate color. Alice expects this of Samuel, that he will say something enlarging, something that makes this or that ordinary person fascinating—in fact, she harbors a secret shame that she does not so transform the world for him, that she does not see beyond surfaces as he does, that once he is beyond the thrall of their physical love, she too will fall prey to his incisive remarks, only in her case, since all of her best is lovely and obvious and not a secret to anyone, he will one day whisper of her in another woman's ear, "So ample a bosom, so small a heart." She seeks to postpone that day, to broaden her interests, to become a woman Samuel might truly love before he notices that she is not, and so she rearranges herself for him, offering a fuller view, a sweeter smile, a squeeze of her hand. But he is not looking at her. Intelligent! Seldom does Samuel acknowledge that of others.

"Am I to be flattered?" Mary asks.

Edwin raises a hand and lowers it. He smiles nervously, a silent apology for the gaze with which his wife affixes Samuel, for the awkwardness that has swooped down from the rafters, as if from nowhere. Go no further, Mary's eyes say. She is a hawk, surveying the field, arresting time as wings hold gravity at bay. The discomfort of this moment goes on and on, a silence hovering, beating its wings over the brothers and Alice, beating, beating, thudding from each a quietly rising alert.

"*Scattering*?" Mary draws out the sounds, as if each syllable is so worthy of disdain that the uttering of the word entire is an affront beyond the reach of the most liberal imagination. "Exactly what do you propose by that?"

"Come, now. You and I—we're not like Edwin. It's hard for us to stick to one thing. Admit—you've said it yourself—when you look back at your gardening notebooks, some seasons it appears that every crop has died. Did your garden truly fail? Never. Nature keeps busy even as we lapse. You just stopped writing. Perhaps an interesting houseguest arrived." Samuel raises a hand and brow both to that possibility, and fixes Mary with a stare as intent as her own. "Or some other project. You start; you stop. Your concentration leaves. But when everything converges, ah—"

"Leave it, Samuel," Edwin says.

And now it is Edwin's warning that Alice does not like. In Samuel's family, she has no place. She forces a smile again, at her own table a foreigner, ever congenial in recompense for not understanding a single word.

"What? She's said it herself, Eddie. I meant no harm. I love her enthusiasms. Don't misunderstand. The Anti-Imperialist League. The notebooks. The library lecture series—I wouldn't have her any other way."

"Not any way," mouths Edwin.

"Are you suggesting"—Mary raises her voice—"that you and I scatter our seeds too widely?"

With that, Samuel stops in midrise and sits back down, his eyes on her. Then he turns deliberately toward Alice, who relaxes a bit to have him back, except that she fears her chest is flushed. She cannot look down to check because she does not wish to look away from him; she takes care not to blink, hoping her own unbroken gaze can pull him from his brother and sister-in-law. *I am the one who loves you,* she wills him to see. Though perhaps it had been foolish of her to wear such a dress. Next to the sober Mary, she feels silly. But then, she has neither manufactured nor lost a child.

"This sister of mine—I may call you that, Mary?"—Samuel pauses barely long enough for Mary to wave her hand in agreement or dismissal, it matters not what she thinks, he will not stop now—"has long charmed everyone on both sides of the river. The Deerfield, that is, not the Mississippi, though I dare say if she'd traveled West, she'd have had her share of admirers there, too."

"Samuel, hush."

She doesn't mean hush at all, Alice thinks. She means say more, but discreetly. No need to drag the West into it. Keep the references local and polite.

"It's true. This brother of mine plucked himself quite a woman."

"Speaking of which," says Edwin, "we haven't properly congratulated you. The both of you."

"Well, well. Are you ready now for me to stand with my bride for your blessing?"

"Samuel, you know I'm not much for ceremony."

"I do know."

"Forgive me that, Alice. We would have liked to come—but the weather was so bad, and—" Edwin's voice falters as he searches his memory for what had two years earlier made the trip they had now completed appear impossible. The hard frost that May, the portraits to be finished. "We can see how happy you are together. How lucky for you both. Please—accept our congratulations."

Alaska. He had meant then to go to Alaska. He had been selling off his stock of frames, his picture cart. That was it.

Alice inclines her head, a flush of gratitude creeping over her. He is kind, this brother. She finds her eyes wet. Is it kindness that makes her cry? Kindness a pocket she wishes to huddle inside, burying her face, hibernating all the long winter. But she is the hostess; she is the wife of Samuel Elmer. She blinks hard, that her lashes might dry her tears, and raises her head again to face the family.

Tuesday

In her green book, Mary could tell the story herself, but for now she is only a woman walking. There is always a woman. And a man. *Treat the men and women well; treat them as if they were real; perhaps they are.* These lines of Emerson's come to her. A kind of curse, she thinks, to move through the world with so many words strung together. She could spend a lifetime unraveling and tying on a warp of another's scraps, never to arrive at her own weaving. *Why should not we also enjoy an original relation to the universe?* Emerson again. Indeed: Why not?

Samuel was right. He is right about her always.

He exposes her. Her pretense that she belongs on First Avenue, that her errand is ordinary and no reckoning, that the weight of her carpetbag is only domestic: coin for meat and fabric she has brought out to match in a shop on Rivington, and not a book, whose pages, were she to fill them, would tell—that, she is not prepared to say.

So far she has spent her days in New York walking (and making whip-snaps, of course; they'd brought the machine with them; they needed some income; they could not let Samuel provide all), from east to west and back until she had lost track of logic amid the crooked streets of lower Manhattan. She sees with certainty now how impossible her task. Even if she were to walk every street of Manhattan, doing so would not yield up every resident. Anyone who didn't wish to be found would stay hidden. And to be honest, some small relief she feels in that. She may just as well stop looking, lean back into the plump, goose-down pillow of

Chance. *Goosey goosey gander, where shall I wander?* she mocks herself. Chance at least something she believes in. *Accept whatsoever befalls.* Emerson.

But she cannot—quite.

It was as if Samuel had been looking in her window as she'd packed and not only had seen how she'd wrapped the green book in her night-gown and tucked it at the bottom of her bag but had surmised from that her every thought—and laughed. With Samuel, that danger existed. That he might dump the things he knew of her through the sieve of his mockery, and then show her—how thin the water that runs through, how ordinary the soil caught in the screen. Why indeed write in notebooks at all? Trying to extricate meaning from day, when the days were all—*marching single in an endless file.* She is easy prey. For him, at least.

"Still the same girl," he had whispered to her as she and Edwin were leaving after dinner. And she—she could not say that by her experience, she should have earned more respect than he showed her. Instead she was left speechless, or rather, speechless-feeling (for hadn't she said something?). She was the same, after all; with that she could not argue. And by that he meant the girl who'd talked with him on Sunday afternoons while his brother sketched by the window. The girl who'd talked of the Stoics, of natural history and the reproduction of worms—of anything. "Edwin acts, while you and I fritter the hours away." She is the girl who talks with him, instead of filling any notebook. "And what, my dear Mary, do you make of our city?" Always he stakes his claim—"my" Mary, "our" city.

Mary resolves that at the very least—say Samuel what he may—she will be the object of derision to no stranger. She will not ask for directions, or stare as though she is unaccustomed to crowds, or to any sort of chaos, or to the smudgy black of coal dust, as though she has never seen such a fine boot withdraw itself under a cascade of orange silk, or a dead horse stepped over as if an irregular cobblestone, or the boys in their tattered clothes sitting atop cans and crates, staring. Though if anyone cared to watch Mary long enough, he would see the hesitations in her purposeful stride (how easily distracted), the agitated pauses—here adjusting her hat, there unfastening the buttons of her gloves. And how, when she arrives at 51 First Avenue, she tips back her umbrella and looks full on the sky, as though expecting sustenance there.

She offers herself to the steady November rain. Here, thinks Mary. Here is all—and none of it Samuel's. "You'll catch death," her mother would say to her and Lucy when they were young and stayed out in rainstorms or ran barefoot on dares through April snow. Not "You'll catch pneumonia," or "That'll be the death of you," but "You'll catch death."

"So be it," she whispers aloud, taking in the breadth of gray sky—the finality of the clouds, the inconsequent fringe of building-tops around. *Sky, in which the private earth is buried.*

Jimmy Roberts must have written her that. Suppose somewhere close by he thinks of her.

Perfectly plausible, she reassures herself, wiping rain from her eyes. Having once loved, do we ever stop? Maybe it was foolishness to call the throbbing in her temple *love* when she should know better. She is old enough: old enough to know how trouble comes. All naming a bedevilment and surprise. She is always surprised. The lines that have begun to mark her face these last few winters are arches across her forehead: She must have, more than any other impulse, frown, or squint, widened her eyes at the world she sees. Like an animal at the edge of the woods, stilled by a human scent, tail up, ears perked, eyes wide, whites showing. Call it alarm, fright—or wonder: Why not?

Peas inside a pod surprise her. She had not taken the peas off the fence before she and Edwin left for New York. That carelessness born of Samuel's new wealth. It was no longer necessary. They hung there still for all she knew, many more unharvested than needed for seed alone, their tightly twisted vines inky dark, impenetrable as crabbed handwriting, more tenacious than she'd imagined. She had opened one velvety black pod—idly, a scientist now and not a farmer—while Edwin was hitching the horses, and had been surprised to find inside perfect pale-green peas, unharmed by rot, ready to plant come spring. There, without her vigilance. Unruined by her neglect. Samuel was right: Never had her gardens failed. But for that she was not due praise or blame or remarks on her charm across rivers. No gardener dares predict the harvest. So who is she to venture what is to be found, in the story she has carefully tended for so many years.

Jimmy Roberts could be inside the door, here. Now.

Would he recognize her? And if he did, would he be disappointed to see the difference sixteen years have wrought? Though surely he would at least honor what was. His boyhood would come back to him, and the places he'd left, and in her presence time compress to the thinnest line. His heart would skip and race, too; his head bent with dizziness, he would yank off his gloves from the need to do something—is that too much to imagine? He, too, might walk all the way to Union Square, and back down again nearly to Houston Street, just to screw up his courage to speak.

Mary, he would say.

She shivers at his voice on her name.

Is it really you? he would ask. After all these years?

Jimmy Roberts! she would reply (if words came). Imagine that, she would say, as though such imaginings had never before brought him to her side.

Every Past Thing Becomes Strange. That will be her first sentence in the green book. And then, as she has in her garden journals, she will describe and measure the constant rain of these afternoons she has spent walking alone down every street of lower Manhattan. The wide-ocean feeling at the very tip of the island: From here one can sail around the world. (How she would like to carry that air home with her.) The warmth of this strange November makes people stop to unbutton their coats, and pause to look at one another. With such weather, is any human story surprising?

The rain has drenched her, has caught the curls about her neck and pulled them straight, so that the wet dribbles down her neck, along her spine.

Why, in the middle of such a downpour, does she stand, looking heavenward?

As if—

Beseeching? Praying?

Neither, exactly.

Is it a gesture of relief, then?—like that of a child who, after carefully skirting a series of puddles, finally jumps in, trouble be damned.

Maybe. Yet what of the aspect of grief?

As she stands and looks up at the sky, Jimmy Roberts watches her. He must be. If he would be surprised to find her in his neighborhood, at least he would not find the extravagant gesture unfamiliar. That is the Mary I know, he would think, watching her drop her umbrella and turn her face to the sky. Were I to go close enough, she would let me pull a loose thread and unravel secrets and true things, not anything waste, not anything that would let me forget what I belong to (the sky, its fragments of star, the earth below). She might tell me about her girlhood game of grabbing bees in her fist to see how long she could hold them before they stung, or about collecting from the edge of the woods fiddlehead ferns before their unfurling, or about the Spanish singer whose picture her mother kept glued to the inside of her drawer of petticoats and stockings, or that grief and ecstasy are the same in time. And the things she says shift inside and remind him of the great sculptor he once watched work. Of the sharp metallic sound of his chisel and its stop at a tiny chunk of marble spinning off across the floor. She'd cared about what she let drop no more than the sculptor noticed those pebbles whizzing by him, and the commotion, all the visitors, all around.

Did she really share that same spirit, the same concentration, that same gathering in the center as Rodin? Jimmy Roberts had told her that. A silly thing to say.

Say that Jimmy Roberts was just a city dweller romanticizing Nature and one of her daughters. Say that his love (if that is its name) had not been tested by life. But even here, in gray tangling New York, weather surprises people. Love surprises. Thunderstorms come in November without warning. Here, more than he ever had in the country, Jimmy Roberts notices the people who live in accord with the weather, with rain and thunder, crying with the sky, hearts thudding as if to leap out of their casing. (And so forth, Nature all metaphor we need.) Irony, he thinks, that the inhabitants of those windowless, crowded rooms—that is how the reformers always write of them: thirty people, men women children, packed into one room *without even a window*—live most in the weather, its heat and its cold. Wet seeps through, spotting mold and drawing lines across the plaster walls, dripping puddles. Nature wins out—whether or not there's a frame through which to watch it. But there will be time enough for him to tell more of that story, inside with her.

For wouldn't he open the door and say, Shall we? And wouldn't there be chairs for them to sit together? And a table for them to lean across? And years or hours for them to talk?

A trickle of rain has slipped all the way down her spine to her waist. She blinks and takes cover, leaning up against the building, under the awning, bending to withdraw a handkerchief from her bag.

Dare she?

It was all very well for Jimmy Roberts, but could she—did women do such things?—walk straight into Justus Schwab's saloon?

Justus Schwab's saloon was and was not the place the word suggests—cabbage stew and coffee could be had there, not just drink, and after Justus himself died of the tuberculosis in the winter of 1900, his wife (who, like Emerson, survived the disease that took the beloved) carried on for some years in exactly the same manner, until she and many of their friends grew too old for such work and such play.

This demise was yet in the future when Mary Jane Elmer stood outside in the rain. It was no matter to her that chronicles of the anarchist history of the early twentieth century make no mention of Schwab's eventual closing, or that the *Appleton's Dictionary of Greater New York* Samuel had given her failed to list the place among the city's eating establishments. Nor that the woman who walked out the door, laughing in a group of men, was Emma Goldman.

Mary saw only a woman like her—simply, plainly dressed. In late 1899, Emma Goldman had still managed to avoid having her photograph in the daily papers, though she had already done enough time at Blackwell's Island to have begun carrying a good book everywhere, in case the police tried to cart her off again. Didn't she ask for it, clucked the dailies, saying the things she did? Associating with free lovers and bomb-makers. Still, she had yet to be called the worst names (that boy anarchist had not yet shot President McKinley).

Had Mary known it was Emma Goldman, she'd have looked more closely, because she understood from Jimmy Roberts's letters that it was she who had inspired him to abandon the life his family had intended for him. (If the abandonment and resolution of one person can ever be laid at the feet of another.)

As it was, Mary noticed a woman laughing. That was enough. More than enough. The woman whose name she did not know gave both permission—proof the establishment fit for a woman—and lure—laughter: laughter! So it was that Mary Jane Elmer (née Ware) entered Justus Schwab's First Street saloon, shyly.

I'm comfortable here, Jimmy Roberts had written her. *It's become more my place than what's called my own (I am not of this city's Four Hundred, whatever else you might say of my pedigree). Talk here with a person from anywhere in the world, Mary. Writers, artists, anarchists—they all make it home.*

She heads for a back table, a bit away from the crowd, near a man hidden behind a newspaper. She finds herself expecting Edwin (though he must be at the Academy by now). Here in a place where she very well could find Jimmy Roberts, she can no longer imagine him. He is no longer a boy. Perhaps she would not know him.

The giant red-haired man behind the counter raises his brow. When he sees that she won't call her order out to him, he comes over to ask what she would like.

She has money. "Get something for yourself, Mary," Samuel had told her. He probably meant something like one of Alice's dresses.

"Something warm," she answers the man, as though his question were a matter too trivial for her, as though she entered such establishments every day.

She withdraws the green notebook from her carpetbag and carefully folds back the first page, pressing it down to reveal the little nubs of Samuel's red silk that bind the pages, the same color thread as the whipsnaps she's braided all week. After all these years, the same dye lot. She frowns, surveying the writing inside—entries of years, ending with Effie's birth—and flips the book over and opens it from the other side. Slowly, deliberately, she writes:

Every Past Thing Becomes Strange.

She has been thinking that ever since the journey from Shelburne to New York, on that enormous train. It was not the first time she had seen one. She'd gone to the station with Edwin and Effie and Maud to pick up or drop off Samuel several times a month. So it wasn't the only time she'd felt the anticipation, and the rush of air and noise so powerful it obliterated all the nervousness of waiting and replaced it with a pounding audible more in her heart than her ears. A thudding straight through her. But this time it was she and Edwin who stepped aboard. An act tantamount to saying, Yes, I bind myself to this engine and all of its terrible, puffing speed. Yes, I pledge myself to the new century and all strangeness to come.

She had said these things to herself. I am committed to living—she said this, afraid she was courting death. To step on a train! She hadn't any right to expect to survive that first jolt of speed. We are not particularly designed for velocity. Our pace is that of our own two feet. Even a horse's trot could make Mary feel she was fooling time, pulling a sly trick on Mother Nature, who, though generally tolerant of deviance, was nevertheless known to assert her will. Mary might be caught out and punished, like the time her sister Lucy had dared her and she had jumped on Master, no saddle, holding the stallion's mane and gripping his belly with her knees like a wild boy. This train put even that galloping to shame. The only one of her family who'd ever gone this far south was her father, and he had not come back.

As the train pulled out, a wrenching deep in her belly. *Edwin. Husband.* He reached out to hold her hand, and she understood then their leaving. Felt the weight that had been pushed aside by packing and ordering and planning.

She studied his hand closely as the train pulled forward out of the station, as if, before turning her face to the window, she had to take the measure of this ground—the long, bony fingers of his capable hands, his eye's instruments, usually in thrall to his concentrated gaze, but still now, gripping hers.

He has held her hand many times, yet she does not often pause to think of it.

Somewhere in Connecticut, it must have been, she no longer minded the train's speed. Would the past now seem slow? When they returned home next spring, would she be impatient holding the horse's reins up in front of his picture wagon, the back full of frames and photographs and crayons and paints?

She nods her thanks to the red-haired man, who smiles at her and makes a teasing gesture of peeking into her notebook—a motion that at once pays her the compliment, I want to know, and at the same time assures that he would never look. She takes a grateful sip of the steaming cider, and then spreads both her hands on the table. How strange they look. This morning at the whip-snap machine, her right hand gripping the black-handled wheel and left the braided whip, her hands had seemed part of his unwieldy invention and not her own body. She watched the two five-fingered instruments—small, they are, and her fingernails never glowed as pink as he had made them in her portrait—one turning the crank, the other moving back and forth, her eye no longer following the three strands becoming one braid. They had been three: Edwin and Mary and Effie. Two strands don't hold without the third to braid them. No, she chides herself, for harmful metaphor. No. Two strands might very well be plied together; she had done so herself, countless times.

Every Past Thing Becomes Strange. Her sentence has a word for each finger, like Effie's hand on the keys of their upright piano, reciting the notes as she pressed—C, D, E, F, G—and back down G, F, E, D, C. Cat, Dog, Elephant, Finch, Goat. Goat, Finch, Effie did clap.

Come Down Eddie For Good—Good For Eddie Did Come.

She hopes good will come for him. She is not at all sure what sentence she wants to follow *Every Past Thing,* so she contemplates her husband. Her mind a hush, a prayer, she thinks, though she has not prayed since the war of her childhood, the War against the South, when her mother had cursed and forsworn any further mention of God. Mary conjures him, Edwin, as she'd once invented God: with a paintbrush in his hand, of course, his fine dark brows slightly furrowed, his dark eyes fixed on something she can't see. She is interested, suddenly, in this difficulty: how, busy looking so intently at him, she can't possibly see what he sees; staring can bring her no closer to the mystery he is. He would be interested in a puzzle like that. He would line up his magic glass, to see the world upside down and his own stare given back, all of that at once, in one painting.

After she writes *Strange* atop a new page, she stops and looks about. She skips several pages—would that be enough room?—and writes *Becomes.* After delineating this space and thinking for some minutes about Strangeness and Becoming, and what notes she might another day make about both, she turns another leaf. *Thing.* And adds an *S*—for wouldn't that be more fruitful?

Thing(s)—

A business card that says Artist—His.

A Secret—Mine. And one not mine.

Bones—Hers, under the earth, with her woolen blanket embroidered with rosebuds, with Thos. Jefferson's Black Hollyhock seeds and my mother's missing serving spoon with the W atop the handle and clumped roots of Black-Eyed Susans performing their underground winter migration. (But not skin. Not lips or eyes. No longer.) Worms crawl, and stop at our New England rocks and bones.

A letter with a postmark August 1883—from an Undergraduate writing silly nursery poems: Mary, Mary, no longer Wary. (I am, tho', so.)

Blue and ivory eggs in a nest—"Perfection," agreed Edwin and Samuel. And they set out to plumb the mysteries of an egg: the one brother to measure and sketch, the other to describe. (Or entertain, in the event that Perfection proved unattainable.)

Stones—tho' not the gray misshapen monstrosities I stacked to the left of my garden (forgive me if I want something more beautiful than that). Maybe river stones, made round and smooth by water's Constancy. Each perfect as an egg. Effie used to collect them. Those with stripes down their center and those of deep color, all ovaled and polished to the touch, she named magic. Rough-edged rocks, with flecks of mica, "civilized magic." When I asked her what she meant, she said, "You know, Mama, not so much. They don't have the singing." Where on Earth did she learn a word like Civilized, and to put song outside it?

I buried her pouch of magic stones with her.

I can collect more (will chips of cobblestones and other City rocks suffice?) and fashion my own bag. In case I need to drop them one by one behind me.

Wasn't that the trick, in nursery stories, for those who feared becoming lost? But this method will not do for Mary. Anything draws her interest. Stones. Galaxies—that ours might not be the only civilization in the universe, and the corollary: If our civilization is so small, then what of one person? A speck on the earth. All opinion and desire even less.

One year she and Effie had kept the clippings from their fingernails, to see how such tiny slivers might accumulate (a cubic inch per year? Buried, would they decompose?) Then months went by; they forgot about that experiment. Though still a faint shadow of plans conceived and plans abandoned darkens the sky when she brushes nail clippings off the windowsill. Samuel is right about her. About her fits and starts.

Very well. Mary flips the book back over, and—as if possessed, she thinks—adds dates like things:

1849, 1850 Susan Smith Elmer gives birth to her eleventh and twelfth children: Samuel and Edwin Romanzo

1860 Mary Jane Ware born

1876 Elmer Bros. (with help of Cousin John) finish the Bray Road house
Congressional Committee reopens case of the Andersonville prison. Confederates claim they repeatedly sought release of prisoners and movement of surgeons and medical supplies and were denied by the Union government

This clipped information reminds only her and would not convey to anyone else how those hearings had devastated her. The betrayal: Her father had died at Andersonville, and need not have, she understood in her sixteenth summer. His life—anyone's life—worth nothing in the war-makers' strategic equation. She might have written that: *1876 Trust no government.* A realization that turned her more impetuous than she'd already been. More likely to climb out her bedroom window to commune in the fields with a man a decade her senior.

1878 Samuel marries Alma Whiting
2 November 1879 Edwin Romanzo Elmer and Mary Jane Ware, Halifax, Vermont
29 June 1880 Effie Lillian born
1882 Alma dies of pneumonia
1883 Summer visitors in the Buckland house
1884 S. buys our interest in Buckland house and moves to Boston. We remain in the house, Maud with us for meals, Samuel home weekends
1885 Edwin's roof bracket receives patent
Alma's mother, Sarah Whiting, dies
Maud goes to live with Samuel
1886 E. invents machine for twisting and braiding silk thread into whip-snaps (S's company manufactures the horse whips; snaps attached at the factory)

For many years, she'd met the train early Monday morning with a package of 150 snaps to send off to the factory in Westfield. Not that she wishes to dwell on this. Enough that Edwin painted her at his invention, a glow round her head, threads flickering through her fingers. She was not like that. Still, the painting deserves a place in her chronology. *A Lady of Bishop Corner (Wife of the Artist)*. Later. When she gets there. After Effie died, must have been, for she'd worn her mourning clothes.

Whip-snaps are not what she wishes to write about. The pages of a history need not be apportioned as the hours spent. Such a book, if hers, would be devoted one-third to sleep (with its dreams, thank goodness), one-third to food (its growing, its preparation), and one-third to fiber (plying, braiding, weaving, knitting, crocheting, sewing, scrubbing, mending). As for all else—human interaction and reading and walking abroad in the world—mere addenda? Jimmy Roberts only a footnote?

No. She wants another sort of history: The book of what was not. An impossible problem. She sees Samuel laughing. Go ahead, Mary Elmer. Write what cannot be written.

In the book of what was not—there she might write of Jimmy Roberts. But if this is the Elmer family history? The years stand in a line, silent accusers: 1887 1888 1889.

How small a date in a book appears. *Born* four letters same as *dies*. And born a sound more like dying, a thud on the earth. And *dies* more alive—the *I* like fire. One could make quite a bit of nothing. Or nothing of an entire life. Emerson comes to her again: *I forgot my morning wishes. Took a few herbs and apples, and the Day turned and departed silent. I, too late—*

She is in the afternoon of her life, and evening has always startled and saddened her. She does not know how to write what she wants to say. *I, too late—*. Jimmy Roberts came one August and took her heart. Nellie's baby born the same week Ma Whiting died. "You best hold her," she told Samuel, as she put the bundle that was Gracie in his lap. The closest she'd ever come to giving him a child. The strange ticking of complicity when she galloped off after, down Bray Road into town to tell Dave the news.

No, what little she'd managed to write had hardly anything to do with life as she remembered it, let alone as she'd wished it.

She contemplates the page marked *Strange*. She has entered the door at 51 First Avenue, she has opened the pages of the green book, and she is none the different. Jimmy Roberts is nowhere to be seen, nor Nellie. And none of this a dream, unless life is.

Look—there Edwin is, crossing the park on his way to the National Academy of Design, with a painting tucked under his arm.

He stops and bends to the ground, gathers a handful of leaves and brings them up to breathe deeply of their damp. And the facts he uses to order his life fall away: Edwin Romanzo Elmer, student of Walter Satterlee, A.N.A. Admitted to all classes of the Academy save one. Born, Ashfield, Massachusetts. Husband, brother. Father, once.

New York has put him strangely in the mood of retrospect. Strange, because so much new assaults his eye. Isn't that what he wanted, coming here? Retreating into the past now a cowardice he must trounce out of himself. Seeing Samuel last night caused it. And Mary's set face when they left. And being in a city again (little though New York resembles Cleveland): The movement stirs him, unsettles; his thoughts race. They could go—forward—or back.

The leaves have already frozen and melted, and they fall apart in his hands, their skeletal webs only a clue to their original form, their substance reduced to dark crumbs. But the smell of them—slightly sour?—with something rich and loamy buried beneath their first affront.

His shovel had hit the leaves first, and they were harder to break up than the earth below, which was not yet frozen. (They had been lucky in that.) He and Samuel dug without looking up. Not at the sky, not at each other, not at Mary.

When he left that house, he vowed not to ask anything more of the world. *Never again.* Having once, at the Cleveland Public Library, immersed himself in the Greeks, he made note of his own hubris, and, chastened, pledged to need nothing at all. (Though he still had Mary.) He was a person who made such vows. He had enough of the old religion to believe absolutely. *Never again,* he said. And meant it, despite what he'd grown up knowing of the dangers of belief. His own mother had forgiven Pittsfield's Reverend Miller his first miscalculation and waited on October 22, 1844, for the end of the world on the banks of the Wabash River, his sister Emeline a baby in her arms, while Darwin and the others played in the woods within hollering distance. And the newspaper accounts he'd read of his brother Darwin had blamed his death on a mind "unsettled by the Second Advent fanaticism." Not to mention Uncle Alfred's voices. Yet Edwin is capable of conviction—his own, alone, and nobody else's. He had always ignored the gossip of neighbors. He knew, somewhat foggily, about their head-shaking; he didn't allow any of it to come into focus. Though about the big house, he'd come to agree: It was an affront to the land. It was simply too tall. The bracketed roof arrogant. Altogether too much striving for effect. A city effect. It fit neither the grandeur of the mountains behind, nor the slow curve of the road uphill, nor the sprawling Whiting farmhouse across the street.

Never again will I ask for anything. He packed one trunk of clothes, paints and brushes, photographs. Put it in the wagon with chairs, his drawing table, her whip-snap machine, enough blankets and dishes for two. Hammered together a box and gave it to her to pack up Effie's things. And went off down the hill to the center of Shelburne Falls, to settle on a small apartment. No more frescoed walls, no high ceilings, no elaborate moldings, no velvet couches, no tapestries, no billiard room. No orchard with trampled apples underfoot, the brown sweetness everywhere a reminder of ripening and decay.

The house comes to him as a painting already framed, with dark strips of carved walnut splitting the roof from the sky, the house from the orchard, the steps from the grass, the wisteria growing up about the south-facing porch. In the middle, the front door swings open onto a hall and stairs that stretch up alongside a grapevine of a banister. A mad artist's rendering of Greek columns recedes in the shadows of the hall. He was surely mad. To have built that house. Painted those marble columns. Planted the wisteria. And that wife and that child and that brother perched singing on top of the roof. Instead of making the billiard room off the back hallway, he should have left an empty room for getting down on his knees to thank the stars for such life. For their hearts beating and the birds in the morning. But he does not believe in prayer, or even luck.

In the early morning while Mary and Effie slept, he was always startled by the light. Every morning surprised by how it came around the mountain—Goodnow Hill it was called, though it had enough looming presence to block the light of the rising sun until it was so high in the sky as to be everywhere already.

"Be Goodnow," Samuel winked at him when he left Monday mornings. "Take care of Alma and Maud for me."

Be good now. Edwin wonders: When had the tone of that teasing admonition changed? After Alma was gone? Lovely, straight-spined Alma, who saw before anyone else among the village's founding families the appeal of a man such as Samuel Elmer, and took him by the hand into respectability. And bequeathed him its assets.

No, perhaps Samuel's tone had always had a trace of mockery, an older-brother edge of superiority, with its suggestion that because Samuel had seen more of the world, it remained for Edwin to be the good one. As if being good were simpler.

Samuel had mocked his youthful infatuation with Effie Ellsler with the same hint of derision. Encouraged him to trade it in for a real woman. (Samuel, as far as he could tell, had already, even then, subscribed to a few of those.) Still, they were both of them the boys who had come home from Cleveland to take care of their parents. Edwin reminds himself of Samuel's generosity. His encouragement: He had arranged for

Edwin to study at the Academy. Yet beneath Samuel's ostensible willingness, a price. Something Edwin cannot name. And not just a portrait of Alice, though that, he was sure, would do for a start.

The painting under Edwin's arm bothers him. For this one, he has no excuse. Once, he was not bothered by failure. Didn't stop long enough to judge himself harshly. Would simply get up again in the morning and start another painting, another money-making endeavor, another building, another invention. But this painting is so bad that the influence of it has carried over into another day. He—stammers to think of it. He is tempted to kick it under bushes at the edge of the park and cover it over with leaves. He's not signed it. He won't. Its falseness a poison to him. Yet how could he have done any better? The Academy picks the models. The Academy doles out the assignments. This model was the fashion—and what of it? If, in New York, fashion has greater authority than in the countryside, that is no cause for submission. Why then does he bow to it? Because Samuel has paid for their apartment; because this is his last chance; because Mary is at home making whip-snap after whip-snap. Because, because.

Ah that our Genius were a little more of a genius! she'd read to him once, after he'd stumbled out of bed and felt his way down the stairs and then to the kitchen door, where she sat, naked, fire burning in the middle of the night. Reading Emerson. Laughing. She thought that was funny. The whole thing: the passage, his squinting at her. She drew comfort from examinations of human foible and weakness; he did not. But perhaps Emerson had it right: The factories of his youth have exhausted his river, and all that's left to him this trickle.

He does not know how the days passed. Sitting on the steps he and Samuel and Cousin John had put in, he painted in the early dawn while time waited. Nothing else anywhere but the movement of his brush. Until, gradually, their stirring. And then Effie would leap into his arms, bringing back his pulse, and all the seconds ticking away. Mary went on ahead to the kitchen while Effie helped put away his brushes and paints. Then, giddyup! down the stairs on his back. Papa can we grow the same grapes you paint. Papa can we swim today. Papa can I ride Her Excellency. In the kitchen, steam and flame and cornmush and the sweetness of maple sugar and Effie's chatter and constant movement. The city people not far behind, wanting food and advice.

For many mornings he had painted on the walls of that hallway, rendering a grapevine along the banister and, in the foyer, the marble columns of the ancient world. A fashion, too. Still painting someone else's world. Yet then his feeling had been so pure! (Hard to imagine, now, with this poison under his arm). Pure or corrupt, no matter: Could he say the painting of his youth was any better than this Arab tucked under his arm? He'd painted quickly then (a facility he's not lost), wanting to make enough progress to surprise Samuel at the end of the week. The marble columns for him, really. Their grandeur a reminder of the brothers' shared past. Samuel would see them and think of their time in Cleveland. It wasn't Paris—but they'd been away. In Cleveland, life had grown larger than chores and turning the day. Silk thread was going to buy them the world, near enough. Spool after spool traded for freedom. For marble, not New England schist. For scholars' centuries, not a farmer's seasons.

He had found the figures and sketches of the marble columns in his notebooks when he was packing for New York. A record of the precision with which he'd calculated the growing lengths of each column's shadow.

After Effie had died, he had fled that house, with those marble columns rising from floor to ceiling, echoing the Corinthian capitals flanking the front door. He had left behind those particular aspirations. That worship of the Greeks—a fashion the other students in his class mocked now. Satterlee himself already a relic to them—and what, then, of his middle-aged apprentice? But was it any different, really, this new obsession with the Orient?

None of this had mattered then. He had simply painted. There had been, then, the promise of time. There had been Effie. Now, of that promise, only his yellowing notebook remains, with its meticulous numbers and measured shadows in fading pencil. And this Arab under his arm. He forgives himself the columns. He had been so young! He forgives himself and Samuel the billiard room, the oyster rooms in town, the house perched too proudly atop the hill, his portrait of the singer Effie Ellsler—all their showy attempts to bring the city home. To prove their difference from their forebears. Nothing to be gained from that. Not where they all are tending.

The picture of Effie Ellsler—his first portrait—still under sheets in the Whiting attic. Then, his youth was excuse enough for its failings (had he, in those days, admitted either youth or failing). But he has no excuse for this painting under his arm. This, the test to be admitted to the Life class. The latest of the week's three models. The Woman. The Urchin. The Arab. So-called. Misgivings strike him. Something stiff—false—in this practice.

What is this life he has chosen? He—a fifty-year-old man. Probably with more of life behind him than ahead. And he's now one of a circle of pretentious slicks and—. His mother's words come to him. *Give them the benefit of the doubt.* But he is old this morning. Everything irritates. Samuel and his new wife—her smiles, her touch. She'd held his hand until he had felt his palm turn sweaty in hers. Paint's slow to dry. Skies gray, wet everywhere. And it should be colder. It's almost as if the seasons are scrambling—as they had when Effie had died, when the rain had melted January's snow in what should have been its hour of dominion. No, it is not the fault of the other students. He has laughed with them. Shared a drink, once. They are only as young as he and Samuel were, building the house. Already done with Cleveland. Already after first love. They are not so young. It is only that he is old, and he will not see the day—

He has been here before. With cause all the world would grant (their only daughter, dead before her tenth birthday) and none at all. Despondency the same at any age at any place. Worse now. He almost chuckles, to think how bad he feels. Good. Enough light left in him to imagine laughing—if only because now is always the worst and he always the unluckiest.

He had never been convinced that traveling to New York held the promise Mary and Samuel thought. Whatever decision he makes, sadness comes after. To Alaska. To New York. Or taking in his hand the magnifying glass he'd used a hundred times before to inspect the ruffles and wrinkles and eye-sets of the deceased and then turning it upside down in the drinking glass and finding half a tiny world upside down and half a tiny world upright, seeing that and knowing how to paint it, thinking of nothing else until he'd rendered it onto canvas. And then, it was only—a thing done.

"Strange, how absolute the blackness surrounding," she had said to him.

"Meant it," he had grumbled.

She hadn't said she didn't like it.

But it *was* strange, probably—and he was strange, to paint that way, with the facts of his life (logs to be stacked, orchard to tend) seen through the window, shrunken and divided in the magnifying glass, which takes up very little of the canvas where it rests in Alma's glass sugar bowl. Not nearly as much as the expanse of dark around. As if he'd taken it upon himself to embody his father's monocular vision, with its exacting, compensating stare on the one side and dark on the other.

Neither his father nor he will live to see the day.

He will not live to see the day. He does not know why this phrase comes or what future he mourns. But he is not the only one on whom the calendar weighs: With the century about to turn, all the day's greatest minds are bent on summation. He'd read last year Albert Michelson's assessment that most of the grand underlying principles of physical science were firmly established, that further advances were to be sought "chiefly in their rigorous application." Though he does not recall the exact words, he remembers the sense: Though Michelson had granted the possibility that further marvels were in store—it was good science, to admit the limits of one's own knowledge—mourning imbued the rest, and was the true spirit, of his remarks. Mourning that only tinkering remained, and not astonishment. The speed of light always the same whether we are coming or going: Michelson himself could not countenance this, even as he proved it so.

Everything had been for Effie. Every word on every page. The house on the hill, its silk damask curtains. The lace collar she'd not had time to finish. Mary cannot believe that she was ever such—a woman with a child growing inside. With milk and not only blood running. Someone with reason to believe in the future and reason to explain the past. Even her handwriting looks oddly rounded now, plump with optimism. Though she must not have felt so at the time, excavating the family troubles. Brother Darwin's death, Uncle Alfred locked up.

Revelations, she'd quoted for that, as had Alfred himself. *The land will be soaked in blood. The children and the rulers and the generals, everyone, slave and free, will scatter and hide in the hills.* Hadn't he been right, in his way, she had wanted to suggest. Thirty years early.

Questions torment her. (Not Edwin, from the look of it.) Uncertainties about—everything. Why for instance words, unless they are *for* someone? All the earlier pages of the green book had unborn Effie as their audience: *With you inside, my Sympathy cannot help but be with young Annie Catlin, whose baby Alfred took from her.* Or: *Your father emptying Uncle's bucket and bringing his plate. Four times a day out to the cage (your uncle Samuel paid him to take over his turn). And how is Annie? Uncle Alfred sometimes asked. As tho' he'd loved her once.*

This is the abandoned book she has brought to New York. Perhaps Samuel is right: Completion is not in her nature.

When Edwin returned with the mourning picture, full of the vivid colors of a perfect June day, she thought: Here is our difference. I could never have formed it whole. After all our same years there, I could not have put together even the house. Let alone Effie. Or myself. Or him. When she looked at what he'd painted and tried to see in his eyes where he had learned to do such a thing—what knowledge he harbored—he had turned from her gaze. They were separate, she and Edwin.

She had seen then how her own life, too, would slip away. That she would ever after watch it go. That however many days were left to her on this Earth, she would never quite catch up to them, never embrace them—never even begin to lift her arm to wave good-bye. The shadow of the lilac bushes on her side of the painting blankets her in gloom. How *tiny* Edwin had made her. Himself, too. The two of them half the size of their own daughter. Right in that, he was: How tall a child grows!—under your very eyes. Big enough to fill the world.

Today's gray sky and rain the opposite of the clear blue of Edwin's imagined summer day. They'd never the three of them posed in front of the house like that. Though they'd talked of it, when the Howes brothers passed through town, taking pictures of everyone who could afford the dollar for three prints. Her Totwell cousins won the bean-counting contest and posed for free. But Edwin was opposed to paying someone else to do what he could just as well take care of himself.

She had stopped before writing 1890. But what if she simply wrote: *January 1890 The book of no Effie.*

Was there no star that could be sent? House and tenant go to ground—

She follows Emerson's lament for his own young son that far. But she had not any God for comfort, nor conclusion to any verse.

Under *Strange,* she writes: *The last November of the century had a strange heat to it from the start.* The past tense, though the month has just begun. The pretense makes her delirious with bravery. *The weather was nothing tropical, exactly, but with too much wet for good sense or Capitalists. Not every storm changes the landscape, of course. But tell that to the caterpillar.*

She is small, after all. She is three inches high and resides in a single plane. Here is the beginning and the end: a blue sky filled with fractured clouds; the shadow of their lilac bush; red clover and buttercups scattered throughout the lawn; Effie, petting Her Excellency, the oldest sheep. These are the edges of her existence.

Edwin made a box. And she put Effie's things in it.

She and Edwin sit, in their Sunday-morning best, together. Edwin with the Sunday paper with his beloved weekly math puzzle (of all respondents, only he will answer correctly), she with a fresh ball of pale blue yarn and needles. But not knitting. Staring. Into the eyes of those who will come, who will not know or care who she and Edwin and Effie were.

The house looms behind them, empty. (Was it the painting that made Edwin decide that the scale of the house had been wrong for that curve of land, the pitch of the roof too severe?) Empty, save for a formal arrangement of flowers in the parlor window. The last time she had managed such elegance was in the days of the summer guests. Empty, save the shadow in the upstairs bedroom. For a long time, whenever Edwin left the Shelburne apartment, she would squint into the tiny rectangles he had made of the windows, trying to see into the darkness, trying to understand what he had made there. The shape in Effie's window reptilian, something creeping and prehistoric. One morning it seemed a giant lizard, devouring its young. And then she did not look again. *If one person sees God in the sky and another Storm; what is the use of argument?* She will put that, somewhere.

Edwin is near Mary, and near the shadows, but not obscured by them as she is. Energy restrained in the cross of his legs, the sun glinting off his shiny best shoes. It was as if he'd taken Effie's liveliness into himself—crossed his own legs exactly as she'd crossed hers and stared hard, sassy, right at Mr. J. K. Patch when she'd stood for her studio photograph.

The new Effie is under a summer sky, far away, near almost to stepping out of the painting altogether, and taking Her Excellency with her.

Did he think that he was leading her out of our realm and into another? When he contemplates all those photographs of the Dearly-Departeds and breathes color into their countenances, does he imagine himself Charon, performing a service, ferrying those who've been left behind across the River Styx, for a last look?

She does not understand him. When she looks at what he sees—the Dearly-Departeds rendered in albumin and silver, and his hand, dusting them with the color of life and then framing them in somber, funereal black—she cannot imagine how he thinks of them. "A roof and corn-mush," he said. "Shelter and sustenance." But she never believed that was all. His close peering at those tiny photographs of the Departeds through his magnifying glass belied such disinterest. No, she knew (if she knew anything of him at all) that he searched for clues, there, in the reproductions. What did you know? she imagines him asking each person.

He painted Effie wearing the lace collar Mary hadn't had time to finish. Such a thing a luxury, after all. And luxury after everything, even in winter, when time swelled in the long dark evenings around the stove. Luxury after fire and food and socks and comfort when she fell. She had left the crochet hook in the last row when Effie's fever rose.

He knew that.

If someone had asked her, Does Edwin notice what you're doing?—she would not have guessed he knew by heart what she was crocheting before she'd even stopped and shaken the lace out and held it high. Yet he had. He'd picked up her last row and bound it off, held it up complete, smoothing it over Effie's shoulders.

That is her husband. Gone, and then surprising her with observations that only one present could have gleaned. Her powers of observation are not as great, she knows very well, without Samuel's mocking her. She forgets even Effie. Every day she loses her further, until it seems that only her deep-brown eyes remain, painted in permanent inquiry. She can no longer hear her voice. If she remembers things Effie said—that she called mica "civilized magic" or asked, "If the year zero didn't begin the world, what happened to people to make them count?"—these words come to her now as something hardened for having been repeated so many times, no longer Effie's own.

It starts to be as if she never lived. And if Effie, her dearest, whose death she thought she would not survive, had been but a dream, she must be herself something even less. "Come now," she hears Emeline saying. "You don't mean that."

Depend upon it: There are always the Sensibles to comfort the Aggrieved. (She would write that.) She once suspected Emerson's sincerity about his son Waldo, and longed to surpass the years and miles to bang on his study door and voice her protest. Or was it comfort she wanted to give? (*The intertwining of comfort and protest*—that may be useful.) He had been left too long alone among his books. Though surely he had Emelines of his own to dust off his desk and dispense the occasional "Nonsense!"

What is Thought, what an Idea, at the family table. (She could start there: all the family at dinner.) If daughters and sons are but dreams, then words less still. Less than dust. Anyone knows that. Emerson, the most dearly beloved professor of her college by the stove, gone from this world longer than Effie. Yet his words seem real inside her: *It does not touch me; something which I fancied was a part of me, which could not be torn away without tearing me nor enlarged without enriching me, falls off from me and leaves no scar.* So he'd said of his son Waldo. (Though Emerson was lucky to have another, and daughters, too.) He grieved that grief could teach him nothing.

Mary, full of admiration, hesitates to argue. She sits, at 51 First Avenue. She has a pen, and a book, whose pages are mostly empty.

Emerson's great scouring instinct—the vigorous circles of his thought, scrubbing away crust and convention—the light he shines on his own appetites and ways give her a vision. He is a man who found a Method (*conversion of thought to object,* she names it, her hand on her pen.) If

Edwin can bind off the last row of her lace collar, and Emerson get up his old heart again, then why shouldn't she impart and invest her own ounce? As he puts it.

Here is my Grief, she will write.

And here are its lessons, she would like very much to tell Samuel.

“Sketch quickly,” the drawing instructor says, as he weaves in and out of the row of students’ easels. In front of one; behind the next. Such deliberate pattern amuses him. He holds a chalk in his hand and taps it against his palm as though he is a musical master marking tempo.

“When your time is up,” he tells the class, “commit the Arab to memory.”

Ward the Lesser, the students call him, in unkind comparison to his older brother, the sculptor John Q. A.

“When your time is up,” Edwin mutters. “Sketch quickly”—that’s what he’s done his whole life, so why should he sit in a classroom to be so instructed? The framing for the bay windows drawn in dirt with his foot. First drawings for the Patent Office finished one night while everyone else slept. “The Arab.” Ward’s tone no different than if he’d said “the vase” or “the rose” or any inanimate thing. “Commit to memory.” To the asylum, more like.

Edwin is irrevocably, poisonously, irritable, and though his irritation did not begin in this class, Ward has deepened it, distracted it, blown it up into a bluster of angry confusion. Edwin takes Ward as interlocutor—though he does not want him, does not want his terms, and knows that in accepting them he has lost, whatever argument he makes.

Does he have a name? Edwin thinks to ask. Because he admires the model’s concentration. Especially in such circumstances. For an hour, his hand nestled in his thick beard, holding up his head, he has appeared to think deeply—about—what?

Edwin will never know. The man’s own language must have gestures of title and respect and without knowing even these, without any place to start, Edwin sees very little reason to speak of memory or its committal.

He wants a fight (Samuel would not be so easily pushed to fury). Show us what you can do, Lesser brother.

While Edwin imagines what Ward might do, with paper and chalk and memory, a picture comes to him: He is in the middle of Goodnow stream in the early spring, carefully balanced atop a moss-slicked rock, trying to divert the water's path with a log. What is he doing there? He does not remember. Memory holds only this: a heavy, man-sized shape of futility, shivering, holding a log at an impossible angle, and the water bubbling on around him, unfatigued. In the picture, his own figure would be secondary to the churn of river. (Men could harness the power of water—he had only to walk down the hill into Shelburne to see that. But that is not what interests him.) *Feeding the Trout,* he will call it.

"Quickly." Ward jolts Edwin from his reverie, and he bristles.

If he wants quick, let him go to the photographers. If it's a race, Edwin would rather bow out now. The drone of his uncle praying comes to him: *He shall come to judge the quick and the dead.* Here, he has come to be an artist. Everything is wrong about the Academy—stale and old and used up. This much he knows. He should not have left home. He should not have come to New York.

But Mary had wanted it. Mary and Samuel both. Though it is no recompense to be near his brother again. Edwin halfheartedly scribbles in the jagged edges around the man's headband. The cloth has been cut with pinking shears. Must be from a costume shop.

Samuel would be perfectly comfortable with Ward. They would sit together in some paneled clubroom, drinks in hand. Samuel would lean back, stretch his feet out, listen without judgment—he would let Ward be a fool, or not. Under his steady gaze, the shape of Ward's character would emerge.

That's not the only place he's seen her with her clothes off, I'll warrant, Edwin had heard another student say of Ward and one of the models.

It had startled him.

"Why do you think he keeps having her back? The light's better in the studio."

The students laughed, but Edwin did not join them.

He wants to see Ward alone on the world's most beautiful hill with his paper and chalk. See what he is made of there, under the unforgiving sky.

Wednesday

Edwin conceived of a form for our memories. He stopped Time.

For me those days went on, tho' better if they had stopped for all I was alive—without her, and then without him, too, gone who knows where, and with Samuel and Maud set to return to New York City—alone in that house with only deafening slow Eternity. Until Emeline came and fed me and wound the grandfather clock in the front hall. I did nothing, while he made our world again, in miniature. He wrestled all of it into place. He even brought back our long-lost Buck, restored to her curious kitten-self. No longer was she the fat, pregnant cat whose mourning for her kittens had so haunted us when Effie was little. The last we saw her, she was sitting atop the stone wall, mewing a strange, bereft sound, while it rained and thundered and her big belly hung low. She stayed on that wall for one long day and night—through all the rain. And then she disappeared—to give birth, we supposed. Except that was the last we saw her. Next day, Effie saw a fox slink away, a tiny ball of fur in her maw. The fate of Buck herself, we never knew. Had she suffered in the rain that day a premonition of the loss of her litter and her own life? So we read her story, backward.

We talked then about such domesticities, keeping an account of what we laughed to call our Estate. Four kittens, six new red Astrichans planted at Effie's birth, Dody the chicken and her brood, Her Excellency the elder sheep, whose fleece had made Effie's first warm clothes. Is that everyone? And old

Master, the workhorse. And CC, the cow. (SeeSee?) Then, we worried about Buck together.

"Never known a cat to love water like that," Edwin said, coming in through the kitchen door, shaking his head, stamping the mud from his boots.

Bless him: he made her a kitten.

Bless him and curse him both. For here, in the privacy of my own chance, I cannot help but start with his version of us three, as we were at the beginning of the last decade of the century. As we were and as we were not—Which of us is dead, in his painting? Not the one with the glossy black mustache, for what use would Death have of such shine, such manly exuberance? And not she, whose eyes are beseeching still.

"Here," he said, propping the painting against the wall for her to see. "I did all I could."

This was our world—our hilltop, our view of the mountains, the fruits of our love, the flowers spring still has the audacity to bring.

"I did all I could."

How many times had she told herself the same thing? And despite what they did or didn't do, the century is nearly over. And as for us, Mary thinks: Who are we, without her?

Is there anything to be said about us alone?

She remembers, suddenly self-conscious, where she is. And takes her pen out of her mouth. Here, Jimmy Roberts might walk in the door. What would he say? Her imagination meager, she knows very well: She can only supply the words of a man in love. And that can no longer be true, after all this time. If it were, it would be a tragedy—the story of two lives, ill-lived. Is that what she wants? Can she choose?

She likes the big window behind her, though it looks out on nothing: Just the bricks of the next building, an arm's length away. And rain. She likes it all, though there is nothing, particularly, to like. Everything plain, the room dark. The tables long and solid oak. Above dark wainscoting, walls the indistinct chalky color of unfinished plaster. A wide mirror with coats and hats hung below doubles the narrow space Justus Schwab and his wife have carved out of this city. If two people stood side by side and stretched out their arms, they would span the width of this room. That is all. Though the length of the place, with its door ajar to a back room dark even at midday, a place from which an occasional exclamation or laugh emanates, holds the promise of something yet to be discovered. She supposes she can understand why those Boston people always turned so rapturous standing outside the grand house Edwin had built, looking out over the hills, breathing deeply of the country air. But for herself, she likes all the city's shades of gray. She likes the feeling of being held by this narrow room. She likes even the dirtiness of the rain. And the ballast of strangers: People are alive, all around.

Boisterous young men sit down at the table next to her. "Yoostus!" they yell. Finally the red-haired man comes out from behind the bar, and such a commotion they make. She turns away from their noisiness (though she cannot help looking over occasionally), shifts instead toward the man on the other side lodged behind his newspaper. Same man as yesterday. Not Jimmy Roberts. Not Edwin.

Edwin's memories are the air he breathes, a path he strolls down knowing exactly where the next turn comes. But something solid stopped him yesterday. Ward's command: "Commit to memory." Always this moment comes, when he stands back from his drawing, and sees clearly what is missing. Something he can't reach. Stepping back, everything he does not know, and must invent, weighs on him. He does not know. His instruments of measurement no longer of use. *There will always be need of judgment,* Ruskin wrote. Damn him if it isn't judgment he lacks. He sees his sketch in all its tiny pieces. He has divided up the three-dimensional man and put him together in two. Naturally, something is missing.

Is more speed, as Ward insists, what he needs? As Ruskin had it, *Speed to seize certain things that are principal or fugitive*—

"Can I do it?" Effie had asked while he painted the grapevine along the banister. A child's clumsy fingers, he had thought. A smudge atop this precision. "Very well," he'd said, hoping she hadn't seen him hesitate. He'd watched her squeeze the brush with her fist, as she'd squeezed his finger when Alma had carried her out for him to see the first time. "Easy," he had said. "Easy." When he painted her, she was with him still, she and her apple-tree song and her cocked head and those brown eyes that could fish answers out of the darkness in him.

Then she was gone. Is always gone.

Edwin feels the back of his neck burning. He quickly vexes the Arab's eyebrows with a series of tiny flicks. He feels Ward's eyes hot on him. But he will betray nothing. He will make it look easy: there—the man's brow, into oil. Edwin steps back, as if he is considering his own work for his own reasons, as if Ward were not watching over his shoulder.

The teacher nods, and Edwin lifts the brush again, watching his own hand suspiciously. Come. He has been permanently admitted to the school when hundreds are waiting outside. He is in New York, and here he supposes he can believe what they say about his talents. And what good does it serve? He can divide and divide and he will never reach the end of division. What then, when he has carved his subject to pieces and can't put him back together?

Edwin puts down his brush. Better to stop.

He forces himself to consider the folds of the headdress. Only the headdress. From no Bedouin's loom, with this zigzagged edge. Concentration, the one good, he reminds himself. He is glad that he has noticed the cuts of the pinking shears. Ward's voice instructional, even-toned. Substitute "memorize" for any other word—lie, scrape, cheat. Makes no difference. Ward does not care—he is half here, half somewhere else. Edwin is furious. And then amazed at this fury's impotence. His, a child's tantrum. Betrayed, bereft, ashamed, and all in the space of an hour. He is too hot in this cool clime. To want in such circumstances an indignity he cannot bear.

He picks up the brush, though of its use he knows nothing.

"Competent," notes Ward. And that is all.

We were secret lovers. I was sixteen and my father over a decade dead or at least gone, and my mother long married to the man we were told to call Father. *That man had two cousins. Younger enough to make them interesting. Young enough to provide a perfect stepping-stone to all the womanly knowledge I wanted, to everything hidden from girls. Halfway, the Elmer brothers were, between me and my elders in years.*

John Elmer, my mother's husband, was a careful man. When he acted, no one doubted that he had debated the consequences, sitting alone in the evenings, his long fingers meeting at the tips, forming a steep-pitched roof that held within his only church. (Alfred, who'd heard the angel's commandment to kill three people, was his uncle, too.) Tho' they were of the same generation and family, the younger brothers had then none of my stepfather's carefulness about them. They had been out West and lived in Cleveland and they were both Artists. At least, the younger was, and the elder could build up a city, populate it, and put it to sleep by the end of the evening with just his talk. With Father's help, they'd built a grand house the likes of which had never been seen in our town. And then Billiard Rooms and Oyster Rooms down in Shelburne, the former heartily and the latter silently disdained by the churchgoers.

I knew even then, with a girl's unarticulated knowledge, that the town was faintly, albeit lovingly, scandalized by the Elmers. I didn't mind. Mary, Mary, quite contrary*: I liked it. When Samuel told me of his mother's days as Mary Lyon's assistant teacher, I thought, Let me be a woman of that family. Mary Lyon was the founder of an entire Seminary. If Ashfield's oldest could remember why Alfred lived in a cage, or when their father, Erastus, lost his left eye, if there was anything unusual, something hidden and dangerous in their lives—well, there was sympathy for that. Darkness fell early and hard for everyone. The snow, when it came, lasted until the end of many a life. On winter nights the Quiet was so deep that I rejoiced to hear the howling wolves.*

Their Melody gave assurance of Life beyond our own quiet household. And if John Elmer, hearing their howls, rose from his bed, lit a candle, and paced downstairs, thinking of fences and chickens and how cold this deep might crack the eggs, I, his stepdaughter, only shivered. Shivering!—under all the wool quilts and the eiderdown.

Was I shivering in Fear? Only if Fear is a kind of Pleasure.

When there was a knock at the window, I thought it was my own heart's pounding.

When I saw the top of his head, I thought it was Samuel come back for me. Samuel with his snow-lit eyes. He made the family's decisions.

But if, as a boy, Edwin walked three miles every Tuesday night to the Sanderson Academy and three miles home, even without a moon—because he wanted to learn to draw—why hadn't I suspected that he would be the one to act? He and Samuel had bidden us good evening after a family dinner, gone out into the night with their lantern, and then Edwin had walked all the way back, alone in the dark and the cold.

Edwin came, not Samuel. To my window, not to Lucy's. First in the deep of winter, when nothing grows.

Mary had once heard a grave-robbing narrated as though it were a great joke. One of the Truth-in-Art men of whom Edwin was so enamored told the story of Dante Gabriel Rossetti and his friends and the ceremony in which they exhumed Lizzie Siddal's grave to retrieve the manuscript of his poetry that he had buried with her. They discovered that her nails and hair had continued growing. Which of them, Mary wonders, had lifted the stiff hand with its monstrous nails away from the sheaf of poems, had slid the crinkly papers from under the drape of her velvet sleeve and delivered them out of the coffin into the world of the living? Mary cannot imagine Rossetti with the courage. Not like Emerson, who never spoke of what he had found inside the grave. It makes her cross to think of the lot of those English dandies. Lizzie Siddal's hair, its golden red rippling out across Millais's *Ophelia* canvas, an accusation. She'd nearly frozen to death, the Truth-in-Art men said. Never recovered from the pneumonia afterward. They'd shaken their heads. In awe. Of Millais. Of what he was willing to sacrifice in the name of Art.

They would have denied her interpretation. Very well. The Truth-in-Art men had never been particularly kind to her when they'd come to Ashfield for the summer. They'd been too busy rhapsodizing over her flowers, talking about Vision and Lord knows what else, to raise an eye to the woman who placed them on the table.

It is the melodrama of Rossetti's grief that galls her. Grief cannot speak. She is not like those men, and neither is Edwin. She had not let anyone put Effie in a box. She had wrapped her in her rosebud blanket only. The soft wool for her comfort—not theirs. Because soon after she'd learned to walk, Mary had found Effie asleep beside Her Excellency and the baby lambs. Effie had been born of that earth—those fields, those woods—and Mary had wanted to let her return to it, the handspun wool from her cradle her only cerement. So she would not be cold and achy. She will not wake; Mary knows. Of course she knows.

Nestle, girl half-grown, into your future, though it is not the one we dreamed for you. Where to write that? Maybe when the new pages—*Thing(s)—Becoming—Strange*—fill up and she arrives back at the start of the book.

Who is she, to judge another's mourning. Perhaps Gabriel Rossetti thought that Lizzie would draw comfort from his poems. Still. It seems an indulgence. Edwin does not expect such result from his paintings, and she admires in him that strength of character. That he labors for the sake of the work itself, for no other earthly reward but hours well-spent. What is sensible, if not that? she wants to ask of all the family. Her husband is an eminently practical man.

Rossetti is a distraction. Wishing she had Effie's bag of stones (she will never dig them up) a diversion from the question she herself has posed: *What are we alone?* She sits next to Edwin, across the table from Samuel and Alice, and she is Edwin's wife, though she might have been anyone at all.

She fishes in her bag for the maroon pebbles she picked up on the street and drops one into her saucer. One, he loves me. Two, he loves me not. If Jimmy Roberts walked in the door, would he recognize her? He who promised, *I will remember you all my days.*

What did any promise mean, if one were false? She examines her own. To collect nail clippings, stones, dates, newspaper notices; to fill the green book with what she knows of life. To find her own Method. Yet she does not put away the pebbles and take the cap off her pen; instead, she rolls the stones about between her fingers, examining their contours with her fingertips.

Why does she so love rocks? She first loved Edwin (promising nothing) because of the way he looked at eggs. "Perfection," he had whispered to Samuel, who murmured a hushed assent. Rocks not anything like eggs. The one with life about to burst out—the other, hard as death. Put under *Thing(s):*

> *As little as I know of Natural History, I know enough to see that rocks are nothing living. If some are formed in Fire, most are the children of Monotony: the wind that brushes by again and again, the water that tumbles down along a course whose variety only Years reveal. Their slow Settling—that is not a story human patience can stand.*

She is not nearly so steady as all that, so perhaps it is ill-conceived to think of the stories she might write as stones, for that makes their author water (and she is not so free). Something hard is in her, and needs to find a corresponding hardness in the world. Would that her products were as elegant as the oyster's! She feels kinship with that repetitive mollusk, who makes such a production of injury and intruders, wrapping the innocent grain. The guilt of the oyster is hers.

The end of the sand, and the start of the pearl. Jimmy Roberts entered her world, and she has ever after been embroidering him with her own substance. If he knew what worlds were made of his words—

If, what?

That is what she has come to find out. She can imagine the end of the story. She has lived nearly four decades, and watched all the while. The mollusk makes something else altogether of a grain of sand, and the pearl never again rests on the beach, a grain among grains. The man never again a man among fellows. Yes, she knows that this wrapping of her own substance around this foreign body, Jimmy Roberts—no one hers, no one she has any claim to touch or hold or keep—is a long violence, the wrapping a killing, her words a winding-sheet about one who lives. She hopes he lives. But it has been years since his last letter.

She should be content to watch him from afar. To see him bend to tie his shoe or laugh at a joke. Or push up his cuff and scratch his arm, so she might see the veins through which his blood courses. The best she should hope for is to see that he lives, to discover how insignificant her thoughts, that they have not wrapped him tight, that they have squeezed no life from him. To find that Jimmy Roberts has gone on all these years without her. Is it misery she seeks, then, when she dreams of him in her arms?

One—(she moves a pebble into her saucer) we are in New York because Edwin was admitted to the National Academy of Design.

Two—(she moves another) we are in New York because Jimmy Roberts came here first, and I conspired to follow.

"Another?" the red-haired giant asks her.

She should not. But before he takes her cup, she scoops the two maroon pebbles she has been moving in and out of the saucer and places them in her beaded purse.

He mistakes it for a show of poverty.

"It's on the house, *liebchen*."

"How can I refuse?"

It would be easy to say that the cider frees her, but it is not that. There is, after all, a gap between the offer and the delivery, and then again between the delivery and the heat's slow coursing through her, its limbering of fingers, loosening of tongues. It is the words *How can I refuse*. It is the idea that refusal is impossible, here. She accepts. *Nothing refuse*. She leaves the pebbles in her purse. Under *Strange*, she writes:

We are in New York because I wanted to come, I simply Wanted to Come, because I'd left the eight square miles of my birthplace only once (when we eloped), and that was only just over the border in Vermont, where they are more lenient about Rules and Licenses but not much different in scenery than my own dear Home.

I am sitting in Justus Schwab's saloon because Jimmy Roberts wrote a kind letter to a—I nearly called myself a Widow! (Edwin, forgive me.) Why is there no name for a mother who has lost a child? (Would that Nature avoided what Words abstain.)

Because he wrote a kind letter after Effie's death, telling me of his life since I had last seen him in my garden, and the children he struggled to save as one of the ghetto's Summer Doctors. Because he said to me, Such suffering is everywhere, when everyone else said, This will pass. All I knew of him was this address—51 First Avenue. Where else was I to come after Edwin set off for the Academy?

What we love, we lose.

Mary is at first not sure if she's heard or imagined these words.

"Sakes alive," she says, and then feels her face turn hot, as she understands she has spoken aloud. What gave her the feeling she could interrupt these men? That they were interrupting her, she supposes.

They turn toward her, and one man answers as if she had always been part of their conversation, as if they'd all ducked out of the rain and into Schwab's together, laughing and shaking off their coats, standing in the center of the room long enough for everyone to look up, note their arrival, make a space for them.

"You disagree?" the man smiles. A student, she thinks. With that self-satisfied look Edwin had found so grating in Jimmy Roberts. His hair tousled, his clothes unpressed, as though he had not time for society's requirements.

"What's to disagree? But you talk—as though it's a game, something you undergraduates debate in class while the rest of us . . . Oh, curse it."

"No, you're right. We are a pompous lot," he agrees. "But tell me: What were you going to say about the rest of—the rest of whom, exactly?"

She looks straight into his blue eyes. They are not unlike Samuel's. He could pin her to the wall.

"Fine. I'll speak for myself. We lose what we love. But maybe we find—" She stops midsentence. Damn! *We*—what *we* is she talking about? She grabs her coat and umbrella.

"I'm sorry I interrupted," she says. "Forgive me."

When she gets to the street corner, and stops to consider where—where now?—she finds herself poised, toes to the edge, and then her feet hold to the ground beneath them. This is the ground: slippery wet leaves and dark dirt, the dirt from the shovel flying past her and the brothers she loves best in the world digging together, each not looking at the other, two shovels thudding into the earth, metal ringing against rock, worms shocked into tiny knots, a pile of dirt growing as large as a girl.

As she steps into the road, a man blocks her way, clearing his throat, and she steps back up onto the curb.

She sees first an envelope in his hand. And then his sandy hair, flying up as he removes his cap. The man from Schwab's. His eyes, gentler now.

"Did you drop this?"

She grabs the envelope and looks at him hard—has he read the letter?

"I wanted to apologize—" he says, holding his now-empty hands in the air.

"For what?"

Even to herself she sounds terribly hard-hearted. She dropped the envelope—not he. And anger, not gratitude, her first emotion. How on earth had the letter fallen from her book? Perhaps he's read it. And she doesn't even know which one it is—1883, 1888?—She cannot look again while he is watching her. Who knows what he has already learned of her? No choice but to raise a barricade. Though, holding his gaze, she dares him to climb over.

Which he does, admirably, for he is a lovely young man—well-brought-up, as they say, by a mother who loved him and managed in the years she had to instill in him a profound respect for the mysterious other sex. He raises his hands and says, simply, "For making you sad. I felt that we made you sad. And don't blame my arrogance: I'm not saying that we were the cause of your sadness."

Mary finds that she has neither words nor bluster to answer this young man. Hadn't Samuel said that she had charmed—whom? after all. Her famous beauty and wit—so where was her quick tongue now? That was so long ago—all that faded.

"Please do come back," he continues. "Don't let us scare you off—we'll be more quiet. Justus chastised us, you know. Rightfully."

"Yoostus? Who—"

"Schwab," he adds. "The man himself." He offers Mary his arm.

Mary waves him away.

"Yoostus Schwab?" she frowns at him. "I thought . . ." her voice trails off. "Yoostus," she repeats.

"Truly—I'm sorry. A cider?"

"No."

"Come."

"Well—I will walk back with you, thank you. So the red-haired man is . . . Yoostus?"

"Yes, of course."

"I didn't know."

"Is it your first time in Schwab's, then? However did you find us?"

Us? Mary thinks. Whom is he talking about? What else had she gotten wrong, besides pronunciation? Some—nuance—or some essential fact. *Whom* had she found?

"An old friend recommended the place," she finally says.

"Who?"

"Why?"

My, she is prickly. About Jimmy Roberts, she still cannot manage her feelings. Though the letter is in her bag now, this stranger's handprints are on it, and she is not herself. *Yoo-stus.* How could she have known.

"I might know him. Or her."

She is sure he has read the letter. The "her" an afterthought to cover up what he knows. A man named Jimmy Roberts, her lover, he probably thinks. She could be anyone's lover, then.

"He hasn't been around in years. You wouldn't know him."

With every word, her flush deepens. Surely he sees through her lie—Isn't she here to find him? Probably he saw the name on the envelope. Maybe he knows Jimmy Roberts, and that is why he has followed her into the street, doing his friend a favor. She wants to be alone—to look inside her bag, to see what he has seen.

"Thank you," she says, as he holds open the door to Schwab's. "You have been very kind."

"I promised you a cider."

"No, no. I must get to work."

"Another time, then."

"You are very kind," she repeats, and ducks her head.

In the back corner of Schwab's, all the day's anxiety narrows itself and squeezes into the swelling that is her heart. She hears its thudding as she fishes for the letter in her bag. They've all come loose. Impossible to know which he's seen. Touched, in any case. She attempts to order them by date.

27 August 1883
Mary, Mary, no longer Ware-y,
reigning over Castle Elmer,
where the cabbages grow—
and the sun rises slow—
knows all that she must demur.

Wild boys in her garden,
who study Latin, they tell her:
The root of that word is Linger.
Hesitate, pause—cut lettuces for dinner,
Kiss your child, if you must—but Stay
(with me).

I'm no poet, and they're calling my station—Five Minutes, Grand Central, Five Minutes—but Mary I will remember you all my days. And the sky, the air lifting the edges of things, the horses' heads bowed with sleep, the hollyhock shadows, your handfuls of blueberries & cream—(Presently comes a day, or is it only a half-hour, with its angel-whispering,—which discomfits the conclusions of nations and of years! *So writes our Concord sage.)*

Can I say such a thing to you, who knows so much more than I do, about days and their passing and what to do with the flax to make it soft? You will probably laugh. Laugh, then! You tell me what rhymes with you, Mary. As I count it, the second to the last of my possibilities is Woo (but you are Wooed already), and the final is Zoo, where your husband would be sure to put me if I made a spectacle of myself. So I will simply thank you, ma'am, for your kindness. Off to Columbia College. Posting this shall be the first action in my new life—JR

P.S. Tear this up and throw it in the pot, Mary; feed it to the crowd. Your words still have me full.

She is no longer that young woman, "Good Mary," flush with motherhood and boughten sheets and Goodwin & Webster jugs all in a row according to their cobalt numbers. She has no garden in bloom.

"Say hello to New York for me," she had told Jimmy Roberts. And put her hand in Edwin's.

"Effie," she had called. "Let's play a song."

The piano was out of tune that fall. One of the guests had left the windows open during a storm. She and Edwin blamed it on him.

Yet she rather liked it that way. She found it—interesting. The way a note slipping just a notch off true, not sharp nor flat nor plain, suggested a world of unknown sounds. Where is the tuner who can find those notes?

He was not the one Edwin found. "But can't you imagine another sort of music, with the piano left to determine its own ideal?"—or some such, she ventured to Edwin, who took it as an outrage and an insult. For he had worked with particular care on his portrait of the Tuner's deceased Mother.

Neither of them had anticipated her sadness. The piano tuning was his gift to her. There will still be music, he meant. He was sorry. For the blood, for the baby who might have been.

And he forgave her that boy and that night.

Neither the departure of the summer guests, nor the empty rooms, nor the next summer's blueberries, nor sheets rinsed clean of blood had broken her down like the sound of those clear notes. They had lost something, forever. Yet nothing she could name. Through all those days, Effie played still, skipping down the stairs, past that very piano. What did she know then of grief?

But she remembers this: It was as if she'd been catapulted to the end of her time—past all choice and love, her companions on this Earth gone, her will nothing. She was like their wild cat Buck, who'd stayed in the rain, arching her back and mewing at the sky, mourning the loss of her kits before they'd even come into the world.

Who cries over the tuning of a piano?

She smooths the letter in between pages and writes: *Press your Living Specimens between pages, if you will, but Beware! if you dare touch. I saved this letter so I would always be sure there was a person named Jimmy Roberts, who was only seventeen when I met him. Who after all stepped on my lettuces, and was terribly arrogant and silly, Edwin thought. I saved his letter, tho' he'd told me to rip it to pieces. Tho' the holding on was a kind of Betrayal. To Jimmy, I mean. The Bivalve has no choice—I did.*

She wonders how the piano sounds now, left in the empty apartment in Shelburne Falls, and wraps her shawl close. Perhaps in *Things,* she might find a truer history than in dates, events. She could write about the piano. Or Effie's pouch. Effie's cream wool blanket with the embroidered rose-buds. The braided rug by the fireplace in her girlhood home. The blueberry bushes down the hill from the big house. The first time she spoke to Jimmy Roberts, it was out in the blueberry bushes. What had they said to each other that had mattered so? She cannot imagine what intercourse between people might bear the weight of the significance she's given it since.

She watches the letter-bearer talk to Justus Schwab. The younger man gesticulating. His hands come together and apart, drawing a line across the air, his fingers stretched wide in emphasis. Then his hands linger in the center, elaborating a series of fluttering, smaller movements—building something up, she thinks. Building the argument on the ground he's cleared. Then he closes his fingers in two fists and bursts them open, brushing away what's come before.

So much alive when a person speaks. She cannot bring herself to put her pen to the page. Though she has rehearsed their parts for years, the first words she and Jimmy Roberts exchanged are obscure. She cannot anymore summon his voice. What could his words have been, when he was nothing to her? None can bear the weight.

"I dreamed," Jimmy Roberts said (but later: This was not introductory), "that we met out past the orchard where the land levels out. You know the spot: a tree must've been planted there, and not survived. So there's a place for us. We met there and lay down on our backs, with only the tops of our heads touching. As we looked at the sky, you spoke to me. When you were finished, I spoke to you. And when I awoke, I imagined a life in which we could go on meeting like that. Whatever else happened, we'd know where to find each other in the orchard."

"Easy for you," she told him. "But rather complicated for me—I'm always needed. Someone always knows my whereabouts. You're on your summer holiday, but this is my life."

"Mine, too."

"I am afraid," she said, by way of apology (hadn't she made his life seem smaller?), "that I would forever be making apple pies. Eventually someone would wonder why."

"Aren't apple pies excuse enough?" he asked.

The letter-bearer sets down in front of her a full, steaming cup of cider.

"I won't intrude if you'd rather keep at your work—"

"Goodness," Mary says. "Thank you. I'm not really—working. Please, sit down." May as well; she has no idea how to write the words she and Jimmy Roberts first spoke.

"I'm afraid we haven't even—" She unclenches her hands and offers him one. "I'm Jane Ware," she surprises herself. Jane Ware. It's not a lie, exactly: Before eloping to Halifax with Edwin to become Mrs. Elmer, her surname had been Ware. She had been Mary Jane Ware. She has only halved her own name, shed the edges of it, and found—is it an accident?—her mother's. (Her mother's name, that is, before Mary's father died, before she married John Elmer.) And Samuel had for a time called her Janey. She'd forgotten that. After the surprise of hearing Jane Ware come from her own lips, Mary finds herself exceedingly comfortable, like a butterfly, she thinks, who, having shaken its cocoon and stiffened its wings, finds itself aloft.

"Frank Tannenbaum," he tells her.

And they sit for a minute, smiling. The shapes of those names settle in the air around them, the syllables of his long last name stretching out along his shoulders and around his neck: This is the coat he wears.

"Jane," he says. Its directness like her gaze. "Are you a journalist? Or one of those scribbling women who feed their families by writing domestic tragedies?"

Her eyes widen to contemplate these choices. That he assumes such a life for her. That he has no idea where she comes from. She sees herself bent over a bucket of lye and ashes. He imagines her a woman wrapping up her pages and scurrying off to an editor's desk.

She cannot help herself: She starts to laugh. "Oh—no." She shakes her head. "No."

My husband, she thinks to explain, is a student at the National Academy of Design. But these words don't come. She wants no Mary, and no Edwin either.

"Surely it is not such a strange assumption?"

"Maybe not. But no—I am neither."

"You were scribbling away."

"At nothing."

"Hmm." He doesn't believe her, but he won't press. "Well: I'm afraid I am a student," he leans forward and says in a low voice, as if making a terrible confession. "As you guessed."

"Columbia?"

"No, no. Please. The Cooper Union."

"Ah."

"I'll finish this year."

"And then—?"

"Become a journalist, I think. Perhaps a war correspondent in the Philippines. Though this doesn't please my father." He gives a short laugh. "I was to have become something practical. An engineer. A bridge-builder."

She studies him closely. Wants to detect what, exactly, his tone mocks. His own ambition? His father? Journalism itself, somehow? President McKinley?—for he does not call what is happening in the Philippines a war.

People say his wife never recovered from their daughter's death.

"And your mother?"

"She's dead."

"Oh." Mary sees her hands, withdrawn again, tight in her lap. "I'm sorry."

"Well. What we love, we lose," he says, meeting her gaze, until they both look away.

"If she were alive, she wouldn't let you go to the Philippines."

Immediately, Mary cannot believe she has said such a thing, to a stranger—how dare she make any such assumption?—and so reaches out, to touch his hand in apology—and bumps her cider.

He says nothing.

"Islands are almost impossible for me to imagine," Mary says, wiping up the spill with her napkin. "Though we are on one, I suppose. Somehow I don't think of it the same way."

"Well—the bridges. The El. It gets easier to forget where we stand all the time."

"I suppose the Philippines are no harder to imagine than Andersonville."

"Andersonville? Georgia, you mean?" he asks. "Why Andersonville?"

"Your becoming a war correspondent. And speaking of islands, I suppose. A prison's a kind of island."

"I suppose an island's the original prison. Maybe geography gave man the idea. Surround the ones we don't want with water—and we'll take the mainland. And look at Blackwell's. The perfect prison."

"I haven't seen it."

"Well, you and I are probably the only ones in here who haven't seen it from the inside."

"Is that true?"

Frank leans back and surveys the room. "Very well might be. But forgive me. You were talking about Andersonville."

"Have you seen those pictures?"

He nods. "Of course." Everyone, at least everyone in the North, had seen the photographs of the infamous war prison, the men so skeletal their frames seemed to have grown a part of the fence caging them. They were trapped by the camera, too, it seemed to him—forever they stare, bony fingers grasp the wooden posts, hollow eyes ask, *How far home across this divide between us.*

"Kept them in a pen like beasts, my aunts said. Of course they built the fences the same way they do for their animals—how else is a fence built? And only mud to protect them from the heat. Their own skin to warm them when night came. They would wake covered with dew, fevered. This is what you'll have to think about as a war correspondent: all the ways the body has to die. Is that interesting to you, Frank Tannenbaum?" She raises her right eyebrow: another challenge issued.

"Yes."

He does not elaborate. *Yes* stands for itself only. Is itself. Frank Tannenbaum does nothing but wait intently. Waiting and silence as natural to him as his own breath.

It makes her nervous, his silence. Yes. Yes. This boy does not mind the contemplation of the body dying. He does not shirk from saying so, and does not elaborate. That he must know its opposite—the body living—makes her blush. That and her own talk. Why on earth had she said such a thing?—to a boy who's lost his own mother. And suppose her father had died alone, lying in the mud—why, then, would she speak of it to a stranger? Why would she ever speak of such a thing? They don't know. They never knew about his last days, and there is no finding out now, no matter what congressman inquires.

"Fine," she says. "You want to be a journalist—I'll tell you a story. Do you need paper?"

He points to his ears, and folds his hands under his chin, leaning in.

Where will she start? Why had her father come to her now? As if she thought to match loss for loss. His mother for her father. She sits for a moment, studying him. His eyes the pale of Samuel's, all ice and light and crackle.

"Where are you from, Frank Tannenbaum?"

"Right here."

"The saloon?"

They both laugh, relieved. Of what, she cannot say, exactly.

"Manhattan."

"And have you ever left?"

"Most years, we've gotten away at some point or another."

"Who's 'we'?"

"My sister and I. My father, once. Friends."

She nods quickly, vaguely embarrassed that she'd asked. Of course there would have been many trips, and people—what does she know of him? "I don't suppose . . . Have you gone north on the train?"

He nods.

"Imagine, then, a place in the hills, a day's train-ride north. I suppose distance doesn't matter. I suppose landscape doesn't either. Do you think—?"

"Certainly. The farther north, the more need of buttons."

How happy she is to laugh.

"On the other hand," he says then, "blood's blood. Life, life. You tell me what matters. It's your story."

"Very well, Frank Tannenbaum." She does not know what else to say. She cannot refuse him—he looks at her too intently. Though she hears a weakness creep into her voice. Is the pounding of her heart audible? She looks down at her hands and sees one clenched and the other rubbing it, as if to comfort. How did one side get so strong and the other so timid?

She stops and uncurls the tight fist.

"It's a winter story. Do you like sleigh season?"

"Very much," he says, not shifting his gaze, or his hands; only his words raise his chin imperceptibly.

"You really do?"

"Yes. I really do."

"Me, too." She surprises herself with that. As though she'd never quite known it was true. "In the hills, where I was a girl, winter was the season of words. *Our time,* my grandfather used to call it. I would sit on an oval braided rug in front of the fireplace, playing a game of picking out the hidden ends, seeing how many I could find before the talking of the grown-ups quieted, and my mother would notice me, and give me a needle and make me tuck them all back in, and firmly, too. You know the sort of rug I mean?"

"Of course."

She smiles at him. He is comforting.

"I'd follow the rug's tiny wedges of color around and around, all the while words—above and beyond me, a steady hum, a kind of music, 'Samuel always said,' 'Do you suppose Samuel'—that was my father. Samuel."

Mary pauses, embarrassed. Does he notice her tripping over the name Samuel? She is telling about her life before the Elmer brothers came into it. She wishes she remembered what her grandparents and her mother and the aunts had been speaking of—the aunts who disappeared after the War, too, as if they'd died with their brother. They spoke of letters: whose letter had made it back, and from what state. What Lincoln had said. And the Union's prospects—she'd thought the North a man (what else was he, but her father and his brothers and all the others, grave in blue?) and the South his bride. And then the words turned to whispers that she and Lucy could not hear. Silence right in the middle of the season of words. The silence of an empty midsummer house. The seasons toppled and feelings came all ajumble—new feelings, and fear, and dizziness, and notunderstanding in place of what she'd never before had to name as understanding. *You can call him Father,* her mother said, of the man who sat at the end of the table looking at them gravely, touching the tips of his fingers together.

"The words around you," Frank prompts gently.

"Do you have that feeling about winter—that it's full of words?"

When she sees him hesitate, she tries to explain: "It must be a country feeling. In the summer, everybody spreads out—into the fields, down the paths to town or maybe to the river—and wherever they go, they leave behind a silence. Only noises the frogs and the crickets. The clopping of horses' hooves. Tires of a bike going down the hill. Only outside noises. All human voices, all words, go out the open windows, get lost in the sky and the heat and the fields."

"Yes," he says, "I can see that."

"But in the winter there, when the snows fall long enough and the drifts pile high up past the windows and there is nothing left to be had from field or forest, nothing left but to stay inside and talk, repair, make amends—then, my mother took us. Over the snow-packed roads, the biting gray-blue sky descending and becoming bitter white wind against which we had only our eyelashes. Mother must have realized that she couldn't drive the horses with a sled and two small girls a thousand miles, so we returned home and she started another fire. Trying to melt the knowledge that absent him, absent our home clapboarded tight against the cold, and the shed cobbled on, and the barn, without our iron firehouse, without each other and our animals—alone in the howling wind we were nothing, and our tiny eyelash-hairs, slimmer than the slightest word, were all sentence we could muster against the storm."

He watches her, but she does not see him. Her eyes look past him—not to the brick wall behind him, but past that, through anything solid. He catches himself turning to look, as if by turning he would see the horse-drawn sleigh, the city rain turned to blizzard. And then she meets his eye.

"I stopped picking at the rug on my own, because Mother no longer noticed what I was doing. I didn't want to end with a pile of tatters. I saw for myself then—I must have been only six—that the end of war had brought no glory. Our father was dead, and only shabbiness was ahead of us. Shabbiness and poverty. Less of everything. Less song, less talk, less laughter. My aunts no longer came. It wasn't until I was sixteen that I heard someone say that most of the men hadn't even died fighting, but afterward and in the prisons, of wounds not healing of course, but more often the malaria, and diarrhea. Diarrhea! The Northern prisoners were fed the same rations as the Southern soldiers, they said, but their guts didn't take to the uncooked cornmeal. But all this you probably read in the inquiry. That's my war story, Frank Tannenbaum. What do you think they are dying of in the Philippines?"

He rubs his hands over his face. "Our bullets, for one. But, wait—Jane." He looks into her eyes, as if by looking there he will see more of the girl by the fire and the mother driving horses to see the father far away in prison. He sees instead something icy. She is done with speaking of it.

"It's admirable of you, Frank Tannenbaum. To be a war correspondent. Very brave. We have to know, the rest of us at home. To me, war is only a dream. I must not be the only woman who feels that. Fathers—wars—faraway places—I don't quite believe any of it. I'm not a believer, Frank Tannenbaum."

"You're not one of those anarchists, are you?" he says, his eyes crinkling up again. Smiling as he had when he first sat down. For he sees she will accept only this lightness now.

But she does not smile back.

"Why do you say that?"

He is puzzled. Here they are—in one of the most famous anarchist gathering places in all New York, and she wonders why—

She slams shut her book and taps down the edges of the envelopes that stick out of it. Had he read the letter he had returned to her? Which of Jimmy Roberts's love letters had it been? (Love letters!) What had this young man learned of her?

"I only meant"—he stretches out both arms—"look at this place. Justus is the one who brought Johann Most—you know him, yes, the *Freiheit* publisher?—to New York. When she's in town, Emma Goldman uses the back as her sitting-room. I just assumed. I thought if you came in here, you were an anarchist. At the very least a sympathizer. Otherwise, you'd go somewhere else."

"Call me that, then. A sympathizer." She has never liked a word so much as this. If one must have a label attached to one's name. Her suspicion dispels. Such a lovely young man.

"Well, Jane Ware, sympathizer. Will you be back tomorrow? I'd like you to meet my sister."

"Maybe," she tells him. It is the closest she can come to saying yes.

Late in the afternoon is posted a paper on the drawing-studio door. At the top of the page are very few names: those who have been accepted, without further ado, to the Life class, the highest at the Academy. E. R. Elmer is not among them. Further down the page, a longer list: the students who have not been rejected altogether, but will instead face another round of trials. Of these twenty-five, five more will be selected in the next few days; these five, along with the First Five (who will always be so marked), will together inhabit the Life studio with Ward and his models.

The prize is not that, thinks Edwin. But the glow conferred upon the First Five that calls out the patrons and collectors. He has very few more chances. Though he is the seventh name on the second list of twenty-five. Now he has a one-in-five chance, better than the odds from the start. Perhaps the order is neither random nor alphabetical, but some sort of preliminary ranking. Either way, his mathematics bring little consolation.

As he sometimes does, he wonders about his brother Darwin. If there had been a failure for him. He had already moved to Ohio when Edwin was just a baby, so Edwin had never known his brother from anything but story. (Darwin had walked alone the entire seventy-five miles home to Ashfield from Troy, New York, when he was just fifteen; he was "stubborn, stubborn, stubborn—but enterprising!") Yet however knowledge had come, in story or blood or the silence that crossed their mother's face when she learned of his death, Edwin understood his own fate to be linked to Darwin's. He and Samuel would never have gone to Cleveland if it hadn't been for Darwin's first settling himself there many years before, and the family connection he had established with the silk-thread merchants.

Without telling Samuel, Edwin had gone to the offices of the *Cleveland Plain Dealer* to read the report. The newspaper facts he ever after dwelled with in silence: the Second Advent tracts with underlinings at the feet of his dead brother; the cord tied to a drawer knob only three feet off the ground (his will killed him, not his weight, surmised the reporter, without having heard the family story "stubborn, stubborn"); the letter from their mother chastising Darwin for turning his back on the "family religion." Edwin had guffawed here—a nervous laugh: What religion would that be? Gone, anything like it, before he and Samuel had come along. The reporter had drawn these conclusions: It was the Millerite cult, of which his mother had been a passionate adherent, and not any sort of money problem (several hundred dollars right there in the drawer).

But Edwin, who has as little complaint against his mother as a son can have, has no explanation. He'd heard it said once that a mother of twelve was twelve different mothers. So he granted the possibility that the reporter had insights not available in his line of vision. Still, they answered nothing for him. What despair had so filled Darwin, and what portion of it is Edwin's own? *An imperial affliction / Sent us of the Air*—a poem Mary likes comes to him. Something about landscape, shadows. *The Distance / On the look of Death.* He had looked into Effie's eyes before he had shut them, and could understand nothing that separated him from her. Had it been so for Darwin, who had seen five younger siblings die, before Edwin and Samuel were born? Death might have seemed to him like walking home to Ashfield: another place to go, where family was.

If they were home now, he would put an apple and sketchbook in the basket and ride his bicycle over to Put's Hill for the afternoon—who knows, maybe he would even go up that other hill, ride by the too-big house of dreams and the Whiting farm. Under the sky on Put's Hill, where their farm had once stood, it does not matter what he is or is not. No despair is too large to make even a puff of difference under that vast sky. There he is not inventor, portrait artist, miller, farmer, father, husband, but a creature of nature, whose facts and ways surpass any civilization's.

He is reasonable; he understands that the artists accepted to the Life class were very likely artists enough for one country and one time. Even of one so booming; even at the millennium: This flurry will pass, he thinks, the grandiosity, the sermons preached from horseback. It would be best if he and Mary went home before winter sets in. He should think soon about how they will manage in old age. Painting is no profession. The apple trees at John and Mother Jane's might turn a profit with a bit of attention. He could graft new trees for the lower meadow. Still some money trickles in from the double-acting butter churns. That helps. And the whip-snap machine. But he can't expect Mary to keep at that, ruining her eyes very likely. Well, if it is true what people say, that the student imitations of the Masters turn a brisk business during the holidays, perhaps he can put his "very fine color sense" to use. The thought of going to the printer for another business card makes him so weary that when he sighs the force of his expiration so startles him that he hesitates before drawing another breath. So much energy necessary even for that.

He knows that the painting of the Arab isn't any good: Why be disappointed that his own standards match the Academy's? They were kind not to have rejected him entirely: That is what he would have done, had he been the arbiter. Such falsity in its lines. This could be forgiven in a young man. In the case of a young man the faults might be balanced by the apparent technical skill, the breadth (hadn't he painted more, in the allotted time, than anyone else?)

Funny, how embarrassment can flourish even internally, spoken to no one, growing in the darkness like a mold. It needs neither audience nor light of day, for its fantasies are filled to capacity with both. Here, a row of the Truth-in-Art men allotting him a phrase within parentheses in their docket *(Kindly hosted by local amateur E. R. Elmer)*. "Local amateur." Here, an aisle of churchgoers wagging their fingers about the billiard rooms: "Idle hands the Devil's own"—and the way "Devil" lingered, nothing else need be said. Everyone knew those Elmers were acquainted with Him. (He unlocked the gate and emptied his uncle's bucket, avoiding his eyes, as if that could preserve the old man's dignity.) Here Mary, here Samuel, sitting across from him the morning his new mill burned to the ground. "It's not your fault, Eddie." In Samuel's eyes, Edwin saw a strange self emerge: a failure. A burden, probably. At least needful of protection. So talented, my brother, but too sensitive for his own good. The world is not slow, or gentle. Daughters die and buildings burn to the ground. "No," Samuel spoke to the newspaper for him. "Mr. Elmer will not rebuild."

Samuel does not know what classes Edwin had hoped to take at the Academy. He was not even sure he had told Mary. No one at home need know. Still, the intensity of his shame at the failure stuns him. That, and how familiar the feeling.

It reminds him of the portrait of Effie Ellsler. Of standing in the Ellslers' library waiting to return the money her father had paid for his daughter's portrait. He had opened the new book on the desk before him: The Fuller Worthies' Library *Complete Poems of Dr. John Donne.* Every printed word on the frontispiece had seemed to march in line against him, mocking him, increasing his shame as he waited, rehearsing his speech: I am returning your money. I'm not painter enough to (could he speak to a father of capturing his daughter's beauty?)—This is all I have of Effie, and all I ever will, so if I can't have her hand, I will return your payment and keep my crude approximation of her image—

The Fuller Worthies. Printed for Private Circulation. Only 106 copies. He didn't know what the Fuller Worthies Library was, but he understood this: If he were more Fully Worthy, he *would* know, and then he might be son to this man and stand in his library not importuning but conversing as equals about the poetry of Dr. John Donne. To be one of the 106! He stood there reminding himself that he was not asking for anything, he was not begging—he was simply returning the man's money; where was the dishonor in that?

He only had time to read the beginning of "The Triple Fool" (where else could his eyes have fallen but to Fool?)

I am two fooles, I knowe,
For lovinge, and for saying soe

"What are you up to, young man? I've just received those books from England."

He cringes even now, to think of it. No, embarrassment is nothing new. He can still feel the visceral disappointment of looking at his canvas and finding a portrait not of her, but of his own inadequacy. Still—the thrill of considering the edge of her neck against her violet dress. The right to do that. He was sure that he saw her as no man had before or would again.

It is another embarrassment to remember his behavior in the theater. He thought people would take note of him as her portraitist. As if that explained his presence in the theater every other night. Or the impressions in the thick velvet cushion, where he pressed his thumbs when he could no longer bear to watch her. He would grip the edge of his second-row seat, watching the sharpness of his own knuckles, feeling the condensed power in his hands, looking down surprised to see the long, bony hands of a man—a man! when had his hands become a man's?—whose thumbs were regularly bearing down into the velvet, down and up, down and up, holding himself to a rhythm, regulating his breath, keeping himself in the seat where he belonged. He didn't know his was the rhythm of lovemaking. He didn't know anything—this is what shames him still. That he had been blind to the winks of the men who watched him waiting outside her stage door. Samuel knew. All he knew himself was that he and his brother drank very smart whisky and their suits were as fashionable as anyone's, and all the future ahead of them, so he supposed they could do what they wanted with their free time. They actually had time. And she had said yes. So he was her portraitist, not just any member of the audience at Cleveland's famous Academy of Music, at the seventeenth matinee performance of *Bertha, the Sewing Machine Girl, or Death at the Wheel.*

Death at the Wheel. Yes, that was it. Reminds him of Mary, back on 23rd Street, turning the crank of the whip-snap machine. Mary, the Whip-Snap Machine Girl. At least that was a better painting. But for the moment he wants to contemplate female beauty not his wife's. Is it still possible to conjure Effie Ellsler? Her long throat. Her lips curling around a long O, holding back and delivering at once. If he is absolutely still, does her voice still sing inside him?

. . . where's that wise man that wo'ld not bee I,
If she would not deny?

He had unveiled the portrait in the attic and showed it to Mary the morning he'd found her outside with the Roberts boy, watching the sunrise like lovers. After, in place of Effie Ellsler's voice, he heard Mary's. "Oh Edwin. She must have been very beautiful." With her words, something tightly sprung inside him loosened. And Effie Ellsler was lost to him. The part of her he had held for years slipped away. She no longer roused him with her song, her eyes closed, her concentration and abandonment finding a way inside him, the tremor at the center of her soft throat his own pulse, a knot of ecstasy, another world. Not her fingers touching his shoulder, but Mary's. Of Effie Ellsler's voice, there remained only the memory that he had tried to make what he knew of light and color and shadow into something as beautiful as her song.

Now, of all that, only embarrassment remains. To have wished such a grand thing! Even Ruskin told beginners: *Don't draw what you love.* An Englishman, anticipating his mistake from across the ocean. Though Ruskin was not without his own troubles—his own wife, Effie, stolen right from under his nose by that young painter—what was his name? The one who'd painted *Ophelia.*

"You must know," he heard Samuel bringing one of his boarding-house tales to a close: "Always the artist steals the woman. But rarely does he keep her!"

"It's a joke," Samuel hissed under his breath.

How could he have been such a fool? Still he asks himself, *Was it my fault?* To have named my only daughter after impossibility?

Should not, should not—these words are soft as petals, one by one plucked and tossed to the wind. *Should not, should not*—

Yet here Mary is, walking with Frank Tannenbaum, no—half running. Laughing about something as they rush along the street, Mary holding her coat closed at the neck. She had not stopped to button up when they left Schwab's. A tiny fear? That the pause inserted into the stream of their words and their gathering of things, their leaving together when they had come in alone, might grow into a larger pause that would give them time to look at each other, and remember: *I hardly know you.* Apologies would be made and promises about another day. But she did not then think of her buttons, or why she started to do them up, or why she stopped.

They had not noticed how close and still the atmosphere in Schwab's until they emerged from its dark into the last light of day. Her coat flies wide in the wind and hits him. Two strangers, in such a breeze, under such a sky. That could be the reason for their laughing. No ceiling! Save the El with its clatter overhead.

Down the street three or four blocks—she keeps track enough to find her way back—and west one and a half. When Frank pushes the door open to a dark hall, *Should not, should not* beats louder and harder. Here, in this hallway, no wind moves; no petals fly. What does she know of Frank Tannenbaum, really? His mother is dead. He can listen. Entirely still. And with even his eyes.

She looks into those eyes. For too long? Perhaps. But what she sees there reassures her. Something familiar, though she cannot say what.

It is Frank who breaks their gaze, looking down as he fits his key in the lock. He pushes and the door swings open.

Here live Susana and Frank Tannenbaum, brother and sister. One bed, a stove, a table, a few shelves. Brother and sister, she repeats to herself, because it looks so matrimonial, because it is so like hers and Edwin's, only plainer, sparser, without the promise of the opening to an extra room.

A tousled blond head moves at the edge of the bed. Susana. She rises from the floor, on the other side of the bed, as though she had been hiding.

"Frank! Where have you—Hello." Susana stops midsentence and smiles at Mary. She didn't have to: They had interrupted her (though what was she doing on the floor?); she had expected only her brother; she was wearing only a shift. She might, very well, have frowned. "I gave up on you."

"Don't say so. I want you to meet someone. Jane, this is Susana. Forgive her—my sister keeps odd hours, she uses the floor as her desk. . . ."

"You've not left her much choice, I see." Mary nods in the direction of the little table by the window, whose surface is entirely taken by stacks of books and dirty dishes. Her comment on his housekeeping a response to the sun of Susana's smile. It is impossible not to smile back at her. Impossible not to wish to establish an alliance with her. Frank, charming though he is, forgotten for the moment, as Mary flusters under Susana's gaze. Frank had wished for her to see Susana, and he must have known how she would respond. It must be disconcerting for him, always, to watch people bask in his sister's beauty.

Though not just beauty, Mary thinks. A kind of radiance. Her mouth too wide to be classically beautiful. But it is the wideness Mary likes.

"Shall we go to Justus and Marianna's?" Susana asks, her eyes on Mary, as she herself stands dressing in the corner of the room.

Mary busies herself next to the table, reading the titles of books instead of looking at Susana. She undresses in front of them both. Unashamed. Well—where is she to go? At the edge of her vision, Mary sees a blur of white undergarments, an expanse of warm skin.

"We've been there all afternoon already, Susie," says Frank. "We haven't—"

Mary hears his hesitation. Does he not want to be seen there with her twice on the same day? Or is it—is he worried about money?

"Perhaps we could . . ." Mary stops at the edge of her sudden presumption and takes in both sets of expectant Tannenbaum eyes—Susana's she looks at rather nervously, trying not to see the nakedness below; Frank's more fully, that is safer—and sees *Yes* to whatever she might say already written in their eyes. She almost says, I will cook dinner for you right here. She and Susana could go out to the market, and—but this is mad! How tempting it is, to slip into this place, to start washing their dishes.

"Perhaps we could meet there tomorrow?" she asks instead. They would have said *Yes* to dinner, had she asked. But in place of today, tomorrow will do. Only the details are in question; not the fact that they will see each other again. Where they will meet, and in what combination of three.

When Edwin comes in the door, Mary is not home. He is early, he knows. He'd left the Academy as soon as he'd seen the list posted. No point in lingering there.

Where could she have gone at this hour? The storm ushering in the November dark earlier than usual. Is it safe for her to be out? A question part genuine and part effort at distraction from his deeper alarm, which is about his own lack of knowledge rather than any real fear for her safety. Perhaps if he'd come home early other days, he'd not have found her here a single evening. Perhaps this has been going on since his classes began. In any case: She'll be drenched.

Is anything on the stove? Nothing.

He sits down and puts his head in his hands.

"Go with him," he had said to her. "Effie and I will stay here."

He had steeled his entire being to say that. If he had sounded cold, it was only from the effort of keeping himself from—he does not know what. Dissolution. He insulted her, she had said later. He hadn't meant to. He had simply wanted to tell her: I have had my impossible love. And I am done with it. I have memorized the poem—*Grief brought to numbers cannot be so fierce;* I have ordered my longings and my sadnesses. I have chosen you. But I would not keep you against your will.

He had put his hand on the back of her waist and made her go up the attic stairs in front of him—he did not want her behind him, out of his range of vision. Holding her in front of him, he was surprised, by how soft the back of her waist, her hips—that she could be soft at such a moment. How soft she was, and how strong and steady his own hand. No one would guess from the hand how his heart was pounding. He spread his fingers and concentrated all of his power in the five fingers and blunt palm; with this hand he forced her up the steps. Up, up, up. They would have an end to this nonsense. At the top of the house, in the hot summer attic, while the summer guests slept. Or some of them. The early-morning light streamed in the east window, shining on the dust they'd whirled up, the thick latticework of spiders. Just seven years old, this house, and already its attic held an intransigent mass of belongings whose place they could not settle. White sheets covered a row of paintings. He folded back the sheet and then carefully lifted up the first. "Come," he said again, and motioned her over.

"This," he told her, "is Effie Ellsler."

"Effie?" she whispered.

"Ask Samuel about her if you wish."

Did he, then, wonder at the way she looked at him? In retrospect he sees a puzzle of innocence and confusion cross her face, and it is in this light, now, that he observes his own character. How full of the importance of his own confession he had been! How little he had understood what she would think.

"Oh Edwin. She must have been very beautiful."

Astonished, he had been. The sweetness of what she said. She was not angry at all. She was without shame.

"I've got to go back. I've breakfast to make for the guests."

Breakfast! She had no idea why he'd brought her here.

That Roberts boy surely knew! Guilty, guilty, he had looked as he ran off toward the orchard, his tail between his legs. Let him keep it there. As if every day one finds one's wife at daybreak, her hair all unwound, with another man. Not even a man!—a boy.

"Is she Ruskin's wife? How did Samuel know her? Was he in love with her?"

"*Whose* wife?" he said. "And what does Samuel have to do with—"

"John Ruskin's wife. Isn't she called Effie? And *you* said, Ask Samuel—"

"I only meant he was there in Cleveland."

She had no idea what he was trying to tell her. How could he have painted Ruskin's wife in Cleveland? That was absurd. Had John Ruskin ever traveled to Ohio? Well—not when he and Samuel were there. Who does she think he is? She must have overheard some snatch of the Truth-in-Art men's conversation the other night, and confused it all. Totwell had known the Ruskins in London. He had been a friend of that young painter—the one who had stolen Effie Ruskin. Mary must have overheard that story. It had surprised him, too, to hear of Ruskin and his loveless marriage (he seemed a man of great passion). But he saw that though they had, perhaps, heard the same story, she had taken it differently and imagined him, Edwin, an actor inside the tale, as though it had taken place in his world, not one he, too, watched from the outside. He saw that he was himself a stranger to his own wife, that what he did—his time with Samuel in Cleveland, his painting, the people and places he talked about—might as well have been across the Atlantic Ocean, for all Mary knew.

"You named *our* daughter after Ruskin's wife?"

"This is *not* Ruskin's wife. When I was young—" he began and stopped. He started over. "When Samuel and I lived in Cleveland, I loved this woman. After I painted this portrait of her, I made a vow to myself that I would never again—"

He wanted to show her that one must live with compromise, without that particular kind of love, even if she might think, might really even feel, the fineness of a particular sort of conversation (he had seen himself that Jimmy Roberts would make a fine man one day), still the ecstasy of sunrise or midnight or the profundity of mutual confession, whatever they had been about outside, was nothing to build a life upon. Tom Paine had written as much, about the good sense one must employ when choosing the wife (or the husband, he had intended to tell her, had she let him) of your home—how it was utterly different from other kinds of romance. This is *real*, he was about to tell her, except he did not get to that part, for she interrupted him just as he was trying to explain to her what he had learned and what he had vowed to himself—Never again Foolishness, Never again Sick unto Dawn—with yelling about the beastliness of all "his sort." (She had done him that strange favor, aligning him with the Truth-in-Art men, who had themselves relegated him to initials inside parentheses.) The *beastliness* and the *blindness*—Were she and Effie mere chattel, then?—His own daughter the name of some secret pact he had made with his own devils: Was that fair for a baby? And as for her—Wife, she was, Mother of the Vow, was that how she would have to live, from now until the end? Was conversation with the guests not allowed? She and Nellie should stay in the kitchen, keep silent and simply finish the chores, was that his point? And so forth, bringing in even her father, and the futility of his death, the futility of the War itself and the bleakness and cowardliness of their lives ever since, and Uncle, and other things Edwin felt she need not have said. As she yelled, he saw his present painted over in black. A ruin. Everything he believed, everything he had carefully worked to put in place, dashed by this woman turned suddenly a stranger who colored shadows across what had been light and scrawled dark connections (madly, it seemed to him) from every corner of their lives to every other. Who is this woman? he thought, as a sentence below hummed *contrapposto*, This is my wife. This is my wife. How could he have failed so utterly to imagine her response? He—the cuckold! He—the man who had caught his wife blushing, her hair loose, with a college boy at sunrise. Was such vehemence really due him?

Never again would guests return to their house on the hill, for it was unpleasant to awake in the morning to the domestic squabbles of others, to trunks being dragged overhead and shouting in the attic that clearly implicated people one would have to face at breakfast (which was already late and would probably be burnt). Well: That was fine. It had been her idea to turn their home into a guest house in the first place. They—could he anymore envision what they would do together?—would find other ways to pay their way in the world.

In the end, he lost all idea of what he had hoped to say. He wanted only to weep. He hoped only that she would stay. He hoped that she would see how foolhardy it would be for her to go to New York. There was nothing in it for her. He was only seventeen—a boy off to college. And a boy like that quickly would have found a woman in his gentleman's quarters a problem. Where would he have kept her? What would have become of her in this city?

If she had left him then, she would never have come back, Edwin knows. She is that stubborn. Yet—what of Effie? How could she ever have lived without Effie?

What a stupid question. What a stupid, stupid question.

When Mary comes in, just a half hour later, she finds Edwin sitting at the table motionless, his hands covering his face. When he looks up, her lightness deflates.

"Where were you?"

"Out. Out for a walk. The rain let up, and I wanted to—breathe. What's wrong with you?"

"Do you think that's a good idea?"

"Breathing?"

"Going out alone. Do you really suppose it's safe for a woman like you—"

"A woman like me? What do you mean by that?"

"A married—respectable—"

"Are you suggesting that when you are out all day, the only women you meet are not respectable?" Mary slams the iron kettle onto the stove. "Artists, artists' models—" she waves her hand in the air.

"I'm sorry. Sometimes I worry. About where—about how—you are."

"I'd rather you didn't. Is that why you are sitting there scowling?"

"There's another week of trials for the Life class."

"Oh, Edwin. Whatever for? What are they going to find out in a week that they don't already know?"

He opens his hands wide to show her he knows nothing.

"So that's why you look so gloomy. But I thought you didn't like the teacher. What's his name? The Younger?"

"The Lesser."

"Oh. Right."

"I don't like him."

"Well, then. Forget it."

"You're right. Will you go to Samuel's with me tomorrow?"

She feels her shoulders suddenly sink—without thought she transforms herself into a smaller woman. "I really don't feel—"

He narrows his eyes at her. "Decide in the morning."

In bed, he recites the poem he'd written out on the back of Effie Ellsler's portrait:

> *Then, as the earth's inward narrow crooked lanes*
> *Do purge sea-water's fretful salt away,*
> *I thought, if I would draw my pains*
> *Through rhymes vexation I should them allay.*
> *Grief brought to numbers cannot be so fierce,*
> *For he tames it that fetters it in verse.*

"What makes you think of that poem now?" she asks. She keeps her tone light. As though she has forgotten when she first saw those words. Though she has no reason to feel guilty.

He twists his mouth: No answer comes. He shrugs.

If what had drawn him many years ago to this poem (after the word "Fool," that is), was the idea that grief might be tamed by art, this night in New York it is the "inward narrow crooked lanes" and the "sea-water's fretful salt" that interest him. He wants to get away again, go on a journey. He falls asleep thinking of the East and Hudson rivers, of tributaries and rivulets and docks, and how it is that civilization makes its way from the shore. He has not seen the ocean in his life: And why not? Shouldn't he take the opportunity, here? Though it is not the expanse of sea that attracts him, but how the water makes its way inland. Since he has been small, he has soothed himself by constructing different versions of the same ideal landscape: verdant hills, cleaved by a river that flows to a distant sea (never the subject, always the background), where perhaps a dhow sails, far off, near the setting sun. Close by, some flowers, some trees (this night a patch of bright oriental poppies and a quince orchard just to the left of the house), the house small, humble, with the aspect of summer. All that a house truly needs is a porch, and windows that light streams from, and a woman and a child at the door. Someone there is, who lives in that house with them, someone who must come inside from work, into the warmth of that light, answering the call of that woman, whose brown hair streams long down her back. He cannot help what he finds beautiful.

He hadn't need of the fortune-teller who for pennies read his classmates' palms, showing them how the fate-lines and heart-lines of the hand they used were different from those of their weaker hand. Here you have been, she said to that one. And here you are going. He hadn't need of that to recognize how, to make this landscape, he'd split and doubled the hill where he was born and made a river run through to a sea, such as he'd only seen in reproductions of paintings.

"Do you believe it?" she asks. "Do you think it's true?"

The river thunders toward them: all black and glinting light and rumble. He does not follow her question, so he says, "I don't know," and then, thinking she must mean the river, he says, "Of course. What else could it be?"

Thursday

Edwin is always the first to rise. But this morning, when he hears Mary get out of bed, he pretends to sleep. She goes to the whip-snap machine before anything else—before even boiling water for tea. The silken ends of the whips are red this batch. Almost the vermilion he had used for the ribbon on Effie's hat. She always left the hat tossed aside somewhere in the grass, unruined only because of Mary's diligence, that way she'd sweep her eye over all as the sun went down. Last chance to bestow order, to do the best by the day. That year Effie had begun to behave like a smaller version of Mary—all neat and capable and womanly. Shipshape! Brushing flour from her hands, catching a wisp of hair behind her ear. Whip-snap!

Mary tosses a finished whip-snap onto the floor, and Edwin sits up with a start.

"Good morning."

"You're finished so quick?"

"You were asleep for most of it."

"I was awake."

"Didn't you sleep well?"

"No."

"Is it that class?" She hears in her voice, and so must he, that she does not have any store of sympathy for him; she will tolerate no complaint. If he doesn't like the Academy, why does he go? Why does he not do what he wishes? With all the city before him, and his living paid until spring.

"I know it's foolish to be bothered," he concedes.

Mary turns the crank; her fingers fly.

He tries a new tack: "Do you find Samuel changed?"

"Not particularly."

Edwin gets dressed and then stands in front of the whip-snap machine. "How do you spend your time while I'm out?"

"Making whip-snaps."

"Then why aren't there more?"

"Are you the factory foreman now? Did Samuel say I'm not making enough?"

"No. Sorry. I just—"

"I read; I walk. What do you think? I can't be cooped up here all day."

"And you're comfortable walking about alone?"

"More than."

"At home, I could understand, your liking to walk."

"I like it here just as much. Maybe more." Though as she says *maybe more,* she knows it's not true—there's no comparing.

"I would rather be home, myself."

"If you get into that class?"

He considers. "Yes. Still. I'd rather be home." With this repetition, his certainty gathers.

"One day, we will be," she acquiesces. (But it is false; it is ambivalent; she has not emptied her voice of annoyance.)

"Yes." He bends to kiss her. And she knows that her softening has come too late. But did he think to agitate her with visions of home?

"You're not working here this morning?"

"No."

His kiss delineates refusal: what he will not do, what he will not countenance. This kiss—though he has still to shave, and breakfast, and polish his shoes as he always polishes his shoes—is the sealing of a resolution that does not include her. He will not work in the studio near her, though the light coming through the skylight is best in the morning, though there is very little sense in Samuel paying the rent on this place if Edwin does not make use of the light. With the kiss, he breaks the agreement they'd contracted—that they would work here together in the mornings. Hadn't they said as much? Hadn't that been the order of their days?

"Will you go by Samuel's after the Academy?"

"Perhaps. Don't worry—if I do, I'll say you didn't sleep well, and wanted rest."

The fault is hers: His kiss says that, too. She has been walking about this city without him, unbeknownst to him. Very well. She has betrayed his trust, and he cannot abide that. He had expected her to be home last night, so now he shows her what it is to expect, and be mistaken. How small the motion that conveys all this to her. What particular hardness about his mouth, what firm line expresses this particular variety of anger? She touches her own lips, as to find the answer there. An anger that has no words, for to speak it would be to unburden it of its very essence, which is the ritual elaboration of silence, where once might have grown argument, defense, conversation. He is not an ungenerous man; his views are progressive and open; he is capable of change, as much as anyone, and more than most. He would never say to her that he forbade her to leave the apartment without him. Never would he utter such words. More: He would never again say that he had ever so much as expected she would not. And yet. This silence between them; the uncompromising line of his lips.

Here she could place a stone. To mark a path not taken. For she does not explain or query or pardon. She does not ask again what troubles him, or rise from her chair, or stop her braiding, to stand in front of him, take him by the shoulders, and say, Edwin, I should tell you. The strangest thing happened to me yesterday—

About reality, she thinks, a wife and a husband have nothing to say. As for the truth of her soul, or reason, or gesture—perhaps she could explain elsewhere; someone else might understand why she'd folded up her umbrella and lifted her face to the rain.

What stops her? What makes her turn from him, silent? She turns the wheel as quickly as she can, until her wrist begins to ache. He should have added a mechanism by which she could turn the crank with both her feet instead; that would have balanced her body, and saved her hand.

Nevertheless, if she can finish the snaps quickly, she may have time enough to write the story pell-mell, anyway it comes (not by date, not in things either)—that would fit the little time she has, and be true to her subject, too. She will forget propriety and form.

For Jimmy Roberts loved motion. He alone among mortals of her acquaintance accepted that one minute follows the next and never returns. (Letters not to be saved but shredded into stew.) Yes, she will write of him now, with the daffodils starting to push up through the soil at the edge of the park. The green shoots of the crocuses and daffodils are mistaken, and she is mistaken with them. She piles leaves around them to shelter them from the cold that, when it comes (if it comes?), will burn their green tips yellow. She should, perhaps, make some show of caution in her own life: Her coat all unbuttoned, as foolish as the flower. What is she up to, slipping herself inside another family? (And a family of two, at that.) Edwin senses something. His irritation not only about the class, she can tell. But what should she have said? "I met a young man in a saloon." "I went home with a young man and met his sister." Surely he has met people and not spoken of them to her. "I went looking for Jimmy Roberts, and Nellie and Gracie, and it's too late for either you or Samuel to stop me." That, she could never say.

She wants winter to come, if only to ensure their staying in New York for a season more. Whatever Edwin may wish, he will not force anything that goes against the logic of the seasons. It makes no sense to return home in the dead of winter.

She must have thought life would stop. That it had stopped already. That these months in New York with Edwin painting were outside of time, deprived of season or necessity. Now her chance to fill the green book. The only chance she may ever have. But why do it? Is it just a way of giving the past its proper burial? She thinks of that local saying that ends any complaint people have about the problems of their ever-shifting farmhouses: House finished, life over. No wonder she has never brought herself to fill her book. May as well put her own self aside in the attic, and give all her clothes over to Maud while she's at it.

Thank goodness, life intrudes. Here are Frank and Susana Tannenbaum to say, Living does not stop, no matter what introspection, no matter what pause one seeks to puff into the balloon of one small moment.

The notebook's green is not the color of death. It is the green that one spring morning alights on dark branches and blurs their sharp angles. An improbable color, like so many nature has to offer. Who knew that pouring cider vinegar in with the bracken and boiling diapers would make such a shade? Edwin had been so delighted he insisted on soaking in it every last strand of that winter's spun wool and flax. And then scraping the bottom of the tub for pigment. *May the pages pressed between likewise turn into something unexpected by their Agitator.* She should write that inside the piss-green cover.

Maud will be the one left after she and Edwin are gone. Unless she finds Gracie. But Nellie and Dave had left Massachusetts when Gracie was just a baby, so Mary has no claim to be the aunt she might have been. Not now. Proximity might have made that possible, but the tenuousness of their relationship has not borne distance. Distance opened up the tear their shared days had once stitched close. Yes, the days together had done that. She and Nellie had been closer than sisters for a time. Stitched close the right words. The days side by side providing opportunity for tiny piercings of difference—Nellie had no time to go to the library; Mary's father had died in the War, but Nellie's entire family had been lost and her home, too, if it could be said that she had ever known one—and then, mending here, a patch there. Sneaking off to the stream to swim in the August heat. Laughing together to see Jimmy Roberts work so hard and so clumsily at the tasks the two of them could do with their eyes closed. (Did do in their sleep, practically, such were the days.) After they stopped taking in summer guests, no money left to come between them. No longer employer and employed. Still Nellie kept coming over to the big house. "Habit stronger than sense," said Dave. His own habit was to chuckle. Which often meant that it was only later, when his bare words were drained of the warmth of his voice and his punctuating laughter—that she understood how serious his intent. When she and Dave had gone out to walk the perimeter of the pasture, to see where it was the new mare had got out, he had chuckled to see Master galloping over the hillside and returning to snort and shake his mane before galloping off again in the same direction. "Master's got a junior notion of what it means to be a married man. A junior notion."

After Nellie and Dave left for New York, she realized he was telling her that he knew. He knew everything about Samuel. And Nellie. And that word, Master, a brand on them all. They were every one complicit. Though who'd named the stallion? Dave himself, she thought.

Before that, but after Nellie finally stopped coming over to the big house, Mary went to find her. Who had ever been her friend, if not Nellie?

"Do you miss that boy?" Nellie asked her, as they made her pies. No one else would have asked. Nellie herself would not have asked in Mary's house. But in her own kitchen, she bossed imperiously. "Miss your chicken scratching?" she asked Mary when she fidgeted, to have nothing in her hands. "A stack of darning right here."

"Do you miss Samuel?" Mary asked in reply. He had moved to Boston already then.

Nellie stopped rolling the dough and looked at her. That boy, Samuel, the silence, stitches taking up the distance between them. They didn't speak of it again.

To assure herself of the devotion that once existed (though how could it have, with what happened after?), Mary conjures Effie some months later, playing with baby Gracie, leaning over the basket, tickling under her neck.

Turned out Nellie and Dave had been planning all those months to leave. Plotting behind her back. And one day left, all matter-of-fact and thank you, ma'am. She could have written, Mary thinks. Even now, something burns inside her chest. Samuel had taught Nellie to read and yet she had never once bothered to write to let Mary know that they'd arrived safely, or to ask after Effie. For all Nellie cared, they were all dead.

Mary could see—anyone who came along the road at night could have seen—Nellie and Samuel, sitting at the big table, two heads bent over one book. Yes, she knew how to write. So it is really not Mary's place to search for her. She cannot find them if they do not wish to be found. A person could hide in New York City until the end of her days, if that is what she wants. They were gone, and that was all. She had hoped, though. That, by chance—

On the other hand, to find Jimmy Roberts, she has only to ask Justus. But she cannot bring herself to it. Had she thought that when she arrived at 51 First Avenue, all her life would be written? Everything said—about Nellie and Samuel and the secrets that walked abroad at night, while Edwin dreamed of Effie Ellsler or his Dearly-Departeds and the big cats prowled and she hung the kitchen towel out on the porch rail to dry.

If one day she were to find Jimmy Roberts, it would be the end of nothing that was not over already, long ago.

Very well. Edwin will go to meet Samuel after the Academy, and he will make excuses for her: Mary did not sleep well (though he is the one who turned and muttered in his sleep, he who paced by the window in the dead of night). They have made a silent pact to blame Mary for the restlessness of them both. If she had been home when he arrived, Edwin thinks but does not say; if she had been home as she ought to have been, peace would have remained. In order not to disturb their silent agreement, which holds out the promise that the subtraction of one simple action might restore domestic harmony, Edwin accepts without argument last night's plea of weariness. Both, for different reasons, are happy to let Samuel worry that Mary is ill with making whip-snaps.

Though it is not true about the arsenic on the thread, as Dr. Fessenden had accused. The court had cleared Samuel's name in that regard. Indeed, Mary had taken a starring role in Samuel's defense: "Am I a man," Samuel had asked, "who would allow his own sister-in-law to work with a known poison?"

But one needn't look for a malignancy to explain weariness. Reading *English Traits* one night, she'd left the book open on the kitchen table for Edwin, to the page about how the incessant repetition of hand-work dwarfs a man. *Robs him of his strength, wit, and versatility.* She recognized herself thus, with the pin-polishers and buckle-makers. She, a whip-snapper, whatever her life might have been.

"What would you like me to do?" he had asked, pushing the book back across the table.

And to that, she had no answer. What right had she? To hope for anything different.

She and Edwin are lucky. Samuel struck it rich. Here is the world, he said to them. Or at least, Here is New York City. When twenty-four red whip-snaps are done, Mary can meet Frank Tannenbaum and his sister Susana at Schwab's. Noon, they'd said.

She talked too much yesterday.

For that, she blames Emerson. *To live truly is to give any stranger—*

Mary stops in the middle of a snap to thumb through her collections of essays. *To live truly is to give any stranger*—but she cannot find it. Could get lost for years looking, she well knows. Perhaps if she sits very still, it will come. *To live truly. To live truly is to*—

She was to write of Jimmy Roberts. Of going to look for him at Schwab's. Before yesterday, she knew nothing.

8 November 1899

Before yesterday I knew nothing of sisters and brothers living on their own in this City or the German anarchist newspaper Freiheit *or how easy it is to mock the President—*

"Why is McKinley's mind like his bed?

—They're both made up for him."

I was uncomfortable to laugh about the President and his bed. (His poor wife, I thought: Surely she was not to blame?) Yet I loved to listen to Schwab, proprietor and supporter of the anarchists, making jokes with the men. He brought me a beer foaming over the top of the mug—without my even asking. On the house, he said, in an accent that made me slightly unsure of each word. His rich Melody made me wish I could start language over again.

I have always styled myself the Listener (to Samuel's talk, I suppose). Yet what words came from me under Frank Tannenbaum's gaze! Who is he, this college boy? Before yesterday, I knew nothing of him or Susana, and now they crowd my thoughts, pushing aside the ones who have long lived there. I did not even realize, until late last night, watching Edwin standing by the window: Susana is just the age Effie would be now. Also the age I was when she was born. Twenty years and abloom with Life.

Effie would be courting age. Older, already, than Mary had been when Edwin scratched at her window. And at twenty he'd been a boy off to make his fortune in the West. If Effie had lived, perhaps now, there'd be a pair of eyes, steady on her, attentive as Frank Tannenbaum's. *Beholding and beholden.* Mary loves this small tenderness of Emerson's—to think of being and holding equal and consummated. *Beholding and beholden.* Effie might have studied at a college, and read books to talk about over dinner. Perhaps she'd be waiting with Maud to take a train across the continent to teach the children there (as if there were not already young ones on this coast, to be found without such commotion).

Maud may die there, she thinks, setting down her pen entirely.

Mary sees herself, as Edwin had painted her, grief-stricken and dour: a black-clad woman standing in the way of time. We will all die, she tells herself. This, her only comfort. Nieces and daughters will depart for other cities and other centuries. What sensible woman sets herself against that? Grief-stricken and dour she sits in that painting, staring out from the shadows of the lilac tree. And instead of a ball of yarn—cerulean, like the sky—she holds a tiny box, big enough to hold a clenched human fist.

The keys to my castle. The phrase suddenly comes to her. *To live truly is to give any stranger the keys to my castle.* Any stranger. Summoning these words, she takes them as directive. (Books should be taken away from her, before her belief does some harm.) A babe in language, she is.

It must have been only a season, so quickly it passed, when Effie had tested every word, weighing her elders' use against her own, eager to prove that she had mastered more than what they had taught her. "No, little one," she overhead Effie say to her doll, when she paused, listening outside the door. "Don't fly so close to the sun. Your wings have been fastened with sealing wax."

"You want me to *fly* over to fetch Uncle Samuel and Maud for dinner?" Effie looked up, smirking happily. "With my wings?" She had given them notice: Henceforth words are mine, and I will argue with all I hear. Once, Mary would have known Effie's voice anywhere. The part of her that answered to it has atrophied and fallen away, and Mary has only ideas left—that she understands Emerson as Effie once heard her. A babe in language, fresh with accusation: He calls a stranger "lord." He calls his son "caducous."

How one writes is nothing Mary knows. *Every. Past. Thing(s). Becom(ing). Strange.* Learning something new is what makes the familiar strange. Writing speeds that alienation. (*Ignorance soothes*—she must consider this.) She does not remember ever having been soothed. She abides in no comfort. Excitable, her mother always called her. *You could never sit still. You could never accept.*

Poor Emerson and poor me, she thinks, as she puts on her coat. (She cannot sit still.) Baneberry and fig and the curse on us all.

Already what came before yesterday, before Frank Tannenbaum, is strange to her (she cannot reconstruct what'd she had been trying to write before she ran out of Schwab's). She calls him that: *Yesterday's man. Who makes everything else Past.* Though she should not choose such romantic language. For do not words create facts?—Isn't that her trouble? To Edwin, she had promised: If the unacceptable thing you see between your wife and the young boy off to college is what the world calls passion, we shall put it aside. We shall not know it in our tidy house.

Edwin built a box to contain all of Effie's things. But years before, Mary had built a box for her own unacceptable heart. Therein her guilt. That when death came, in the everyday clothes of the New England catarrh, she was prepared. Dour, he had painted her, for all the world to see. Dour, with lines creased into permanent disappointment. Susceptible, she adds, to poetry and visions of another world. And she knocks three times on the doorframe before she leaves, by which she means, Wake up.

Edwin grants that it is no fault of Mary's that a particular memory assaults him at a particular time. She had freely chosen to stay with him those many years ago, and against her he has no true complaint. Yet this morning he cannot carry on as usual. He doesn't want to face the noise and the height of the El, speeding atop a world rendered invisible to him. If he were a different person, he might find himself drawn to the scenes that clatter by at eye level: the boy lying on his back on the fire escape, the woman tending the red geranium at her windowsill. Paintings could be made of these subjects. But he will not make them. What interests him is the feeling of an entire world passing by beneath the train. It causes him extreme visceral discomfort to think of the people below. The boy selling newspapers. All the boy's customers walking by, clutching bags and gathering up their skirts. A painting could be made of these people, too. But that is only slightly more likely. Imaginable. (There: He has imagined it.) Though even as he arranges its pieces—the boy, with his back to the column; the woman in the lower left corner, dipping down, stepping off the curb—he knows he will not paint this scene either. He is hardly more comfortable underneath the train than he is on it. He wants none of this invention on stilts.

For himself, he is quite sure he would have been better off without trains, fantastic though they are. Harbinger of progress, he supposes. He and Mary would not have come to New York. Very well. Perhaps he would not have dreamed of Alaska. Very well. Samuel would not have worked away from home. And if he had stayed nearby? A different life, only. Maybe better. As far as Edwin is concerned, he would have preferred less money and less commotion and more time. Now Samuel has a scheme about a cable railway to a lake and mountain resort where New Yorkers might go to indulge in country pleasures for a weekend. As though a weekend were time enough.

Samuel makes him feel old-fashioned. A step behind.

"I am not against innovation," he says aloud, though his brother is nowhere nearby. In any case, Samuel could not very well have supported any contrary stance, with what he has seen over the years of Edwin's cameras and gadgets and interest in the latest contraptions.

Nevertheless. He is against speed. Ruskin, Ward, all of them, be damned. Against men racing time. His contraptions, as Samuel calls them, are all different tools for securing or deepening a moment's activity. For moving more slowly. Another name for increasing precision. The roof brackets that can be adjusted to the cant of every roof, so that one putting on the shingles has a stable, level platform on which to stand. The double-acting butter churns, whose gears shift for the last, nearly solid finish. And certainly all the tools of his chosen trade: his cameras, the magic lantern, the airbrush. The whip-snap machine alone is different. Nothing to recommend it save speed: Mary makes twenty snaps in the time she used to make one. He wonders if Mary feels bossed by him at that machine as he feels bossed by Samuel to marvel at the speed and convenience of trains.

He only really wants to paint what he loves. (Ruskin be damned.) The woods, and trees, and mountains, and light—sunlight and lamp-glow, both. And also streams and rivers that carve inlets and paths through the land. *Inward narrow crooked lanes.* Must be some edge of this island he could find that would be tolerably right.

Maybe. He has an idea. Heavy and overhead like the train, yet with the roughness of sketch—not what he loves, but something *his*, nevertheless: fear, a strange foreboding that has put a new hunch into his walk. How might a canvas hold the weight of that? The train all shadow and gray, a streak across the canvas. If he put a huge pile of carbon black directly on the canvas to begin—first with his knife, spreading a giant glob of it, damn the waste, in one painting he would use what had before lasted him a decade—that would be accurate; that would approximate his sense of the train's inevitability and his own no-luck. He imagines pushing that much paint across the canvas. He does not know what it would look like, but in a sudden exhilaration to think about the action of pulling across an empty canvas such paint—lampblack would do; in any case Samuel can well afford whatever he asks—he turns abruptly from the stairs leading up to the El and picks up his pace. He will walk to the Academy. The edges of the canvas could stay raw. Once he has spread the black—and how he does that will be the painting's story: hurried and broad, shooting off the top left of the canvas, perhaps just a suggestion below of human shapes—in that darkness he could stay for days, pulling a train from it, pulling up speed and fear, and wonder, too, he supposes.

The decision not to ride the train at first seems no kind of evasion on Edwin's part, but the opposite, a coherence: Here is the way Edwin can find himself in this city. He is accustomed to walking everywhere at home; here he can do the same. Walking briskly, he can make the Academy well before nine. The Academy is eighty-six blocks to the north, and west several long blocks, too.

An omen upon arrival: All his and Samuel's plans had been based on information everyone else seemed to know was no longer true. The Academy had moved—hadn't he heard?—from 23rd Street, way up to Amsterdam and 110th. Walk? He supposed Mr. Elmer could, but it was at least five miles.

"I should have returned home then."

He has spoken aloud.

No one notices.

He had gone back to the carriage to tell Samuel's driver to go on to 165 West 23rd Street. "But where is the Academy?" Mary had asked. "Don't you have the address?"

"It's moved."

"Moved?" Her voice expressed all the incredulity his would not allow.

He revealed to her nothing of his rising panic—what else had he and Samuel gotten wrong? Would he be late to the first class? Exactly how far was Amsterdam and 110th Street? In this city he is powerless; he must do whatever he is told; he is at the mercy of the first stranger. Not to mention Samuel, his teachers at the Academy.

Though whatever he and Mary had felt as they'd silently carried their luggage up five flights to the top floor of the brownstone at 165 West 23rd Street, when Edwin had seen the windows and the skylight, he had silently thanked his brother. (What Samuel had paid for it, he would not have believed.)

Thinking of Samuel and the skylight and of black paint so thick he must spread it with a knife, he begins to walk east. The wrong direction, by any accounting. He wants to get off the island, or come close to its edge, be able to see beyond it. From the dead center, under the Sixth Avenue El, either river is beyond his sight. Instinct, is it? Rebellion? In any case, he walks away from the Academy, and toward the East River and the rising sun, which is too obscured by clouds to blind.

Beside the river, the weight pressing on the top and back right of his head lessens—yes, there he feels it, on the right, which is why he pulls the blackness across the canvas from the right to left, sweeping it off the edge and out of sight. The heaviness in his head lightens by the river. He is glad to be near its movement. Under all the other sounds, he can hear, or at least sense, the flow of water. At 26th Street he stops for a moment to look out over the river to the collection of stone buildings on the island in the middle.

"Which one?"

"Excuse me?" Edwin startles to realize the man beside him—when had he crept so close?—is addressing him.

"Which building—Incurables? Charity? Paralytic? Epileptic? Maternity—eh? Is it maternity?"

Edwin shakes his head and looks back resolutely at the water and not the buildings. So they were all hospitals out there in the middle of the river?

The man jabs his index finger in front of Edwin. "Lunatic asylum for women?" He winks.

Edwin glares at the man now.

"Prison? Almshouse? Workhouse?" the man offers, in retreat.

When Edwin walks away, he hears the man laughing behind him. And these words trail after him, faint gray shapes—prison almshouse workhouse lunatic asylum—written in fading newspaper-type, almost falling off the raw-edged bottom of the painting, but sticking. Some things he will never escape. Always he is the same boy, with the same uncle, the same family curse.

He fancied himself commissioned from Heaven to kill three persons and derived his warrant, as he says, from the eleventh chapter of Revelations.

He is tempted to turn around and tell the man that Uncle was right in his way. The land *had* been soaked in blood. Children and the rulers and the generals—everyone, slave and free—scattered and hid in the hills. But there was no hiding.

Walking to Schwab's, Mary's heart races with a speed her mind cannot catch. She'd meant to write the story of Jimmy Roberts, and had not gotten to it at all, for thinking of Emerson's exhortation: *Give any stranger the keys to your castle.* She cannot shake the thrum of pleasure to think of Frank and Susana Tannenbaum. That they will talk together and—perhaps—walk along the river. Admit, Mary Jane Ware Elmer, you are no different from Samuel. Drawn astray. Lured by this or that idea, this or that person. Jimmy Roberts was once such a stranger. "Goodness," she must have exclaimed when he startled her in the blueberry bushes. "Excuse me, ma'am," he must have said. Though that is hardly an auspicious beginning.

How many years she has stayed in the blueberry bushes with Jimmy Roberts! Reliving (a strange word, when it is not living at all) gestures and sentences that had formed and dispersed. Trying to hold a cloud. And now, as she approaches telling that story (to resume it, does she think?—he must be somewhere close by), she skitters off, thinking of Emerson in the neighborhood with vagabonds, and how a young man like Frank Tannenbaum might have fallen in love with Effie. And what would Edwin have said to that!

To tell the story of Jimmy Roberts, she should spill it all in a tumble and flash. That would be faithful to the one whose hours of companionship she can count on her fingers. Is this why she finds herself stepping instead into another story, at the brink of telling the old one? Because to tell it truly would be to lose him. The effort of narration—its slowing—seems to make all the world around pick up speed. This is not what I wanted, she thinks. I only wanted him.

She surprises herself with that. *Only?* So melodramatic. All these years? Then what a sad story is hers! The sadness of it (which is not precisely sadness now, but something else—a promise floats in the air, the chance to see him, or else someone like him, or someone who knows him) carries her all the way to Schwab's, ahead of her feet. Who is this Susana? And her brother?—what will they speak of today? Perhaps their quick intimacy will have caught up to all three of them during the night and today make them stutter and slow, awkward as strangers.

By the time she arrives at Schwab's, Mary can hardly countenance sitting, let alone opening her book to write. *"Excuse me, ma'am," came a voice.* No. That isn't quite right. Susana and Frank nowhere to be seen. Cider, she'll have, to settle her nerves. She sits around the corner from the bar, where she cannot see the door. She doesn't need its opening and closing to further agitate her. She will sort his letters by date.

8 Nov 1884

Here is what the poets say, Mary.

They gather in the smoky back of an alehouse on Broadway and speak of Ideals.

"Better not to love, but to imagine love," said the one with the curly hair and generous girth settling around his youthful bones. (How does a young man acquire such placid heft?) "Actual women get in the way of poetry."

He was my friend, from the first day of our seminar on Milton. He offered a great many insights into the poetry; he studied; he offered comparisons to Hafez, whom he was translating from the Persian, via the German, which he was teaching himself. All very well. But on that night I began to hate him (tho' this much feeling seems undue). I should say: I do not imagine our friendship will continue.

"Better not to love, but to imagine love." That he repeated, daubing the sweat from his hot forehead. Better that he wipe his foaming mouth.

"Love?" I asked him. "What do you know of it?"

"More than I need know," he replied.

I cannot say what offended me more—his words or the sight of him, so pleased with himself. What an unbearable old Professor he will make!

I am not a poet! I said to myself with happiness as I walked home alone. But I have Mary. Not a poet, but I mean the present tense when I choose it. I have.

Whatever comes, you are inside. "What is in me dark/Illumine . . ." Milton, I should have told him, would have plucked that apple himself, if Eve hadn't already.

Tonight I wish I could meet you in your orchard. My pulse quickens at the sound of your bare feet touching the earth. Would the universe have cared a whit, Mary?—had we listened to its imperatives.

I shall be a student of the body. That is to say: a doctor. Do I surprise you?—JR

Smooth hands cover Mary's eyes. And for an instant, in the cool darkness, Mary has no idea—it cannot be Jimmy Roberts, whose words still make her blush, however young he was then, however old the paper, however much he would never say any of those things were he to find her today (she should not let herself imagine!), but these hands are too gentle for any man's.

Mary manages only a small sound—"Oh!"—more breath than word.

Susana Tannenbaum withdraws her hands and steps around to kiss her cheek. "Surprise!"

"Hello, my dear." Mary is startled by her voice—how calm despite the story racing inside (here, in Justus Schwab's saloon, Jimmy Roberts may walk in at any moment). How like her own mother she sounds—the calm in her voice, the "dear." Susana is right: A surprise she is, a surprise Frank is, however much she was expecting them. "Hello, Frank."

"Jane." Frank nods and sits down all at once, a seamless gesture of release.

Mary smiles at them both, unaware, particularly, that as she smiles at him, she absorbs entire the slowness of his movement, the continuity between his saying her name and his legs stretching out straight toward her and his arms back behind his head. All stillness and steady gaze.

"What would you like to do?" he asks.

What a question, Mary thinks. Goodness.

"Susana's got to go soon to pose for her class." Seeing Mary's puzzled expression, he elaborates, "She's earning money as a model for the life drawing at the Union."

"You are an artist's model?" Mary turns to Susana.

"Not exactly."

"Pardon?"

"I'm not an artist's anything. Here I am, Susana Tannenbaum, and there I sit, Susana Tannenbaum—being paid for it." She laughs, as though the world had told a good joke for her benefit. "Justus!" she calls.

A roof and cornmush, Mary hears Edwin saying. *It's a job.* But she didn't believe it then and doesn't now, either—there are many other ways to make a living besides breathing color into the countenances of the dead and sitting still as death with all eyes upon you.

"However do you keep still? That's what is hard for me—to imagine," Mary adds, for she hadn't meant to suggest that she had any experience in that position. That part of her life she wishes to keep from this place.

Schwab is over to take Susana's order.

"Do you want to go with me?" Frank asks Mary, whose concentration frays next to Susana and Justus's animated low laughter and whispers about someone who had made a fool of himself over so-and-so's wife. "But we'll see," says Susana. "I think she likes him."

"Me? I don't draw. Do you?"

Frank shrugs. "Not well. But I like the mental exercise of it. Perspective's useful. Even for a journalist."

"Of course." Is it obvious to him she lacks it? Coming from where she does. One small place. Why she had been drawn to the Elmer brothers like a body to greens in spring. They offered her other perspectives—Edwin, sitting and sketching, Samuel, talking of worlds she'd never seen. The promise of that was something she wanted so desperately that any step toward them was pure instinct. Same as when the days began to lengthen, however much work it was, they would dig through a stubborn bank of snow to get to the sturdiest greens—the spring onions they'd left over winter, chicory, dandelion—answers to questions the body articulates in its own insistent language. She had been as desperate. Was still. Is. Lovers lack perspective, wish to be transported into the life of another, skipping all logic, she thinks, skipping the mathematical facts (she sees Edwin hunched over his sketches, measuring lines and angles) of the distance between two people.

Mary does not look at Frank (though she knows she has been silent for too long, that conceding that perspective has its place is not adequate for conversation), but she is aware of his eyes on her, as she herself watches Susana's wrist below a tracery of white ruffled cuff pushed partway up her arm. Susana's fingers rub the surface of the table as she talks to Justus.

How could I possibly draw her? Mary thinks. If she measured the distances from cuff to wrist bone, from cuff to elbow crook—then what? Before putting a pencil to the paper, wouldn't she have to know exactly what it is that makes Susana's fingers so graceful? She would need to resuscitate a history of hands, and not only hands, but seasons, too—her mother's hands in summer were another thing altogether from their winter red and cracking. John Elmer's long fingers pressed together at the top, his index tips opening and shutting to stroke the center, shortest hairs of his graying mustache. Could she say what made his different from Edwin's? From Samuel's? Samuel's hands softer than Edwin's. Edwin's all bone and lank, as if their perpetual motion gave flesh not time enough to settle. Susana's hand.

"Plantagenet," she says, looking at Susana's hand. That word came to her: Plantagenet. What had kings of England to do with Susana's hand?

"Pardon?"

"Who were they? I mean, I know Henry the Some-Number, and Richard, but why that name? Where does it come from? What does it mean? I find I have no idea."

Frank rolls out of his slouch, pulls his legs in toward himself, folds his hands on the table, and leans toward Mary. "Why do you ask?"

"I have no idea. I was looking at your sister's hands, wondering what I would have to know to be able to draw them—hands are famously very hard to draw, are they not?—and I thought, Plantagenet. That word, the sound of her hands."

Susana holds up her hands to reconsider them in this light. They all three look.

"*Planta* in Latin is the sole. Of the foot, that is," Susana says.

"Ah," says Mary. "You studied Latin?"

"I took Frank's book. It was of no interest to him."

"I see. I wonder what our word *plant* has to do with the sole of the foot," Mary says.

The three of them look at Susana's hands—do they see?—something of how stems grow and branches fork, how babies plant their hands first on the ground, the mounds at the base of fat fingers pressing the earth, the soles of the feet still facing heavenward, pulled along behind.

"I'll go," Mary says. "But I can't promise anything."

"When can any of us?" Frank responds.

"Jane! I am so glad."

"Usually I'm her only guardian," Frank says, as Susana makes a face at him.

"And who guards *you?*" Mary cannot help but ask.

"Would you like the job?"

Fairly dark it is, in Schwab's, so Frank cannot see her flush. Whatever had she said? She had meant—what *had* she meant? To point out the years between them, to remind him of his youth and his place. She is old enough to be his mother.

Edwin decides to go to the Museum of Art, instead of the Academy. He takes the steps quickly—but not as some men might, bounding two or three at a time—no. He does not skip over any step; his boots simply brush rather than land on the marble. He is capable of a delicate touch. And lightness. And speed, if it is warranted.

He wants to see the Rembrandt—of which he remembers no detail save the darkness surrounding a man with brown eyes. A half-circle smudge of gray gives the shape of an eye. Tiny wet triangles of pink wedged in the corner of the whites. Just these small triangles, thinks Edwin, convey his corporeality. In the two brown globes that are his eyes, two tiny squares of white. That's all. And with these two squares, the Dutchman says, His world lit by our same light. The brown-eyed man is looking at something. Near each square, a round dot of black for pupil. These small dark circles, the depth of them, suffice to put the man and the world together. He looks at us.

The painter's art poor here about the eyes, where Edwin least expects poverty. Smudges and triangles, squares, circles. Even Rembrandt with only these tools. But the velvety background, with its riot of brushstrokes and layers! Edwin could get lost in it for days. That is what is odd about him, and why he finds it difficult to explain himself to Samuel, who would remember the name of the subject of the painting, and something of the man's social relations: He was a prosperous merchant from Rembrandt's adopted city, nephew of royalty, patron of the young Rembrandt and several other Dutch painters whose names even Samuel would forget.

Edwin steps back from the painting, as if from a different perspective he might gain what people call the long view—what a man like Samuel has, peering forward into time and seeing clearly which industry has a future and which does not; which facts to withhold and which to release in order to draw people to him. And here Edwin is, watching the way his own movement shifts the angle of light coming in from the doorway. Cliffs and edges of brown, of maroon, odd peaks of light—all of these Rembrandt's countless strokes. He catches himself starting to count brushstrokes per square inch. How Mary would mock him. Numbers we have, Edwin defends himself silently. Numbers. A finite number of breaths. Our very lives can be counted—by years, or months, or days, as he used to practice mathematics with Effie. One hundred and fifteen months she lived. Always it falls to someone else to make the sum of our years—he checks behind him to see if anyone is watching, and puts his finger forward to trace a peak of red that rises from the background of the painting—to mark the turning point, where the days behind are more than the days ahead. His must have already come. His, and Samuel's, maybe even Mary's. For all they know.

He will not go to the Academy today. He prefers Rembrandt and the East River. Such moments come, after all: the turning points we make ourselves, without aid of any calendar or calamity. To proceed in the established way becomes impossible. He must shift his daily routine. (How will he and Mary support themselves when they return home?) Today, he will avoid the Academy, answer though it once was to the flight of seasons, to the everyday questions the days do not answer.

Avoid the Academy, but he cannot avoid Samuel. Though going back there means facing Alice. And her promised portrait.

It is undoubtedly his own failing that he does not like Alice. A kind of jealousy, perhaps. That Sam has, with his grand new wife, put the past behind him. The past, and all the rest of them with it. Grand the word for her in more ways than one. What did she intend with such a color dress? What dye must have been invented, what alchemist's mixing of factory refuse and nature's indiscretion, what hours the silk drenched in his potion, to make an orange so vivid as that of the dress she had worn

Monday evening? "What do you think, Eddie?" Samuel had asked. "Won't it be splendid in oils?"

The extravagance and expense lavished on the fabric somehow magnified by its skimping in the construction of the bodice, which had shocked him with its tightness (wasn't she afraid of it tearing if she let out a breath?) and also its presumption—that so little could restrain what threatened to tumble out. He found Alice's voluptuousness distracting. Troubling, rather. He and Mary had been expected to converse with Samuel and this milkmaid of his, as though there were just four individuals at the table and not the additional twins Alice harbored between her sleeves, nestling, rubbing against each other throughout the meal, making with their silent presence certain feelings and suspicions more palpable than the conversation that floated through the air. Such is the effect always of those who are silent among us: They have a way of trivializing the audible—What news did they bring of home? And how had they found their trip?—bringing attention to all that can never be said. "Exciting," Mary offered at first, and then grew awkward as she tried to describe the strangeness of the speed of trains, and Alice interrupted to say, "But they're not so thrilling, once you get used to them."

Samuel, obviously, is used to them. To those breasts large enough to feed a man. A baby would be killed by them, squashed or drowned in their milk. He could not look at his brother without imagining the things Samuel would do with them—for something had to be done, such objects surely required some bulwark, some extraordinary efforts at self-defense for anyone who existed near them—even for Alice herself, he thinks, charitably. The permanent presence of them. At least that obvious trumpet of animal desire that is a man's hardening was not something one had to live with all the time. But her breasts! Held up like that, on display! Perhaps the day would come when contrivances would be invented—surely there is money in it—to hold up so, to plump and show off the male offering.

Samuel, child that he is, Edwin does not doubt, child at heart is his brother, frolics there in her ample landscape, licking and sucking and pretending he is a man-baby, innocent of all, happy in nature's bounty, that orange silk worth every penny.

Here is the life you're missing, Eddie, Samuel winks.

Edwin's feelings were no different sitting across the table with his wife in New York City than when Sam had brought him to the—salon, he'd called it—in Cleveland, and after Sam had bent to kiss a certain lady's hand he had kissed her breast, too, on the way up, and then looked back at him, and winked, as if to say, See, Eddie? Here's how it's done. Samuel had left the woman standing there in front of him. But he had missed the cue, and followed Samuel out. Samuel had mocked him afterward for his cowardice. Get yourself a real woman, why don't you, Eddie?

So he did. And then Samuel married Alma. Alma, whose presence (even in death) had made a long and lasting peace between the brothers. The two of them married men. Then their own mother died, and one girl baby and another on the way. Fathers themselves.

Edwin tries to picture Alice's face, but cannot. She is not unattractive, he knows—regular features, light hair, fine skin, he supposes. But he cannot think of one interesting or charitable word to say of her. He cannot think of anything but how she positions herself carefully, for each viewer to find the most charming angle. How could he ever paint her? How would the result not reveal to Samuel what he cannot say? He does not want to fight that ancient battle.

Nevertheless, he rings the bell.

Samuel himself answers.

"Eddie!" And he is folded into his brother's arms, into his back-slapping exuberance and infectious joy. There is nothing like Samuel's light, when he chooses to shine it on you.

"Uncle Edwin!" Maud pushes past her father to him.

And Edwin, despite himself—despite the day and his doubts—suddenly hoots with joy to see her. Laughs and spins her around, though she is a woman now, all grown.

"Whoa!" he protests. "I can barely lift you! Have I shrunk or have you—" And then he sees her tears. "My darling one, what is it?"

He looks to Samuel for some clue, but Samuel avoids his eye.

"I'm leaving for Seattle on Tuesday."

"This Tuesday? But why so soon? I thought you weren't going to start teaching until next fall."

"Well—the person I was to replace died. If I want the job, I go now."

"Goodness. Well. Seattle, it is, then."

"Yes. Across the entire continent. Let's not think about it. How is it at the Academy? Is it true what they say—that teaching art is anathema to true artistic expression?"

"Is that what they say?"

Maud shrugs.

"Is that what you think?"

"Oh, I don't know. I just think it is impossible that I should have anything to teach anyone."

"My dear. You are the loveliest, most open-hearted . . . we all have something to learn from you."

At this Maud starts to sob in earnest, and Samuel backs away, making gestures over her head that say, You see—and, I can do nothing—and, *You* try to cheer her.

Edwin is helpless before the tears of a woman. He thinks of Emeline hitting him over the head and crying her tears of furious relief to have found him (as far as he was concerned, he had not been missing, so to imagine her worry was only that: an imagining, an effort at conjuring, nothing as real as his own feeling). His mother did not cry. Or if she did, she kept it to herself. She turned and left the room. What she did alone her own matter, and if she came back with her eyes glittering, they could not say whether it was sadness or poem. A visitation, she called it. And praise be. It is not that he is unfeeling or unsympathetic; he simply takes his cues from his mother. Sorrows a private mystery. Tears come. And need not be remarked upon, for the only comfort to be had must be found in solitude. Not in another's arms. If he had believed his arms could have eased Mary's pain, he would have given them.

So when Maud buries her face in his shoulder, he strokes her hair awkwardly. "Maud. My sweet one. Life is a great mystery. Full of tricks. Just when you are saddest, happiness comes. You never know. You're afraid—and why not? Embarking on such a great journey." He steps back and holds her face in his hands. She is grown. He kisses her on each wet cheek, though he feels himself to be an imposter; she will sense the falseness of his comfort, know what his reassurances lack. "We should be so afraid every day. Even in familiar surrounding, we never know tomorrow."

"But perhaps I will never swim in the stream behind Grandmother's again."

"My dear. Shhh."

She is right. She would be surprised to see how the stream had changed course after the long winter that stretched into May year before last. How long had it been since they'd picnicked there? She had still been a girl. Five years ago? Six?

"Now, now. The train that goes west also comes east."

Maud tries to smile.

"You will come back in the summers, and you and Aunt Mary and I will camp out on Put's Hill and sketch trees and hills and eat all the berries we can pick."

"Really?"

"Yes." Edwin hands her his handkerchief.

"You didn't answer me about the Academy."

"Ah, well." Edwin looks around, to make sure Samuel's not anywhere nearby, and lowers his voice anyway: "I hate it."

Maud emits a sound that's half gasp and half laugh, and Edwin cannot help laughing himself.

"Why? Tell me what I should not do."

"Stay yourself, Maud. That's all. Whatever system, whatever method—keep the idea that another might work as well. You know, for years I believed Ruskin's advice never to draw what one loves. Of course, it's a contradiction if you're like us, and love trees and woods and grasses and all the little summer lawn flowers, which he says *to* draw." Edwin waves his hand in the air in dismissal. "Forget Ruskin. After a certain point, a person cannot listen anymore. Cannot take advice. However. That's my problem. It has nothing to do with you."

"I wish you were coming with me."

"Ah, well. Maybe one day I will persuade your aunt to take the train across the continent."

"Do you think she would?"

"You never know."

Any time now, Susana will sit on the stool. She will sit down, and she will be without clothes, and she will read Emerson's *Nature,* while the men and women desiring to be artists competent in the execution of the human form will consider hers for two and a half hours.

Mary says these facts to herself. She traces the most ordinary of details—the wooden stool where Susana will sit, the scraping of the chair legs across the floor as the students drag chairs and easels into the center of the room, the lines they draw through the dark varnish (doesn't anyone care that the floor is being worn so?), Frank's tying Emerson's essays in place on a music stand for Susana to read as she sits, the fringes of her own green woolen shawl—because she feels herself to be unmoored by physical fact. Me? she wants to ask again. A tremor. I don't belong here. I am not an artist. Wooden furniture, string, yarn—these are familiar. Her mind focuses on the edges of things, as if all the room and the people in it have been reduced to lines. She cannot go deeper than the physical facts; her mind hovers there, afraid. Yes, afraid.

She and Lucy had never stood inside their bodies as Susana does, blithely undressing in front of strangers, brothers even—no matter sex or age or familiarity. She suspects that brothers (for she and Lucy might very well have had those ordinary companions) would have made no difference to her life in this regard; without them, she and Lucy rushed through the cold to dress by the stove, hiding whatever they could, shunning the affront of air and eye. She can imagine nothing but shame and hurry for her and Lucy, their shoulders hunched forward to hide what made their new dresses too small too quickly one year. And the growth of a wild darkness between her legs, under her arms. All this hidden. Every day hidden. Toes hidden, too. Once dressed, she and Lucy were rapped on their shoulders—Sit up straight! Shoulders back!—to improve their postures. But theirs seem stiff, compared to Susana's regal bearing.

Here she is. She makes herself comfortable on the stool, leans forward to adjust the book, and drops her long wrap.

Of course Susana's mother is dead. Otherwise she would have been taught shame. If only Effie could have gone on without her! How splendidly, how like Susana, Effie might have gone into the future. Standing unconcerned, turning her stockings inside out along her arm, her body grown tall, her changed parts of no particular concern.

Here is sorrow's nectar. To be twenty, and lovely, and healthy. Mary bends close over her notebook. She cannot look up again. She cannot. If she were a painter, her canvas would be the forgiving miniature. For what can be wrong, kept small enough? She would paint a girl perched high up among the tree's new apples. Jimmy Roberts had lifted Effie into the apple tree. And there she had stayed, among the not-yet-full-grown summer's apples. So steep and green and precise, those apples. Mary's mouth tightens to a parch to think of them. The townsfolk whispered, "Mary Elmer cannot bear the sight of any child. They've boarded up that house and taken an apartment in town." Give them the benefit of the doubt, she thinks. Do not hear judgment that the Elmer ambition had wrought it. "That house, too tall. And such fancy windows." Maybe she was as they said, as Edwin had painted her. Her mouth puckered. It was true that grief had made the sweetness of apples indigestible. True that she'd declined food. True that the next summer, she'd eaten half a dozen unripe apples and been sick after. She could taste them, at least. No sweetness would have reached her.

She looks up at Susana, and when she meets her eye, ducks her head again. Why hadn't she known—how the world went on. Nellie's voice comes to her. Her song floating out the window to where Mary stood hanging laundry. And the breeze in the evening on top of Goodnow Hill, when the sun sets on the mountains opposite. And the grease of a sheep as she slid her hand snug into the wool and held her tight for shearing.

Susana does not move. Her lips make nearly a straight line, yet a smile plays at the ends—for Mary? She winks at her, and Mary looks down again, embarrassed, though Susana does not wish it so.

Susana lifts her hair from her shoulders and twists it up into a knot, and all the pencils in the room come to a stop. The room is silent for an instant before she replaces her hands and the scratching begins again. How can Susana sit there with nothing between her and everyone else? Mary tucks her head further, to hide what will otherwise show on her—everything, she thinks, everything I don't know—everything restrained threatening to flow. Water quickens and comes to her eyes, but she does not cry. No sounds must mar the quiet. Words forbidden from lips. Though the silence is not silence but the scratching of pencils and chalks. No one would object if she were to write in her book, and not draw. Frank not close enough to see, though her arm still feels warm where he touched it to indicate the chair he'd saved for her. He is not looking at her; he concentrates on his own piece of paper. Along the edges of everything Mary senses a heady perfume, something thick and palpable but impossible to touch. Across the palm of her hand she holds a thickness of hair, soft from brushing, ready to be criss-crossed into a long, smooth braid. Sit still. I can't brush your hair with you twitching like a robin. Maud, stop your faces. Stop egging her on. She had been a mother, and a daughter, once, herself. She had been that young.

"I'm sorry," Mary whispers to Frank. "I must go."

The city's lights are Edwin's problem. He can't find pure darkness anywhere, though it is late by the time he leaves Samuel's. He closes his eyes. A corridor of orange shimmering light—the East River implanted on his retina—snakes across his vision and disappears. Darkness settles under his lids. He stands still, then opens his eyes long enough to hoist himself up on the rail next to the 28th Street bath sign. He makes himself as comfortable as someone sitting atop a fence can be. The bath's closed for the winter. Though it's just early November, and warm again. But the calendar is the calendar: No more bathing in the river until Memorial Day. Edwin closes his eyes again and imagines darkness. The cold depths of a river—this river, any river, Goodnow Stream. The game he'd played when he was young, walking the three miles home from Sanderson Academy without a lantern. It was nothing when the moon was full, that first Tuesday. Each week of the moon's waning an apprenticeship in darkness, a training for the night that was to come. After cleaning the school to pay his tuition, long after the other students and even Farrer himself had gone home, Edwin stepped out from the school into total darkness. Alone, without any lamp or moon. He locked the door and pushed the key under so that he couldn't change his mind and retrieve the lamp. Alone. No snow to reflect and no moon to be reflected. No home unless he found it. Only himself and the darkness and what might emerge.

First other eyes. Of wild creatures. Then rectangles of paired sets of windows that told him when he was approaching the farm—what had been the name of that fellow who'd gone out West before him and Samuel? His family's place, and then Cousin John's, and then home, if Emeline had remembered to leave a lantern lit for him. By the end of the journey, his eyes had grown preternaturally sensitive, capable of distinguishing the different darknesses of ordinary trees and stone walls and barns and sloping pasture from the deeper black that nestled all the shapes of his world.

How little light he needed.

Easy to say with the streetlights and years intervening. Terror fades. What of how he'd huddled on the ground, pulled himself tight as a baby in the womb? Now, he sees himself from above—a skinny kid curled up, waiting for the sun to rise, shivering. Then, he'd seen nothing. Scratched at the dirt, patted down the grass, to be sure he wasn't in the middle of the road or someone's rosebush. Rubbed the dirt between his thumb and fingers, for the comfort of sensation. Hummed himself his mother's lullaby, *Soft the drowsy hours creeping/Hill and vale in slumber steeping*. It had seemed a foolish bravery to interrupt the silence so.

Of what sadness is bravery descendant? he asks now. The darkness not velvety, not like the black velvet stitched into the borders of the crazy quilt Mary kept over the back of the rocking chair. Golden thread biting into its edges like chicken prints in the mud. The night was not soft, was not velvet, but spoke to him of something hard and cold, the carbonized remains of an ancient fire. Beyond his knowing. Would not accept impressions, but make them.

No noise but the peepers far off. The pond, that way. Best to stay still, where he would not drown. It occurred to him later, when he woke, stiff and cold with the sun's first rays, that though nothing there was in the darkness of human comfort, he had been held. And born again to the daylight, with a holler and stretch.

Knowing very well how rash, Edwin strips down to his next-to-nothings, climbs over the rail and jumps. The splash for an instant the night's loudest noise, that end of 28th Street.

It is as if Mary can feel the final criss-crossing of hair at the bottom of the braid, and the ribbon on her fingertips, and one last touch, testing its weight and smoothness, before the full, thick braid slips through her hand.

"You next," she told Maud.

Maud. Perhaps the green book could be for her. Perhaps that is the way. *Maud, dear as my daughter. Do not judge me. I hope you will agree that Truth is itself Good.* How will she not? Maud, with her wide eyes and kindnesses; Maud, who will travel so far as to make the Pacific Ocean her Goodnow Stream.

Mary wonders if Maud remembers the Roberts family. The last summer guests. Or Nellie and Dave, who helped with—everything.

Accept the Days as Gods, she will write. But Maud already knows that. *So succinct, the wisdom of the Concord sages. But what whey must have been left behind such hard nourishment! Let me tell you the whey*—no, she crosses that out. No matter what their drab apparel, she should have said. Days as Gods too grand without that. *Accept the Days as Gods, no matter what their drab apparel, Maud—then you will not be so distracted by the din of retrospect in the middle of your life.*

That will do. She was not there to greet the Roberts family when Dave drove up and Jimmy Roberts climbed down from the back of the wagon. Dave had to come fetch her from the garden to say they'd come, and didn't she want to show them to their rooms?

She had wanted the season to end. *Never wish for a season to end, Maud.* They were the last guests; she was exhausted. She and Edwin had, in the Yankee custom, taken on too much work. The gardens flourished, and all summer long Dave ferried the Boston people back and forth from the train station. Maud and Effie chattering questions in the kitchen when they awoke. How many children are coming this week? Are the blueberries ripe? Will the raspberry man come in his wagon today? Can we play in the stream after lunch?

It was my idea, taking in summer guests. With you across the street, and Samuel only on weekends, and your Elmer grandparents living at the farm with Emeline, we had space in the big house. When I was just a girl, younger than you are today, drying a pan in the door to the kitchen at one of Charles Eliot Norton's town dinners, when he thanked the "good people of Ashfield for their hospitality," I thought, if I had a house like those Elmer brothers, I would be host to these City people, invite them every summer. To listen to their talk!—and turn an easy nickel at the same time.

It was not as easy as I had presumed. Your mother, dear Alma, had died two winters earlier, and your father was gone most weeks. It was as if I were the mother of two girls. (As my own mother had been.) The last summer we took in guests, you must have been only four or five, and Effie a year younger, yet I put you both to work, shelling peas and snapping beans, putting fresh flowers in the vases for every room, carrying piles of laundered sheets up the stairs to put outside the door to each room in the back hallway. We were so busy we hired Dave's wife, Nellie, to help with the laundry and cooking.

Perhaps that was the beginning of the trouble. I did not like to see another woman doing the job I had set for myself. And Nellie even less than me receiving benefit—she never socialized with the Guests or rested her body on those soft linens. Of course we paid her as well as we could. But I began to think that summer of the secrets money could hide: bills exchanging hands an obscuring of Facts. People still being bought. Father died to set them free—my cradlesong. Well, I knew that all was hogwash. Now I wondered, weren't we doing the buying?—Cut rate, at that. By the day instead of the life. And the guests who came bought us. Their country pets. They thought us charming. Or at least your Uncle Edwin, who spoke to them of Ruskin and performed his trick of staring and rendering in charcoal a precise likeness of the maiden aunt, the favored son—who next? (That his gifts and his charms were then and remain to this day remarkable, I do not deny. But still there was shame in me, to watch the buying and selling.)

Who were we to have set up a scheme bigger than human size? And it had been my idea. I began to acquaint myself that summer with the consequences of Folly.

By the time you read this, you may have had occasion to observe firsthand how one person's revelations (so-called) might, in changing all her landscape, cause her to drift from those closest to her. So it was that I hardly spoke to your father or your uncle by the end of that summer. What, had I stopped to say it, would I have said? That something was rotten in our hilltop kingdom?

Anyone wiser would have known that nothing was ever going to be as I had imagined it while Charles Eliot Norton stroked my hand. And, if I'd considered more carefully, hadn't I been humiliated even then, when he'd brought me forward, for all the town to see, to thank me for my dish-cleaning? He'd heard only part of my name—Let us thank Jane Ware, he said, leading the room in a round of applause.

I shouldn't have been surprised that the guests kept their own company, taking long strolls into town or along the river, gathering mushrooms in the woods. They drove carts over to Ashfield to visit with Norton and Belding and those folks. Tho' you and Effie played with their children. A Democracy of mud, at least. (They were kind people, Maud. I fear a Judgment against them coming through in my narration, when it is only my own board I mean to mark. How earnestly and how mistakenly I once aspired.)

Here in New York, I remember this. To see the poverty!—and to see how your father and Alice live! I do not know much about politics and economies, but as I walked about Manhattan this fall—surely if you are reading this, your father and Edwin and I are gone, and History has marched on, and you will be accustomed to women on streets with intentions all their own—I felt my heart likely to explode. I knew already, from having the summer guests, that some people float through this life, buoyed by labor not their own. Was it Luck? I thought. Standing at the kitchen door in the Ashfield Town Hall, wiping my hands on my soiled apron, I was charmed by it. I wanted what Norton and his guests had. The luck to think. How they spoke!—in long elegances fastened by words whose shapes I tried to remember for long enough to consult the Library's dictionary. I wanted what they had: the luck to wonder and gaze, to slide about the puzzle pieces of this world until I had arranged a picture of my own.

The Truth-in-Art men changed me. Those cataloguers of the true curve of the mature Oak, the false lines of So-and-So's sloppy approximation of the woods from afar. More kin to Alice, with no idea the number of stitches in any one of her probably dozen gowns, than any relation to Emerson's Poet.

Labor—by which I mean the simple work of the world, the work of providing shelter and sustenance—was invisible in that place for which I had been preparing my mind with secret study, with my happen-upon-occasion book learning. I had begun to yearn for a world in which the efforts of our hands and bodies were erased. Strange, where Desire takes us.

I think of Mother Susan, cold in the earth since the year Edwin rapped at my window, and I am sorry I cannot ask about the Topic on which Emeline anyway said her mother would not be approached—the Prophet Miller's Second Advent. How had she prepared herself? How had she reconciled herself afterward to Life-No-Different, after the Day came and passed and no one in any Promised Land but the ones who already lived in the big houses? Children died before that day, and children died after. How did that change her?

Here I am, living in the Day, thinks Mary. Only a different Paradise. She believes that when she finds Jimmy Roberts, they will fall into one another's arms and, wiser for all the years of want, live in love's bounty. That Paradise is where this tunnel leads, if only one follows the light. Paradise maybe the place she'd find if only, when her body startles at the edge of sleep, she lets herself tumble down the stairs, into the other world just beyond.

Yet she does not ask Justus if he knows the whereabouts of Dr. James Roberts. Who, after all, welcomes the earth's quaking? Who dismantles the roof? She is not Susan Elmer's child. Yet neither is she the child of any Enlightenment.

Bear with what seems digression, Maud, dear, and you shall have some family history in the mean.

Mother Susan was drawn, said Edwin, to the Reverend Miller's careful mathematics. To the way he read the Book for a message locked inside, available only to those who studied with rigor and precision. She enjoyed searching its pages for all the clues available in human assignation—the sounds and counts of syllables, the numbers of generations recorded and buried. For what other tools have we been given for deciphering a Divine design? She admired what she called the Reverend's humility, for she believed the truth of a Prophet's words to be in direct proportion to his reluctance to speak.

How then did she bear the Reverend Miller's mistake?

It only increased her faith in the mystery beyond, to see such a sincere man doomed to miscalculate. Any day, it could be then. Any day the Messiah would come and Wrong be made Right. What else to do but answer each day as if it were Chosen? She was an immensely practical woman, I always felt when I encountered her as a child, when I knew nothing about her religion and so did not try to match this Philosophy to that Action. She was kind, and taken with small things: with insects, and when best to cut flowers, with stretching an idea to fit a rhyme, with each of her children's particular gifts.

The Puzzle is vast, and my writing only a slender line bending itself to the mystery of a sphere. To understand myself not so different from Mother Susan, whose meticulousnesses and privacies her sons were known to mock (if gently, if secretly), does not widen my course; it simply brings me to the brink of another grave. Am I necromancer any less than those Truth-in-Art men? If only Edwin and Samuel had not misplaced her book of poetry!—I say, blaming them rather than asking myself why I suddenly want it so: What answer do I hope to find in the lives and words of the dead?

I said the Truth-in-Art men changed me—made me see the poverty of our (my and Edwin's) different versions of the same yearning. But perhaps it is too easy, my indignation with those men, who must be dead themselves by now, or across the sea; with Alice; with two brothers and their weaknesses.

It is not Alice's fault she is not your mother. (Of her, *I cannot bring myself to speak, tho' I know that you should like it. Nor of Effie, either. Alma and Effie are long gone, and there is no point.) We should not make Alice's name the abbreviation of Greed and Indifference, as if she were nothing else. Besides, am I not floating now, myself—do I not have it easy, the afternoons my own? I am becoming one of Them (like Alice, we have accepted your father's money—my morning hours at the whip-snap machine a small price to pay for the privilege of placing some Difference between us and her). Well, even we laborers manage to extract moments from the rest of Time. Can anyone steal Joy forever from another human being? People in Schwab's talk of such things. Of Pleasure and Thought, not as privilege but man and woman's rightful heritage.*

The truth is, Mary is surprised to find Schwab's real, and exactly as Jimmy Roberts had written about it. Perhaps in some way she had ceased believing in him or his ideas—a fantasy he was, her college boy. Last she knew, he had become a tired doctor who no longer had time to row on rivers at dawn.

Once, he had written to her about testimony he'd overheard someone in Schwab's translating, about the Blackwell Island dungeon—how the East River seeped through the rock walls of the cells, how long the prisoners were without light. *Inside that dungeon, has the jailer won? Consider that,* Jimmy Roberts had written. And she'd shivered to read it, in her armchair next to the perfect piano. Reason enough for loving Jimmy Roberts, she supposes.

But that is not all. She has thought on his toes just as much as on his words, truth be known. What if she writes (and Maud reads one day) what she has never before said? She comes close, mentioning Schwab's. She thinks of Samuel touching Alice's lip. Winding his finger in a tendril escaped at her neck as he speaks. What dare she say of Samuel to his daughter?

She can say nothing.

Not how she heard a woman's voice startlingly close as she hung the kitchen towel to dry over the porch railing. And the rumble of laughter followed that could only be Samuel. Then quiet, as if all the world were woven of whispers not her lot to decipher. Three silhouettes became one: the maple at the edge of Bray Road, Nellie, Samuel. She peered farther into the night to understand this new configuration, though every scratch of detail—a line humping itself up into the top of a triangle, a wedge of light, a sudden thrash of branch—caused her pain that she had not known possible. She held the porch railing, unaware she was holding it, until she looked down, as surprised by its ballast as she would have been to find a rail in the middle of an ocean. That a railing stood for her to hold, that a house with a door opened behind her, that a man and a child slept upstairs, that a houseful of summer guests would rise in several hours and want feeding, all were facts of no consequence whatsoever.

Maud, I have gotten ahead of my story. Justus Schwab's another year, another place. It is the summer of 1883—your mother gone less than two years. In the wake of her death, Grief drew lines everywhere. As later the clouds split and fractured nearly as soon as your uncle had painted them in our blue sky. (He cursed himself, for not planning the layering of the paint more carefully, but I said: How could it be otherwise? Our world cracked. Why should paint dry properly, or anything else go smoothly.)

You will judge for yourself, Maud, which fault-lines were inevitable, and which of our own making.

How much could she explain? Perhaps she is wrong to try. Had Maud ever asked it of her?—to explain her father, to explain men, or women, anything. What need had she to know of the follies of her parents' generation? As she asks herself these questions, Mary sees the sky, as it was above their hill, but not in the daylight, not as Edwin painted it. And she wants to ask Maud: Do you remember that sky? Did you ever wake in the summer to find everyone gone to the fields to work under the full moon? And walk down the hall in a dressing gown, down the stairs, out across the lawn, looking? And did you notice how sweet the air? As if the world had drawn its breath, and was waiting.

I've written of the distance between me and Edwin and your father. And from the start, the divide between us and the Guests, for they were City people, friends of Norton and those folks. And between us and Nellie and Dave, whom we paid in cash and whose dark skin was a reminder of the War everyone wanted to forget. And of the barbarity of people who look like us. Between our two families (you and Samuel, and the three of us) and the rest of the Elmer clan, who'd never hired a Negro or anyone else as even temporary summer help. Never hired a person at all: They were not of the hiring class, and they suspected anyone who was of deep Mischief. And between Edwin and Samuel, for your father was never around when things went wrong. Of course he worked very hard selling thread. He did—he would say—what had to be done. In any case we were never so happy as when we all—you and Effie, your uncle and I—drove into town on Friday evenings to pick him up at the train.

Late that August, the Roberts clan arrived, when I was worn to the bone—every morning waking with the crows, thinking: Rest will come again. Rest will come. The scent of fall in the air, promising earlier and earlier evenings. And then, maybe, time to sit by the stove and read. The last family of the season, with three little girls and their older brother. I noticed how he played with his sisters, for I thought: Good that the season is nearly over and last week's Henry and that John are not here to distract him from taking care of the girls. He was kind and made his sisters find a part in their play for you little ones. Effie, Princess of the Lady-bugs; and you, Maud, Queen of the Dragon-flies. But I was all irritation by then—feeling ill-used (and by whom? Hadn't it been my idea to play host?)—and did not care for these games that brought children frolicking through my garden when I was gathering dinner's vegetables.

When the moon was full one night soon after, I went down the hill to the blueberry bushes. A noise startled me. A bear!—I thought. Quiet. Its cubs may be nearby. When I heard nothing else, I thought maybe it was Nellie, on her way home. I didn't want her to find me.

It was Jimmy Roberts.

"Goodness!" I exclaimed.

"Pardon, ma'am."

"Whatever are you doing out here at this hour?" I asked him sternly—for I was shocked, and embarrassed—I'd left my dress behind, soaking in to-morrow's first batch of laundry, and was outside only in my dressing gown. For efficiency's sake. I'd already undressed to nurse Effie, who'd woken with a bad dream, suckled a bit, and fallen promptly back to sleep. I had laundry to soak and berries to pick before the next morning came. But if I'd dressed again to pick the berries, and only afterward started to soak the laundry, still having to work it—Well! At that rate, I would not have slept until the sun rose. Perhaps you are thinking that it was foolish to go picking blueberries all in white. But I didn't care about the clothing no one but Edwin would ever see.

As I write this, you are twenty, poised to begin your life as a teacher. I once thought that I would have liked to teach school, like your grandmother Elmer. In your profession, you'll need mercy—keep your generous heart, dear

Maud: it is hard to know what to say about what people do and why. I knew that it was not the sort of thing one should do—go barely clothed outside in the moonlight, with a house full of guests. A foolishness I can't quite explain, to myself, let alone you.

The house had been silent. Not a noise; not a candle lit in any window. She had believed herself to be alone, preparing for the day to come. A peace in that quiet almost as good as rest. In loosening her braid and letting her dress drop to the floor. In walking out into the soft night alone, red clover and timothy brushing her ankles. If efficiency had brought her to the blueberry bushes at midnight, pleasure held her there. She did not pick quickly, coaxing whole handfuls at once, but only single berries that had been overlooked in the daylight. The white dust of them glowing with the moon.

I was angered by the noise and the sight of him. As if Demand itself had awoken. "What do you need?" I snapped.

"Blueberries?" he said so timidly I should have known he wanted to please rather than anger.

There was no accounting for what she did next.

"Do you like your blueberries with cream?" she asked.

"Yes, ma'am."

"Do you like the moonlight?"

"It's beautiful."

"Yes," she told him. "It is."

I picked up a tiny tin cup you or Effie had left with the buckets, scooped up a cupful of berries from my big one—each of my motions abrupt, the movement of anger.

Then she had pulled the string at the neck of her dressing gown and lifted out a breast and squeezed herself as anyone squeezes an udder—and why not? she would have to do that, too, in the morning, for the butter—what made her any grander a creature than a cow? And she looked Jimmy Roberts in the eye, and handed him the cup of blueberries and cream.

"This is where your fruit comes from, and here your cream, and this is when it's gathered, by the light of the moon, while Cities sleep."

I ran into the house, and stirred the sinkful of laundry, brushing away hot, pitiful tears. I was that badly behaved. I expected Jimmy Roberts would avoid me in the morning. That perhaps his family would leave early, and Edwin would be hurt and then worried about the loss of income. If I felt any remorse, it was only that by my rudeness I had taken from you and Effie all his stories of the fairies and the brownies and the bug-royalty.

But he was the first one awake. We said not a word to each other, yet he hovered about the kitchen. When Nellie arrived, he said, "Hello, ma'am"—to her, not me. "Put me to work," he addressed Nellie, who looked at me quizzically. I shrugged. "Put him to work. Sometimes the city folk are curious what we do with ourselves out here in the wild," I told her, refusing to look his way. And he labored by our sides all that day, while his sisters occupied you little girls.

Thereby passed one of the summer's most peaceful days. None of the work too much with one extra set of hands. We decided to have a picnic for dinner—no-one said so, but celebration ruffled the air. Jimmy and Edwin set up a table long enough for everyone at the edge of the orchard, using boards Edwin was drying in the barn. Nellie and Jimmy and I carried food out to the tables, and everyone shared the roasted chicken and biscuits and sweet corn and long stringed beans. Edwin stood at the head of the table and ladled berries into bowls and we passed them, down one long bench and up the other, followed by short-cakes and a pitcher full of cream. Ah, everyone said. Stretching out their feet and smiling. Wasn't it bounty; wasn't it peace.

To think of it at all, I am strung with melancholy. You know sweet corn is the last crop of Summer.

After dinner, Jimmy Roberts lined up you five girls in a row. As I passed by, clearing the table, I heard him say: "Act I. Sunflowers. Stand up straight and tall. Turn your heads to the sun. Now. Here comes the wind"—and he leaned back, filled his cheeks with air, and blew. "Look out—a terrible storm!" He blew and blew until the sunflowers collapsed into giggles, at which point he feigned sternness and helped you to your feet. Act II: Jimmy Roberts whistled his way into the flower patch, pretending to be a little girl, come to cut down a flower to place indoors beside her piano. "Me! Me!" Effie volunteered over and over again, despite what he tried to tell her, without straying from character (was he Wind or Child?) about the lesser aspects of indoor life, the certainty of premature death. "Why do you want to be picked?" he finally asked her directly. "Out in the fields, you'll have a long life among all the other flowers."

I paused to hear the answer, for altho' I was shooting puzzled and sympathetic glances his way—yes, of course, with you I would choose the field; I don't know what I've conveyed about Civilization and Nature to deserve this child's response, but children are their own mystery, Jimmy Roberts—I was chagrined beyond my concern about what he would think of my mothering. Why did Effie refuse to be won by his depiction of the life to be had in Nature's arms? What was Jimmy Roberts discovering about my daughter that I did not know myself? "I don't care if I die at the end of the week," said Effie. "I want to be with the little girl."

Strange it is to remember that.

Five sunflowers in a row, and Jimmy Roberts, looking up at me to see if I'd noticed him, and Edwin lingering at the head of the table afterward, beaming with the fullness of the evening—that the guests hadn't gone without him to the meeting of the League Devoted to Truth-in-Art, that they had dined here, that Dave's hand was going to be all right after all and Nellie was smiling and seemed full of ease, and maybe everything would be fine still when your father came home the next day. Such peacefulness reigned that I had a moment to feel your mother's presence, and say, Do not worry, Alma. There is love enough for Maud. This rocky soil below us is bountiful in its own way. Here nearly thirty sustained by this patch of earth.

I like to think that you and Effie felt the throbbing of that joy, too. That the differences and pains slid around you, bounced off your sturdy little bodies. I lifted you onto one knee, and Effie onto the other, and vowed to love you as much as I loved my own child. Didn't matter who was the child of one brother and who the child of the other. Mr. Roberts stood and sang, with both hands crossed over his chest, and I bowed my head so no one would see the tears his lovely tenor drew. I'll take you home again, he sang.

Across the ocean wild and wide
To where your heart has ever been . . .

And then Nellie answered his song with her own, fit almost to make me a believer. No one interrupted. You girls didn't say, No one can live ten thousand years, silly!

When she sang, she could make us believe anything: We'd be here in ten thousand years, bright shining as the sun. Or was it the sea?—the sparkling atop waves what we saw in each others' eyes. The sea might one day come and roll on over the fields. Not to fear—there's a God big enough to hold the earth and all its oceans in the palm of His hand. And we are beloved of even the sky.

Everyone went to bed late that night, abuzz with song and chatter.

Edwin pressed himself to her as he'd first surprised her on Put's Hill, as if he'd forgotten himself and fallen in love again. And then, after he fell asleep, she crept downstairs, gathered the baskets, and set off for the bushes, humming Nellie's last song. *I know moon-rise, I know star-rise/Lay this body down.*

Of course that time she expected him.

The black of the water breaks into a glittering, and Edwin begins to swim, fast, for the other shore. What of November, in this southern clime. He'd been in Goodnow Stream this late in the season. Though not by his choice. Their mother would have none of their blaming one or the other, and maybe she was right that his and Samuel's tussles were of their own making—equally—and should be of their own resolution. It must have tried her, saint though she was, near enough, not to blame Samuel just a little bit for his health in the face of Edwin's pneumonia. They'd all survived the incident in any case. He and his brother, and their mother.

He swims for the opposite shore, a glittering of buildings. There Dr. Roberts stands at the window, taking a break between surgeries, looking out over the river. Is that someone swimming? The night guard at Blackwell's (who allows the Doctor's packages to reach certain inmates) paces to stay awake, and then peers out into the water. Is that someone swimming? He rubs his eyes to be sure. Have they broken through down below? He should sound an alarm.

The black of the water breaks into a glittering, and Edwin comes up quick, whirling about, spitting water, wiping his eyes. Near enough freezing to kill a man. And though he'd meant to swim across and back, after just a few seconds of slapping, thrashing crawl out toward the center of the river, he lunges back for the edge and heaves himself quickly to the fence that the city had erected around the bathing area, climbing as fast as he can, grabbing for his bundle of clothing, rolling it out, glancing up to see if anyone's coming, shaking his pants out and pulling them up fast as he can, damn! his wet feet catching at every inch as he tries to jump his trousers on. He flings his shirt and then coat about him and shakes the water out of his hair before replacing his top hat. And then tries to tie his boots, calmly, as though he had been strolling beside the river and happened to see that his laces had come undone. His fingers nearly useless with the cold.

Rebellion enough. Rembrandt. River. His body shakes all over. The water glitters. He will pull black paint from the very bottom of the canvas, and when it dries and cracks, he will examine the paths of its dividing under his magnifying glass, and then start over, making them bigger, tracing them with all the colors that shine in water drops, and then again, and again, until when he finishes, he will have painted a river.

When Effie was born, Mary thought, What did I ever do to deserve such a gift? As folks circled and clucked their congratulations, she thought, I have done nothing. Such cheap glory. She did not study, nor labor more than a day, nor decide—Let her eyes be the brown of her lashes; let her bite her lower lip when she thinks; let her be charming and quick.

Something like that she felt in the blueberry bushes the next night when she saw Jimmy Roberts standing all flushed before her. She hadn't meant—she hadn't thought—and then she saw the cruelty in her actions. So she said, "Every woman can do that, Jimmy Roberts. Don't make too much of it."

For she saw then that she had done another easy thing with her womanhood. He was young and impressionable, and probably never before had seen a breast with his man's eyes, and was apt to be too impressed by its fullness, by that difference between them.

It wasn't just that she had been overworked that she'd gone out like that. There was Samuel by the side of the road with Nellie. There were the Truth-in-Art men quoting their poetry around the dining table ("That he might see her beauty unespied," recited Totwell, as she refilled his lemonade) and bemoaning the strictures of contemporary fashion (Why didn't they realize how much more graceful their undergarments, their uncombed hair? said Gibbon, as she refilled his). Maybe she wanted to be seen like that—an artist's vision in the moonlight. Maybe she wanted to disturb the fellows' rest. Or Samuel's. But only poor Jimmy Roberts was watching.

His feet were bare, for she remembers thinking: How lovely and absurd to have a second toe that much longer than the first. That long toe seemed the embodiment of his entire being—his eagerness, his stepping a bit out of the place where he should have been. Just like her.

"Look." She showed him. "Perfectly symmetrical. How dull, next to yours."

"Well, you know what they say," he laughed. "A long second toe is a mark of aristocracy."

"Really?" She was suddenly ashamed. He'd put her in her place: She was a servant to him.

He laughed. "You believe me?"

She smiled back at him, shrugged, and thought of Lucy. The intimacy of comparing toes seemed rather like an activity for sisters.

"You are a terribly arrogant young man," I told him. "Trampling my lettuces."

And we both laughed again.

"Might I fill one of those baskets?" he asked.

So it was that Jimmy Roberts and I were picking blueberries in the middle of the night, with a moon just the waning side of full. (Ever at the fullest moment begins the Decline.)

I don't remember all that we spoke about.

Must not something remain secret?

I told him how to catch bumblebees in his fist without getting stung. And where to look for fiddleheads in the woods at the start of spring, and about the picture of a handsome Spanish singer hidden in my mother's drawer of undergarments. "Does your father know?" he asked. He meant, Does John Elmer know?

He told me of seeing the great sculptor Rodin at work in his studio, and how he could not afterward forget the small chunks of marble that whizzed by him, how Rodin himself paid no heed to what flew about, but only to something in the center of the great bulk of rock invisible to everyone else in the room.

"It was the most frightening and astonishing thing I have ever seen. To see someone believe that strongly—in what is not."

"We've seen a bit of that around here," I said. And I told him the story I'd never uttered aloud (why would I tell it, when everyone knew?) about Edwin and Samuel's Uncle Alfred, and how he'd received a Sign from the Third Angel that he had been chosen to offer three lives. Three lives—his duty. Story ends with Annie Catlin's baby dead and Uncle Alfred confined for life to the four sides and roof of a handmade cage. Cage made, in a strange twist of fate, by the father of the dead baby—it was he who had that contract with the state, making iron bar for criminals. I wonder what he thought forging them. What Uncle Alfred thought sharpening his ax. All we know is that he heard and believed. Believed with all his reasoning heart that the lives of the next three he saw were to be sacrificed. Given, he called it. His difficult lot to perform the Sacrifice. "I didn't ask to be the one," he told Edwin later. "I didn't ask for this fate. I didn't ask to be born in these troubled times."

Brutal, what he did. Outlandishly brutal. Wrong by all human account. What Boston fears those wild country folk are up to out in the uncivilized Woods. But the story's old, you know. Tho' by that I do not mean to belittle it. Uncle Alfred like Abraham, going to Isaac, only the child not his own (except people forget now, how he'd loved Annie before Catlin ever came to town and wooed her). That Abraham received different final instructions—that was his luck, and not Uncle Alfred's. What is luck, that marks a man Insane when the census-takers come. Or father of his Nation. Or Freed, when none of us is that. Justice of the Peace or Wife or Soldier. I wonder, did my father hear a voice from Above, like Uncle Alfred, or did he know it was only Lincoln? My mother always used the same words as Uncle Alfred: "Your father believed." End of sentence. Believed that he was saving the Union and ending Slavery, and we must remember how brave he was. Period and no more questions. You know that tone? That stern motherly tone.

"You're a mother yourself, Mary."

He made me laugh when nothing was funny.

"In any case," I told Jimmy Roberts. "You were wise. To beware of the flying debris."

"You look like Rodin," he said. "Talking, now. Picking blueberries."

He embarrassed me, with that.

Yet I've told myself that ever since. All my life since. You look like Rodin, the way you knit that sock. You look like Rodin, the way you fry that cake. You look like Rodin, the way you turn those pages. And why not? A harmless trick to increase my own life's Meaning. "Your Truth-in-Art meetings are all very well," I imagined telling Edwin, "but I look like Rodin." And then I laughed, to think myself a picture of manly concentration, clay smudged across my forehead and halfway up my arms, tools for chipping and smashing and hammering hanging about my waist.

Jimmy Roberts told me about how, after his great-uncle heard Emerson at the Divinity School, he'd declined his pulpit and gone out West, following the path that Scott's men had forced on the Cherokees, sending back reports to his sympathetic sister, who read them to her grandson. Those were his boyhood stories. And he told me about rowing on the Charles River at dawn, how there were only three sounds in the world: the oars entering and leaving the water, his breath, his heart pounding. That was the first time, he said, that he'd felt he was part of something beyond himself. As important and unimportant as any other part of the Universe.

I don't know how or if I spoke my delight, to stand there next to him, pulling berries from the same bush, listening to him tell me about Rodin and Emerson and his uncle with the Cherokees and the Universe and the air around us pulsing.

"The second time's now."

"You mustn't talk like that," she told him.

"Then I won't talk."

And he said nothing more. Nothing. All noise the sound of his fingers and hers, touching the berries.

Hear, if you can, the sound of a berry leaving its stem, and the whisper of long fingers brushing past the gray-green leaves no bigger than the fruit they protect. There must be a sound when a berry disengages from its stem. When red clover bends under the weight of feet coming closer. In the catch and the skip and the going on of two separate breaths.

When Edwin comes in, teeth chattering, hair still wet, he finds Mary asleep, the covers kicked off, her gown loose around the neck. He is amazed to find warmth so expendable. Asleep, no frown or sadness mars her face, and when he bends to kiss her, his bottom lip touches her forehead and his top lip catches her hair: this is how he first kissed her, at the line between flesh and hair, and as then, a few hairs stick to his lips as he pulls himself away.

He has not been the husband his eyes must have promised her. When he went to her, he had been emboldened by Samuel's example, cocky with the achievement of the house on the hill, absorbed in finishing his self-portrait of Samuel. Yes, self-portrait. Samuel's was the face he looked at when he arose every morning. To substitute blue eyes for brown a trivial matter. The spirit of the thing—the sketch of Ruskin's he'd made the background, the American flag he had staked in the ground of European painting—was all him, and not Samuel. It was as if, instead of embodying Samuel in his portrait, he'd taken on something of him in the flesh. Tapping on Mary's window. As if he would know what to do when she answered. Though it was simple enough, at first.

Samuel has no need of the wine his table offers—the physical ease that escapes Edwin never leaves Samuel. Even without wine, his words flow smoothly. His evident ease with women proven again with Alice, that he should attract a woman so different from himself, so different from his other wife, that even with nothing to say to one another, in fact with a painful obstacle between them—that he loves Maud with the half of his heart he reserves for fatherhood, the half of his heart that will not be brooked, that does not sway or open or close, and that Alice does not care a whit about this part of him or about Maud herself—even with every reason for there to be no connection between them at all, still

Samuel finds his way, dogged, across the divide of their two unlikely persons, and something strong passes between them that Edwin sees in Samuel's twisting of the hairs at her neck, in the way her eyes follow him. What is in Samuel expanse in Edwin shrinks.

It had been easy for him not to bother Mary with his physical needs after she strode down the stairs with an armful of bloody sheets that fall, after they'd closed their house to guests once and for all. What good would come of it?—what steadiness in their household?—for them to swim together in the soup of physical intermingling, the blood and the terrors, the pulsings of such small internal pleasures, the stickiness, the extra wash—all for a little ride, him deep within her, both of them with their eyes shut waiting for a throbbing and shaking at long last. An end of sorts. He took it to be for her as it was for him, though such assumptions are generally mistaken. Let him speak for himself then—a shame and a weariness, it was. Weariness that he could not find expression and elegance in the act, could not live in the offering that was Mary's presence in his life without feeling a miserable inadequacy.

Paint is what he does. He is not himself, painting. Is not burdened by Edwin Romanzo Elmer, brother of Samuel, husband of Mary, whose spirit he does not move; son of Susan, who believed the predictions of the Reverend Miller, and Erasmus, missing an eye and declared insane in the census of 1870; father of Effie Lillian, who died before her tenth birthday, though she was the liveliest of them all. He is all of those, and none, when he paints—not for love or money or glory—but because here he moves best. Here he can swim in life's current. And in it, despite life's command to sink or swim, he manages a gesture now and then that is his alone, an extra stroke not required by the distance to be traveled but inserted simply for the joy of it. For joy he pulls the vermilion up to a peak and down again and it is the ribbon on her hat. It is the ribbon on her hat though Effie will not toss it up in the air again or catch it before it falls to earth, though Mary has put the real hat away in the box he built. For joy he pushes the bristles into the brilliant red and, stroke and lurch, unfurls a ribbon across a lawn edged with clover and buttercups.

Edwin walks to the window to pull shut the curtains, and then hesitates. Why close them? The light from the gas lamps is faint by the time it rises to their window, and with the fog and wet the effect is rather pleasant. Such a filtered, soft light should not keep him from sleep. And what harm would come to them to receive the full force of sun in the morning? If indeed the sun can make its way down these streets. If it is not deflected by the water towers and ducts, the jagged angles of roofs one taller than the next, sent back to some kinder human environment, some land left more receptive to nature's bounty.

No good in that line of thinking. Even at home they closed the curtains every night, and what on earth did they have to keep out there? Some sliver of moon caught in the branches of the line of black locusts. A wolf, howling. Mary had, with her sister, sewn curtains for the entire house out of heavy silk damask Samuel had arranged to order at discount from Belding. None finer. Travel all the world, and you will not find a lovelier damask in any Old World palace. They did not doubt him, though he himself had not crossed any ocean nor been to the workshops outside Florence.

Edwin supposed that had he paid attention—vigilant, vigilant attention—he might have noticed before Mary made her anger palpable that she preferred that he not close the curtains at night, preferred he let that task fall to her, to perform in her own time. He had at first untied the cords rather absently, helpfully, he would have thought, had it been thought and not ritual carrying him forward to the bed, pulling shut behind him door, stove, window, curtain, until he blew out the candle at his side and darkness settled all around. Her resistance sweet at first: Leave them, dear—I'm not tired. I have hours left in me. I'll close up. He could fall asleep like that, too, with the curtains open, and the last light of his day the candle and its doubling in the window. The last sounds, her moving downstairs—a few notes on the piano, a line of melody, the clank of the stove door, the squeak of floorboards. More activity than necessary to finish chores. Nor could he fathom how book-reading could be such a noisy business. During their years in the big house, it was the mystery he lived with, what she did downstairs at night.

After the Roberts family left, for a time Mary would yank the curtains open when she finally came upstairs, the violent rustle startling him out of his sleep. How many hours or miles he'd dreamed, he didn't know. The anchor that held him to the shore of his temporal life had been lifted and he was somewhere else—swaying in an enormous wooden crate with his Uncle Alfred, borne with heavy straps onto a great ship that rocks with the waves of a brewing storm. He tilts, swings back and forth, rocking as he'd once been adrift in his mother's sea, as helpless then to stop his own growth and expulsion as he is still.

These curtains do not reach all the way to the floor; their opening and shutting make no sound. He will not wake her. When she'd yanked the curtains open in their tiny bedroom at the top of the stair, he'd sat bolt upright, late for the day, he'd thought, shaking all over. A relief to find it still dark, and Mary slipping into bed beside him. Before day was still to come the long matrimonial night, with its tossing and rubbing and then startling to find they'd run aground and this sharp word had to be recalled and explicated and then retracted, if that's how you understand it, Mary—of course I hadn't meant to suggest my love for you and Effie was less than my love for her—it's nonsense, you must see. Yet always the bleak outposts of the voyage's language accompanied by physical facts both milder and more constant: He warms her cold toes with his long-bedded warmth, and her body seems only softer, more accustomed to the world, than when he first touched her on Put's Hill.

Their foundation rock—*we were secret lovers*—suggests a unity that has long obscured the muddier facts of what they were not, even then: what was in them both tightness and resistance and a fear unto God (were they believers, Edwin adds). Snake the personification of evil because of its shape: here a line, there a curve, here twisting into a perfect circle, whatever it appears one moment changing the next before anyone can name it. Making itself invisible. Their secret activities concealed secrets that lay even deeper than they themselves could say. They could not see what their choice would bring. They held hands and walked out into the fields, and made themselves known—a part of themselves known—to each other on the cold earth. Afterward, returned to the dirt under their bodies, icy mud had seeped through his thick woolen pants and the rumple of her skirts, and the dry grasses that must have been brushing against them all along were twitchy against their skin. Their slowed pulses made them the relics of something that had passed through and vanished, and the whispers of their own awkward language seemed to him at one with the insects' buzzing. He wondered if the earth and the sky above pitied them as he pitied the crickets, for their short life span. Under the perfect sky, he sensed something weighty and broad, as if the sky were settling itself over them and they might stay forever on that hill. Except that is not life. They both had to return home. So he said, "Dear Mary, the sky will not fall." By which he meant simply, *We have to go in soon,* but she took to mean, *Our families will adapt,* will configure themselves around what we have done. Life will go on, despite our having shattered everything. Indeed, why should her mother be unhappy to have her daughter marry the favorite cousin of her own husband? And how could Samuel truly protest, when Edwin had gone and done what he had advised all along, and taken a real woman? But about the sky, Edwin had also meant, if words can approximate feeling: that even in that place whose horizons had been known to him before he could talk, no story would find its resolution; comfort would pass; even then, they could not make themselves understood to each other. An agitation remained inside the kind of peace they'd found. No matter how they touched one another, still the gap between them throbbed as wide as the space between themselves and the sky.

A marriage between two people a commitment to impossibility, Edwin thinks. Then habit. And habit a man's undoing or his making. Edwin draws the curtain toward him and inspects the fabric's weave, as though he will find in its pattern—a plain weave, not the complicated damask of home, with its rich patterning and tricks of light—an answer to his own questions. What had they made of themselves? Of each other? To be someone else no longer possible for either of them. She will not take him to a place he has never been. He will not show her any other world. But his mind stretches, it bends, it arcs its way back to her, and he leaves the curtains open.

Friday

Mary cannot tell whether the heat and light are dream or poem or the real world, so-called. Edwin is next to her asleep, in their Manhattan aerie. So high they are in the sky here. A brightness through the window pitches her forward. She must have forgotten to close the curtains. *I rubbed my eyes a little to see if this sunbeam were no illusion.* She shuts and then opens her eyes again. For there he stands.

Stop this day and night with me. There he stands. The air coming from the window the same air on top of the hill, where they left the windows open all summer, until frost crept up over the ledges. Here, the rectangle of city framed by the window glows with a strange steamy light that is the sun just beginning to burn off fog. All shapes still indistinct. Wetness seeps through the walls, moves inside her. He must have climbed in the window.

Jimmy Roberts is before her, baring himself. He unbuttons his shirt, watching her all the while. She steps closer, as they both know she will. When he pulls off his second sleeve, she moves close enough to touch his barestript shoulders. She holds him apart, as if looking were all, as if she were a mother bidding a son good-bye. The war comes to her, as if it had never ended—leave-taking, bloodshed, and all about a great darkness, in which she does not know what will come. Except that this man is not her husband, and not her son. Did she see such a scene from her cradle, when her father left?

This is what men call desire, Mary thinks. Dream or wake, incontrovertible desire. And though she does not say anything, he watches her and knows. Every fact of her life falls away except his pulse under her fingers. This is his body. It really is Jimmy Roberts—she recognizes his arms. They are not Edwin's or Samuel's or Dave's or those of any other man she's ever seen by right or accident. They are the same arms that lifted up Maud and Effie to reach the apple-tree branch. He is the person she watched on that August day when the sun hovered in the sky long enough for the two of them to live an idea of a whole lifetime in its glow. She, picking dinner's vegetables. He, telling the children stories for her to overhear.

How had it happened? In no time from strangers to whisperers of secrets. In no time she parted his pants and pressed her face into the heat of him, the quickest way to say, *I take all,* every part she had never dared imagine, broken teeth and sweat and afternoon secrets and trouble with the law, all. *If we've no time, then let me touch you everywhere.*

Then he was gone. That much happened in not even an instant, in no time that can rightly be called minute, second, or any fraction thereof. She knew she was dreaming him. Yet her hands held the shape of him: the muscles of his arms he'd got from rowing the Charles at dawn, the hard coil of him she needn't have parted his pants to know.

Mary holds her hands up and watches how they tremble. She shakes all over, as if she'd just loved him in the grasses and climbed in the window after, trying to still her heart, to not wake Lucy. If this shaking is real (Edwin will wake and see this trembling and ask what troubles her) why should the cause not be what it seems? That she has made love to Jimmy Roberts this morning.

In some scullery of Time, she writes, *tucked away in the basement of the grand house of Years. The activities of this dark corner easily forgotten or overlooked, yet without them the inhabitants of the house would starve. Starve to death.*

And if she has made love to Jimmy Roberts, why not believe that this pulse has passed through him, too? She feels him close beside her, in agreement. "Mary," he says. "Mary." He has only to say her name, and she shakes all over. But she is not afraid of this power he has over her. *She* can create life. He is not here in her ordinary daytime world—she knows he is not—but the veins threading his muscles pulse under her fingers, and she sees brown hairs growing sparsely over his lips and feels his breath. If she were to speak, her breath would meet his.

Another world exists. In it, he is with her. There is only astonishment, to be holding him after so long. She cannot write; she cannot think; she cannot talk. Too many words will break the spell, pull her back to this world she daily calls ours.

He disappears—

and she lets him go.

(Shred it into your stew, Mary; Feed it to the crowd.)

She lets him go, as if she is herself a New Woman, like Susana Tannenbaum, like the spectacled woman laughing outside Schwab's. His naked self retreats, until he is clothed and respectable, as though she has not been holding him tight around his hardness (it is the vein that snakes along the top of him there whose pulse beats in her fingers). She smiles, as thought it is easy—to come and go, to love or not love, as though none of it could change a life.

Then she brings him back. (And why not? She knows she is dreaming.) Only this time, it is Jimmy Roberts in his daytime garb. She pictures the chalky-golden wall at Schwab's, the door that opens onto the street, and she summons him. She concentrates. Gives her whole attention. He pushes open the door, and he is there, as she knew all along he would be, lifting his hand in greeting, his eyes meeting hers, entering her through her eyes, through her fingertips, coming through her until she shivers all over. He puts his arms around her to settle her quaking, and they lean their two heads together, as if thoughts move from one to the other like that.

But then she is shaking too hard to sit. Someone has seen straight through her: Her body is no longer solid, or hers. She stands carefully, holding her arms out for balance, and takes baby steps toward the bed. Best to lie down. Though she may wake Edwin. Careful. If he wakes, she will ask, Is this what you felt when you painted her?

Some disorder has entered their lives, waking her and not him at dawn and keeping him, not her, up at night. He had still not come home when she fell asleep last night, though she is nearly always the last one awake, unless she is ill. Ill? She is not ill. If her body feels strange, she will reassemble its elements. *What the body can feel!* Seemingly unprovoked. How is it possible that what he'd once described so starkly—*Better to listen to the prostitute's account of man, than the medical doctor's*—could alive be the conduit for this strange energy, this unbiddable, this—she does not have the words. She kneels next to the bed, and bows her head to it. Not to pray. So that she will not tip. So that she will not wake him.

Though she is in some small way glad for the chance Edwin's sleep gives her to compose herself, more of her wishes not to be alone with this feeling, which she sees could turn into terror. She will ask him, After she died, where did you go? Where were you inside. What was it like to touch your brush to brown and make her eyes?

That Mary cannot imagine.

She closes her eyes to hold the thought of it: a brush stirring, its tip coated with oily brown. Then held aloft. Then coming down again. The bristles touching the canvas. The brown smoothed into two circles that make Effie's eyes, looking up at the sky.

"There is no heaven, Effie."

"But then where will you be?" she asked Mary. "How will I talk to you when you die?"

"I don't know, sweetheart. When it happens, we'll find out."

Was she with you? Did you feel her breath? Her weight on your back? Did you stand together in the grass out front by the road, looking across at the Whiting farm, telling her, Next week, I'll cut the hay. You and

Maud mustn't run like hooligans through the windrows this year. You doubled my work, you scamps.

Mary looks at Edwin. Maybe he'd known Effie better than she had. He carries the same satisfaction with life that she had. The same certainty. *I could die now,* he had said once, atop Put's Hill. Though she had made herself imagine what he meant—taking into consideration not only the words, but the contentment in his eyes and his hand stroking her back—she had felt a horror of abandonment. Not just to imagine Edwin dead (such a thing was impossible even to contemplate, when she was so young) but to see how far apart their understanding. Learning to love Edwin had given her a fresh horror of death. *No matter how many years we have, they will never be enough to love you.* She had said that, once. Her only regret then that she had not been with him sooner, had not traveled to Cleveland with him and Samuel, had not shared their youth. Her regret now that she should have lost that conviction. It was not the years that were lacking. Perhaps Edwin's view was really more like Effie's. Jimmy Roberts had made her say it: "I don't care if I die as long as I have what I want now."

If she can feel Jimmy Roberts's breath on her lips, then perhaps—

If Mary were to hold Effie in her arms, would she still be only nine, as small as when she'd left? Or would she have grown? *There is another world,* Mary whispers. Though she holds her hands up again to observe their shaking, she thinks, Now I know. From this shaking, a stillness will radiate. The day will come. Something is new inside her.

Edwin still does not stir, and, as her hands settle, Mary tires. She elides her dream's impossible feats, supplying stairs between down there and up here. Jimmy Roberts must have aged, could not be the inhabitant of that young man's body.

She will not know how to speak when Edwin awakes. How can she ask questions about Effie without explaining the places she has been? "I made love to Jimmy Roberts last night." Impossible. No words for such things. Was Edwin silent, sometimes, for the same reason—fear of what he has to say. Maybe fear plucks the words from him, has stolen so many times he has vowed to offer nothing precious. Emeline had warned Mary about his silences. His disappearances. "He doesn't mean any harm. It just happens. His time not the same as ours." Then she had shaken her head at Mary, with an expression something like pity and something like puzzlement. "I know you think now that he'll tell you everything. But one day, you'll see. He'll go away. Leave—entirely. When it happens, don't blame yourself."

Emeline said that Edwin might go away.

"Go away?" I asked. Did she mean his and Samuel's business was not done in Cleveland, or that he might insist after all on traveling all the way to Washington, D.C., to deliver by hand his patent application for the double-acting butter churn?

"You heard, I suppose, about how the Elmers left." She ignored my question and phrased her own as tho' it were not one.

"Left?"

"Moved out West to New York State. And then farther, to the Wabash River."

"I didn't know."

"Of course not. What was I thinking?—We were back by '47 or '48, long before your time. Before even Edwin was born. Your Edwin, I mean. Not the other one."

"The other?" (I was all questions, then, just sixteen; I must have seemed—dimwitted. I had been meeting Edwin outside for only a few months, and Emeline had seen him from birth to Cleveland and back and, besides that, had lived twice as long as I. I thought that "the other" was a woman—tho' that is Love's sense, not Grammar's.)

"Died," said Emeline.

"She died?"

"Not 'she'—whom do you think I'm talking about? The first Edwin. There was an Edwin Elmer before yours. He died the year before I was born. Year of the Second Advent, it was. Come to think of it, without his dying, maybe there'd been none of us—Samuel or Edwin or I."

"I'm sorry."

Emeline's laughter taught me this: Think! Don't mouth the platitudes you've been taught. The people of this family will see right through them. Sorry?

Was I sorry there was Edwin, who kissed me under the stars? Or Emeline, who answered any question I had the temerity to ask? Or Samuel?

When she finished laughing, I asked, "Did he love someone before me?"

"That's not what you need to worry yourself about, Mary Jane." (So I knew, yes, he had.)

"What should I worry about?"

"That's what I'm trying to tell you. He disappears. Goes away."

"Where?"

"Put's Hill. The bank of the river where they used to catch the salmon. The roof of the Whitings' barn. Doesn't much matter where. Could be anyplace. Has he shown you where our farmhouse used to stand? The old Mary Lyon place?"

I nodded. (She must have seen the pink creep up my neck.)

"You heard Father destroyed the place?"

I nodded again, tho' I hadn't known the Elmers had anything to do with the building's demise.

"A matter of Time before it would've fallen of its own accord. So my father decided to burn it and no one came up with energy enough to stop him. He and Mother went to live with Delilah, and Sammy and Eddie to live with me. There I was—just five years older than Samuel and now mother to them both. And isn't that just when Eddie decides to disappear for the first time. For an entire two days, no one knew where he was. So I went over to where the old house had been. I knew he'd loved that place. We all had. And at sunset, there he was, sitting where he'd always sat on the wall out in front. He didn't even hear me until I smacked him hard atop the head. That woke him good."

Emeline finished cutting the tips off the green beans. "He'd been there the whole time, conjuring that old place. He'd drawn it exactly as it had stood, board by board, as if the flames had never burned.

"I see your eyes. You find that romantic." She opened the woodbox of the stove, and poked at the fire. "You will see. He is not like the rest of us, Mary Jane. He'll make you cry for certain. You don't care about that now—you think love can carry anything. But you will see."

"You are up early."

She turns to face Edwin, with a slight frown. "Or you are up late."

"I went to Samuel's last night."

A heaviness inside her returns. She cannot ask him anything. Nor can she describe the supernatural stillness at her core—the steady buzz of it. Another presence in the room. Now there is another fact: Edwin is angry, unsettled. She did not go to Samuel's with him last night. She has shirked her duty. (Not to mention, made love to Jimmy Roberts.)

"Maud's leaving."

"What?"

"Maud. Is. Leaving. She's going to Seattle next week."

"Maud?"

"Yes. Maud. Our niece." He hears the exasperation in his voice and makes an effort to quell it. Perhaps this cramping weather is why his temper is so short. With Ward, with the other students, with Samuel, with Mary. And what have they all done to him? Nothing that he can think of. So he is not one of the First Five; how could he expect it, with that wretched impersonation of a painting? He has to start the other, maintain the clarity of last night. "She has a position teaching in the Seattle public schools—remember?"

"Of course I remember," Mary snaps. "But I thought she would begin next September, at the start of a school year—Why, that's nearly a year away. I thought she'd be here through the summer, at the very least. I always assumed she'd be here as long as us—we. As long as we would be."

We? Us? A grammatical problem. Which is it? He hears her stumble, but decides—if one can call anything so quick a decision—to ignore what the break in her sentence allows into the room.

I always assumed she would be here. Giving birth means signing an agreement no one takes the trouble to decipher: Part of you has gone forever. If you're lucky, she will stay close for a while, and inhabit your lap and home, greet you at daybreak with song. In time, you may forget the contract you signed with your own blood: Yes, I understand that I may die before my own death. *Born we are between piss and shit,* Jimmy Roberts had written her. But they are speaking of Maud, Samuel's Maud.

Maud's tear-filled eyes come to Edwin, and he feels a duty and a desire both to alleviate her pain. They can do it best together, he knows. Uncle Edwin and Aunt Mary. Mary still with a mother's touch, when she deigns to use it.

"I didn't know either. She didn't know herself. The person she was to replace in September died suddenly. She just found out, and of course she's desperate to leave."

"What do you mean—'of course she's desperate'? Because of Alice?"

"You know she hasn't been happy."

"But I thought—oh, Edwin. I don't know what I thought."

"She expected you, Mary. She was waiting to tell us both."

"Of course."

"I'm sure she would love to see you. Why don't I take you there after lunch, and you can walk in the park together while I go to class? If the weather continues like this, it should be—"

"Edwin, I don't know. With so many whip-snaps to do . . ."

"Mary, you must rest, too. You must rest, and you must make an effort to enjoy yourself. I know you haven't been sleeping well. Does the noise bother you?"

"Not particularly."

"Well: What is it? Another of your spells?" Edwin sees her lips tighten. "I'm sorry."

"What exactly do you mean by *spells?*" His name for the shaking. For when she sees—what he does not. Very well: She will reveal nothing. Not waiting for an answer (she does not want his definition), she asks instead, "Are *you* happy here?"

Edwin thinks of hitting the icy water, the shock of it nearly heart-stopping, the heat of his body after. He is easily irritated, true, he is bothered by Ward, by the atmosphere of the studio, by Samuel, by his wife's twitching, that Mary had left him alone with Maud—but isn't this irritation by its very nature something on the surface? Something to be brushed aside, like May flies. The flies don't obscure the joy of that season's long, unwinding days. Would he trade in this opportunity for any other year? No.

"Perhaps it is something akin to happiness, to be as occupied as I am."

"Good."

"I hope it is not too much to ask of you—to be here?"

"Not at all. Despite my 'spells.' " And she gives him that look he knows to beware, a brisk, Very well; I shall not speak of this subject again.

"Mary, please." He studies her closely. He does not know what he meant by *spells*. He fears the part of her he does not understand. Who is he to know what is sensible? He can't imagine how she fills her days. She can make the whip-snaps with her eyes closed—it takes nothing of her. So what does she think of as she turns the wheel? She encouraged him to come to New York. He would never have come here on his own. It wasn't his idea that they take Samuel's offer. Yet her clipped "good" has the air of a threat: You had better make use of this education you're getting at our expense. (Though there was no tuition; though his own work had earned him the place.) Like Samuel, she cannot help but suggest, Look at all we are giving you.

"I like being here," she says.

He breathes.

And she softens. "Isn't it good, to be surrounded by so much unknown?" She feels a warmth creep back into her.

He considers. "That's one way of looking at it."

And his coolness returns. Why must it always be? One waxes and the other wanes. Go, she wants to tell him. Go. Lift this gloom. When they are together she cannot see anything but—what is. The room, bare of any trace of home save their quilt. A man who looks older this morning than he did yesterday. The two of them, only.

~

She hides under the quilt when Edwin leaves. In notebooks or whip-snaps, there is no point. She is too tired. "Jimmy," she says very softly. Not that she thinks he'll hear. She is not crazy. Spells, indeed. She just wants to hear a sound. *Jimmy*. Darling, he replies. Darling Mary. She closes her eyes, to keep him.

Justus Schwab laughs. Throws back his great red-bearded head and laughs. Everyone in the front room looks up at him, and at Mary, who stands before him, shamed.

I've come to pick up Jimmy Roberts's mail, all she'd said.

You and who else? he wants to know. You'll not be able to carry it in one trip, did he tell you that? Come.

He takes her through the door at the back of the saloon, into another room, and opens a closet in the corner. Here, stacked as tall as Schwab himself, divided into manageable packets tied with string: 1884, 1885, 1886, all the way to eye level: 1898, 1899.

Which year would you like?

As they survey the years, Justus fades: His red beard turns white and his bulk withers.

Father, she calls him. She stands with him at the edge of the Battery, at the very tip of Manhattan. She unknots a string, tears back the year's wrapper, and then takes each envelope, rips it in half, and throws the pieces over the rail to the sea. Tear them up, Mary; feed them to the gulls.

In her dream, years are burdens that might be dropped, as the gulls drop shells to smash them open on the rock pilings below.

The letters she'd written to Jimmy Roberts, late at night, sitting beside the stove, gathering the day's meaning, were gone long ago. Sealed and stamped and carried to this city. He would not have saved her letters;

it was not his way. Though they would've filled the green book ten times over; there'd have been no need of it.

Perhaps she will put the letters he sent her all in order, read them one last time, and ask Justus if she might leave the packet of letters with him. For Dr. Roberts. No, he's not expecting them. But they're his.

Otherwise she will grow white surveying them.

9 September 1886

My dear Mary—

With which sense would you first like to apprehend my subject: Smell? Curiosity flares your nostrils; something acrid fills the air. Sight? White sheet with an expanding splotch of pus-yellow. Sound? The echo of footsteps in the basement corridor. Here come the cadavers. Our Selves, when we are no more. Put out your lovely long-fingered hands (twenty-seven bones each) and lift the cloth. Or perhaps taste is the best introduction. No stopping the bitter liquid rising, despite seeing from which meaty mass, from which flimsy gourd it will travel backward, through which tube, to the tongue, which says good-bye in all our invented languages. Which pulp is language's organ? How does the mind tell the heart to thud at gallop-speed? How do the glands say slow down, cool off, Young Doctor?— The sweat drips from your forehead into the cavity from which your partner has disengaged the right lung, and is now carefully carrying it to the Lung Table, on which it will join its compatriots and submit to the inevitable comparisons, as do men in the baths along the river. (More splendid than they know, hearts beating and minds planning this or that diversion.) Pinned to the table, histories such as we know them: twenty-four years; miner in youth (Poland?), most recently employed Gorham's factory at 226 Orchard. With our limited time, we read the stories only to answer one question—What on Earth?—and then only if they label one of the prizes: the blackest lungs, the most atrophied, the tiniest.

Apprehend the heart, Mary, dear—still at last. Is this where love once resided? 'Twas sooner born of the air. What is lost, to know what we are? I ask, and cannot seem to answer, tho' it is certain that something has been taken from me. Experience, *literally: snatched from danger. But sometimes danger destroys.*

My former self seems unwieldy with innocence—as if not-knowing has a physical component, is something soft and yielding (what the Pornographers say of women) before lacerating knowledge. The loss of innocence might as well be a finger cut off (as I nearly did). Now, to catch sight of myself in the glass, or in the greeting of a colleague, I feel a mere stump. (Who was the boy before? Can you tell me?)

Pointless, it is, to mourn the tender capacity of the missing fingertip. Here I am, alone, unmoored by sorrow. Where does it come from, my sadness? To see the corporeal facts. What delusions did I hold?

Do you remember how heavy and round a berry, between the tip of the index finger and thumb? Along what passageway does the sensation of that firm roundness reach you? And you—who are you? Where are you? Not gone with the fingertip, where a blueberry's purple ink once charted the vulnerable gully between nail and skin and marked the whorl that belongs to no other. The finger is gone, but the wound remains—that is only one of the problems of the doctor.

(Nothing serious happened to my own finger, Mary. To yours either, I trust. Our particular wholenesses go on, I hope, if miles apart. Tho' one can never be certain.)

I cannot transcribe my heightened awareness. Everything I am rushes into my fingers; these ten digits must carry all knowledge. If the weight of this heart in my hands sends something impossible through me, all the better. Next time, it may be beating, and I responsible for it. I must spot and correct the slightest of deviations. My fingers feel what I can't see.

To know the colors of a decaying human form—the blackness of lungs; the spring yellow of fat; whitish gray of bone and ligament; all the hues of pink and blood—of what use is this to my training? A child pushed from a window otherwise teaches us the story of human perfection—how tiny yet capable the heart, how pink and healthy her lungs, without yet the cavities made by the tuberculosis, how precise the proportions of her organs before life set in to make of her a drunkard or the mother of seventeen (four surviving), her story pinned to that loose winesack of a uterus rather than this tiny precision.

Two boys, each with their own end of rope, beginning together with toes touching—Go! one, two, three, four . . . until they've stretched it long. What do you say, Roberts? Eleven. Ten for me. Twenty-one feet. Shorter than the last, but it's got some heft to it, heh? Lumps of what wasn't quick enough to make it into our City's fine sewer system. First of our jokes (between shit and piss we fall into the world), least of our humiliations. This length worn away in places, we notice, as we coil it back and place it on the table. I write down everything I see. Become accustomed to seeing. (If we trust anything to the doctors, we should go to the prostitutes to learn the true Nature of Man. That is what I wish to say to Mr. Comstock, who will end up like the rest of us, poor fellow.)

Perhaps none of this shocks one who has grown up on a farm. Allow me to hope that you will write back and tell me of the first time you saw a lamb slaughtered, and comfort me. Because I am ashamed. Of my horror at these bodies. Allow me to think that perhaps you, Mary, can look unflinching at anything. You should be the doctor, not I.

For comfort last night, I searched for how Emerson had mocked the materialists—the witty physician his vehicle. What is a physician to be if not witty? He found the creed in the biliary duct. If the liver was diseased, the man became a Calvinist; if the organ was sound, he became a Unitarian. Let us hope that I can find wit in my fingertips, along with everything else.

At school, they must have decided: Lost Roberts. Shame, they have muttered, passing in the hall. But they have not. I have just not decided how to return. On what terms? What pact shall I make with my own body? When, how—shall I begin to fill myself again? I will eat only greens, like some pre-Historic man who pulls leaves from a tree and sleeps in his cave. The Vegetarians have a point: Their food does not linger in our bodies as do the bodies of our fellow animals. Something in me craves that lightness. I am done with flesh.

As a child I pored over my uncle's Geography *whenever we went to visit him. Imagine the map with the greatest detail, in which the cartographer has shrunk thousands of miles of countryside into the space of a page, and the coursing of a river to the peregrination of a thick black line, its sources many spidery threads. If you can imagine a confluence of waters running into one mighty course along which pockets of human civilization have grown and flourished, then perhaps you can imagine the ganglia of nerve and vein and artery that meet together at the human heart, each tiny spray of branches representing Life—still it seems as tho' it must be a representation, for to think that emotion or thought or impulse or any of what seems to cause pain or exultation passes through, is here, in this splendid organ (How else can it ache?) is as hard to imagine as the rivers of Mesopotamia meeting together and flowing to the sea in Great-Uncle's library. We are conduits, all. But for what?*

It is plain that Life is supernatural. That we have, from inside our jungle of bones and organs and attachments, conceived of anything—such wild Thought! Such poetry and play, such scene-painting and subterfuge, such talk, such cities and turnpikes—is Strange, only.

All right, Mary, dear. I am ashamed of myself—I am the laughingstock of my fellows!—and I can see why, surveying this letter. But do you mind if I honor that fingertip? The too-muchness of conviction and innocence. Pray do not judge me.

I am going back. I am going through certain doors, tho' I will not come out the same. Do we ever? I hope you and yours are very, very well.

—As ever, JR

There did not have to be trouble. Or was that naive, to think that the authorities might look the other way? Frank Tannenbaum knows older and wiser anarchists who would laugh at such hopefulness. Our friend here has not yet been beaten, they would say. Has not yet spent time in the dungeon. Whom do you suppose the police are paid to protect? Not you, boy. Not you or yours.

The police and what they might do with their horses and their clubs and guns carry the jittery upper registers of Frank's mind. And was it really true, as someone had said, that America had sunk the *Maine* herself? And incredible as that is, only a detail. All Cuba as good as stolen. United Fruit with its two million acres of fertile war booty. He resolves to go to the Philippines. Someone has to write what is happening there.

Frank wonders how early to pass out leaflets for the rally. A balance to be struck between maximizing the crowd and exciting the authorities, who after all had vowed never to let Emma Goldman speak on American soil again. He doesn't want to see anyone trampled by horses. Or shot.

He wonders what Justus would advise. Can he excuse going there now? Jane will not be there this early. Though what does he really know of her habits. He does know that he wants to bask in her presence. Rare people, he finds like that. This Jane. And Justus. Ease drapes itself around his shoulders, and whatever Justus is doing—lifting boxes, explaining a fine point of anarchist philosophy, kissing his wife, serving water to a drunk, introducing a sullen stranger to a friend—whatever it is, he looks born to it. As though nothing else in life mattered before or after.

Susana has a similar quality, which may make Frank so susceptible to it in others. She is the ground of his existence. If all of his nervousness about the rally, about the *Maine*, about the extent of the power he wishes to oppose and the price such opposition will entail, about what makes a man as powerful as Justus and how he might develop such power in himself, jags and lurches along the treble clef, Susana is the bass line of the symphony in Frank Tannenbaum's brain. Promised Mother, promised Father. He does not want to stay in New York any longer. He does not wish to study anymore (though he is just six months from graduation). He will never be an engineer; he will not design buildings or bridges. What he wants to do—it's true, what he told Jane in Justus's place—is be a journalist. He likes to ask questions. He likes listening. Why not in Manila? He has come to the point in his life where he should be making decisions on his own, about a solitary future. But can he leave Susana, neglect his promise to their parents to care for her? Maybe she would come with him.

With the woman at Justus's, he found his words coming before he could catch them, as new to him as to her. And the wanting to bask. To sit at her feet and put his head into her lap and explain his problem. What should he do? Could he drag his sister around the world? Maybe Susana would find the tropics agreeable. There you go, he imagines Jane saying, as she strokes his hair. Why don't you ask Susana what she thinks?

As she strokes his hair. And more than just two lines of song, more than just treble and bass, an explosion of sound all around and inside him: the El overhead, a newspaper boy shouting, his watch ticking, his heart beating up into his throat. So much to do before the rally. What is the harm in stopping by Schwab's? Perhaps, if it is quiet, he will ask Justus's advice.

Mary holds her hands up to inspect them, but no visual sign remains. Her trembling has stopped. Under her ring, a strong pulse beats, and she slides the band up to release it. Something strange there, where she has held him. Though already the effort of reconstructing the feeling is too much that: an effort, and not an ecstasy.

Ordinarily, she enjoys solitude. But this morning she is nervous with emptiness. Something has moved through her and left. Was it like that for Edwin when he finished a painting? Then why would anyone wish for such an experience? And afterward to be so lonely.

To her left, the green book. To the right, the stack of letters and newspaper clippings. One a coherence, the other a ruffled pile. She looks at the two and sees what is to be done.

From her sewing bag she retrieves her seam ripper. Such a task cannot be undertaken as whim: to wiggle the ripper into the tight Coptic stitching of the book's binding is too difficult, the silken cord too strong. Always a humiliation to rip out stitches. To labor, the dupe of time. Longer to tear stitches out, longer by far, than to have esteemed correctly from the first. Why hadn't she kept all the papers loose, and left their binding for some later date, some day of wisdom (would it ever come)? Some pages for Maud. Who is leaving soon—she could, perhaps, give them to her. Just hand them over.

She applies the hook to the stubborn red stitches, and pulls, until all the signatures of the book come free. Those clippings and letters she has no need of saving for Maud, she will throw to the sea. Here in New York, a sea for housecleaning. A sea and not the burial ground of earth or fire that is theirs at home.

She could just burn his letters in the stove. But she will not. Like Samuel, she is. That is: all talk. Talk, and a careening after magic. Ever after. Torn pages might float upstream. Wasn't it possible that he'd find them (and her)? The universe made of pattern: tracings and retracings. *Mary*. Jimmy Roberts would say. *Is it really you?*

She brushes the tiny curls of thread off the edge of the table into her hand, raises the window, and blows the scraps out of her palms. Wish-making. A young man below whistles up at her. A wish, a kiss. She shakes a fist at him. And laughs, to think she looks fierce. What a crock. If only he knew.

The Doctor sits at the end of the long bar. A thin man, comfortable in shadows. He has come from the Charity Hospital, where he labored through the night, tending to the emergencies come his way. He has always loved the rigor and quiet of the night work; daylight's ills seem petty by comparison. In the dark, no one pretends that the enemy is anything other than Death itself. And in the morning, the Doctor's solace comes: to walk outside at dawn. He usually sees a few other people, but they are alone like him, and serve only to magnify the strange solitude of the streets as the city gathers itself and the sky broadens into light. When the sky lightens, his heart lifts and seems to swell; *Nature says,—he is my creature, and maugre all his impertinent griefs, he shall be glad with me.* And he is glad, indeed. The Doctor is glad, and he breathes deeply of the river air. If it weren't for these mornings, he doesn't think he would survive (very close despair lies in him under vigor and habit). But when the sun rises, the body's sturdy instincts take over. Coals are stirred, fire sparked, water boiled, dough kneaded. So the Doctor walks home, via Justus's, usually: for Marianna's *brötchen* and the men's own brand of conversation, which bridges night and day—single words, surrounded by long silences, and then monologues, broken by laughter and coughing and regaining themselves, and silence again, and coffee, and chores interspersed with comment.

How easily he takes all things, thinks the Doctor, watching Justus tease his wife. Perhaps his own associates say the same of him, but he knows the internal cost. Only dawn he takes easily. So he comes to Justus, to laugh. As for Schwab?—the Doctor brings him news of the world. He doesn't have time to read a paper, and no one else comes in this early. Justus and Marianna depend on him, for the opening to the world he provides.

Frank Tannenbaum is made shy by their friendship, feels the inadequacy of his own twenty years. He should have gone to class. But Justus greets him warmly, if the Doctor's nod and smile has a whimsy about it, a whimsy and something sardonic that makes Frank dip his head in shame: Which of his thoughts has he left untucked?

"She's not here yet, Mr. Tannenbaum," Justus says.

Frank blushes furiously as the Doctor turns to scrutinize him.

Ignoring his embarrassment, Justus asks, "You'll join us?"

Before Frank has the chance to decline, Justus puts a warm roll and a steaming cup of coffee in front of him.

"Thank you." Frank keeps his eyes on his plate.

"Aren't you supposed to be in class?" Justus continues.

"Bother class," the Doctor intones. "On a morning like this?"

"Precisely!" Frank turns to the Doctor, relieved to find support from this unexpected corner.

"But aren't you nearly finished?" Justus pursues.

"I'm not—" Frank pauses to consider what he is not. He was about to say that he is not interested—but he cannot say that to these men; *everything* interests them. They, he feels certain, would not dismiss anything so lightly as he has done—especially a chance to learn. His education is free. Given to him. A responsibility that he is shirking. And whatever the dailies might claim, this is not the proper application of the anarchist impulse. He's operating from a position of weakness, he knows. They will see it. How he moves out of confusion and not power.

"Can't you see he's a man of action, Justus?" says the Doctor. "Of course he doesn't want to sit in a lecture hall on a morning like this, when there is so much to be done—am I right?"

Frank does not know what to say to these men, each old enough to be his father: He does not know how to strike the proper tone. He knows the Doctor is baiting him, and that he should respond with something light, something edged with self-mockery—he should abscond with that role himself. That is what is called for in such situations. But finally the world of men is alien to him. After his mother's death, his father had stopped drinking with his friends around the fire in the evenings—no longer time for those pleasures. Pleasures Frank otherwise would have grown old enough to share so that he could have heard the actual words exchanged, rather than just their rhythm through the floorboards. His mother's world, the one he had shared with her as a child, remained real. A world of conversations and hands kept busy and comfort: He and Susanna together re-created it every day, even as their father drifted away.

"You're a student, of something obviously—so what is it that really interests you, if not this morning's lecture?" the Doctor persists.

Now the Doctor has turned himself fully to face Frank, and Frank senses that, for some reason, he wants to know. He has dispensed with his mocking tone. The patient before him is a person. But Frank decides that he will give nothing away.

"Women," Frank answers.

Justus and the Doctor laugh until Justus starts coughing again.

Frank cannot help but smile a bit, too.

"Ah . . ." says the Doctor sadly, when he stops laughing.

And then they are quiet again, the two of them; Justus, seeing that they will be comfortable without him, has excused himself.

It occurs to Frank that he might ask the Doctor what he thinks of his plans, but he stops himself. He should ask instead about his work. Perhaps he could do a story about the hospital for the *Pioneer*. Or about the boys' school the Doctor had helped fund.

The Doctor fingers one of Frank's leaflets.

"Have you heard our Emma before?"

"Oh, yes. Of course." Frank feels himself flush. The Doctor is her friend.

"What is she like, really?" he asks, cursing himself as he hears his question; he had meant to devise one more subtle. "I find it hard to . . . imagine her."

The Doctor throws his head back and laughs. "You needn't imagine her. She's real enough! Were you there when she horsewhipped poor Most?"

"I heard about it."

"Well, she was ashamed of that. But that is what she's like." The Doctor sits back and looks up, as if he were considering a number of Emma Goldmans and choosing which one to show Frank.

"I shouldn't have asked," Frank says. What did he expect the Doctor to say? Any little story a kind of betrayal—this way she prefers chicken cooked, or that one is her favorite of Ibsen's plays, or, though it's hard to talk about now with all his years in prison, she did once abandon her Sasha for that painter. Much of this Frank knows. What he wants to find out is what she thinks when the crowd yells for her and stamps their feet. He is used to thinking of life, his own or anyone's, as defined and held by a solitary body. But with Emma Goldman, words leave her and *do something.* Though she is only as tall as his chest, her words do something beyond her reckoning. He supposes it might be true of anyone. Jane talks inside his head now: *I was six years old and knew only shabbiness was ahead.* Her words making him look differently at the children he's seen since: What things do they know, he finds himself asking, and who will love them enough one day to find out? What Frank wants to ask the Doctor is, How does Emma Goldman live with herself, with her words loose in the world, effecting plots of someone else's devising? How does she sleep, after stirring a rally? There are people he knows, other students, who would do anything to be near her, to pretend if only for the space of a brief conversation, to be an intimate like everyone knows this Doctor is. Frank can understand—really, does he not feel it himself?—but a dignified stiffness in him usually does not allow the desire to be manifest. He doesn't want simply to be near her, or to gossip about which man is her companion. He wants to understand her. He will not shout or prostrate himself. The call of *There's Emma!* from one of her enraptured supporters had led the police to her in Philadelphia. It occurs to him, now, to pity Judas.

"No—not at all," says the Doctor. "I hesitate only because I have no answer. What is she like? To be with her makes me think about what is hidden, and need not be. Like you, she's not good at hiding her feelings."

"Like me?"

"Yes."

"I didn't think that I was—particularly revealing." Frank feels himself flush as the Doctor begins to laugh again. He should never have come in at this hour.

"Mr. Tannenbaum, forgive me. I mean that in the best possible way."

"Then I should thank you," Frank says, standing. "Perhaps I'll see you at the rally." He wraps his scarf tight and makes of the question a statement, deepening his voice at the end into opaque resolution, as if to say, No—don't answer. I don't expect it. I will not ask it of you. And the Doctor, who notes the dismissal in the young man's tone, the lurch out of their quiet and unsought camaraderie, is saddened. Off Frank Tannenbaum goes, into the light of the rest of his day. If the Doctor thinks of their encounter as he falls asleep for the afternoon, he will ask himself, What got at that young man? and shake his head. For that is how people are with him. They come close and shy away. He sleeps while the world around him hums. He remains apart.

51 First Avenue, New York City
11 January 1891

Dearest Mary,

I have heard from my mother about Effie. Now I have explanation for your silence this year. I had thought that you, too, had grown tired of letters.

You, *too*. Had she skipped over that tiny, three-lettered word? He had tired of her letters. She had not noticed—or not remembered—that.

I cannot bear to think of you, Mary, you with your talent for life, laying your body alongside Effie's, willing all the healthy substance of your own to flow into hers. And understanding that you could do nothing. Your finding that you could not feed life to the child you delivered into the world and nourished with your very essence. Love does not animate life. Good deeds do not. Kindness does not. Nor intelligence; nor beauty. Nothing we are, and nothing we have invented.

I often see mothers who will not let go of their dead children. Why should they?—as long as they hold them, their flesh is still warm; they remain in the circle of life. These mothers give of their very being, would give anything at all—self, husband, all other children—to save the life of the one already lost. And there I would stand, Hope come too late to the doorway, through which that beloved child would be carried feet first down the stairs, round the corner, down more stairs, out onto the street and across the Bridge to her resting place.

How you must have suffered, Mary. How you must still. Does it help or hurt for me to tell you, This suffering is everywhere.

That is in the air between us.

That is in the space between my idea of you, and you. (For we are only ideas to each other, are we not?) What else, Mary, is a life of letters? What is it but anticipation and then memory? Our lives—yours and mine together—happen only inside. Where we sit, what food passes our lips, what words we speak aloud—all these worldly details have nothing to do with us. Yet who is to say that our shadow life is not real? And Effie with us.

At first, when time was slower, I would return to visit the families of children who had died. Sometimes I could help: Once I saved, if I can call it that, the family's third son. And sometimes I would visit to find the mother's pledge to death forgotten: The empty bed filled by a boarder, she was again determined to survive, cooking a stew with discarded cabbage leaves and raising her right brow at me with suspicion when I asked if I might move the baby's crib outside to the fire escape.

Who was I to speak of fresh air? I could sooner have told them to fix a poultice of sunbeam.

Effie had everything a child needs, and more besides—air, sun & moon, music, laughter, food grown by her own mother's hands. You gave her everything possible.

"If you don't lift me up, Jimmy Roberts," Effie said, shaking her finger at me, "I'll jump myself to the tallest branch, and you'll be sorry."

"Why would I be sorry?" I asked her.

"Because I'll step on your head."

I wouldn't have told you this at the time, because you would have been dismayed by her lack of decorum. I personally liked her forcefulness (it was not unlike her mother's).

Do you remember how she wiggled her finger like that, with her eyes twinkling a warning?

She's with me still, you know. As are you—despite my strange isolated life. It is slim consolation I know, but I send you all of my sympathy, along with this slender volume (the Roberts bros. back in Boston keep busy without me) that came into the world the same year your Effie left.

An imperial affliction
Sent us of the Air—
When it comes, the Landscape listens—
Shadows—hold their breath—

Yours—J. Roberts

He had made her laugh, almost. "I'll step on your head." She had clung to his words and to the poems. Effie's finger wiggling: With his help, she could see that much clearly. The shape of her small hands, with ten fingernails square like Edwin's and Samuel's and Maud's. The mole on her left hand that she called her hand's eyeball. And the green apples growing all over the trees, perfect miniatures yet. And almost—almost, Mary can see the shape of a young girl, a blur of dark dress and petticoat, perched on the branch of a tree. Effie's weight nearly knocking her over when she jumped down out of the tree into her arms.

You, too. He had grown tired of her. Of course his life had gone on.

16 January 1892

You are wrong to set so much store by me. An envelope from Massachusetts has come to seem admonition rather than joy: like the eyes that greet me at the doors of the apartments I visit. The Doctor has come. Savior, I am to be. I am an idea to them, as I am to you. Something beyond. (I see this register in their gestures: hurriedly collecting pins in the pincushion, dusting off a chair, as if I could only enter the room after something was improved to make a place for me.) And were they, too, only ideas to me? Here is my Calling—my own Salvation more than I was ever theirs, probably.

I have floated in this life for several years now. "Grave," the eldest daughters say of me. Friends tell me I should eat more, but as you know, I cannot eat steaks and other cuts of animal. Truth is, we need less than you'd think to subsist. Someone accused me of enjoying the feeling of wasting, of hovering somewhere at the boundary between life and death. Do you have another suggestion? I asked her. Well, I am not beyond enjoying the picture of myself that an eldest daughter creates, one still young enough to think position and weariness something to be desired. I have been known, on occasion, to make myself available to listen to her ideas of me, to have her bring me back to the community of the living.

But you know, don't you: I am not life, Mary dearest. I am not Love. You cannot bury yourself with Effie, nor find yourself with me.

Didn't you offer yourself up for sacrifice, if only Effie were saved? She was not. So what of you? And what of Edwin, who shares your bed. What of the sweaty, incontinent body of love? Not the dream of it, Mary. Not the dream. The flesh is our substance: our sweat and boils and itches and daily defecation. This is all we are. (And if not, why be a doctor at all? And wherefore grief, were spirit all?)

I have done with letters, Mary. Send them no more. I am sorry. Perhaps I would not be writing this had I slept yesterday, had I not made the rounds at Blackwell's Island last night, had I not attended a young girl dying in childbirth.

I assured her she would not die.

But with you Mary, I promised to speak the truth as I find it, or say nothing.

—JR

His initials alone. She is alone. Alone as a child, sitting in the middle of the hearth-rug, picking out the ends. She has made one Jimmy Roberts; he is another. He the letter writer, he the one who has for sixteen years lived in

New York City, he who takes a knife to human flesh, he who has embraced women she has never seen. One he is, and however much she wants to get to that whole, she cannot. Hadn't there been other letters?—records of his daily life, treatises on East Village politics, medical school accounts of this or that doctor's feud, the business of men she has never met. If she had really wanted to write in her green book about him, she has lost all the useful information. Of him, she can make only fragments. She has made love to him under the skylight on the floor of a painter's studio on West 23rd Street.

No, Mary, he tells her.

Mary shivers. Jimmy Roberts's refusal, like the distance on the look of death. That poem comes again. Shadows hold their breath. A slant of light, a winter afternoon. A certain slant. To think of him once a delight that carried her through all. Through cleaning, pruning, stirring a batter. Spinning Her Excellency's creamy fleece, the thin strand slipping across the tips of her fingers as Jimmy Roberts's bare foot stepped close. Excuse me, ma'am, he would have said, if their feet had touched. As the wool passed from fleece to strand through her fingers, she was alive to it, to the grease of it, to its softness: Jimmy Roberts's skin she felt.

I have done with it, Mary.

He was done with her. And she had not believed him, though he had never in her experience lied. To the sea with this letter. Yes, to the sea. Could he have made his intent more plain? Yet she had not understood. *(What opium is distilled into all disaster!)*

Was it Boscovich who found out that bodies never come into contact? she copies out. *Well, souls never touch their objects. An unnavigable sea washes with silent waves between us and the things we aim at.*

What a fool she'd been, to think of how he would embrace her in Schwab's.

She circles the word *sea* and puts that paper on top of his letters, and then goes over to the window. She settles herself on the floor and leans out, surveying the street. That Jimmy Roberts had sent her a book of poetry does not make him the universe's only poem. She thinks of Samuel, turning back to wave at her, as he crossed the road with Alma and Maud in her arms. One hand waving free. No one need know. She can write anything. It need not be bound.

"You don't approve of Samuel and me," Alice says.

Edwin looks down at the pencil he sharpens. He watches the shavings fall away and then blows, slowly, deliberately, on the point. "What gives you that idea?"

"You refuse to meet my eye. Your wife will not address me directly. 'Samuel, perhaps you and Alice would like to join us . . .' "

"Husbands and wives agree in all matters?"

"You agree in this one."

"Ah." Edwin looks down into his bag, considering the pencils and brushes.

"Am I . . . am I sitting as you'd like?"

"Are you sitting as *you* like?"

In response Alice softens her spine and stares at Edwin, her eyes punctuating the movement with a challenge.

"Now?" he asks.

She shrugs, and looks at him with the same eyes: an aggression and a challenge. You tell me, she wills silently. If the visual impression is his, the shape of conversation will be hers. She will own the silence. She may as well: Samuel's family will make of her what they will. Her husband's brother will paint her as he likes. She has only to defend herself.

He has a pencil in hand, about to make a quick sketch, as he's always done before. Except a decision intrudes. Luck descends. The decision or the luck is refusal and embrace all at once, so much the same impulse that he does not feel it to be divisible.

Alice knows nothing of how an artist might work, and imagines the concentration she watches simply as an intensification of something she has felt herself. The abruptness with which he exchanges the pencil for brush reminds her of when she first met Samuel Elmer. How she took off his hat. She had never done such a thing before, and has not since.

Alice wants to know if painting every portrait is the same for Edwin. And if not (as she suspects), how is he different with her? What does it mean that he puts the pencil he so carefully sharpened back in his bag without so much as making a line, and begins instead to squeeze out a brilliant red paint onto his palette? Then yellow. He slices into the paint to mix the colors as though he is trying to hurt something.

For Alice's portrait, he will not sketch in pencil first; he will not consider and study and measure. He will not take a photograph (he has not brought any camera with him to New York), which he would then be free to consult in private, as he had done with the portrait of his brother, and every other since. He will begin with color—this orange of her dress that he cannot get around—and he will paint the portrait from start to finish in her company. He mixes the colors of fire and then softens them with lead white.

"Just like that?" Alice asks. "You start right in with my dress?"

"Happen to, yes."

He softens the brilliance of the orange because something in him has softened, standing across from her—to see her pride so visible, her vulnerability, her attention to him. In this room with its closed door, something shifts. Though they are in Samuel's house, what transpires now is apart from Samuel, apart from Mary, apart from anyone. The fear Edwin had of being placed in this position, of Samuel's heavy hand forcing him to his wife, dissipates. "Don't interrupt," he'd told him. You brought me to this room—Edwin's eyes conveyed warning—now I will inhabit it as I see fit.

Edwin is aware now of Alice's own presence, as if she were a woman he had just met, whose proximity he is duty-bound to honor with the rituals of attention men have accustomed themselves to paying women. As for Alice, she is part nerve and part solicitous gratitude. She loves Samuel with so much new conviction that to stand before this man who is his closest brother makes her feel her beloved with a double intensity: as if she were standing in front of another Samuel, this one sterner, one she cannot reach with the usual charms, with a touch or breath or suggestion of more to come. There is no more to come. He sees all of her in a glance. Will what she is suffice?

All of anyone suffices. Edwin feels something he has not working at the Academy. Does it come from Alice? From the flush rising to her cheeks? That announcement, unbidden, that what he might make of her matters more deeply than she can hide.

I am his, she thinks, immediately rephrasing it thus: He paints my fortune.

"Have you read Ruskin, Alice?"

"Yes, of course."

"The Seven Lamps?"

"No." Alice's flush deepens.

Edwin stops and looks at her even more closely. She is afraid of him. Afraid of him!

"Forget Ruskin. He's not important. I was just thinking that the other day at the Academy, the teacher lectured that we must strive to acquire 'innocence of the eye.' Imagine that. Asking someone to cultivate innocence." He chuckles.

Alice widens her eyes, shrugs her shoulders, starts to speak—and then is quiet again, as Edwin continues, without noticing her effort.

"It is Ruskin's phrase, 'innocence of the eye,' though the teacher didn't mention that. I'm not saying that credit must be paid for every idea. Individual men, working in their own corners of the world, make the same discoveries every day. But this teacher—" Edwin stops to consider. "He's so—pompous. Has about him the air of unearned glory. As if being an artist were a lark. Some child's game."

"Well, Edwin." Alice smiles. "Some members of this household have already left for work."

"And others stay behind doing nothing at all. Imagine."

"If you are suggesting that sitting here is idleness—"

"Not at all, Alice. On the contrary. It is difficult to be still—difficult to hold a pose—difficult to reveal yourself."

"Is that what I'm doing?"

"Don't you think so?"

"Then what do you see?"

"Don't worry." He winks. "I won't tell Samuel."

Alice harrumphs and refocuses her eyes on Edwin's, determined to get the best of this brother. What is the secret of an artist's gaze? He narrows his eyes, and she narrows hers.

"Effie and I used to lie in the grass and squint like this—are you, too?" He stops and looks at her. "Squint until your lashes make everything hazy. See?"

"Hmm."

"Effie and I used to lie in the grass and squint like this, and Her Excellency—that was her favorite sheep—became a cloud, and all still things dancing—dancing patterns—and not—meaning. Or not the usual meanings. And Effie would shake her head, she had this way of shaking her head, and only saying 'oh, oh, oh,' slowly, as if what she'd just discovered so stunned her that to speak it would not be possible. Of course, she had her audience completely rapt. Me. Right here." Edwin taps his palm. "And finally she said, 'It's just so green.' That's all. 'It's just so green.' I couldn't very well worry then about the fact that the grass had to be mowed before the rain came, could I? Or anything else." Edwin smiles at Alice. "Not with the world all"—he pauses and shakes his hand like an old-time preacher—"ashimmer. Ready to be made again. Green the first green." He laughs at himself. "She was the one teaching me." Edwin looks off into the distance: not Alice, not canvas.

"She must have been very happy with you." Alice looks down at her own hands and holds them up, smiling, shaking them back at Edwin, as if to say, At least it's nice to think about fingers like that.

"I suppose so." He makes an effort to gather a smile for her. Of course he knows that joy is everywhere, anywhere, still. *Life is an ecstasy,* Emerson said. And genius only knowing that. Emerson speaks of everyone's Genius, Mary said one night. At the Academy, genius is a rare commodity, to be hoarded, taken out only for display and boasting. He is angry at himself for agreeing to such terms. At himself, not anyone else. To have wasted any days, suspecting that success lay somewhere else. He'd already had it, sitting on the steps, working in those early mornings before anyone else awoke. And after hardly a week in New York, he sees what he might have known all along: That no one can teach him what he cannot learn. Or what he must. Ward, full of bombast, preaching what Edwin had already discovered for himself, lying in the grass with Effie nearly two decades ago, in no sermon but accident.

Can he find his way back? No. He knows that regret and retrospect are the wrong path. Onward, he must go. Forward. But something is missing now; and then—it wasn't. Perhaps his moment has passed. Creative power allotted like the days and never anyone to know when his own light is brightest. To mark his peak and his decline will be left to someone else—poor Maud, most likely.

He can do nothing but try his hand at the canvas in front of him. Brush in midair, he considers Alice's face. What moment in her life is this day? She is no longer young exactly, but still her skin derives its structure from the bone only. No deep lines her face has made for itself yet, except maybe just the hint of what will one day be a line between her brows, as though she has often furrowed them, trying to see farther into the distance.

"I see Samuel," Alice says.

"Excuse me?"

"Blur your edges and I see Samuel."

It is Edwin's turn to blush. To think of Samuel's wife regarding him as her husband. "Family resemblance, Alice. It is hard to get around."

"What does that tell about you, Edwin?"

His face narrows into concentration. He was right before. He cannot paint Alice for Samuel. He paints X's across Samuel's voice, which comes unheeded—joking, mocking. His humor cruel sometimes. Everyone in the room laughing, but Edwin left feeling as though something sharp had bitten into him. Samuel poking him, prodding. "Come on, Eddie." He'd thought that was all past. Only because proximity had no longer given Samuel the opportunity. As soon as they arrived in New York, Samuel began pushing him to paint Alice. What next, Edwin fears. It was the worst when they were in Cleveland. Running the business, instructing him how to spend his free time, too. Sam telling jokes to the cigar men and the waiting women: "Did you hear the one about the medieval lord who was called to battle? He gave the key to his wife's chastity belt to his brother for safekeeping." Here, Samuel had dramatically fished about in his pocket, and, with a flourish, handed Edwin his copy of their apartment key. "Hardly had he been riding a mile, when his brother rode up behind him, to say: 'You gave me the wrong key!' "

When Edwin had met the startled and shamed eyes of the young woman on Samuel's arm—was there always a woman on his arm?—all the resentments he had ever felt against Samuel-a-year-ahead, Samuel-do-this-Eddie had flared into a blaze of anger. And he had looked into that woman's eyes and felt an accord and a sorrow for them both, that they would both do whatever Samuel asked, however much they squirmed and resisted. Except he didn't that time. He left. His first successful resistance to Samuel. His second: Mary. And the house. How surprised Samuel was, coming home every weekend and seeing the progress he and Cousin John had made in his absence. With his two hands he had built what Samuel could only imagine, impressing Samuel—and Mary, too, he mustn't forget—rather than pleasing himself. It took him a good many years to realize what he didn't like about the shape of the house.

Anger flares up. Easily. At Samuel, at Alice, at them both. What game were they playing with him? She is beautiful, he sees, as his brush sketches an orange shape. Of course. An image of Alma comes to him. Alice looks down into her lap. She will not meet his eye. She confirms no suspicion.

"Fine, Alice," he says. "Pretend I'm Samuel. After all, he will be the one looking at your portrait, not I. Do you suppose he'll hang it in his office, so he can look at you all day long, before he gets home to the real woman? Show me, Alice. Strike whatever pose he likes best."

Alice widens her eyes, and then looks at him with contempt and fury, in equal measure, and Edwin is as surprised to find himself indifferent to both as he was to hear the tone of those particular words fall from his own lips, their implication ripe.

"Come. Surely he doesn't enjoy you glaring at him like that?"

Who is this man he hears? Some puffed-up man of the world, pleased to make others squirm. He wants to laugh, to hear his voice in this particular guise. It is not his own. It is that of a man perfectly well acquainted with human foibles. With perversity. With inserting himself into his brother's private life. Instead of laughing, he paints. He does not stop to soften his words (which anyway do not feel like his) or apologize. If he is lucky, the portrait will say what he cannot. Perhaps. He has begun, no matter what is volatile between them—an anger may live in this portrait; what had they expected with such an orange, with her twin provocations, with Samuel's demands?—but perhaps his brush will find something else.

He is trying something he never has before, spending the oils without a plan to govern their use. Mary called him too much a mathematician. She is right: He is precise where he longs to stumble and bloom. Look at this, he wants to say to her. Swimming in this color, he has no idea where it will take him, what mistake might, in its refusal to be unmade, reveal himself. He can paint over anything; that is the nature of oil. Anyone with a modicum of talent can make something beautiful in oil, say the watercolorists. But he disagrees. The mistake—if it be that—is still there, no matter how many times covered. Covered so many times the error is built up, elaborated, becomes its own statement. What will Samuel discover, then, about them both, by the time he is done with Alice's portrait?

He thinks of that woman in Cleveland, the gentle openness of her brown eyes. Before Samuel made his joke, he had been drawn to her sweetness, to something innocent in her, however Samuel saw it. With Samuel's women, this happens: He becomes a boy, as if to see them in his thrall he himself feels it all over again—Samuel bigger, funnier; Samuel the success of the family—and the women, finding an ally in Edwin, take to him, becoming girls themselves, as if they were his sisters and had grown up suffering the same injuries. An intimate bond, to share with a stranger: This is what it is to live by Samuel's side. I know you, Edwin's brush says. I know that, Alice's eyes concur.

They are silent for a long interval. She can hear his brush touching the canvas. If she thinks too much about that—about how he drags or pushes the bristles against the canvas—she starts to twitch.

"Samuel says you are quite the mathematician."

"He's not bad with numbers himself."

"I'm at a loss with them."

"Oh, I doubt that, Alice." Another time, he might have meant, Don't feign innocence; your calculations are exact and hard, but now he simply means to take her side, to refute anything disparaging she might say of herself. He pauses to smile at her. Alice's spine softens again.

"You are a beautiful woman, Alice," he says, coming close. "May I?"

"Yes," she says.

He takes her head in his hands, his palms cupping her ears, his fingers settling in her hair and his two thumbs on her cheekbones. Call it a way of measuring. His thumbs bring burning pink spots to the centers of her cheeks. He moves her head slightly to the right and then just as slightly to the left.

"That's all?" she asks when he drops his hands and returns to his easel.

He nods.

As he traces the oval that will become her face, he imagines himself returning home, a man who might say to a woman, Take off your clothes. Though he cannot imagine what might transpire after that sentence. What if she agreed? He can only see images isolated in time: Mary bent over, unlacing her shoes. Her head to one side, caught in mid-circle as she unwinds her hair. Her hands at her shirt buttons. But he cannot connect these images one to another, or to himself. In each she concentrates on the task at hand—unhooking, untying, unwrapping. He cannot make her eyes meet his. He cannot even imagine her fully undressed, standing, facing him. She would slip quickly under the covers and wait for him there. And where would he be? Would he all the while sit on one of the chairs by the window, and watch, like a man in a theater, his hands nervous in his lap?

He does not see his own hands on Alice, or how his touch startles her, so he does not imagine that he knows as well as anyone a way of beginning. How hands, in honoring the body's symmetry—moving from the ears to frame the neck, sliding four fingers under each shoulder strap to lift and slip them down, making of his palms the skin of a second corset, holding her breasts firm to her—might make of the one he touched a willing partner, with ideas of her own that, like symmetry, would have a logic he could follow. Would there be words? What would he say? What would she? He cannot imagine action or sentence that connects one image to the next, or any man to any woman. (Should it be so difficult? Did not the propagation of the race depend on it?) Lean forward and touch her—where?—where was the place? What could possibly bridge the gulf between his sudden, surprising desire and a woman? Yes, Samuel: a real woman.

Maud might very well have been Edwin's own daughter. His eye she'd inherited; his proclivities. Perhaps Maud would want to know something of his first drawing teacher. Edwin had kept a letter Farrer had sent the *Nation* tucked in his book of Tom Paine essays. For no reason Mary knew. Because he agreed with his old teacher. Or because Farrer's precision amused him. Keep for now. (Two piles: one marked Maud; the other, Sea.)

11 January 1866

The summing-up of the criticism is in these words: "The inevitable tendency of this sort of work is shown by the drawing of the three little eggs. But, in doing this, the painter has been compelled to lower the tone of the whole, and they are not white eggs that we have. That they were meant to be, the high light seems to show."

Now, they were not meant for white eggs. The central one was, as it appears in the drawing, white; but the other two were the pale buff color always to be found in any large number of city eggs.

I would not trouble you with this were it not that in criticisms that profess to be accurate and just, and which help to form public opinion, any misstatement is important.—Farrer

The porch was wide and low, hardly above the ground, so that visitors had two ways to stumble: Lifting a foot in anticipation of a regular step or paying the half-step no mind and tripping flat out. That could spill an entire basket of eggs all over the porch. Lucky I saved even the one.

The older brother came out first.

"What the—? What on earth are you up to? Edwin! Come see. We have a mess here."

Samuel folded his arms and laughed at me.

"I was looking at the door."

"You like it? Edwin spent all day mixing the color."

"It's beautiful. The green of old copper."

"Perhaps too beautiful."

"No. I'm sorry—it was stupid of me."

"Don't worry, sweetheart."

Samuel picked a lacy trail of maple pollen off my shoulder and kissed my forehead. I am not a child, I wanted to say. Or was this what people meant: Samuel's easy with women. Even Father John said so. Here he was calling me sweetheart and bending himself double.

"Come in." Samuel stepped out onto the porch and took my arm, drawing me in just as Edwin came out.

"Let me see if I can save the yolks," Edwin said and turned back into the house.

"For paint," Samuel said.

"Is that how he made this color?" I started to touch the door, but Samuel grabbed my hand.

"Wet." Samuel smiled. "You ruined the eggs already." He let my hand slide out of his.

"I'm sorry," Edwin came back to say. "I should have said hello."

"I should have been more careful."

He crouched and began to scrape an egg yolk into a cup.

I knelt down beside him. "May I help?"

"Sure. But only the whole yolks. The egg whites'll harden too quickly for the brush."

"Look at that." Samuel's voice came from somewhere above our heads. Edwin and I looked up. "One perfect egg."

Edwin and I stood up and we all peered into the basket. It was one of the speckled chicken's beige-pink eggs.

"Look at that," Edwin repeated. "It's beautiful."

Edwin and Samuel stood looking at the egg while I scooped the yolks into the cup and tried to sneak away.

"Wait!" Samuel called after me. "Won't you have tea?"

I saw that Edwin was still looking at the egg. How could I stay for tea? I'd be sure to say some stupid thing or break a saucer.

"I've got to get home," I called, and began to run.

"Another time," Samuel cupped his hands around his mouth and called from the edge of the porch.

My heart beat with that invitation. Another time.

So it came to be that I spent Sunday afternoons at that Elmer residence, which was only different from ours in that on Sundays idleness was enforced (except for Emeline's bustling about in the kitchen) tho' they didn't believe in the rest of the church teachings.

"We pledge ourselves to do nothing useful all day long. Something must remain sacred," Samuel said, as he took my hand and bowed to greet me. Edwin sketched in the corner of the room, by the window.

I wanted to be one of them. A man with them. Not Emeline in the kitchen. I was like a younger sister, I suppose. Except not exactly. And not a cousin, really, except by marriage. But nothing like a sweetheart, no matter what Samuel said. That would have ruined everything.

Did I sense even then that our Sunday afternoons were stitched of a fragile fabric? I was allowed to go only because the Elmer brothers were kin, almost. Lucy didn't go with me only because I didn't tell her what she was missing—if she had known what fun, my sister would have come along, too, and bossed me until I ended in the corner with Edwin, crocheting something useless with nothing to do but listen while Samuel plied Lucy with his attentive questions. Except here I may as well say, her answers would not have been as interesting as mine, for both the Elmer brothers were attracted to what Lucy called my "oddnesses"; they would have found her conventional attitudes dull. She would have hushed him instead of laughing, as I did, when he tried to shock me with his City tales. (Tho' he succeeded at times. And he must have known that I could hardly have been as worldly as I pretended. One dinner at the Nortons' had not made me into the sophisticate I wished to be.) In any case, the presence of one more person—or one less, if either brother had been courting and making of us two plus one instead of the three we were—would have torn apart those afternoons.

Edwin hardly looked up from his sketching, except the afternoon he made Samuel sit still for him.

"For my self-portrait," he joked.

Every once in a while, Edwin offered a comment that would let us know he'd been listening all along.

That I knew about Samuel and his women (tho' what, exactly? Only rumor) is certainly true. That I was not sure whether his affection was that of an older brother's (was he kissing me on the head because he thought me a child?) or an instance of his larger affection for womankind (his "sweetheart" profligate, and not mine alone) is also true. Only Samuel knows.

As for me, I was sixteen years old and in love with Samuel Elmer. That is all there is to be said. Perhaps sixteen-year-olds know nothing of love. Well—then Jimmy Roberts knew nothing either.

Friday

What should I have done, when I got outside and saw it was Edwin, and not Samuel, who'd come back for me? I thought they had spoken and agreed what was to become of us. Who was I, the interloper, to quarrel? Either way, Sunday afternoons were excised from the book of days. Edwin did not seem to notice that I'd called out his brother's name before he turned around. We did not speak again, of how it had been, we three in our Eden.

Edwin takes the steps at a dash, as if he's been hurled inside by the wind, and he runs, two at a time, up the first three flights. The last two, he slows, curses his age. Not so strong as once. Easily winded. Careful. Not. To. Press. Too. Hard.

At the top of the stairs, the door to their apartment seems to him a reproach. For what, he cannot say. He aligns his eye with the slit of the keyhole. All he can see a gray, clear light, as if the room were uninhabited. The I-shaped lock accepts his key. I, the latch, he thinks. And therein, treasure. If he can unlock it.

A mistake, probably. To come home in this state. He should have kept at the painting, but something in him had bowed to convention. The workday was drawing to a close. Alice was tired and should be left in peace to collect herself before Samuel returned from work. Edwin did not want to intrude on them at the end of the day. But once outside, he saw that the sky had darkened prematurely with storm. He need not have left so soon. The clouds' admonition: *I have this against you, Edwin Elmer.* A fear had made him dump his brushes and colors so precipitously into his bag and flee his brother's house.

He has to push hard to open the door. The wind presses back. Once inside, he finds the window wide open and the wind howling through, and Mary nowhere to be seen. Edwin stands and looks around for a minute—where has she gone? He takes note of the chaos: a giant spool of silk tipped over and rolled out across the floor, the quilt flipped up across one corner of the bed, and papers strewn about. He brings the window down with a bang, bumping his head with the force. He should pick up this mess before she returns.

13 July 1829, Ashfield, he begins to read. *People stopped Uncle Alfred before it was done. The angel had commanded Three, and he got one. The Messenger had said, You are strong, Alfred Elmer, and your eyes are sharp. Remember the time you felled four partridges with one shot? But I have this against you: You have abandoned the love you had at first. Remember then, from what you have fallen. Join the Celestial Army, and you shall eat from the Tree of Life.*

Alfred started back from the fields toward the barn, then stopped by the wall he'd been meaning to repair since spring.

Did Annie see him leaning there, holding his head?

Belief did not come easily to him. He was plagued by doubts: What made him so beloved of God? Anyone (and surely God) knew that such a feat as the partridges involved luck as well as skill. The birds had startled, and all flown up together. He was strong—yet not out of the ordinary, he argued. Strength such as anyone might have from work.

Did Annie notice how his muscles moved beneath his sleeves? Did his strength frighten or please her? Did she see him lifting the top rock off the wall, then standing back to judge how far the wall had to be dismantled before it could be raised again, straight?

"I am only a man," he spoke.

Yet do other men of your strength hear me, Alfred Elmer? Let anyone who has an ear listen.

He could not still that voice.

As he unstacked and then shimmed and pushed and rebuilt the wall, he tried not to hear anything but the stones, and his own hands, brushing off dirt, nudging them over to inspect each side. He held himself to the stones, to their heft and the peculiar demand of each: this gash and then falling-off at the right requiring a flat wedge of a rock about the size of his hand to compensate. The horses heard—all the animals heard—whinnying and braying and pacing as if before a storm. And he began crying with them: crying from certainty over the destruction to come.

The land will be soaked in blood. The children and the rulers and the generals, everyone, slave and free, will scatter and hide in the hills. But there will be no hiding from the wrath of the Righteous One.

. . .

All the world is strange to Edwin. Too full—of meanings. Those words from Revelations in him, and then written, here. His mother had viewed coincidence as divine, looped her worldview around its posts. "God's instruction, my child." Though at first he thinks he should not have opened the door, he is not a coward—he believes nothing can be unleashed worse than what he has already seen. Not a coward. *(Yet not out of the ordinary.)* He is curious. Of course he is curious.

Alfred's was a strange kind of blessing: to hear voices, while he was alone in the field. But he chose neither blessing nor voices. He did not choose. He wondered if others had heard, too, and done nothing. It made no sense to him, that he alone should hear God's Will. At least the animals, too, were restless, as if they sensed a presence in the air.

He could not stop thinking of her, holding her tiny new baby. Must this terrible fate come to her, too? And to the babe in her arms? For if there were innocence on this Earth, surely the child—

He must save her and her child.

Though every bone in his body had been anticipating it, the thunder startled him. And he knew then that there could be no denying the voices. No denying his duty. He had not asked to be born in these times. He had not asked for this lot in life. Or for the chanting that would not stop: The land shall be soaked in blood. The land shall be soaked in blood.

Leaving the stones (only one more and the capstone would have completed the job), he went to the barn for his ax.

Edwin had told her that. He'd told her that three decades after, Uncle had asked him to check the stone wall by the old barn: Was the capstone at the back still missing?

Did Annie see him coming, and wonder why?

Newspaper accounts are available—I bring them up because you surely will hear the whispers before you are even grown, for children are not shy of Detail.

Was his wife mad?—"before you are even grown"? As if these pages were spread out for Effie.

They will say he murdered the Catlin baby and afterward tried to take his own amd the life of his grandfather with the very same ax.) Greenfield Courier, *14 July 1829.) You should know, though, what a newspaper does not print: about sorrow. About quiet. About how long his life after, carving tiny blocks of wood, and rocking back and forth on the stool in his cage. Your father emptying his bucket and bringing his plate. Four times a day, when your uncle Samuel paid him to take his own turn, which was usually.*

Edwin sits down at the table.

Uncle had died in that cage. Of course he had. There was no other place.

More papers in front of him. *We did not speak again, of how it had been, we three in our Eden.* He sees envelopes, with New York City postmarks. *What of Edwin who shares your bed? What of the sweaty, incontinent body of love.*

He can read no further. He is not a coward, but not a fool, either. He sees Mary's arms wrapped around a pile of bedclothes, and Samuel's arms wrapped around her, the two of them rocking back and forth in the bed that had been Effie's. Damn him, he thinks, as he picks up page after page from the floor and pushes them into a pile. He can look no further. He puts the kettle down atop them: to hold the pages in one place, to say, I've been here.

He locks the door again. Eye, the opening, the latch.

Mary had left without her bag or any of its contents, with only the key and a single bill folded inside her coat pocket. She does not know where she will walk.

That she tells herself. No destination in mind. Without her notebook, she has no reason to go to Schwab's. She may go to Maud. East, at first, holds both possibilities. And they are not the only two. There is what she does not know. She has superstitions—about a luminiferous ether; about worlds beyond worlds or worlds inside worlds (the governance of prepositions attempts to pinpoint the location of these realms; each word misdirects). She tries to sharpen her hearing, as though with ear trumpets. She watches those she passes, as through a magnifying glass. All the people on the street. Always when she walks out into the city, she hears this hum: perhaps Jimmy Roberts. Perhaps Nellie. Perhaps Nellie or Dave or Grace. One never knows—how fate may turn.

She turns downtown. For Schwab's. She will pass by and not go in.

"Jane! Jane. Jane." Susana Tannenbaum suddenly close behind.

"Oh! Goodness. Hello."

"I've been shouting to you for blocks."

"I'm so sorry. I had no idea."

"Will you go in with me?"

"In? Well. I—"

"Come." Susana takes Mary by the arm, and holds the door open.

"Frank says that you are a writer."

"Oh, no. No."

"Can you tell me—wait a second. Justus!"

"Susana." He bows low. She bows back.

"How is Marianna?"

"Fine, *liebchen*."

"She isn't working too hard?"

"Of course she is—always."

"You must take care of her. Of yourself, too. How is that cough? You are thinner every time I see you. I'm getting my own drink. And I'll go back and help Marianna after I talk to Jane. What are you having, Jane?"

"Cider." To Mary's surprise, Justus does not protest, but steps aside to let Susana behind the bar, where she looks perfectly at home.

"Me, too, then. What are you writing? Can you say? Hold on—wait until I sit down."

Can she say? She thinks of Samuel and Edwin. Of Effie sitting on a limb of an apple tree. Of her pouch of river stones. How she had wanted them to hold, to roll about in her hands, to line up in a row and name. Here, a rug by the fire. Here, Mother says, You may call him Father. Here, I dry off my hands and listen to Mr. Norton. Edwin raps at my window. We four—Edwin, Maud, Effie, and I—stand waiting at the train station for Samuel to come home. Jimmy Roberts whispers in the blueberry bushes. Nellie stands and sings. Edwin opens the door in the early morning, and looks from me to Jimmy and back. A portrait of a woman in the attic. *I am two fools . . . for loving and for saying so,* on the back, in Edwin's elegant hand. Let us call her Effie. Her rosebud blanket wrapped about her shoulders as she is lowered into the ground.

"I am not sure I can," Mary answers, when Susana settles herself across from her. "Do you know Emerson's 'Experience'?"

"Of course. *We do not know today whether we are busy or idle*—I like to remember that, when I am idle."

Mary laughs. "Yes. It is some consolation."

She looks down at Susana's hands, and at her own. Hers with tiny lines across the knuckles, the backs a hieroglyph of veins. Susana's hands are smooth, the skin rising to knuckles without such fuss, as supple in demand as in repose. So much possible for the young, Mary thinks. She should have written—what had Frank said? Domestic tragedies?—when she was younger, when she still had youth's audacity in her. Alas. What is left to her? Wrinkles, loosening. Though the lines the skin makes are themselves interesting—the angles at which they cross each other to form tiny boxes and triangles, each intersection different from the next. Complexity the fate of age. Is that solace?

"Jane. About Emerson." Susana takes her hand.

Susana's touch startles Mary. Though this is just how Susana is. She reaches toward people. She smooths lapels into line as she says hello; behind the bar, she pats a tuft of Justus's hair that points skyward. It amazes Mary that such a one as Susana—full of such warmth and steadfastness—should be interested in her. She embodies Emerson's advice: *In the midst of the crowd keep with perfect sweetness the independence of solitude.* That is Susana. As for her, introduce another and she begins to watch, tilted and askew and forgetful of all before. Her soul ajitter. She is not steady, but ever inclined.

"My dear, you must not call me Jane."

"Pardon?" Susana thinks she will propose a term that will make formal their blooming affection. Aunt, perhaps.

"Really, my name is Mary Jane. Most people call me Mary. When I met your brother—"

Mary breaks off, not knowing how to end her thought. When she met Frank Tannenbaum—what? She had been afraid to give him her real name. She wanted a different self. Were the two the same?

Susana watches a pained look come across the other woman's face. "You needn't explain. Mary."

They both smile, to hear her name. And that is that.

"It was my first time in Schwab's. Actually, my first time alone in any place like this."

"Really? But you seem so—"

"Experienced? Old enough to be your mother? What is there to say? I've led a different life. I grew up on a farm, in a town with as many inhabitants as are in this room right now. No, I exaggerate"—Mary presses Susana's hand to still her protest, and notes how her gesture is one of Susana's; she is under her spell; how easily she falls under anyone's spell; that is her only consistency—"Still, in winter, we hibernated as sure as any creature. So this is all very strange to me."

"What brought you to New York? And to Schwab's? And where is your family? There, still?"

Mary hesitates.

"Forgive me. You needn't answer. If I am prying, tell me to hush."

"They are—well, here and there." (There, in the earth, curled in her blanket.) Mary is surprised how like evasion the precise truth sounds. "I suppose I came because I was looking for someone."

"A man, you mean?"

Mary looks at Susana, startled, and blushes. She sees that Susana and Frank have indeed presumed her to be—as she herself had wished, isn't it, giving only her maiden name?—a woman alone. Here she is, with no Edwin, with a past to be revealed only as she chooses.

"Well, yes—though I don't mean that I am looking for—he was an old friend, actually, and he had written to us"—oh dear; to what us is she referring?—"about Schwab's, even used the address as his own, and so—"

"Then I must know him. What is his name?"

"Oh, my dear. That was years ago."

The calm of her own voice almost convinces her that it is foolishness to imagine Jimmy Roberts might be found here. But she knows from the thudding of blood in her neck that her body holds out the opposite conviction, whatever the evidence, however many years intervene, whatever her civilized voice proposes.

"Oh." Susana sits back, disappointed.

The two women sip their cider.

"Emerson, then," Susanna says. "Unless you want to tell me about your family."

"Emerson's always interesting."

"You know that Emma Goldman finds him one of the most liberating of American voices?"

"So your brother tells me," Mary says. So Jimmy Roberts told me, she thinks.

"Altogether too perpendicular, Margaret Fuller called him. But she was his friend."

"Really? She said that?" Mary puts her cup down; she cannot fully contemplate such criticism while holding anything.

"So the story goes."

Too perpendicular. Mary supposes all his imperatives make him seem so. He's only trying to convince himself, she almost says aloud. And what about—his lightnesses? Sprinkled everywhere. *Life is not dialectics*. But Margaret Fuller had something right. "I wish I'd said that."

"Yes," smiles Susana. "How about calling his son *caducous?*"

Mary's eyes widen in delight. "I can't believe"—she reaches for Susana's hands—"that bothers you, too." She has never heard the word aloud before, though she knows, having looked it up in Ashfield's Belding Memorial Library, that it comes from the Latin *cadere,* to fall. She long ago turned the dictionary definition into an image—a yellow, withered part falls from a sturdy branch. Naturally children leave their parents. Though she wonders, thinking of this season at home, of seeds blowing from the fragile insides of flowers dried upright in the field, if caducous might be a seed, and not the end of anything after all. Wasn't it the apostle Paul, who called the human corpse a seed? Though she generally has no use for his philosophies.

"And it's dreadful what he says about orgasms—a waste, doesn't he say?"

"Goodness," Mary says, turns red, and withdraws her hands.

"That's his problem in a nutshell."

"You think so?"

"I do. Control is one thing—of course it has its place in our lives, but a waste? It's as if . . . Should all rivers be dammed? What if all nature's power were harnessed to serve some direct, quantifiable benefit to human beings?"

"Okay—you're right. But I don't think Emerson means—"

"Oh, of course not. In theory. He resists extrapolating any ideas from this coldness at his center. Except that its opposite exists. So he looks outside himself, thank goodness. And everything hovers between these two poles. Where is it he says that he lacks sufficient 'animal spirits'? Of course he makes up for it. With energy, will, attention. Oh, he makes up for his every deficit. And we've ever after been chasing him."

Mary is shy now before Susana, who has ventured in casual conversation to a place where she might never have arrived in a lifetime. For Susana, this must be nothing unusual. For Mary, as if a secret spoken aloud. A secret laid open between them, to be dissected, its components noted. People took other views. People had spoken of such things before—of Emerson's failings, of private pleasure. She thinks to tell Susana of Jimmy Roberts stepping in her window. What does it mean? she wants to ask her. That our bodies are capable of such pleasure and people live and die not going mad with it, not speaking a whit of it. The experience locked away. Emerson not the only one. The idea everywhere about the dangers of indulgence, even among those who believe themselves free-thinkers. Like the young Elmers, rejecting the religion of their forebears, bringing an oyster bar and billiard rooms to town. Proposing those pleasures. Yet: Edwin's frowning at Samuel and Alice. Look where chasing after pleasure got Samuel—blind to the welfare of his only child. True. She agrees with Edwin there. But what of Edwin's long-held belief, before Alice, before Jimmy Roberts, before her, even: Alone he preserves something of himself. He does not spend it in the grasses.

Mary suddenly finds herself about to cry, to think of them there, so young. So young, in all their not-knowing. What it would have been, not to be confused or ashamed. To have let the pleasure be, the expansion in her the earth's own, as the beetle crawling across her thigh after was no annoyance, but a small representative of all the earth's gifts, the pricks of its tiny feet salutes to the miracle of sensation. All the things a body can feel. Yes—the creep of insect feet. The heart beating hard against its frame. She cannot now quite remember the first feeling of him inside her. All power in her compressed, and then rolling, thudding through her, making of her body's solidity a lightness. And blood trickling. Samuel refusing to look at her the next day.

"But it is different for women, Susana."

"What do you mean?"

Mary takes a breath. "Pleasure, like that. Physical pleasure."

"Why?"

"Come, my dear. Think of us, pregnant and bleeding, pregnant and bleeding, until one day our weary womb comes out wrapped around the final child's head." She thinks of the mess of sheets. "Maybe Emerson was just being considerate of womankind, to speak for restraint."

Susana shudders. "Well, there's that. Which is why—why don't you come to a birth-control meeting with me?"

Mary is silent.

"Or the rally. Come to the rally. You will love listening to Emma Goldman, I'm sure."

"Maybe."

The two women are quiet.

"Susana?"

"Yes?"

"Would you have a lover instead of a husband?"

"Would I?" Susana bursts into laughter. "Why the conditional? As if my life were a theory. If what? If a lover and a husband both presented themselves before me, which would I choose? I do have a lover, if that is what you are asking."

"Oh." Mary stares at her cider. "I suppose everyone does. Frank, too."

"You'll have to ask him yourself."

Mary flushes. She cannot imagine the words, let alone—What is it like? She wants to ask. To come together without law or habit. Well, Susana is New. A New Woman. Next to her, Mary feels very, very old. Old, and ashamed of what she does not know.

"Susana, do you think that it's true, that someone who spends his energy making, say a writer or maybe a painter—would necessarily have to deny, or else lack—" Mary starts to gesture instead of speak. "The—what shall I say?—animal spirits." And her hands fall to the table, as if they had been suspended in the sentence, and finally, hearing its conclusion, slump from the effort of getting there. What does she hope to learn from this twenty-year-old girl—about Edwin, or about herself, about mysteries she has long observed in silence, alone?

"What do I know, Mary? Each person—artist or no—finds his or her way. A general rule? I can't imagine. I don't know that I even believe Emerson's idea about the two poles. I mean, it's useful, maybe. As a picture. But I don't like it, somehow. Though I suppose the only reason to have a theory is to disprove it."

Mary smiles at this.

"But where does that get us?" Susana continues. "Where are we going? All of us, I mean. Articulating and then—dis-articulating. Leaving behind us a sea of language. Every year more of it, a flood of propositions and their refinings. I doubt it's heading anywhere. Or that it improves anyone's life."

"Of course it does. I can't imagine my life without books. They have been such solace. I wouldn't have survived without them. At night, after everything—" Mary shakes her head. "I never thought to disagree with Emerson, as you do. I was only grateful. Grateful to have those essays with me at night. Grateful that there was the gas lamp, and the silence all around, and those words, and what they made—"

Why does her voice waver?

"Another world," says Susana, stroking Mary's hand, wondering whether to explain that she hadn't meant, exactly—but it doesn't matter.

Mary bends her head so Susana will not see the tears that have filled her eyes—and why? Why does sadness come when it does?—though it is not the tears she hides, the tears Susana has already seen and heard catch her words, but what she might see reflected back in Susana's eyes. Sympathy? Pity? Susana's own sadness? She cannot look up into the eyes of this lovely woman who holds her hand, who is just the age Effie would have been. *And Effie is with us,* Jimmy Roberts had written. She cannot look at Susana, though all of Susana's presence asks it of her. Another of her spells, she hears Edwin say. *Mary Elmer grew neurotic,* people said. *They shut up their home and moved to a town apartment.* She has read of joy. She has seen Susana, throwing her head back, laughing with Justus. But Mary does not know such happiness.

"I'm sorry," she whispers. "I'm sorry." And to hear her own voice—so fragile, so extremely vulnerable—brings more tears. Where does sadness come from? She knows only this: It is a liquid, and it threatens to drown her. It sweeps down over the hills, makes of all the land she knows an unrecognizable sea. For all she knows Nellie is dead, too.

"I'm sorry," she repeats. She cannot wipe the tears that cover her cheeks, for Susana holds both her hands.

"You needn't apologize."

"I must go," Mary says, pulling her hands away.

"No."

"I must."

"Will you meet us later? Please. Frank will be so disappointed if you don't. Not to mention me."

"I'll see."

Alice raises her eyebrows in a silent question when she sees him standing ragged and winded at her door.

"I'm sorry," Edwin says. "I wondered if—"

All possible conclusions to his sentence leave him. He does not know—He simply does not know how he meant to finish. Her silence surprises him. She had been expecting him, then, and sees no need of a greeting to punctuate a conversation that as far as she is concerned has continued all along. Before she opened the door, she knew it would be Edwin. Now, she waits for him to speak.

"—if—"

Her brows arch further.

"Could we continue?"

"Right now?"

"I'm sorry," Edwin says again. "I shouldn't have come back."

"No. It's fine. Do you mind if we eat something first?"

"Of course not," he says. Though he is disappointed even by this minor delay.

"You'll have to come down with me to the kitchen. Everyone's off this afternoon. We've a party to go to this evening, so for now you and I are on our own."

Edwin does not want to go to the kitchen with her, but he feels that the choice is not his. If she is hungry, she must eat, and letting her out of his sight seems more disruption than letting the painting sit for a little while longer without him.

He follows Alice through the narrow hall and down the stairs, to where the kitchen is tucked at the back of the ground floor. She is aware that he must be watching her, now, from behind, and curiosity and embarrassment both plague her. He sees what she cannot. What does he make of her? Does her form please him? Or does he think she is rather too round everywhere?

The ceiling is lower here. And the walls yellow, as though someone has pulled the sunlight they've hardly seen this week through the single back window and spread it thin across the entire downstairs. He nearly walks into her when she turns around suddenly on the landing. As if the bottom step had marked a boundary they'd not known existed until they crossed it, Edwin feels distinctly that he has stepped too far; that he does not have the resources for survival in this territory. He can feel the heat of her. Her breath. He needn't put his palm on her chest to feel her heart beat: Without touching, he feels the pulse of her. She is too close for him to see her clearly. He steps backward up a step. She moves forward into the kitchen.

"Surely you are not intending to cook in that dress."

Her hand flies up to her mouth. "I hadn't thought. Of course—I can't."

They survey one another. He stands in the door and considers the impossibility of their situation. She thinks of taking the dress off. Of not taking the dress off. She wants to ask, Isn't that how it's done in studios? But it is too hot by the stove; she cannot bring herself to suggest what he does not.

"You can't take it off. Sit down," he says. "I'll cook for you." Though he does not know the first thing about the preparation of food.

"Madam," Edwin bows. "Please." He pulls out a chair for Alice at the slender rectangle of table that must be where the servants eat, they who are off today. Though if he and Mary lived in this house, they would eat at this table. Everything but size recommends it: the sunny yellow of the walls, the back door to the patch of garden behind the house, the proximity to the stove.

He shifts out of his make-believe voice, realizing the difficulty that might otherwise ensue. "Don't expect anything fancy," he warns.

"Why don't you just cook some eggs? Contrary to what you might think, I am not fussy. My dress notwithstanding."

"And what's growing inside is very demanding," she adds further, though she had not known she meant to say it.

"Really?" Edwin turns back from the pantry.

"Really," Alice blushes. "But—" she puts her finger to her lips. "I haven't told Samuel yet."

"I won't say a word."

Edwin goes back to the pantry for the eggs, and to collect his thoughts, which surprise him as much as her news. For what he feels is a mix of alarm (and for what? It is not his child to bear or raise) and pride (and for what? It is not his child), some pulse of implication—she has told him before Samuel. He is alone in the kitchen with her and the baby growing inside her belly. No wonder she is so full. He realizes that he had suspected as much, though he would not have presumed to say it aloud. To do so would have been too intimate an admission. A lover's or a husband's words.

"Here," he tells her. "Put this apron over yourself."

Edwin tosses it from across the room, and it lands flat against her, straps flying up into her face. "I'm sorry." He is always sorry. And for what? "Here. Let me tie it." Though he did not want to come so close. He had meant to stand back from her, to judge the space between her neck and shoulders.

She holds the apron flat against her belly and chest and turns for him, her head bowed.

As he pulls tight the cloth at her middle, he hesitates. Doesn't want to squeeze the baby. When he sees how the muslin still curves in about her waist, he feels the blood in him rush down. As though—He ties the ribbon at her neck quickly, trying not to register the effect in him of her pose. Which is of submission. And for a second he wonders. What would happen if he kept his hand on the back of her neck and reached forward, to turn her toward him? What is it to be Samuel, next to her? Yet her bent head also a kind of trust. A daughter's. Effie bending her head forward exactly so, sitting on the piano bench, while Mary brushed her hair out. He must have been drawing, at the table he'd put by the northern window, facing the line of locusts.

She is waiting for him.

"What do you want from me?" he says, when she doesn't move, though he is done with tying.

"Prickly, you are," she turns to say. "I want some eggs. And then a painting."

"Hmm," grunts Edwin.

"In the meantime, civility."

"Ah—civility. Is that the prize?"

"Respect, then."

"It's yours." He inclines his head. "Certainly," he says, half to himself, breaking one egg after another into a white porcelain bowl. Good—they are fresh. Each a deeper yellow than the walls. The last with a spot of blood in it. Superstitious, he is: He holds his breath when he sees the crimson knot. Holds his breath as Maud and Effie did at the graveyard when they sat up beside him on the way to pick up Samuel. "Or the ghosts'll come into you." When they passed on the way back, Samuel teased them by taking in loud rapid breaths. And when they least expected it, moaning in a voice not his own.

Edwin fries the eggs in butter, and watches as the clear albumen hardens to white and the yolks grow paler with the heat. He tries not to feel Alice's eyes on him, or panic to think of what to say. He need say nothing. Samuel's child grows in her. Well, well.

He puts the buttered eggs on the table and looks at her, until she breaks his gaze to survey the plate.

What does he see? What will he paint when he comes to the corners of her lips and to her eyes?

All our blows glance. All objects slip through our fingers when we clutch hardest. That is what she had started to tell Susana about Emerson. She might have answered her question, tried to tell her what she was aiming at—but what would it matter? *All our blows glance.* For comfort, she repeats these words. She is not alone in failure. She cannot really speak to Susana of what she has been trying to write. To speak of it has no meaning. Is the very opposite of meaning. To write him is to let him disappear. To pin him to the page, specimen of her youth, her life not chosen. Her Jimmy Roberts is not real, or alive. The Jimmy Roberts who somewhere in this city goes about his daily business is not who she imagines him to be, but someone else—himself, alone. If she were to find him, their meeting would not be anything like last night's. He is no longer the boy who said, "Then I will not speak," and looked at her with the longing she has not known since. That, of the people they were, will not come again, not in heaven or hell (she believes in neither).

Mary turns the metal catch on the inside of the door to their brownstone with an ease that does not predict the finality of the sound in the door's frame as she sinks the deadbolt back into place. She has come home, to her and Edwin's home of the moment, though she has not thought once during the walk across town of where she was heading. As she climbs the five flights of stairs, she thinks of Edwin. So much refusal in them both. And the exhaustion of that. Of affirming disbelief. The two of them. They do not believe in any God, in heaven or hell, in angels or messengers who boast any relationship to the divine different from that of any other mortal. Oh Edwin, she wants to say. I am sorry. Her tears are all the expression she can manage. I have wronged you. Wronged life.

But Edwin—who loves her, too, she supposes, though he does not know her—is nowhere to be found.

Feeling at home in the strange emptiness, she stands directly under the skylight, in front of a painting Edwin has covered with a white cloth. A sentence lodges itself in her: *All that you seek will come.* Perhaps that was what Jimmy Roberts meant, coming in through their window. Though as anyone of any experience knows: not in the guise you expect. Jimmy Roberts will never come back to her. How had this realization come? Because she'd said to Susana, "That was years ago," that he'd used Schwab's address. *It was,* she hears. It *was,* she hears the truth in her own voice. Correct use of the past tense. If she had incorrectly used the conditional. However she'd put it, they all have lovers. Susana and Frank, and Jimmy Roberts, too. In any case, she has arrived at the end of the scene in the blueberry bushes. *Hear, if you can, the going-on of two separate breaths.* Two separate. Two. She thinks of Edwin's imaginary landscapes, and how he always makes two hills, with a river running through. As if he'd split Goodnow Hill with its stream and made it run to the sea. We two stand, with life passing between. I am sorry, she wants to tell him.

Dream delivers us to dream.

Wind blows in the open windows—

Here is the window, on the north side of the house. Bang hard, and it flies up. The leaves of the line of black locust trees rustle. The heavy cranberry damask of the curtains lifts slightly with the air, as if the house itself were breathing. The heart of the house lifting. And the storm comes.

"I didn't leave the window open," she had answered Edwin's accusation.

"Roberts, then."

"I know you love me, Mary, dear/Your heart was ever fond and true—" Edwin had sung, his hand over his chest, mocking Mr. Roberts and his son and his own wife at once. And then he had left her alone, with the piano out of tune. (Weren't people like those heavy instruments?—sensitive to changes in weather, incapable of harmony without regular adjustment, without the careful attention of tender fingers and acute ears?) It is all very well, Mary thinks, to remember the discord, the notes that jar and assert themselves as though they are something solid offending the air—but what of song? What of the life that skips and moves? Here her pen falters. After Effie died, Edwin had the piano moved to Shelburne with them. Traded the moving and tuning for a portrait of the piano tuner's dead mother. That was to be said for her husband: He had insisted there still be music. It was not his fault she could not lift the cover to touch any one of the keys.

Music she lacks now.

She can remember the words Jimmy Roberts's father sang—*my heart is ever fond and true*—but she cannot match them to a melody.

Why had she concerned herself with stones—what can be held—when she might have tried to write of what disappears? About the chances gone, the life spent—chipping here, patching there, with nary an effect. With nary an effect—on an *impression so grand as that of the world on the human mind.* Was that how he'd put it? Emerson's words all strung through her own.

My heart is ever fond and true—she tries again to find the melody. She walks over and stands under the skylight, where the cool greenish-blue light stretches out in an octagon around her, its regularity making her feel as if she were a woman on a stage—except never would a stage hold a singer with so sad a sound. She was no Effie Ellsler. She cannot find the notes to this simple song, a tune that had been popular for years. Jimmy Roberts's father had sung it; people across the country had hummed it. She herself had. But that melody is gone to her now, and in its place, something wavers: Each time she sings, the final few notes change slightly. Why not call such uncertainty song? Why not? Surely she is not so unusual. Surely the medical students, cutting into her remains, would only find gray matter like any other gray matter; a heart like any other heart.

My heart is ever fond and true—she sings again, and she tries to listen to the voice that is, instead of straining to hear a far-off melody. Her heart is not true—that is the problem. Even Jimmy Roberts, she does not love. Not love as she'd thought of it, an unchanging force. What had given her such an idea? Rivers swell and trickle with the seasons. She thinks of Jimmy Roberts with effort; she turns her mind to him. Here, where he might pass her on the street at any moment. It is Susana she thinks of now unbidden, Susana with her words tumbling out. Susana and Frank smiling at her. And Edwin an ache inside. She has wronged him.

She examines the pile of completed whip-snaps. One in progress in the machine. She lines the finished snaps up on the floor to see if they are identical. This one or that, one revolution of the wheel longer than others. A length nearly invisible—invisible indeed to industry's coarse instruments, though someone with a more subtle rule might detect it. Here and there, a slight tightening or loosening of the threads. That would never matter in sale or in use, raised aloft and then coming down on the horse's back end.

She sits back down at her machine. How it had pleased Edwin to make it! She had been impressed with his ingenuity herself. Enabled her to braid twenty snaps in the time she used to make one by hand. Though she had rather liked the slow handwork. It was conducive to daydreaming. Something else happens at the machine—a dullness creeps into her mind. She does not know what she thinks as she works, but after, as she splashes water on her face and raises her head to the looking-glass, what she sees startles her every time: a frown, as Edwin had painted her in mourning. Lines that bite into her brow and tug down the corners of her mouth, settling into furrows that deepen with every hour she watches the threads make of themselves one braid.

She stands. Away from the machine, the mirror, the sky-lit stage, at the table again, pieces of the green book and letters to the side, she again inspects her skin's cracking along the knuckles. Perhaps she could draw these lines. Not try to draw hands but instead the lines on them. Perhaps if she and Frank were to go with Susana again, she might draw instead of write, but not what was expected—never if she lived to be one hundred and sixty could she transfer anything of the true life of Susana Tannenbaum to the page. No: she would draw only the slant graphs her knuckles animate.

She begins again to cry—because she cannot draw, because she has wronged Edwin. So much emotion comes that she can no longer think, as though the tears (which come only from her) threaten to obliterate their very source. As if to feel what she is risks annihilating her very being. This cannot be, she tells herself. Get up, and wash your face.

And then? She cannot very well go back to Schwab's now. Perhaps Edwin is right: She should go see Maud. Maybe invite her to the rally tomorrow. Though the thought of Maud meeting Frank and Susana makes her nervous. Why should it? The three of the same generation and inclination. Introductions would fall to her. She would have to establish the ground on which they might converse; she would have to watch and tend whatever grew there.

Yet her nervousness is not only that. A whisper says: What kind of trouble are you making, Mary Elmer? What kind of trouble? Frank thinks her name is Jane. She will have to explain to him—if Susana hasn't already—that she told him only the half of it. Well, maybe Frank would take a fancy to Maud.

Why would she want to suggest such a thing, with him so full of itch and agitation to leave? What if Maud ended up a teacher in the Philippines instead of Seattle? Though for that, they probably wanted Christians. Or what if he left her behind and her life shaped itself around a yearning for a man not anywhere near? Did Mary wish that life for her?—Alone, and wondering. She should know better.

Yet a matchmaker's scruples do not explain Mary's sudden agitation. She wants to keep her activities at Schwab's separate from her family. She wants to keep a secret. One thing it is to write, *Dearest Maud*—all the while holding the image of her niece in front of her—it would be another altogether to speak the same story to Maud herself. She could never, face to face, tell Maud of Jimmy Roberts, let alone all she knows of Samuel.

Are secrets the frame we build our lives upon?

Mary rehearses one sequence of events—knocking on Maud's door, though it is not only Maud's, of course; Samuel himself might open it; all three of them walking in the direction of Union Square, encountering there Susana and Frank. Her head starts to hurt, and she abandons her relations mid-story. Doctors knock at her skull, as carpenters tap to find framing beneath plaster. And then, upon finding the softest spot, her vulnerability, one quick rap! The doctor cuts.

"Secrets our only solidity," Mary whispers aloud. The unspoken a web that holds us in place. In what organs do secrets reside, Jimmy Roberts? She has seen only a drawing of the human heart, but with this aid she pictures her own, after the cutting, and sees a tiny spider of charred black incised upon it. Here, she has already died. And death's heart reaches out into her own, like the rays of an inverted sun or the stitching of a wound.

She unwinds a length of silk three times the breadth of her outstretched arms, breaks it off with her teeth, slides her papers out from under the kettle and wraps the thread around and around and around. Edges of the papers tear where she tightens the silk, though she doesn't rip them deliberately. She lets the mummified book sit and goes to bed. Nothing left for her.

She could take a walk.

To the Battery, maybe. Even back from the wharves, the air moves differently. The rain there carries the salt of oceans and other lands. But as if she were under an iron weight, she cannot bring herself to get up.

Tear it up, Mary. Feed it to the gulls.

Eventually, for the second time in the same day, she leaves their building carrying almost nothing.

Alone by the sea, something fills her and she is as near to content as is possible on this earth. Her tears nothing to the ocean. Worth coming to New York for this alone, she thinks. The clearing of her landlocked soul. Outside, she no longer succumbs to bleakness. The birds are disks of light over a gray, choppy sea. Where she sees only flash and shadow, she invents wings.

She thinks of Frank Tannenbaum, and whether landscape changes a person. Who would she be if she had been born, like him, on this island, within sight of this view? Or if she'd sailed on that ship? She watches the work of a crew, who carry plants she does not recognize up a ramp and onto the wharf. What if she walked aboard now, while everyone was busy, and secreted herself below? After they'd pulled out of the harbor, she'd make herself known. I can cook, she would offer. I can be an ocean-wife. (Would another man want her?) I can keep a log of your journey.

What does she have to lose? Nothing. Though she had once refused Edwin when he had asked her to travel to Alaska.

She thinks of Jimmy Roberts's cadavers lined up for dissection, and how she had not been able to answer him, or at least not been able to give him the answer she imagined he wanted (whatever it was he thought the farm daughter's view), but instead had been overcome with his feeling, and bundled it confused into her own. Now she thinks that the horror she'd felt reading his letter had nothing to do with blood or gristle or organ but with the deafening silence of the corpse. That we all will be mute one day. What we could not utter alive will not be said. Something there is, she must say, even if she can say it to no one. Not even Maud. It is about the sky. About the wings we once had. About the fire of the sun. And how what we have known in time becomes strange.

"I have an idea," Edwin says, watching Alice eat the buttered eggs. "Be right back."

"All right," she says so quickly that he senses he has hurt her feelings. He should have waited until she finished. Mary would have understood that by *idea* he meant he had to be alone. He could no longer make words that might be construed as half a conversation—he has set off on another course. It's not Alice's fault. Nothing to do with her. He will have to make it up to her somehow later.

Upstairs in Samuel's sitting-room, Edwin paces before the canvas. A bowl of eggs on a table to the side of her, in the foreground. No need to have her sit for that; he could work on it at home. Except—he doesn't actually want a bowl of pristine pale eggs. In fact, he wants to remove the blue-and-white china vase from the sideboard and crack a single egg open in its place. What pleasure to paint its yolk vivid and yellow beside the orange of her. He begins to chuckle. The urge to juxtapose this with that irresistible. Might be trouble, egg yolk on mahogany. Probably make a bad stain.

He walks into the hall to look at the portrait he had made of Samuel. Perhaps the two could hang together. A gesture in that direction might make all the difference. Formally acknowledging their marriage might excuse the blotch on the table. Now with her news especially.

Squinting at the portrait of Samuel, he is surprised to see that the background is not what he had begun painting behind Alice. That is: surprised that he is surprised. Of course these ponderous dark shelves (albeit lightened by the china vases) are not the background of a portrait two—no, three—decades old. Samuel had not then been the man of this house. Had not yet set foot in Manhattan, for that matter. Had not yet married Alma, let alone this one. They'd been hardly more than boys when he'd painted his brother.

Had Samuel kept the little books Uncle had made for them when they were young? Perhaps in a trunk in the Whiting attic. He wishes he had his. He remembers on one page an Arctic landscape, with reindeer and a sled. The seed, maybe, of his Klondike fever a few years back. After the barn had burned down, he had nearly convinced Mary to pack up everything and set off for Alaska. Men found gold there. For him, that was just something to tell Samuel and Mary. Perhaps he should have tried to tell her the truth, which would have been something else entirely.

He laughs again—the truth, indeed. He is upstairs laughing at himself, while Alice eats his buttered eggs in her yellow kitchen. He should have tried to explain to Mary that he'd thought the part of him missing might be found somewhere else. Who could say about such things. Maybe if he had not looked at all those books and pictures of other landscapes, of mountains and ice and unknown turquoise coves, the space inside him would not have opened. But it was as if a wind had blown through him. And he wanted ice and white cold and Northern distance. Do pictures make desire more than they come from it, he wonders. Photographs make no hardship of Alaska, or anywhere else. Look long enough at this picture of Samuel, and it's as if they were both home. Home in the little house with the door he'd painted pale coppery green.

He will not be in this world forever. So—he will paint a basket of eggs. One, cracked open on the table beside her.

Where had Uncle's ideas for his pictures come from? Edwin can remember no photographs or pictures in the family until his uncle's. All the hand-sewn book's pages equally foreign, now that Edwin thinks of it. Riders bareback, boomerangs flying overhead. Uncle had carved him one of those, to show in three dimensions what he had meant by the picture. Throw it away from you, and it comes back. Magic, Edwin had marveled.

Magic that could only have come from his strange uncle who lived down the road in an iron-barred cage. Who else would carve both release and return into the same slender curve of wood? No one had known more of wood than his uncle. He would have liked to have said this. To whom, Edwin does not know. The Patent Office? He would like to have entered something in the public record of Alfred Elmer's hands besides blood. Blood was not all. Accident and death not all. Confusion not all, nor belief. Who has not listened to voices he should have shouted down. Who among us knows for certain which voices to heed and which to strangle.

Edwin realizes he is gripping hard on the back of the chair. He watches his hand release the wood, cracks his knuckles. It was something, what Uncle had made of fallen trees. Edwin's knuckle-cracking deliberate this time. One on the left, one on the right.

It had seemed to him as a boy that Uncle spent all his days carving. Edwin's favorite toys were the delicate horses he had made: herds of them, mares and stallions and tiny stilt-legged foals. When he was a bit older, the puzzles fascinated him. "Here," Uncle would say. "Hold out your hand. Come closer." Only when Edwin's both hands slid through the bars would his uncle open his own, and roll a wooden ball into his nephew's waiting palm. Had disappointment at first clouded his eyes? Uncle held up a finger to show him patience. Then into Edwin's other hand he rolled a round wooden cage with a ball identical to the first inside it, etched with the same marks of his tiniest plane. Edwin shook it, but the tiny ball only knocked against its cage. What a lovely sound wood makes against wood. "How did you do it?" he yelled, jumping. "How?"

"Think," Uncle told him. "Think."

A cage with a ball inside it. Then more elaborate tricks: Four heads of horses atop a tangle of wooden limbs. Bring the heads together, and all the limbs below shift, a braid of wood. Yet not exactly a braid, Edwin corrects. Each horse-head first branches into two legs and later resolves into a single hoof. An entwining of eight wood-limbs, all carved of one block of wood, released by his uncle's knife into separate legs that clatter and shift against each other. Then human forms, too, when Uncle adjudged him man enough. Two men and a woman embracing, their limbs all sinew and twist, the pose suspended with the spikes of the men in the holes of the woman.

He should get back to work. But he takes one more look at the painting of Samuel, and thinks of them both, as Uncle must have seen them, skinny-legged, jumping. Though Edwin doesn't know, really, what he looked like as a boy. The face and body he imagines are always Samuel's. The first time he'd had his own photograph taken he had been disconcerted by the darkness of his own eyes, by a gentleness around the lips, an innocent lift to the brow—What lack there is in this method! he had thought. How inexact!—until he saw Samuel's picture with the resolve bracing his lower lip, the light of his eyes, the slight glower downward of the brow, and thought: *Here I am.* So it may have been Samuel who had jumped up and down upon rattling Uncle's first ball in its cage. But it was Edwin who had heard him say, "Think," and tried to do it.

Now he wants this, too: to paint a wooden toy of Uncle's next to the egg yolk, next to Alice. Desire has taken hold. An idea. He picks up his paints and canvas. He will paint her in her yellow kitchen. All around as yellow as yolk and sunshine, which will surely come again one of these days.

Mary dreams she meets Waldo, Emerson's little son, at Heaven's gate. A brown-eyed cherub he is, playing a fretted instrument with such joy that he arcs backward, flipping through the air, his round belly leading, his arms wild with the joy of music—he needn't look over the strings to see where his fingers fall. So *this* is the music of the spheres, she turns to say. Imagine, a Concord son. In such a place of honor. She'd never thought the world so congenial.

Not (to speak precisely) the *world*, corrects her guide.

She has no choice but to follow this man across the sky, so she pushes off with the pads of her feet, stretches her arms wide, and cupping each hand slightly to gather the wind, finds herself aloft.

When she awakes, night is falling across the city. Where on earth is Edwin? Extraordinary, he had said to her once about her dreams of flying. No—it's easy, she had said, and tried to show him. Stretch your arms wide. Like this, she rolled his shoulders back, securing the wings of his shoulder blades deep in the center of his back. Demonstrating herself, she had felt again how it is to be airborne. What you have to understand, she'd told him, is that flying is *ordinary*. Ordinary. No great mystery. We learn to walk and run and skip and swim—it's hardly different. When she thinks now of how he'd shaken his head and smiled at her, an understanding comes to her from far off, as if she were another woman and he another man: how once his love had burnished her, polished her up until she glowed. And standing beside the window now, looking out at the rain, that seems to her a stranger mystery than any other. That he'd sat in the corner sketching and watching, and that he had chosen her and never left.

But he is not home now, and the fire in the stove has gone out. "He disappears." She hears Emeline's flat voice. "Goes away. His time not like ours." It was maddening, really. Always had been. But tonight she is not angry, to think of how Edwin loses time when he works. How much he loves light. He'd painted a glow all around her at the whip-snap machine. Though Edwin would probably say that the light that made a halo about her head was simply a faithful rendering of the light coming from the machine lamp. Love or a touch of cadmium yellow? Lucky him, to have that work. Especially when Effie died. She had only been able to stumble through those days. Why life at all? she would have asked, had asking come. Edwin had shaved off fine splinters of the same question: With what paint shall I make the maple-syrup pools of Effie's eyes? How does Mary hold the machine lever; how does the light come through the pine trees and fall across the rug?

Emeline must have that painting. It had been out on Edwin's table when Samuel came back for the first time after Effie died. Nearly two years he'd stayed away. Samuel had stood and looked and shaken his head and whistled admiration. "Such fine contrast between the dark folds of your dress. The light around your head. And the rug!—How did he make his brushstrokes disappear like that?" They had leaned forward into the painting, squinting. "Edwin," Samuel had said, shaking his head. And the way he'd said it, *Edwin*, just *Edwin* by itself, only he could say to her.

Where had Edwin gone? Could not have been far. He would not have wanted to leave them alone for long. Maybe he'd stepped out to post a letter. To pick up more photographs of the Dearly-Departeds for coloring. Wherever he and Maud had gone, he and his painting filled the space between her and Samuel. "Mary," Samuel said. And that, too—the way Samuel said *Mary*—only he could have said to her, and it meant: We were young then. And even younger before. Remember, across the road from each other, Alma with us and every night dinner the four of us, and then six of us Effie and Maud on our laps. Her tears were running to hear his voice, and she bent so that he would not see. But he knows her. He lifted his hand to her chin and turned her to face him. She cannot hide from him. He always sees.

She had been unmaking the bed in Effie's room. Pulling out the triangles of white linen tucked under the featherbed, drawing each corner up toward the center into a great bundle of smell that was Effie and never would be her again. She would take this pile downstairs and soak all her bedding in water and soap and that would be the end. Except this she could not bear. She climbed on top of the bundle and then held it, was rocking it to her, when Samuel came to the door and gathered her in his arms and kissed the tears that were the first to fall, though Effie had been dead already three mornings. He kissed the tears from her cheeks, humming, *Mary, Mary,* in a voice that had all scraped from it but the bare consonants of her name. She held him, same as she held on to the sheets, and to the banister walking up to Effie's room, to all solid things. A cup she'd filled very slowly with water. The shawl she drew close about her. She did not understand the significance of touch: that one could—that she could—reach out, crumple the sheet in her hand. She could change and be changed. The fabric relayed a meaning through her fingertips: It was a cloth she'd washed and hung to dry many times. This white sheet an inhabitant of the permanent world she'd lived in once. Now all transient. They are ghosts, themselves, she and Samuel. Nothing lasts. Not the way a person might touch another. Not the hot wet of tears or the tongue that laps them. Not the world or bed or sheets or limbs moving through air, though why this our medium instead of water, she does not remember ever knowing. Not the way something invisible might float up between two people and draw them together or push them apart.

"You may go now, Samuel," Edwin said, at the door to Effie's bedroom.

The chill of his words, *You may go now,* broke the trance of grief. Still hearts beat and quicken and cringe. Still the regulations of earth's civilizations preside over husband and wife, over brother and brother, and something akin to shame washed over Mary.

Samuel took Maud back with him to New York City.

"I've done the best I could," Edwin said, leaning his painting against the wall and resting his own head against the wall above it. She looked at his back as his shoulders shook. She looked down at the canvas and took in Effie and Her Excellency and Buck the kitten with her tail up and the ribboned hat and Edwin with his newspaper and the house all shut up and her own grief-stricken face. She could not speak. She walked down the stairs, holding the banister in her right hand, noting that its solidity was now slightly less strange, as if she herself had grown harder. She saw then how things would progress: She would acclimate herself again to the properties of the physical world, and none of it would touch her so very much again.

It was all long ago. Yet it pains her now to think of Edwin standing there, leaning against the wall, his head bent. In resignation, it had seemed to her. He had tried but not won anything for his efforts. Too bad for him, if he had thought to battle death. She had walked away. Walked away. What kind of woman was she?

His everyday posture comes to her—the little hunch of his shoulders to the left. His clean shirt every day at noontime, and his smile sneaking its way out under his enormous mustache. His feet bare in his shoes for half the year. The steadiness of his gaze under his soft brow. How he pedals his bicycle, with a little quick whirl and flourish of speed before he stops, as if he's still a boy giddy with invention. He and Samuel, the two of them talking, heads bent at the same angle, kicking stones as they walk along the road together. She and Alma behind, carrying babies.

She had turned and gone downstairs without touching him, though his shoulders had been shaking, though she had never before seen him cry—not when his mother or father had died, or Alma, or the baby. That quivering another quality of the physical world: its pulses and leaps. Nothing solid but abuzz. Her fingers might have gone to the center of his back and rubbed him there, where the pain burns sharpest. She might have stayed with him and looked at the grasses and clover and buttercups he'd made. Which after all had taken longer to paint than Effie's eyes. And were themselves love, as much as anything. If love is concentration. And burnishing what another person might have left untouched and unseen. So closely he looked. Each blade of grass a stroke of attention. Every loop of the white lace collar, though she'd left it in a drawer, unfinished. Somehow he had known where the leafy openwork tightened to double crochet near the edge. "Husband," she says aloud. It is different from saying Edwin. She invokes the pact they've made. Solid as anything.

"Edwin?" Alice startles to her feet at a crash overhead.

"I'm sorry." He appears at the door to the basement carrying his paints and canvas. "Tripped on the easel." He puts the canvas on the table, making no effort to hide it from her anymore. She looks at it without comment. A blur, she is only. A confection of orange.

"I'll be right back."

He dashes up the steps, taking them two at a time, and returns with the easel.

"Do you mind?" he asks. "If we stay here."

"Of course not." She reaches up to check her hair. "But soon Samuel will be home. And we're going out this evening."

"At least I can get a bit done. Do you mind?" He holds out an egg.

"Do I mind what?" she starts to put out her hand and then pulls it back when she sees he does not mean to give it to her.

He cracks the egg open on the edge of the table beside her. Good. The yolk is clear of red.

"What on earth—?"

"I want to paint you next to the egg."

"Is this your idea of a joke?"

He laughs. "No."

She looks at him hard.

"What? I like the color of the walls."

"You're the artist," Alice says, as she sits.

"Do you know if Samuel has any little wooden carvings around?"

She blushes. "No."

"Too bad."

"Why?"

"I thought to put one of our uncle's creations in the portrait."

"Whatever for?"

Edwin is peering into his bag. Why doesn't he answer? Does he really not hear her question? Does deep concentration fall upon an artist so quickly? She suspects not. It is maddening.

"Edwin." She raises her voice. "Edwin."

"Hmm?" He looks up, surprised.

His response tells her nothing. She does not know whether he's going deaf, or leaving the place they inhabit together to—what? Perform his magic. Whatever it is the genius brother does with a brush and pigment. (Though his startled look is no different from Samuel's looking up from his newspaper.)

"Can you hear me clearly now?" Alice raises her voice.

"Of course." He spreads his hands wide, as if to say, There are only the two of us here in this tiny room. No need to shout.

"Why do you want a carving of Alfred's in my portrait?"

The directness of her question startles him. She calls Uncle by his name. Mary had once, too. The Elmers never did. Always he was Uncle, though they had others of that relation, and now that he thinks of it, wouldn't names have been useful to distinguish one from the other? Except with Uncle there was never a chance of confusion. Whatever was said of him would be said of no other man—he was always apart. Always Uncle. And why does she call the portrait hers? It is not *your* portrait, he almost says. He checks himself; it is not unreasonable of her. What did he think he was painting?

"Are you comfortable there?" he asks instead.

"You're changing the subject."

"I suppose I am." He takes a breath. "Do you mind? If I start. I don't know why, or I would answer."

"Would you?" she asks.

"A good question," he allows. Because a glimmer of answer comes. It is Samuel's portrait. Alice is in it, yes. But it is Samuel's, and his. Every painting another self-portrait.

"Was it those—I don't know what to call them—those braids of men and women you mean?" She sticks a finger in her fist to demonstrate.

It is Edwin's turn to blush. "Samuel showed you?"

She shrugs.

"Really, any carving of his would do."

"Let me see what I can find."

He works on the egg until he notices a stomping overhead. God, it's loud. Samuel come home. And the light nearly gone. He looks around for a lamp and steps back to look at the picture as he waits for them. Moves his easel over a bit, so that when they enter the kitchen they won't immediately come upon him and the painting. A bit later, when he hears the front door close, he is puzzled. Have they left for the evening without a word? She must not have told Samuel he was here. Or surely he would have come down. Edwin creeps up the stairs to look. Why creep? He is not a criminal.

The house is entirely quiet. Is Maud gone, too? "Hello," he yells. He goes upstairs and pushes open every door. "Hello. Hello." This must be the master bedroom. He shakes his head, to see the size of the bed. It smells of Samuel. And a perfume that is Alice. *Houses and rooms are full of perfumes,* he hears Mary reciting Whitman. *The distillation would intoxicate me also, but I shall not let it.* He steps inside. No one home. What he does his own. He bends over, slips his hand inside one of her stockings and holds it up to watch how the silk catches the last light.

Saturday

It might be dawn, but the curtains are too heavy to let in light. In the air she detects a scent of movement—though that might only be herself, so she takes care not to wake Samuel as she slips out of bed and tiptoes across the room. She still has not told him. Why, she cannot quite say. A fear that he is past babies. That although she has gotten this far, she may not get further, testing the laws of the universe. He is old enough to be a grandfather.

She wants something to eat. And—maybe Edwin has left the painting in the kitchen. She feels exceedingly young and foolish. Like a child sneaking out of bed before everyone else on Christmas morning.

Edwin spins around. Alice stands at the door in a white chemise, her hair falling over her shoulders, her face puffy with sleep, her smile radiant.

He frowns. Such a smile. Doesn't she realize the trouble that will come?

"Good lord," he says. "What time is it? Where's Samuel? Why aren't you dressed?"

"It's not quite five. He's sound asleep, naturally. I was hungry. I wanted to see—"

"See, then. But hush."

Alice looks at the canvas. There is nothing of her but the same swirl of orange. And a glistening egg yolk, atop a wooden table, whose grain, in all its careful, minute detail, seems to have been polished and lifted to the surface. She bites her lip to hide her disappointment. Silly. Of course he had not painted her while she slept. How vain she is. Best to parch herself of such vanity in the coming months—a baby will have no patience for it. She is shamed, that she does not know what to say.

"How unusual," she manages. "And beautiful. An egg, by itself like that."

Edwin shrinks back into the corner, moving away from her. The sleepy warmth of her permeates everything.

"Aren't you cold?" he asks.

The way he looks at her, Alice turns suddenly self-conscious, as though she'd unbuttoned her gown and dropped it in a puddle of white at her feet.

"Is it true what Samuel says, that you can look for a split second only and then draw what you see from perfect memory?"

Samuel must not know he is here. Edwin is one of at least two secrets his brother's wife keeps.

"He exaggerates," Edwin says. "As you surely know."

"I don't believe he does."

"You should."

A creak silences them both, and the door swings open.

"Morning."

"Maud."

Maud takes in Alice's glance and follows it around the door. "Uncle Edwin! Whatever are you—?"

"Her portrait."

"Oh. Yes. Father said that he'd asked you. Can I see?"

"Not yet. Soon. Come," he says, stepping out from behind the easel and opening his arms to her. "How are you, darling one?" Over Maud's shoulder, he raises his brow to Alice in warning. No more of these shenanigans, sister of mine. Tiptoeing about with secrets.

His silence frightens her. So quiet, compared to Samuel. Samuel, for whom words are another kind of breathing. The softness of Edwin's eye has turned hard and inscrutable. Samuel's face would not change so without an explanation. Edwin must think she is not good enough to carry his brother's child.

Hundreds, probably thousands, of people ride the El every day. Do they think they're going to their deaths every time they climb the steps? They could not. Though the rumbling noise alone is enough to shake a body from its path. Still, ever since Mary first saw the trains overhead, she has wanted to ride them. If it is death she seeks, so be it. Edwin sometimes does, though he prefers to walk.

She is full of resolution this morning. She must be. Edwin is gone—and what is left her? Not Jimmy Roberts. Not the green book. (Though she has neatly wrapped a packet of papers for Maud.)

The conductor thinks nothing of the exchange between them. Yes, he says, it'll turn on 23rd. He takes her coin, whether she is a widow or no. She cannot decide whether to go to the Academy and see if he's there, or go straight to Samuel's. She need not worry. In her heart, she suspects that he is off somewhere painting; when he is done he will come home. He always does. Her concern more habit and excuse than actual fear. A reason to take a train ride. But not to despair. Still, a delicate matter, to decide which voice to heed. His heart may have stopped on the street someplace where no one knows his name; he may lie crumpled in the road. For now, it's not that time. Too early to ask at the hospitals or morgues.

No one looks at her, so she tries not to stare at the other passengers. Jimmy Roberts may have taken this train nearly every day of his adult life. Third, Second, First, Delancey—the train is not too fast for her to notice immediately that she is going the wrong way. Past Schwab's. An admonition. Ajangle with apprehension, she counts the streets they pass. She'll have to get out and switch trains, and then she might run into Frank and Susana. With their lovers, this early. Of course Frank must have one, too. He must turn on her, whoever she is, his steady gaze.

Mary's friendship with him, on the other hand, has been from the start a family matter. Inviting her to accompany his sister to the drawing session was no prelude to lovemaking. (Though she cannot invent the man who would not want to lay himself down next to Susana Tannenbaum.) *Pray that life is good to her.* The sudden passion of her wish surprises Mary. She hopes no one will ever have cause to portray Susana grim in mourning. Or bound to a machine.

"You would be surprised," Susana had told her, "what you learn, given over to stillness."

"I'd need something to keep my hands busy, I'm sure."

"You never know," Susana said, smiling and reaching over to hold her hand, which had seemed to Mary to have too hot an agitated pulse, compared to Susana's own cool one. "The painter makes his painting, and there you sit, making you."

Stillness will come in time, Mary very well knows. She has no need of rehearsal.

Disembarking at Second Avenue and 59th Street, on her way to Samuel's, she still thinks of Susana. Of how her touch goes directly to her heart. Yes, she is Effie's age, but that is not enough to explain it. Not every twenty-year-old woman touches her. A mystery, how love grows. Tentatively, she names love. And offers evidence: She had told Susana the truth of how she'd split her name in two. Though it wasn't that she'd lied to Frank. What she'd told him was before language and marriage—another kind of truth. That she was born with the war, and grew to speaking in a fatherless house.

Perhaps she will persuade Samuel and Maud both to walk to Union Square. Samuel is not easily shocked, and Maud might enjoy it. Perhaps they could listen to Emma Goldman together. "It's impossible to disagree with anything she says," Frank had told her. "She's on fire. Sign me up for your army, you want to march up to her and declare." She would like to hear Samuel try to argue.

If she is at the rally with Samuel and Maud, and Frank calls to her?

She could pretend not to hear him. No: Susana's smile comes to her. She could not.

She surprises herself by hoping Samuel will be home. Perhaps she will give Maud her pages of family history before she leaves.

She lifts her fist to the door. Instead of knocking, she uncurls her hand and places the tips of her fingers on the dark-red shellac. It's a gesture that takes both a measure of her intentions—*What* am I doing?—and the pulse of the building. This is Samuel's new home. She thinks of their first door, his and Edwin's and Emeline's—that pale green so light, so suggestive of breath and space that her lungs had filled to see it. When she and Lucy walked by, they would both look, and whisper, the Elmer brothers, and make faces at each other. When they had gone by, and stopped giggling, she imagined her own hand turning the knob. Alone. Without Lucy, without her mother, without John Elmer to accompany her. Samuel would answer, and Edwin would be inside drawing the old Lyon farm.

The door suddenly pulls away from her touch.

"Aunt Mary!"

"Goodness! You startled me—I didn't even have a chance to knock."

"I saw you from the window. I'm so glad you've come—Uncle Edwin said you weren't feeling well, and I was worried I wouldn't see you before—you heard that I'm leaving?"

"Goodness, Maud. I'm fine. You know I wouldn't miss seeing you." Mary reaches up and rubs her thumbs over Maud's eyebrows, smoothing out the furrow in between. "My dear. Don't wrinkle your brow worrying." And then touches her lips. "Let me see your beautiful smile."

Maud's smile is not precisely that, but some softening upward of her lips, a wan acknowledgment for her aunt that things are not so bad as all that: She knows what smiling is, even if it is for the moment memory and not nature.

When Mary sees Maud's expression, she decides that she will not add to her niece's worries. Edwin must be fine. Truly. He must have stayed at the Academy to paint.

"Your uncle is working all the time these days, so I thought the two of us could sneak off for a walk, now that the weather's broken."

"Father says another storm is due."

"Of course another storm is due. Where is your father, anyway? Has he looked out the window this morning? There is a bit of sun. Come"—Mary pulls Maud back to the door, opens it—"See? Let's show him."

Maud shakes her head so awkwardly that Mary steps back.

"The two of us, then. We can keep each other from being blown away. Come. Let's enjoy this peek of sunshine while it lasts."

"Let me just tell—" Maud doesn't know what stops her. Mary must know Edwin is here. If she wanted to see him, she would ask. It seems strange for her to have come all this way and then not see him. But Maud certainly does not want to be the one to interrupt Edwin and Alice again. It had embarrassed her. Her aunt, partly clad. Edwin with deep shadows under his eyes. And her father's office door closed.

"Let's just leave everyone a note. I'll find a card."

The hallway is taller than wide, with dark-brown wainscoting and elaborate trim. Mary wants to push out the walls—something of them all pinch and gloom, despite the loftiness above. Such a foyer, with its only spaciousness above human reach, is not particular to Samuel and Alice; all these brownstones are built so. And the paintings that line it, with their gilt frames, are only what such walls demand. Samuel is there, with his snow-lit eyes, rakish and amused under Edwin's brushstrokes.

Mary stops to look closely—it has been so very long since she has looked at this painting. She searches his face, as if this Sunday portrait might tell her something the man had not. Does he wake in the night and pace, like Edwin? She can see the brushstrokes that make Samuel's hair, keeping it neatly oiled in front, but letting it stray at the side, springing up over his ears. Here is the tracery of the windows of the campanile of Giotto, as Ruskin had sketched it for his *Seven Lamps*. It was a shame, really, that Edwin had not traveled. Though at least he had gone out West. Maybe he'd seen there the imaginary landscapes he sketches and paints over and over again, with water splitting distant hills. She'd forgotten that such a scene is in the background of Samuel's portrait, too. Nothing of this painting suggests Samuel, really. Though at least Edwin had put Samuel in his own clothes. He wears the black wool rep suit he wore the first time he left on Monday and came back on Friday. With only paint, Edwin makes her feel the corded ridges of the fabric under her fingers, as if it were earlier today that they'd stood on the platform, Maud and Effie underfoot, watching Samuel step off the train. Her hand sliding through his proffered elbow after he had embraced them all. The traveling salesman come home. Tell us a story, Maud and Effie would shout, and Edwin smile. They needn't otherwise express the joy that came unbidden. They hadn't thought, let alone said, how they missed him. No time to stop to think, in those days. Dinner on the table same as always. Somehow the two girls made as much noise as before. They filled the table themselves. Only when he arrived did they know the hole he'd left. Listening to the tales of the rooming house—the New Haven storekeeper who stubbornly insisted on carrying only white thread, and Samuel's plying his wife with samples of the rainbow. A salesman's charm his stock in trade. Edwin had, at least, painted Samuel's own blue eyes.

Where is he? The house is so quiet. What does he think of, at the end of days? He has done well for himself. She imagines him drawing a book off the tall bookshelves she glimpses through the door. She pushes it open, curious to see what titles fill the shelves.

They had not gone into this room when they'd come for dinner; Alice had whisked them back to the dining room. She hesitates. A feeling that Samuel himself is behind her. She turns back to look. Only the painting. Still, when she turns back, she is the same woman who looked back over her shoulder at Samuel with his arm around Alma, holding baby Maud, walking across the street to their farmhouse after dinner. Samuel turning back at the same instant and floating a wave high above everyone's heads. *I see you still, Mary Jane.* About some things there are not words. But today he does not appear when she turns around.

Mary looks about the room and notes the canvas at one end just as Maud returns.

"Maud—are you painting?"

Maud looks down and blushes.

"I won't look if you'd rather not, dear."

"Don't."

"I won't. But that's wonderful. Do you like it very much?"

"Oh—I am not very good. Mostly, I waste paint." Why does she not say that the canvases are Edwin's? Why she does not say, Don't you want to say hello to Uncle Edwin?

"Aunt Mary, let's go. I'll leave a note. Where shall I say we've gone?"

"How about Union Square?"

"If we make it that far without losing our hats."

"Let's try."

When they leave, Maud opens and closes the front door quietly, and the frame accepts the door in a complicit, silent embrace.

Alice and Edwin startle at the turn of the doorknob.

"Darling—"

Edwin, who steps back into the corner made by the door's opening as Alice rushes forward, sees only the back of Samuel, his hand coming forward to Alice's cheek, and then sliding down her body, staying at her waist, as his head slips down from hers, moving about in her ample décolletage.

Edwin meets Alice's eyes and watches color flood her cheeks.

"Your brother," she manages to say.

Samuel spins around. "Eddie!"

Alice pulls Samuel farther into the room and shuts the door, freeing Edwin from the corner.

"Your brother, the portrait artist." Introducing him thus, she puts his presence on Samuel. He has asked for the portrait. He is the reason she is wearing her orange silk in the kitchen.

"Here I am," says Edwin.

"When did you arrive?" Samuel asks as he steps toward the easel.

"Yesterday. Don't look yet," Edwin warns.

But Samuel steps toward Edwin to embrace him. As though he had never intended to look at the painting. Edwin is made small by Samuel: a physical fact. Samuel owns no vulnerability. No flush like Alice, to be seen so. Life hits Samuel and stops there. Is absorbed by his solidity. Incorporated into his slow, deliberate steps. Edwin wonders that he didn't hear him outside the door. Had he been that taken up in painting?

"Well, well. I had no idea what was happening around here. My brother in the kitchen with my wife, and my daughter gone to Union Square with yours. Your wife, that is." Samuel directs his clarification toward Edwin. Though it is unnecessary, this delicacy. All their lives, tiptoeing around the central facts. Edwin has no daughter. Mary is Edwin's wife.

"What?" say Alice and Edwin. "Mary and Maud went to Union Square?"

Samuel flourishes the note he's found in the front hall at Edwin. *Gone with Aunt Mary for a walk to Union Square,* he reads.

"With Mary?" Edwin asks, frowning perplexity at Alice and Samuel both. How could it be? What time is it? He is not sure—. His heart begins to clatter in a panic when he considers how darkness fell, long ago, and light came again. He hasn't been home in a day.

"Don't look at me like that," says Alice. "I didn't see her either. They certainly kept quiet about it. Why would they want to walk all the way down to Union Square?—in this weather!"

"Did Mary really come all the way here?"

"Edwin. I didn't see her either," Alice repeats. "But don't panic—working women travel unescorted all about the city."

Edwin feels his nostrils flare. To hear Alice refer to his wife as a "working woman." In front of Samuel. The two of them. To hear himself so described: panicked.

"That's a good walk without the carriage," observes Samuel.

Edwin recovers himself. "With the carriage it's no walk at all." Jabs his brother in the arm.

Samuel looks at Edwin, considering for a split second—and then his eyes crinkle into a smile. "Shall we go after them?"

Edwin combines a nod with a quizzical brow and gesture to Alice. "You?"

"I'll stay, if you don't mind. You two go."

When she is sure they have left, Alice looks at her portrait. The color of it! But she is only faintly shocked. More pleased. That he has given her such light. It seems more than she deserves. Though she does hope he intends to bring some clarity to her figure. He's left his paintbrush on his palette. Alice closes the kitchen door to be sure no one will come up behind her. She steps close and draws a faint line of yellow across the already yellow background. Still, it's visible. She can see the yellow line she's drawn, from her heart out to the right edge of the canvas. Will he notice?

She looks down at the tools before her. She takes his paint-stained cloth to the bottle of spirits and wipes the rest of the paint from his tiny brush, taking care to keep the bristles aligned. They seem impossibly small to her, these hairs. That so much might come from so tiny a tool. That so much is made of whether a person uses such a thing well or not at all. Whatever Samuel does from now until the end of his life will be nothing next to what he thinks of Edwin. Edwin the artist. If he were such a genius, why does Samuel have to pay his way. She puts the brush down and holds her belly. Edwin will know what she has done, but will say nothing, because she has saved his brush. She rubs her belly again. Later, when she wakes from a nap, she will find that she has forgotten what had seemed both so frightening and strangely compelling about her husband's brother.

Mary and Maud walk across town, the buildings shielding them, until they turn down Park Avenue and the wind takes over, rushing down the long corridor, kicking up the dust of dried leaves and horse manure and soot. They link arms and hold their hats and go where the wind blows them. *Nature says,—she is my creature.*

In Union Square, a throng has gathered, despite the wind. Maud and Mary have the ballast of linked arms—with Mary reaching up ever so slightly and Maud down, for she is taller by several inches than the last time they'd been together. They are delighted by the commotion, by each other, by the wind itself, though they forge complaint, squinting their eyes and talking themselves hoarse.

Aunt Mary has come for me! flies up, a joy that waves itself high above the rumble of puzzles and trouble that fill Maud's heart. Why today? And isn't there something strange about Uncle Edwin, shut up in the kitchen with Alice? She is sure her father knows nothing of it. When Maud gets on the train for Seattle, she may very well be bidding her father and Aunt Mary and Uncle Edwin farewell forever. Who knows when she will ever have time or money to return home. By which she means not this city, though she has lived here for almost a decade, but the farmhouse with the stream that curls around Goodnow Hill.

Around her father and Alice, Maud is nothing but a ball of fury, coiled, eager to be sprung from them at the earliest opportunity. But with her aunt and uncle, that anger relaxes into confusion. These people whom she will miss when she is gone—what do they know of her, or she of them? She cannot speak honestly to them of her reading or her interests. Except to Uncle Edwin about art. He softens her feelings for her father. To see them together laughing douses the rage her father otherwise provokes in her. For marrying Alice, for his successes (which she cannot call success). Corrects it and facilitates it both. Maud looks sideways at Mary, who has realized all at once that people are making way for the woman she'd seen leaving Schwab's—the one who laughed—and that—

"It's Emma Goldman!" Maud says.

"You know her?"

"Of course not. But I *have* heard of her. I'm not a child, you know."

"That I know." Had she been condescending? "I just didn't realize—we never discussed—"

"Politics of any sort?" Maud finishes Mary's dropped sentence.

"Oh, politics. We're always complaining—over dinner, over the paper."

"You and Uncle Edwin, maybe."

"Not your father and Alice?"

Maud does not even dignify Mary's question with an answer.

"You are unfair to him, Maud."

"Maybe."

Mary studies Maud's set mouth, and thinks: How could I ever tell her about Samuel? How could I ever. "Tell me what you think of Emma Goldman."

"She has more principles in her pinkie fingernail than McKinley has in his entire body, and—"

Mary cannot help but laugh. Because Maud is so much like Samuel: No hesitation giving her opinion.

"What's funny? It's true."

"You're probably right. I don't know either of them."

"That's not a reason not to have an opinion."

"Isn't it?"

"No. You can read."

"Surely you don't think I should believe the newspapers? In that case, I would think your Emma Goldman some sort of child molester."

"So you have to read more, not less."

Mary laughs again. "You've become a schoolteacher since I last saw you! My dear. It's not that I disagree. I wanted to come hear her myself."

"You did?"

"I did."

"Oh." Maud smiles.

"But it's a problem, isn't it?"

"What?"

"So much disbelief. Can't believe the newspapers, can't believe the president, can't believe the preacher. I can't believe the words coming from my own mouth. Before I speak aloud, it seems I always retract, readjust, find the flaw. Does that happen to you?"

"Wait," Maud says.

Emma Goldman has begun to speak. Maud wiggles her arm a little further into the crook of Mary's elbow. "We'll talk after," Maud whispers.

"To grow with the child is her motto. Mrs. Alving is the ideal mother—"

"Who is Mrs. Alving?" Mary whispers to Maud.

"Ibsen's heroine in *Ghosts*."

"—because she has outgrown marriage and all its horrors, because she has broken her chains."

Mary turns to Maud, widening her eyes, to let her know: This is news to me. I have never even read this Ibsen. She worries how Maud will take such gloom about marriage. She is before all that. But Maud looks straight ahead now, stretching up to see Emma Goldman over the crowd.

"Misunderstood and shunned, love rarely takes root. And if it does—by chance, by luck, by grace—it soon withers and dies."

Mary had not expected this. Love! Emma Goldman talking of love. Not imperialism or economics. *Love withers and dies.* Well, why shouldn't she speak of whatever she wants? What else had she thought an anarchist would do? Why should any boundary stand between home and all other human institutions?

Mary is conscious of two things: Maud's arm through her own and the force of Emma Goldman. She is so short, so small, yet her voice cuts through the wind. Mary listens—and yet it does not feel like listening so much as feeling, as the body responds to song. I was growing with a child, once. She is not alone. Motherhood a subject for a speech. Love's flourishing something to be studied. Susana Tannenbaum was not the only one who had learned to talk so. Maud probably could, too, for all she knew.

By chance, by luck, by grace. She likes those words. She thinks of Jimmy Roberts, jumping from the carriage, holding up his hand to help one of his sisters down. *How has it come to be,* she had written him once, *that your words have become my own?* It must have been his first letter about Emma Goldman that she had been answering. *You gave to me the words I wished to say (had I the experience to find them).* How strange, that when her heart lifts, she finds Jimmy Roberts there still. Except not Jimmy Roberts, exactly (she had not seen his family arrive), but something he left in her, something shifted. Not his voice, but something grown from it.

Why now?—with Maud's arm in hers.

Mary has lost track of Emma Goldman's speech—Jimmy Roberts, and then Emerson, has knocked on her door, and she sees his fly hitting the window-glass, her own stubborn efforts to understand made manifest. Every day the beginning again. What can she give? Has she anything? Her heart pounds so hard she can feel the blood running through her body and she can no longer think, except: Let this moment go on and on, until I catch up to it. Pay attention, Mary Elmer. You have long wished to be here. These days, in which she has fiddled and stumbled, undoing her plans and stalking their opposition, with grief everywhere flickering, here, now, she wants nothing but what she has. Nothing but this tiny woman before her, with a voice stronger than her size should allow, her words edged with the elegance and lilt of other tongues—Russian, Geman, Yiddish. Words at home in the wind. She does not fight what nature offers. And nature cruel at the moment, and loud. Rough and sturdy. *Life is sturdy,* Mary thinks. How is it this woman knows? Rolls up her sleeves and fights back, undeterred. Her speech comes through the lulls in the wind. And Maud's warmth is constant with the promise of after. They will talk. They will talk of this Ibsen she has never read and Emma Goldman's speech and Edwin and Samuel and the canvas in the study. She will give Maud the pages she has written of their family history, and maybe she will write others, too, and send them to her across the continent.

Not everyone is spellbound. From 14th Street, a procession of horses with blue-uniformed policemen riding straight in their saddles. At the edge of the crowd, a fraying. Whistling barefoot boys throw an old hat back and forth. A few workers wander away. Frank Tannenbaum spots Mary from across the crowd and he makes his way toward her, as the shouting all around becomes louder than speech, louder than wind.

The darkness inside Samuel's carriage surprises Edwin.

"Strange, not to be able to see."

"Edwin, don't be ridiculous: There are two windows. One on your side; one on mine. I don't see—well, that's your point, isn't it? That I don't see. I don't see your problem. If you'd rather walk, we can, of course. Though the weather's miserable, and quite frankly, I'd just as soon be home."

Edwin is silent. He had not meant to provoke Samuel. How does such squabbling start so quickly? He should not try to explain himself to Samuel. He can see very well he'd rather be home alone with Alice.

Yet he cannot get out from under the sensation of being trapped in the carriage. His view reduced to two tiny squares. It makes him uneasy; he cannot help it. He should calm himself—Mary will be fine; the painting will wait for him to return—and take advantage of the strangeness of the view. Something new for his eyes. And how unusual, for him to be alone with Samuel.

Though next Edwin's olfactory sense finds complaint. "Uncle Samuel doesn't smell like himself," Effie had said, wrinkling her nose. "That's natural," they'd told her. "He eats different foods and sleeps in different places." She'd only said aloud what they were thinking. Every Friday, he smelled different. Different women, different drinks, different food. Breathing the smell of Samuel in the darkness of the carriage, Edwin panics that his lungs can no longer fill.

"Sam, why don't we walk? Do you mind? You used to—" Edwin breaks off, surprised himself by the accusation he hears coming. You used to like to be outside. You used to walk everywhere I did, swinging the lantern, whistling to warn off the foxes.

Two eyes aglow in the bushes. The snap of the twig. What animal? Someone is there, watching. Had Samuel been watching in the bushes? Had Samuel seen him with Mary in the moonlight, as he had just seen Samuel's head bowing toward Alice? Spying on love. On someone else's desire. Blush and avert your gaze. Do not look at the eclipse of the sun. When Edwin had come back home from scratching at Mary's window and looked in to be sure Sam was asleep, he had startled to feel him at his back, a darkness filling the doorway.

"Caught you."

They never otherwise spoke of that night. Edwin told himself that it was not clear what Sam had meant: maybe just caught him looking into his empty bed, when he should have been long asleep. Samuel didn't necessarily see him walking home from Mary's. Didn't necessarily watch them from the woods there. Didn't necessarily see him kissing her forehead, half his mouth on her skin, half filling with her hair. Didn't hear her ask Samuel of the moonlight. He said nothing. Nothing would have changed his course. Even if he had known his brother's heart. What was to be known about such a heart, that loves everyone? In any case, the next day there Samuel was, courting Alma, and marrying her, too, before the leaves fell again.

"You're right, Eddie." Samuel sticks his head out the window and whistles to catch the attention of the driver, who stops the first stroke of his whip at midblow and looks back.

"Sorry. We've decided to walk." Samuel's good cheer seems unperturbed. "If it rains, it rains." He turns to Edwin. "And if we don't find them, we'll stop and have a drink."

Alice has been watching them through the window all along—as they stood on the lower step, waiting for the carriage to pull around, as they got in, as they got back out a couple of minutes later. She opens the door as they start walking. "Wait!" She waves an envelope. "This letter came for you. I entirely forgot."

Edwin frowns at the return address: The National Academy of Design. How quickly his absence has been relayed.

Mr Elmer:

We should be happy to admit you to the Life class in the Fall of 1900, providing you remain a student in good standing through the Spring. Please know that our selection for this Spring's class has been quite competitive. The faculty urges you to make use, during the intervening nine months, of every subject available to you.

Yours sincerely,

JM Ward

Under his signature, Ward had added, in his own hand: *In addition to your work at the Academy, you may wish to attend some of the city's great number of life drawing sessions (Thursday evenings at Cooper Union; Saturday morning at the Art Students' League, et cetera). I hope to see you in the Fall.*

"Never," spits Edwin. "Never."

Samuel watches his brother. He knows better than to ask. Edwin does not explain. Instead Samuel offers his arm, and Edwin takes it.

Frank Tannenbaum grabs Mary's arm and pulls hard, just as the horses begin to whinny and shriek in terror, and the police, using their clubs on their own horses, seek to calm what cannot be calmed and right what is already falling. Then, as if a shot has been fired (was a shot fired?) at the very center of the crowd, everyone and every standing horse scatters.

They run north on Broadway.

Slowing to a walk, Frank says, "She's lucky."

Mary at first thinks *lucky* means her—for he has pulled her, and Maud, too, away from the horses, saved them both from being trampled. Her gloved hand still in his bare one. No: He is talking to her about someone else.

"Who is?"

"Emma Goldman," he says, as though this were obvious. "Lucky again. The anarchist boys scared off the police."

"The who?" asks Maud.

"Hello," Frank says, ignoring her question, dropping Mary's hand, and offering his to Maud. "And you are?"

"My niece," says Mary, unconsciously mimicking his bow. "Maud Elmer. Maud, Frank and Susana Tannenbaum." And then she feels light-headed. What will Maud think, to discover she knows this man?

"Tell me," says Frank, still holding Maud's hand. "Are you a writer like your aunt?"

Maud withdraws her hand and looks to Mary uncertainly.

"Bother." Mary waves. "He found me writing some letters, and has made far too much of it."

"I'm just an Ibsen-reading schoolteacher," Maud offers.

"Ah. One of those." Frank smiles and winks at her.

"Tell us, Mr. Tannenbaum—Mr. Tannenbaum is an engineering student, Maud, though if you ask him, he'll deny it—who are these anarchist boys?"

"There's a priest in town who's gathered quite a number of boys—orphans, half of them. You will appreciate this, Miss Elmer: He's started a school, a modern school in the anarchist vein: They learn whatever they want, whenever they want. In between working or running from their mothers or their bosses. Rolling bullets at the feet of the police horses the sort of thing they do for play. Serious play, you understand." He winks at Maud. "Father Roberts is always showing up at Blackwell's trying to ease their sentences. Succeeding, too."

"Roberts?" Mary gets out.

"For goodness sakes, Frank. Robbins," Susana says.

"What did I say?"

"Roberts. You're thinking of Dr. Roberts," Susana answers.

"Dr. Roberts?" Mary asks. She feels her blood thinning and running too fast, a swirl in her heart.

"Have you met?" Susana asks. "He's around Schwab's nearly every day. Early, though."

Maud looks with curiosity at her aunt. "Aunt Mary?"

"Mary?" asks Frank, looking from Mary to Maud to Susana in confusion. Susana looks contrite.

"Mary Jane," she corrects him. "Two names." And then, as she watches the shadow his face becomes, she makes light. "One name, two—Robbins, Roberts—what does it matter? *We live among surfaces—*"

"—and the true art of life is to skate well on them," Maud finishes. "Usually Aunt Mary's the one to quote Emerson."

"And Maud, to know what to say next." Mary adjusts her arm in Maud's and smiles at her niece.

Susana moves nearer Maud and Mary as if she, too, were being drawn by the tightening of their linked arms.

"Really?" glowers Frank. "I didn't realize Aunt Mary was a disciple of Emerson's."

"I'm not a disciple of anyone's." Mary glares back. "He never wanted disciples. He quit the ministry, after all."

He has seen this look of hers before: closing up and daring at once. *Aunt Mary,* is she? The air crackles. As for Mary, she has the feeling of being pulled toward the points of darkness in the centers of his pale eyes.

"I'm off," he tells them. "I've got a story to file for the *Pioneer*."

"Why don't we three go to Schwab's?" Susana asks. "Frank can meet us there later."

"If I have time."

"Why are you so surly?" Susana asks.

"I'm not."

"Good. Then walk with us a ways."

"Afraid not." Frank bows to Maud, kisses his sister's forehead, nods to Mary.

When the three women turn away, Frank grabs Mary's hand and pulls her back toward him.

"What?"

He bends forward and kisses her hard, quickly. Their lips, dry from the wind, scratch.

"Good-bye, Aunt Mary." He turns and strides off.

His lips could not have found hers so quickly if she had not leaned toward him. She must have. *Frank Tannenbaum.* The syllables of his name flip inside her and settle as she turns to catch up to Susana and Maud. She will have nothing to add to their conversation. *Frank Tannenbaum.* Who is to say she was not meant to fly?

When Emerson met his second wife, Lydia Jackson, he made much of the fact that he'd seen her years before, across a crowded lecture hall. *There are some occult facts in human nature that are natural magic,* he wrote in his journal. *The chief of these is the glance* (oeillade). *The mysterious communication that is established across a house between two entire strangers, by this means moves all the springs of wonder.*

After his lecture, she discovered that she had all the while held herself rigid, every muscle immobilized by attention. Perhaps her stillness had drawn his eye. She'd been hardly more than a girl—fifteen. "Did you like hearing your own ideas preached?" a friend asked her afterward.

So many ways to tell a story. Some biographers suggest that Emerson never recovered from the loss of his beloved first wife, who died young of tuberculosis a year and a half after they'd married. That she was his great love. That he only made do with Lydia.

Accounts of Lydia's passions paint a different picture. She draped the front of their house in Concord, where the coach stopped for Boston, with all the mourning cloth that could be found to protest the Cherokee removal, while her husband wrote the president: *The name of this nation will stink to the world.* She never stopped insisting to her husband that women were due the same rights as men. She welcomed every eccentric guest. Thoreau loved her completely—too completely, wagged some gossips. Emerson reported that, upon finding their son Waldo's first tower, built of *two spools, a card, an awl case, and a flour-box top, she fell into such a fit of affection that she lay down by the structure and kissed it down.* Kissed it down! What geometry, what secrets there are, in a woman's love.

Thunder came, after the wind. Was a shot fired into the crowd? Or was it thunder that frightened the horses?

What happened first or next, Mary does not know. There was the clap that dispersed the rally, and the clap that stopped conversation. Frank's lips on hers. *Good-bye, Aunt Mary.* The scratch of his lips emphatic. Almost frightening. A glimpse of the brutality that is wind in a forest. And then, Maud waving to two distant figures.

"Uncle Edwin!" Maud calls. "Father!"

A dream, Mary thinks. This must be a dream. Maud looks back at her for an instant, as if she wants to ask her permission or pardon, and then, without waiting for either, starts to run toward Edwin and Samuel, waving an arm high. Had Maud seen—? Frank standing back up to his full height? Her flush?

Edwin and Maud come toward Mary and Susana as if floating—Edwin smiling strangely, Mary thinks, *What a strange smile*—and Maud wide-eyed, *too wide-eyed.* Samuel behind, as if he holds the string that floats the kites of them. Yet he is the first to speak.

"Mary. Hello."

"Samuel." The knowledge they have, what years and not sentences make.

"You had us worried."

"I—? What about—?" She looks over at Edwin, takes in the puffy darkness around his eyes. "Well—everyone's found now."

"My father, Samuel Elmer," says Maud. "Susana Tannenbaum."

Samuel takes Susana's hand in both of his and clasps it to him. And bows. "Lovely to meet you."

"My uncle, Edwin."

He inclines his head.

"Won't you come to Schwab's with us?" Susana asks.

"Schwab's? Why not?" asks Samuel of Edwin and Mary, who both nod and raise their hands in the same gesture: *Yes* but not one of their making.

"You were painting?" Mary asks, offering Edwin her arm.

He nods, and tucks her arm into his. "I'm sorry. I didn't realize—"

She holds up her hand and shakes it to brush off his explanation.

Asked, unasked, the rain comes. The edges of Mary's dress swirl heavy and damp about her ankles. Her left foot grows cold where the sole has worn away, a prick of sense—This is life, it shouts to her. Yet it seems a dream. In front of them, Susana and Maud, under their waxed-cloth umbrellas, skip through the rain, stepping wide over puddles. Next to her, she realizes that Samuel whistles the song she sings. *Life is but a dream.* He takes her other arm, and they walk together, Mary and the two brothers, behind the girls, arms linked three across.

"You both may as well know," Edwin says. "First thaw, I'm going home."

"With or without you," he adds to Mary, when she and Samuel say nothing.

"And if winter never arrives?" asks Mary. "We'll stay?"

"Not a milder November on record so far," says Samuel. "Watch what you ask for. Just because the sun rose this morning—"

"Don't start."

"You never know—"

"Stop, both of you."

Edwin shakes his arm free of Mary's and lengthens his stride. Samuel and Mary drop their arms in response.

"Edwin," Samuel says, "what did that letter say?"

"What letter?" asks Mary.

"From the Academy."

"Edwin! Was it about that class?"

Edwin waves the question aside.

"You didn't get in?"

"I did, but—I'm not going, so it doesn't matter. I'll finish the portrait of Alice, and we'll go home."

"The portrait of Alice?"

"He's been working away."

Facts exist that Mary will sort through at some later time—Edwin's discontent, his making the portrait he'd sworn not to, what seasons would be without him.

"And? How is it going?" she asks.

"We'll see," he says. He will not speak of it. Words like straps weighting his wrists, keeping them to his sides. He cannot paint and talk, both. Must unshackle. Must brook no interference.

"Indeed," she says. "We will."

"Yes," says Samuel. "Deed and not talk for my brother."

At the door to Schwab's, Susana and Maud glance back and give a little wave, fold up their umbrellas, and duck inside.

"After you," says Samuel to Mary and Edwin.

Inside, Mary heads over toward Maud and Susana, who are sitting at the table in front of her favorite one.

Samuel and Edwin watch her make her way across the room.

"You have always loved her."

"I have always loved her," Samuel agrees. If it were accusation, he does not take it so. "And I have always loved you." He holds his brother's gaze until Edwin turns away.

"Strange how at home she seems," Samuel observes.

Does Edwin imagine it? That he's been here before? The red-haired man behind the bar familiar somehow. The man and Samuel start talking immediately; before the man places their drinks down on the bar, they are laughing together. Brother raconteur. His own portion of affability shrinks to accommodate his brother's.

But he is not unhappy with his lot. This is what he wishes he could say to Samuel and Mary. That joy is quiet in him; he cannot speak it. He puts his finger into his mug of beer and swirls the foam about. He had not wished to leave Alice just then, his brush thick with the egg-yolk yellow he'd mixed, her hands moving nervously in her lap, her eyes glittering.

"Don't tell him," she'd said.

"Of course I won't."

Samuel to be a father again, three times over now. He looks for Maud, and spies her bent in conversation with the young blond woman—what was her name again? He watches them—women, they are. Any man would judge them so, he sees at this distance, startled. As Effie's size surprised him the season before she died. She'd gone from being a baby to almost-woman overnight. He shouldn't have been swinging her through the air anymore. The pains in his lower back still with him.

How can he help but see all human effort as mistake? By which he does not mean anything grim. Indeed, he would like to convey to someone, somehow, that by *mistaken* he means lively, and not punishable. A growth spurt, she had. And then died. Nature was that reckless. Human beings would do better submitting to the wildness, than to the urge to neaten, to categorize—

No end or furtherance of his thought, because the sight of everyone talking impresses itself upon him. If Samuel had married Mary, how full of talk their house would have been. Life might have gone that way. Past him. Would it have been so different? All about him runs, though he sits still. One morning atop the big rock in Goodnow Stream, the river had shattered to pieces under his gaze, the sun making of its movement glint and shard, triangles and arcs and parabolas of light. And he one piece among the racing pieces of the universe.

Which is why he cannot grieve. At least properly. He had seen that censure in her and Samuel's eyes. He had done the best he could. Everyone does, he supposes. Everyone—their mouths opening and closing and hairy appurtenances quivering and slanting atop eyes that also open and close—taken together, a thing too large to fathom. He reaches behind him for a chair, misjudges.

"Whoa, now!" says a stranger. "Watch yourself."

"Can't very well do that, can I?" he asks.

"You look a bit unsteady on your feet."

"What man among us isn't?" Edwin rejoins.

The stranger laughs.

Edwin laughs in return, surprised. This is what it must be, to be Samuel.

They don't really look alike, Mary thinks. Edwin's nose thin and angular, where Samuel's is broad and blunt at the tip; Edwin's eyes the dark-brown pools that Effie had inherited, and Samuel's an ice-crackling blue; Edwin shorter and thinner, and so forth. These details can be discerned, would be by a portrait artist of any reckoning. It is something beyond physical appearance that causes her sharp intake of breath and a hurt under her ribs when she surveys the room and them in it—Samuel at the bar engaged in jovial repartee with Justus, Edwin seated alone in a chair across the room. No, not alone. A man pulls a chair up beside him. Good. His eyes crinkle up with pleasure at what the man says, and she warms to see it. She has the feeling that, amidst all the chatter, she can hear them both—not clear words, but a steady hum, as if they share the same note. It is not a harmony they make, precisely, but an intense vibration, as if their spoken voices reside at precisely the same pitch, and duel about its edges. The effect on the listener is only to hear the increase in that note's power. Samuel and Edwin grow larger in each other's presence. Magnified and increased. That is it. Something invisible binds them. Watching, a loneliness wells up in her. How far she has gone from her sister Lucy. How little they know of the women they have become, apart. She isn't sure when or how such distance grew. Steadily, for certain. As a garden, left alone a few seasons, quickly becomes an impassable wildness of bittersweet vines and berry brambles. New England a jungle at heart. Lucy has grown nearly unrecognizable to her, hidden as she is behind children and grandchildren and extra flesh. When Nellie had come to the big house, she had taken Lucy's place in Mary's life. Or more precisely, she'd taken the place of Alma, who first had taken Lucy's. To think of Nellie now hurts worst of all, as if the sorrow of three lost sisters had accumulated into this last. It is not a loneliness that wells up and might rock her to sleep, but a sharp, stabbing, waking pain, for which there is no consolation. No one who doesn't wish to be found will be found.

"What would you like to drink?" Samuel is at her side.

"Do you know where she is?"

He nods in the direction of Maud and Susana.

"I mean Nellie."

Samuel stands up taller. Had he not been standing straight before? Had he been bending solicitously toward her? Now he is rigid.

"No."

"You know very well."

"I assure you, I know nothing *very well*."

"Come, Samuel. I loved her, too. Why should your claim on her prevent all others—"

"*My* claim on her? My claim? You must know I have no—"

"Please don't tell me you haven't provided for Grace all these years."

Samuel looks away from Mary, and tents his hands over his eyes, as though he is warding off a headache, or banishing the room's bustle.

"Well?"

"487 Lexington. That's all I know." He makes a gesture of rubbing together bills in his hand and pats his pocket.

She's seen this look before. Clouds darken and stir his face, until his countenance becomes cruel and foreign and says to her, Of me and the ways of the world, you know nothing.

Samuel leaves her and then returns seconds later with a hot cider.

"I'm sorry," he says, as he hands her the cup.

"No," she says. "You're not sorry. You are sorrow."

And she turns away, without looking at him, shaking with an ancient rage. Though he does not deserve the half of her anger. She betrays him, she knows. Samuel who came home on Fridays and embraced them every one, and made them laugh. Samuel who lifted her up from the pile of bedclothes that were all that was left of Effie's smell and kissed away her tears and held her until she could feel her own pulse, until she knew again that the earth is comprised of living things. Life *is,* he showed her. She turns away from the pain she knows would be in his eyes if she looked again and heads toward the back of Schwab's. At this hour, the back room might still be empty.

She is beside herself. *Beside herself.* The strangeness of the expression catches her. To think of Nellie and Samuel, and that he's always known how to find her and never said so. Why hadn't he told her how she and Gracie and Dave had fared in the city? Though she knows her anger is a swirl of confusion: How easily people fall together, and apart. To apportion blame an inhuman project. Nellie knew where to find her, and had never tried. For that, she cannot blame Samuel. To do so will not bring Nellie back to her side.

Anger and righteousness do not suit Mary; she is not comfortable inhabiting them (or sitting aside while they inhabit her, as the expression has it). She finds only regret in their wake, and nothing the better for it. *Of regret,* she will write, *Nature says nothing.* (She cannot resist loosening the strings of the bundle she's tied up for Maud.) *Of procreation, and profligacy, and excess, and mystery, ample.* And of anger. Thunder crashes and lightning blazes. The high spring river rushes, flooding up over the banks. *Let righteousness roll down like a mighty river.* What words! Of what use prophets, when the world kills them in every generation, when the rains come again. Of what use rhetoric. Or reflection, or regret, when the same stories come again. If beavers under their thatched roof ponder whether or not they'd intended in felling those trees that the valley flood and the river cross the road, still they sleep at night, protected from the weather, and labor at their earthworks until they float belly-up to the bank where their bodies are found. Here the earth moved, and there. To say any creature's part smaller or stranger than our own plain foolishness.

The finish of Uncle Alfred's wooden sculptures like beaver poles. He'd used his tiny blades as the beavers used their big front teeth, steadily wearing away, making of blocks of tree something polished and delicately ridged. On that day, he must have been beside himself, too. Did he feel something running through him that was not him? Was he beside himself when he brought the ax down? And did it run through all the Elmers? She is an Elmer only by name; the problem need not concern her, with Effie gone. Yet it does.

The noise from the front room a buzz, a drone. She must play her part—she stretches her fingers wide. She wants to use her hands. She has missed her chance this fall to dig up the old lavender bush and pry apart its roots. She'd meant to divide it before another year passed. And she should have brought that finespun gray wool with her to New York. What lovely, warm socks it would have made.

Samuel stands alone in the center of the room. For an instant, he is the only one standing—everyone else sitting, talking. Justus is bent over behind the bar. Samuel goes over and taps on the counter. "Drinks for everyone," he says. "On me." And then, as he appraises Justus, "Are you feeling all right?"

"Feeling fine," says the affable Justus, who starts to pouring, though he has just coughed up a towel full of blood. If Marianna had seen, she would have made him sit. But he hates to be still, with life passing.

Who knows what it is to be Samuel? Mary cannot guess, because pictures of his women intrude—his women!—she should not use the possessive. Alma, with her quick black eyes and long, wide-nailed fingers shelling peas as she sang "Grandfather's Clock" cheerily, *His life seconds numbering, Tick, tock, tick, tock . . .* Alma had nearly chirped the song, making it quick and high, using it to pace her pea-snapping. Young pink Alice, all eagerness and voluptuous beauty: What will Edwin make of her in oils? Nellie, laughing by the sink. Or silent by the fireplace, she'd seen her once, gazing into the flames. What he must have done with them all, alone. She could see Nellie's head against the tree and Samuel against her, kissing her he must have been, kissing her face and neck and shoulders before stooping low and standing back up with one hand under her skirt. Maybe Nellie had been crying and he'd kissed her tears away, too. Or the full moon had called them out, and they'd stood, considering its glow and all the stars. Did he love her? And—did she love him? That is what Mary wants to know. All those nights, while he taught her to read, time enough for love. Or was it only the world she wanted, and not Samuel—all the world opened up in those pages. The one who shows you that may as well break your heart, while he's at it.

When Mary starts to cry, she knows that the tears that come are not for Nellie, but for her, and Edwin and Samuel. 487 Lexington. A number and a place. All these years, he's known as much. With Samuel, all that she calls past becomes present. Being is what she and Samuel do best, with their shuffles of word and glance and gesture. *What our eyes carry,* she will write. *Borne by an invisible current such as sows pines on the forest floor or carries the call of hoot-owls through the night.* They will not speak it, ever—how desire branches from a tree that's rooted deep inside. *We're grown from the same stock,*

Samuel Elmer. It is cheap gossip to say that she married the wrong brother. Or that he saw her kissing Frank Tannenbaum, as she'd seen him with Nellie. Though it seems impossible that such a detail would escape him. Quickly and completely their lips matched, edge to edge—Frank's and hers. The years that divide them fell away. She is still the same girl, answering a knock at the window. A scratch of an apple-tree branch. Not a mistake, she thinks. To give yourself to what is offered.

"Child, he is dead," Emerson told little Louisa May Alcott, when she came in the morning, asking after Waldo.

At the big table in the back room, Mary writes, *What Fate had done, this: Taken me in hand and slipped in the tip of a knife, matter-of-factly turning its point, deep inside my Flesh, as if excising the eye of a potato. A wound that deep and that indifferently cut. A swift pivot of the blade. And Effie was gone.*

How are parents bound to their children? If she knew, she would understand what part of her was cut out that day.

Under *Thing(s)*, she lists:

Kitchen knife, eye of potato.

The pain of her loss is physical, and still comes. It is absolute.

From the eye of the potato, grow new shoots. And in the same eye, Time whispers: Come, rot.

Frank Tannenbaum strides into Schwab's place. People notice him—he has a look about him, a little wild, or maybe he's just wet, and out of breath, when inside everyone is warm and slow.

"Him too," says Samuel.

Justus waves Frank over to him. "This gentleman's bought you a drink."

Frank's brow creases in question, and Justus gives him a look that says, Take what comes.

"Thank you," Frank nods. He sloughs his wet wool coat.

"You're quite welcome."

"Frank Tannenbaum." He offers his hand.

"Samuel Elmer."

"What brings you to Schwab's?"

"My daughter." He scans the room for Maud, gestures. "With the dark hair."

"Really! That's my sister with her."

"You don't say." Samuel steps back to take a look at them both.

"Don't bother." Frank waves a hand. "No resemblance whatsoever. She takes after our mother, and I after our father. Rather straightforward, that."

"How do they know each other? They haven't stopped talking. Hardly lifted an eye in any other direction. Well—why should they?"

"Susana's always like that. Captivates her audience."

"Then she's met her match."

"That I would like to see. You came with—" Frank clears his throat "—Aunt Mary, then?"

"Mary? We found them on the street."

"She's your sister?"

"In a way of speaking."

"Your wife's, then?"

Samuel lets out a laugh. "Sorry. It's just that—there are hardly two women less alike. Though in the end, that doesn't much matter, does it?"

"I don't know what end you mean," Frank says stiffly.

"Mr. Tannenbaum. You've a lifetime ahead."

"Part of one." Frank enjoys the new weight of his future—savors the gravitas of the fact that had settled inside him as he was filing his story. He can't resist saying it aloud: "I'm off to the Philippines, next week."

Samuel takes his measure of Frank. "So you come down on the island side, I'll reckon."

"If by that you mean, do I support Aguinaldo, of course—"

"No, no. What I mean is—did you see that Mr. Dooley wrote no one was sure if the Philippines were 'islands or canned goods'?"

Frank sputters his drink.

"Poor taste, wasn't it?" Samuel adds. "Shouldn't have repeated it. Sorry. May I ask what you intend to do there?"

"I'm a journalist."

"Ah—like Mr. Dooley." He holds up his hand. "Forgive me. Not *like* Mr. Dooley."

The two men drink.

"If Mary isn't your sister, or your wife's, then how is she Maud's aunt?"

"She's my brother's wife."

"Of course." And if, before, Frank had felt something pleasingly heavy inside him—the fullness of his decision, its boldness—this man's single sentence has punctured his certainty. To staunch the slow leak, he sits down heavily, perturbed that he should have any such feeling.

As if his movement caught her attention, Susana looks up.

"Maud," she squeezes her hand, "excuse me a minute."

Susana pivots her way across the maze of tables, chairs, umbrellas, people's legs stretching. When she reaches Frank, she put her hands on both his cheeks and pulls his head up to look at her. "Frank. What's wrong?"

"Nothing."

She raises her brow to show that she doesn't believe him. "Did you write your piece already?"

He reaches into his pocket and waves a sheet of paper full of ink at her. When she reaches for it, he folds it back up. "Read it tomorrow," he says. "This copy's too scratched over."

"All right." Still with her raised brow. "Want to join me and Maud?"

"Mary's left?"

She looks at him intently. "Back room," she says. "She didn't look altogether—well, see for yourself."

Slightly embarrassed, Maud is, left in silence when Susana gets up. She has spoken too much: about going to Seattle, and how she'd hardly ever known her mother, and how Mary and Edwin had been more parents to her than her own. Susana had drawn her out. Now that she's left—to say hello to her brother, only!—Maud feels strangely abandoned. What business had she telling her life to a stranger?

Seeing Susana embrace her brother makes Maud even more self-conscious. Everyone else with their families, while little Maud is left alone, in her grandparents' attic room, at the train station, in the Central Park apartment. She watches Susana and Frank—how she touches his cheeks, and Maud flushes and looks quickly away when she notices her father watching her. She does not want him to come over. She wants everything as it was—she wants Susana back. It is her turn. How dreadfully boring, what a waste it was!—that she'd spoken so long of herself and had not learned one thing about Susana. Somehow, Susana had asked all the questions. She had fixed on her such an irresistible look of attention that Maud had not thought to stop, had not thought their hours were numbered. If she gets the chance, she will make up for it. If only her father does not come over. He would get in the way. He would tell stories she has heard before; he would make Susana laugh and shine. Maud wants her own chance. Yet when she looks up again and sees that her father is no longer looking in her direction, it is not only relief she feels, but a tiny thread of sorrow. This is what she knows best—the separateness of people. She, Aunt Mary, Uncle Edwin, her father.

Mary looks up the instant the door opens, and when she sees it is Frank, unbends from her hunch over the table.

"Look at this." She points out words etched into the old oak table: *The world begins here.* Then an arrow leading to another inked point: *and here.* When he reads and then smiles at her, nothing is left in her anymore of anger or sorrow.

He sits down across from her.

If he can tell that she's been crying, she does not care.

She reaches across the table and takes his hands in hers. "How bold I have become."

"Good."

He cannot hear the sadness, she thinks. That she means, as well: *How timid I have been.* Heat rises along her spine and radiates, but now such flames will not catch and burn anything to the ground. Her body a thickness that will hold life as it comes, as long as it does.

Still their hands together make heat. In a winter long ago, she had leaned forward in a sled, grabbed hold of the back of the seat, and Samuel had pressed his shoulder into her hand. She had been shouting into the wind, and had pulled herself forward to be heard. Edwin was driving. Samuel's shoulder completely covered her woolen hand, and she lost her words and felt only the heat of her bundled fist and his shoulder, as if she were ball and he socket, and from that union all the world moved. He covered her hand, and the heat that pulsed there had seemed to her enough to grow an entire life.

"I'm old enough to be your mother."

"So?" He gets out his inky piece of paper from one pocket, and fishes around in another to come up with a short pencil. He writes atop, *For Mary,* carefully underlines something, and signs, *With no apology, Frank.*

"It'll be in the *Pioneer* tomorrow," he interrupts as she's reading, made nervous watching her eyes slide along each line. She looks into his eyes again, and squints a bit, as if that might allow her to travel further in them.

> *Miss Emma Goldman, in a space of twenty minutes on a blustery day, gave a crowd of several hundred a vision of life as we always knew we wanted to have it.*

"What would such a life be?"

"Read," he answers.

> *If any of her detractors, who drape the same dread around her name that children use to speak of Monsters, passed through Union Square at noon-time yesterday, they would have been surprised to find that the small, bespectacled teacher of literature, speaking passionately about Ibsen, the Modern Drama, and the great possibilities of love, was none but the infamous "Red Emma" herself.*
>
> *If one listens with an open heart, what thinking man or woman can resist her message? With Emerson, she tells us that what is of value in the world is each individual (not the government and its law, which were after all invented to protect life, not replace or limit or deny it), with its active soul that, seeing and uttering truth, creates. What interests her is the right of this individual—each of*

us—to food, to shelter, to love and companionship, to happiness. Only in the freedom of this pursuit, she believes, can justice thrive.

Is it any wonder such a woman is off to Vienna to study the arts of healing the human body?—she who wants so strongly to heal our city's (not to say our nation's and even the world's) body politic.

Bon voyage, Red Emma. Your "Scarlet Letters" are the color of the life that courses through us.

"You wrote that very quickly."

"I wanted to get back here."

"You did?"

He nods. "Did you like the part about Emerson?"

"I like it all," she says, as she opens her bag.

"And you? What—" Frank gestures at the papers.

"A family history."

"Could I?—"

"No."

Rebuffed, he sits back.

"It's in pieces. Not fit for another's eyes. One day, maybe." She is very still.

Her thoughts? He watches her closely. Dive and come to the surface.

"Or not. Come. Let's walk." As she stands, Emerson comes to her. Emerson, and Jimmy Roberts. Here, he whispers. Here is a step into real nature. The wind will blow, the water flow, the fire burn. "What would such a life be, Frank Tannenbaum? What is it you've always known you wanted?"

"Time." He stands. "Moments of clarity."

Without having to say, *not out the front,* Frank and Mary head to the back door, which lets out into a narrow alley lined with crates and bottles. Here a person can stretch her arms and touch the bricks of one building and the bricks of another. She reaches wide, and he walks into her arms.

Honestly, Edwin would like to return early enough in the spring to graft new trees for John and Mother Jane's in Baptist Corner. He is ready, now, to go there, to settle into a home again, to see what might be done to improve the farm and orchards. More golden russets, certainly. Perhaps a few black gilliflowers. A variety of shades. And he would like to get a scion of that splendid golden-fruited quince from Norton's, the one that grew such rich golden-yellow fruits from even poor soil. Perhaps, if he judged it correctly, he might make a fruit with the fragrance of that quince and the taste of the apple. At any rate, he would enjoy trying. He will take whatever comes. To get his hands back on his tools satisfaction enough. He particularly misses his knives. And the smell of the melting beeswax and resin. One never knew which grafts would take—he had long ago accepted that.

"Know much about apple trees?" he asks his neighbor.

"Do I know apple trees? When I was a boy in Germany, we had an orchard that stretched as far as I could see—but a child doesn't see very far, eh?"

Edwin stretches out his arms to show how quickly he reaches the wall. "Far enough. What kinds of apples?"

"What apples? Little dark ones like this." The shape of a sheep's nose in the air. "And big yellow." A plump round sphere formed in his hands, which he then tosses up in disgust. "No use. How do you say? I cannot tell—the colors, the shapes. Who can?"

Edwin smiles, and attempts his own: "Red Astrichans, golden russets, Gravensteins, Baldwins, Tallman sweets—"

"Tall? Fruit or tree?" The man gestures height with his hands.

"Neither." Edwin puts up his hands and laughs. "That one didn't take."

"Ah, well." The man shakes his head. "Luck and not luck, the fate of the fruit grower. Gravensteins, you say?"

"Yes."

He points to his chest. "From my country."

Edwin and the man smile that there is one apple they might compare.

"It is—" Edwin draws the shape of the apple in the air, "elegant."

"But not my best fruit."

"Nor mine."

They break out into laughter, that two men who'd failed in such a popular fruit might find one another in a city saloon. He'd thought anyone could grow a decent Gravenstein, except him. Funny. The language they share enough. Not many words actually necessary. *Yes* and *no* and *thank you* carry human discourse as far as it need go, most times. No words describe the particular sweetness of a particular apple, picked ripe from the tree, or cellared the proper length of time, what golden its gold, what red its red. Greenish, he might say. Orangish. Striped or speckled. He'd rather toss one of the tiny Roman apples into his companion's hand. Take a bite. It is just too *good*. Too good to talk about.

He will not paint in oil anymore. He prefers the quickness of pastels. They are—more congenial. More like—apples turning and arraying themselves in the orchard in the late afternoon. He with pastels in hand more like a creature who lives in time, taking every stride his legs make.

Alice will be his last portrait. Perhaps he will not even color more Dearly-Departeds. Unless for a good price. A very good price. Let them be content with photographic likenesses. What relief, to be done with oil paint. Its viscous slowness so like clotting blood. Its infernal fumes. Couldn't be good for a body. He will grow fruit trees, which have not one bad smell nor any other flaw. Not the heat of flame and the beeswax melting with its smoke rising on the breeze, up past the highest branch, where he sets the new into the cleft of the old. About pastels and charcoal, he likewise has no complaint. He smiles broadly at his companion, raises his drink to him. He'll buy back the picture cart from Patch, so that he and Mary might take long rides into the country, keeping an eye out for beautiful trees. They will pack food and blankets and sleep under the stars. With Maud, too, when she comes back.

At first Mary closes her eyes to kiss Frank, closes her eyes to the world, though she had always thought that if Jimmy Roberts came back for her, she would keep her eyes open; they would make love slowly; she would not miss a thing—not her own hesitation or his downward glance or how sorrow comes, despite the syllables of his name on her lips.

So she pulls back to look at Frank, and when she does, it is his youth she sees. Does he, so close, notice that she is twice his age? His reddened cheeks with only the faintest stubble. He is barely a man, with the life she's already used up still to spend. Her life—Edwin and Samuel and Maud—just inside the door. They will not look for her in the back room; Samuel will keep them from that. They will not find her in the alley. Why these thoughts come to her as certainties, she cannot say. Perhaps she does not care. She will not regret. Will not wonder *what if*. Surely she will be forgiven. In all her life—long, it seems, and irrelevant—surely she has done worse than she does now, taking what comes. She cannot stop—her hands cannot stop. She unbuttons his coat and he wraps her inside.

"I can quote Emerson, too, you know," he says.

"I don't doubt it." She pulls back and watches him, sees his hands on the buttons of her shirtwaist. "Go ahead."

"Bring me wine, but wine which never grew/ In the belly of the grape . . ."

"'Bacchus,' " she says.

He nods.

"Are you suggesting that we abandon ourselves?"

It is a not a question he has to answer. Not in words.

With the side of his thumb he traces the bone below her eye out to the edge of her cheek, his fingers stretching out into her hair, tugging it down, to her ears, to her neck, until she feels she is made of a thousand fingerprints.

"And if you are going to tell me you're married, Aunt Mary, I already know."

"You do?"

"Yes."

"You met Edwin?"

"Samuel."

"Oh. Then—"

"I don't care." He surprises himself with that—he, who not ten minutes ago collapsed at the news. But it is true. "Whatever brought you here, I am glad of." Easy to be glad, now, nothing but joy, fingers, pulse. "Though I should tell you *my* secret. No—not what you think." He leans in to kiss her again. "I'm going to the Philippines."

"Now?" He is so close. Bright spots have burned up in the center of his cheeks. The rain comes down in a fine mist. Her fingers move at his waist—rubbing past the line his trousers have made in his skin. Frank is going to the Philippines. She is married to Edwin. These words operate in some far realm, further than her hands.

"Next week."

"But here you are." Though she knows somewhere, far off, that a week is a marker of time, which moves still and like the rain will eventually soak and ruin them. The day of his departure will come. "You're here now. What does Emerson say?—*Nothing refuse*."

"I know that poem, too."

"She left," Susana says. "Quite a while ago."

"Really?" Samuel is surprised.

Maud is surprised, too, but she'd been facing away from the door. Susana would have seen, not her.

"She must have tired," Maud suggests, to herself, as much as to her father.

"Are you?"

"Not at all."

"Me either," adds Susana.

"Right. Well, I've got to get your uncle home. Mary will fend for herself, I am sure."

Maud eyes Edwin, who's leaning against the wall. Asleep maybe.

"Dead drunk," says Samuel.

"Really?" Maud sits forward to take a closer look and shakes her head in amazement.

"Really." Samuel looks stern, and then breaks into laughter. "Will you be all right if I take Edwin across town? Stay here? Stay together?"

"Yes, Father," Maud mimics a child's voice. Then, "I'm about to go across the continent alone, and you're worried—"

"When you go, you're on your own. Until then—"

"Bosh, Father."

"Bosh yourself. Take care of her," he says to Susana, opening his wallet.

She waves him aside. "We don't need anything."

He ignores her and tucks the bills under her napkin.

Maud rolls her eyes.

"Why?" asks Edwin. "I am having such a nice time."

"Any more of a nice time, and you'll find it impossible to walk."

"Must we walk?"

"You're the one who refused the carriage."

"Ah. Right." Edwin leans over, puts his arm about Samuel's shoulder, as if preparing to share an important confidence. "Your carriage is too small for me."

"Really?"

"Yes. Can't see anything from those damn windows."

"I see."

"Without it, you do."

The brothers walk a stretch.

"So you're happy with Quincey."

"Pardon?"

"Quincey. Alice. Like the fruit. Tuck her in, and she'll keep the sheets smelling sweet all season."

"Jesus, Edwin."

"Thank you." Edwin bows. "But I'm not him."

"Good Lord."

"I tell you, I'm not—"

"Stop, please."

Edwin starts chuckling to himself. He can't stop.

"Edwin."

"I'm sorry."

"No you're not—you're sorrow," Samuel says in a mocking whisper.

"What?"

"Nothing."

They walk in silence for a long block.

"These blocks are longer than the others."

"Yes," Samuel agrees.

"We're going home."

"Yes."

"Do you think we should stick to apples, or should we start some pear trees?"

"Whatever you think."

"I thought I'd get a couple scions off that golden quince of Norton's."

"Excellent idea."

"Do you remember the smell of the lilacs in front of the big house?"

"Yes."

"It's enough for me, Samuel. The smells of home. I don't need any of this." He gestures to take in all of New York.

"I see."

"Stop it with that 'I see.' "

"Stand up straight, and walk, and you'll be home, and done with me."

"You're not staying?"

"I've got to get home myself."

"Oh yes—to Quincey."

"Damn it, Edwin. If you weren't my brother, I'd leave you here by the side of the road."

"Leave me, if that's what you want."

"You're a difficult man, Edwin Elmer."

"You think so?"

"Yes."

"I thought I was—endlessly accommodating. Always cleaning up after you."

"Cleaning up after me? You must be joking."

"Taking care of Maud whenever you left. Taking care of Alma's parents. Taking care of the house whenever anything went wrong. Let Edwin figure it out—he's good with tools. Let him fix the roof in the freezing rain. Let him get the cows out of the barn before it burns."

"While I was—off dallying about in New Haven? Is that how you think of it?"

Edwin opens his hands to the sky and raises his brow, to say, Is there any other way to think of it?

Samuel shoves Edwin's arm down and picks up his pace.

Edwin scurries to catch up. "I'm sorry."

"What for? You keep saying so, but you're not. Not at all. What did I expect? I've done nothing but give to you—keep it up, and I'll be lucky to escape with my own hide, let alone any"—he waves his hand in disgust—"cloak of gratitude."

"What about Mary?" Edwin asks. "Where's Mary?"

"How should I know? I am not her keeper."

They've knocked over a stack of crates. Potato skins and purple cabbage hulks fall over her shoulders.

"It's nothing," she says when he starts to brush her off and right the crate. "It doesn't matter." She fastens a cabbage shell to the top of her head like a bonnet and pulls him to her again.

"Should we go somewhere else?" he asks.

"Together?"

"Of course."

Like lovers, they walk, or drunks—flushed, arm in arm, swaying around the puddles, and laughing as though all the things of this world are funny.

"Where are you taking me?"

"487 Lexington."

"Which is?"

"A long story."

"I have all night."

Sorrow clutches her throat.

"What is it?" he asks, and bends to look into her eyes, though she turns away.

"Don't say *all*. Or anything like it."

He searches her face until she looks back. "All right."

"Let's go north along the river."

"Tell me the long story," he says after a while.

How, she muses. "Well. There are—two brothers. Very close in age, in height, in general appearance. Only their eyes different—the younger's brown as maple syrup and the elder's icy blue. A midwinter glint. Rather like yours, in fact."

She stops and looks at him. "Yes—like yours.

"So it happened that the brothers set out from their childhood home to make their fortune together. You see, all their family were poor farmers, with nary a chance in life."

If she wonders herself at the folk-story language of her tale, Frank does not know.

"Their father, who'd lost his left eye before either of them was born, was already helpless. Their mother had turned to religion and poetry—every morning she sat in her room, whispering.

"Not that she didn't do everything else required of a woman," Mary interrupts herself. "Cleaning and cooking, harvesting and stitching. But she was unique, the brothers felt, in the extent of her devotion. A Millerite—you know?"

He nods. "Dismantling the roofs of churches. Preparing for the rapture."

"It was before your time."

"Yours, too."

"True enough." He is right, and Mary wonders, for just a moment, how she has come to feel so old. As though the men on the rooftops something she'd seen as a girl.

"Actually, in her own house, the woman laughed at the other disciples—she thought they were wasting their time with the roofs and all that. 'All future the Lord's,' she said, 'and how do we know how He'd like the furniture of this Earth arranged?' Not having prepared at all, she was in a better position than the others to go on after the day came and went. And go on she did. More fervently, in fact.

"The two brothers were the last children of this woman. Number ten and number eleven. She gave her final child the name of one who'd already died and a middle name all his own—that memorializing first name the only indulgence she ever allowed herself. And no other child had a second name at all, let alone one with a Z and an O—a song and a show on the end. Like all mothers with their last children, she loved him selfishly and extravagantly. And though such a command may not have been uttered, not precisely spoken, the older brother knew himself to be charged with protecting the younger, facilitating in all ways his successful passage in life.

"In time, the brothers met with great success out West, and returned home with riches enough to honor their parents and build a grand house on a hill near their boyhood home. They complemented one another: The elder negotiated with the world, earning coin and favor; the younger kept to himself, solving mechanical problems and mathematical puzzles and rendering the beauty of the living in two dimensions.

"When it came time for the brothers to find brides—"

"Such a time comes," Frank interrupts.

"It does."

Frank brings Mary around to face him and kisses her. "Excuse me. Go on."

"How do you expect—? You can't do that and have me think."

He holds a hand over his mouth to show he'll listen.

"It shouldn't be a surprise that the elder, expert in all ways of the world, should meet with equal success with women."

Frank sighs loudly, and she kisses him again, and then keeps a finger over his lips.

"Yet this brother had been charged—silently, implicitly—with facilitating in all ways his brother's passage through this world. So he set out first to find an appropriate woman for his brother. He courted a young woman of the town, while his brother sat nearby, working at his sketches, overhearing their every word."

"Let me guess."

"Wait," she stops him. "Here, versions of the tale diverge. Some people say that during this courtship, the elder fell in love with this girl, despite himself and despite his brother."

"Of course he did," Frank interrupts.

"They say that the younger brother, knowing this, tricked the girl into believing he was his own brother, and she went with him. Lay with him, as they say in the Bible. And though the elder brother quickly married another woman—as I have said, he was expert in the ways of the world, so he saved himself moping or worse and protected them all from comment—still he could not save their two families from the curse his brother had brought on their house."

"Curse? What sort of curse?"

"I'll get to that."

"And what about the other versions?" he asks.

"So impatient."

"I'll wait." Frank sighs again.

"Well, it could be that the younger brother loves her, plain and simple."

"Plain and simple?"

"You doubt that?"

"Yes."

"Or perhaps the older brother did not love the woman after all, and was only procuring a bride for his brother."

"Not if she were as lovely as you."

"Stop." She pushes him. "In any case, the story always ends the same way: The daughter of the younger brother and the woman . . . dies. The elder's first wife, bless her, dies, and the elder and the woman forever miss the one they should have loved. The woman and the older brother are doomed always to wonder."

"To wonder?"

"Whether—life has passed them by."

"Hmmph."

"You don't think?"

He shrugs. "Passed them by—a bit of an overstatement, isn't? And the younger?"

"He goes through with his part of the bargain. He is one of those unusual people. He takes what comes. Never a complaint or a regret. Always with a mind that matches the task. And entirely self-sufficient. That is what is different about us. Though I shouldn't say us. I don't know you well enough."

They walk in silence.

"Once, when we'd taken a sled ride far out over the hills, the sun was setting, and I pointed out toward the horizon and said, 'Let's go there.' I was joking, of course. But Samuel was all for it. Edwin was furious. Furious. Well, he was driving the horses. I suppose he felt—excluded." Her woolen hand hidden under Samuel's shoulder. "'May as well wish for death,' he said, crossly, to us both.

"It is hard to describe." She has stopped walking. "Our own minds. Or the quality of—the type of—mind we bind ourselves to. I was hurt by his crossness. I wanted to tell him I knew—who doesn't?—that the horizon is a trick of the mind, or the eye, however you put it. Not a real place. Instead, Samuel and I just rolled our eyes and I shut my mouth. I'm not an idiot—it wasn't death, or Constantinople, or Cleveland—and of course not the horizon, for goodness' sake. I just—wondered. It was an idea I had, about how the air might be, where the sun turns purple. Listen to me. Perhaps he was right. Purple."

Was she just the same, all those years, wishing for Jimmy Roberts? And hadn't he said the very same thing as Edwin, when it came to it? That by her desire, she was courting death? *Take off your mourning clothes, or wear them for us all.*

"Where was I?"

"You were telling about the difference between the older and younger brother."

"Oh, bother. It'd be more to the point to talk about how they are the same. In every version, the brothers are bound together until death. The end."

"What of the woman they both loved?"

"As for her—" Mary hesitates. "She loved them both."

"Naturally."

"You think so?"

"Of course."

"Well." The lightening sky surprises her. "Which is why they never killed each other," she is further surprised to hear herself say. "As brothers have been known to do."

"Didn't I ask when we first met if you were the author of domestic tragedies?"

"You did."

"You might consider joining that profession."

She smiles. "But I despise such stories."

"So you say. Look. 487 Lexington. Wasn't that the place—?"

A bank. She peers in the door. Samuel is impossible. Probably he sent money here for her. That is all.

"There's no point now," he ventures. "It won't be open for hours."

As he watches her take in the dimensions of the building, the placement of windows, Frank fears he is in deeper than he'd meant to get. Only found her in Schwab's. Surely she's not planning to attempt a robbery. It would be ludicrous.

Then she starts banging on the door as though she's going to shake the building down.

"Mary. Mary. Stop."

"What choice was left him?" she stops to say. "His wife dead, his brother across the road, married. Why shouldn't he look for happiness?"

"Why not?" Frank agrees.

Mary rests her head against the cold of the door. During the day, Nellie might come here, to collect her money. Or Grace. She would be old enough now for such errands. Early, Dr. Roberts goes to Schwab's. How sharp it is, the pain of breathing.

"Are you all right?" Frank asks, touching the middle of her back.

He makes her think of Edwin, his tentative touch. How kind, he is, to listen.

"Yes," she says, after a time. The air is cool on her face. "Walk some more with me. I've no need of sleep."

As they start down the block, Frank says, "I have one objection to the story. How is it that the one who brings the curse is the only one not to suffer from it? Nothing works like that."

"Pardon?"

"You said the younger brother brought the curse. And also that he is the one who does not wonder—"

Had she said that?

"I said that?"

"You did."

"I suppose you're suggesting it's the woman who brings the curse, when she carries her basket of eggs to their porch. Pandora's basket."

"Not at all. I don't believe in curses."

"What do you believe in, Frank Tannenbaum?"

"Happiness," he says, and starts to laugh at himself. "Laugh if you will." After they grow quiet, he continues. "I believe that—I know nothing. But—the sun will rise. In fact, I know the place. Wait until you see. An actual place, Mary Elmer."

Beside the East River, he bends down and slides his arms up under her skirts and hoists her onto the wooden rail that divides land from river. If he were to push her—

But of course he has no such intention.

The world sways. Dawn rises over the East River, which scatters the sun's fire. Of the sky, Mary wants to sing.

"How beautiful it is," she says. The heat in her like to wrestle the sky to earth and ravish the clouds. She wraps her legs tight around his hips.

"When isn't it?"

Unimpressed, he is then. Their heat a small portion of the fire that keeps the Earth. This is what people do, every day and in every place.

"Do you think the sun's setting in the Philippines now?"

He shrugs and fits himself in closer. "Rising, here."

It is all she will ever know of him. Not what years make. She thinks of Edwin, and how he changes into his best clothes every day at lunch, a small optimism that seems to her well measured. Of human scale. She and Frank cannot make their bodies dissolve, one into another. They are together, and then separate. Ecstasy and grief the same in time.

After, they walk in silence, his arms about her shoulders and hers about his waist, their sides pressed together, as though they'd been stitched close, from ankle to cheek, with sinew for string.

He will sail for the Philippines in a week.

She and Edwin will leave for Massachusetts, come spring.

In the morning, the Doctor's comfort comes: to walk alone at dawn. If he sees other people, they only serve to heighten his solitude. "Good day," he nods to the young man from the café, who appears wrapped in love. "Hard at your studies already, I see."

The city gathers itself, as the sky broadens into light. When the sky lightens, his heart lifts and seems to swell; *maugre all his impertinent Griefs, Nature says,—he shall be glad with me.*

Edwin kneels under the skylight—good for morning work, Samuel had written—and prays, eyes open. *Give me this day.*

A Flitting State,
a Tent for a Night
November 1922

It isn't like they say—whoever they be—about Death, or about Knowledge.

That is Edwin's first thought, on his back, under the apple tree, looking up at the blue sky. The frightening, dear sky. If he is dead, then life has not been so unusual. Is not so strange? Is not so different? The sky, with wisps of clouds like the feathers poking through his pillowcases. These wisps, he sees first. These wisps, and then a spinning darkness, all this world a spinning darkness and the wisps flecks, dancing. He might have caught the branch. He should have been able to catch the branch. But he had not even tried. He had not thought it—necessary. He had leaned—far. He must have been holding to a thin branch overhead, and to the hand-saw. He must have leaned. He must have leaned—too far. He was confused. Up down and down up, and in that case what is gravity, or the distinction between one being and the next. It was as if he were apple tree, as if he grew out of the trunk, a branch from the trunk, which grew from the earth, so heading toward the earth no different from growing out of it. He must have—he opens his eyes again to the sky, the wisps—he must have been holding on to the branch he cut. He must have cut off his own support. He tries to lift his arms to see how he had held them in the air, the saw in his right hand, left hand choosing the branch to prune—but his arms are too heavy, the confusion of lifting and arranging them too great.

So much effort. And the world would not have cared a whit whether some hypothetical apples might one day next spring have had their start in pink-white buds in the space he had made for them in the upper reaches of the tree. He will not see the spring. And that, too, an inconsequence. That one apple falls or a man lives or dies. He in his orchard. Others—elsewhere. Elsewhere, where the river rushes toward the falls, and farther, in all the cities and places he has never been.

"I am so small," he says. "So small."

His words, barely a whisper, do not ruffle the air, do not make any more dent in the landscape than the fallen branches. Tiny nubs of green that will not unfurl. He wants to laugh—to see things come to this. Trees, limbs, ground. That is—he feels laughter in him, but no sound comes.

He will stay on the ground. Unless Mary rescues him. But she will not notice his absence until dinner. No reason for it. And it will turn dark before then, so he'd better save breath enough to call out when she comes looking. By then he may not be—

The ground is so cold. His limbs start to shake. He must be alive. Death surely a more significant rupture. He lives—or he cannot explain the facts: the sky, the cold, his shivering. He laughs, but no sound comes. The sky floats above and he is pinned below, captive, a chattering form upon the earth. If he cannot get himself up, he will die here.

"I will die here," he tries aloud.

But his words do not rend the air. He knows that. Knows that this is the end, and is surprised to find that death is so funny. But a private joke. After all—this. What all foolishness comes to. A figure prone upon the earth. He might have left the last tree a bit shaggier than the others.

Yet why not die? He had not known before how easy it would be. He sees how she could have slipped from them so quietly. Though not like sleep. Not a closing like that, but—something else. His bones shake so hard he is—are—pieces. Pieces see through skin to separate bones, feel each distinct from every other, as if he have not sinew or muscle or flesh. He know then, has not broken the sticks and pegs that hold him together. Failure not mechanical. Something else. Dissolution of the spirit. Shattering of—self. He not—what he had thought himself to be.

He draws a great gasp of air. Arms try again—lift. This arm, this hand with fingers, must have dropped the saw. Fingers bend and unbend: Try to hold. Roll bones to one side. Knees tuck. Gather self. Must gather self. All selves. Laughs again, but no sound comes. Miracle all along it had been. Miracle all along to have held himself in one body. Parts could so easily have gone off on their own, kept their own time. (Something multiplies deep inside him.) Grass blades poke eyes. Other parts, probably, but they do not report. Only eyes mind. Sharp. Strips of viridian too blue. Gold and pink if sun slant under trees. Sun slant and wrap him. Sun slant and wrap and turn him into the earth.

Far across the gallery the colors dazzle. Vermilion ribbon around her hat. Yellow-spoked wheels of her doll carriage. June-green grass, singed gold by the sun. Sky blue as the best day. Freshly painted clapboards. A kitten in midstep. And heavy white clouds, falling. In the darkest corner of the painting, a flicker of motion. Mary lifts a needle and slips a knot up over its point. This, Edwin gave her: yarn the color of the sky, the color of Samuel's eyes. Cast on a thousand stitches, Mary. Sky fills the needle.

Epilogue

Two winters after Mary and Edwin returned home from New York, Samuel Elmer died of pneumonia. His second wife, Alice, was not included in his will, of which Edwin instead was made the executor. (*Your father's last joke,* Mary wrote Maud: *Edwin's elegant hands made paws by the Responsibility.*) The following July 4 weekend, the funicular railway in upstate New York in which Samuel had been a partner collapsed, killing fourteen vacationers. The settlements eradicated all that remained of his estate.

The next year, Charles Eliot Norton (owing to ill health, he said) ended the Ashfield dinner lectures. He was too tired to argue anymore, he allowed to Mary Elmer when she sent him a note asking him to reconsider. His rebuke of the McKinley administration for its travesty in the Philippines had offended a segment of the townsfolk, who had vowed not to attend another evening. (Furthermore, only a man from Cambridge would not see that the new barbed wire kept cows better than stone walls.)

Mary and Edwin lived out their lives on her childhood farm, where Edwin tended the apple orchard and drew landscapes. He did not paint in oils again. One summer, Maud returned from Seattle, and the three of them camped for weeks on Put's Hill, where the rareripes and peaches grew so sweet, and Mt. Holyoke alumnae still make pilgrimages to the place where the farmhouse stood.

Edwin died the spring after he fell from an apple tree—not from the fall (though that turned his hair white), but of stomach cancer. He was sent home from the hospital to die. It was an insult, Maud felt, in the listing of American artists, that his supposed suicide merited mention that otherwise might have gone to his work. What he'd done (doubled pillowcases over his head and a clean shot down the throat, to save mess for Mary), any self-respecting farm boy would. Certainly one so capable.

After Mary's funeral three years later, an auction was held of Edwin's paintings. *At the end of the day, there was still a wagonload of pictures, and these were put under a shed near the barn,* wrote his biographer, Betsy B. Jones. *Years later . . . family members looked for the pictures, but none were found.*

Maud survived them all—mother, father, cousin, uncle, aunt. She made occasional trips home from Seattle, where she was supervisor of art in the public schools, and tried to amass and order what could be found of her uncle's paintings. In 1950, his portrait of Mary at the whip-snap machine was shown in the *American Processional, 1492–1900* exhibit at the Corcoran in Washington, D.C. *The great period of luminism was in the 1860s and '70s, but it lingers on and there is something of it in the curiously unforgettable picture by Edwin R. Elmer.* Two years later, Maud's efforts culminated in a show at the Smith College Museum of Art, where the paintings remain. *Haunting,* the curator wrote, *the oddly large girl in the foreground: so like the Surrealists in their exploration of dreams.*

About all the family at dinner, Emerson wrote in his memorial essay to his dear friend Thoreau: *You seek it like a dream, and, as soon as you find it, you become its prey.*

Of Frank and Susana, Nellie, Grace, Dave, Alice's baby, and Jimmy Roberts, history has no account.

Acknowledgments

This novel would not exist had I not seen Edwin Romanzo Elmer's *Mourning Picture* in the Smith College Museum of Art; to this artist I owe my greatest debt, and to his biographer, the curator Betsy B. Jones, whose meticulous monograph, in which each endnote suggests worlds that want telling, gave me a base of information about the artist and his family to draw from in this fiction.

In thinking about the period, three other works stand out: Emma Goldman's speeches and autobiography, *Living My Life;* Louis Mumford's evocative *The Brown Decades: A Study of the Arts in America 1865–1895;* and *The Souls of Black Folk* by W. E. B. DuBois, brilliant son of the same Berkshire hills.

The lines of Emerson that haunt Mary come primarily from his essays, mostly "Nature" and "Experience," and from his poems, especially "Threnody" (his lament for his son Waldo), "Bacchus," "Give All to Love," and "Days," though an Emerson scholar might find free-floating phrases from other sources, including the journals. Of works on Emerson, none was more essential than Robert D. Richardson's magisterial *Mind on Fire,* which sets the highest standard for bringing the past to blooded life. The portrait of Lydia (Lidian) Emerson and her love for Waldo is drawn from this work.

Thanks to

Those who've generously given their time and wisdom, reading this novel in its various guises: Therese Chehade, Cathy Ciepiela, Justine Dymond, Cathy Edwards, Robin Friedman, Tamara Grogan, Eppie Kreitner, Beth Morrow, Nicole Nemec, Susan O'Neill, Elizabeth Porto, Dan Shapiro, Declan Spring, and Hanna Weg; Keith and Wendy Kreeger for pointing me to the Seymour Durst Old York Library and Madelyn Kent for shepherding me around the collection;

Beth Morrow and Buck McAllister, for sun and snow and Bread Loaf; Hilary Plum, dear literary companion; Andrea Barrett, for sustaining encouragement; Jennifer Gates and Lane Zachary, true believers; Fred Ramey, for saying yes and asking more; Rosa and Amos, my greatest teachers; Mark, for the days and nights.